OMEGA LOST

EVELYN FLOOD

Omega Lost

Evelyn Flood

First published by Evelyn Flood in 2022

ASIN B09R4TLPMB
Copyright ©

2022 by Evelyn Flood
All rights reserved. This book or any portion thereof may not be reproduced or used in any manner whatsoever without the express written permission of the publisher, except for the use of brief quotations in a book review.

Cover and formatting by Diana TC @ Triumph Book Covers

TRIGGER WARNING

This book contains themes and scenes of sexual and physical assault, torture, pregnancy and birth trauma.
All abuse takes place outside of the harem.
Please take care of yourself.
If this is okay with you, then please keep reading!
Evelyn x

About this Book

This book is an **omegaverse**. That means that the characters have some of the characteristics often seen in wolves, but they **do not shift.**

In loving dedication

Sorry fam, you can't read this one either.
Dad, please stop telling your friends I write children's books.

The Omega Creed

1. All omegas become the property of the Omega Compound upon awakening
2. Omegas must obey alpha commands at all times
3. Omegas are not permitted to own or use soft furnishings or participate in any activity that may be considered 'nesting'
4. Omegas are not permitted the use of a bed
5. Omegas are not permitted to initiate bitemarks or participate in heats outside of those permitted by the Omega Compound
6. Omegas must kneel in the presence of alphas unless permission is granted to rise
7. Omegas are not permitted to make eye contact with alphas
8. Omegas must consume food or drink from the approved list compiled by the Omega Compound
9. Omegas are not permitted to own property or drive
10. Omegas must wear the allocated collar when outside of the Omega Compound

Exceptions to the creed may be made under agreed circumstances, such as mating, with the permission of the guardian alpha.

Any Omega found to be in breach of the Omega Creed must be returned to the Omega Compound for correction.

Prologue – Ava

Fire twists in my belly. It burns, the urges rippling down my spine, bowing my back.
It pulses, the burning growing stronger, turning to pain.
Everything hurts.
It's too much. There are too many scents here.
Help me.
Kill me.
Please.

Chapter One
Max

"Will you be gracing us with your presence anytime this century?"

Luc's dry tone sounds casual enough, but his worry bleeds through. My hand reaches up automatically, rubbing at the pack bonding mark on my chest. I'm too far away to pick up Luc's emotions directly, but we've known each other too long for him to hide anything from me.

"Shouldn't be long now." I blow out a frustrated breath, staring up at the hospital in front of me. The high-rise concrete building houses the largest hospital in the area. Hopefully, it'll have what I need.

"How's she doing?" I ask Luc.

"She's okay," he says quietly. I hear the snick of a door closing in the background. "But we really need those meds before we run out, Max."

My throat closes. This hospital is the last one in this area, and I couldn't get into the others. If I don't get Leah her medication on this trip, we'll run out in a matter of weeks.

"I'll be home soon. Give everyone my love."

Disconnecting the call, I pull my bag from the red pickup

truck in the parking lot and head through the double glass doors. The older beta manning the front desk glances up at me and away, a faint blush lining her cheeks.

Well, that makes things easier.

"Hi," I smile ruefully at her, pulling off my cap and running a hand through my hair carelessly. "I'm Daniel Morgan – the on-call locum support for today?"

She twitters and looks down at her notes, her eyes scanning the screen. I mentally cross my fingers – if Bastien has done his part, my name should be there waiting for her. Flicking my eyes to the hospital map on the wall behind her, I make a note of the pharmacy department. Eighth floor.

"Of course, Dr. Morgan," the beta simpers. "If you head up to floor six, it looks like we're down a gynecologist. I'm sure they could use an extra pair of hands."

I shoot her a smile and wait patiently while she bustles around. She slides glances under her lashes towards me as she works, self-importance hanging in the air as she prints off a temporary ID badge and hands me a lanyard. I slide my false ID across the desk to her, watching as she glances over it and takes it for photocopying. Pulling out my phone, I shoot a quick text off to Bastien. I shouldn't raise any alarms if everything goes as it should, but I'd rather not have my face floating around their system.

Thanking the receptionist, I head into the elevator and hit the button for the sixth floor. As the doors slide shut, a black-clad arm thrusts in, forcing them back open. Shuffling over, I make space as two large betas dressed in matching black step inside, glancing at me and the badge around my neck before dismissing me. I catch a handful of their muttered words as the elevator starts to ascend.

"Still in the coma – not sure when…"
"…bored shitless. She's not going to make it."
"He wants to try again."

One of them glances around, catching my eye. I hold his gaze, and he drops his eyes to the floor. It's an expected power play between alphas and betas. Doing anything else would likely raise suspicion, and that's the one thing I need to avoid until I can grab those meds and get back home to my pack.

Nothing to see here, gents.

I briefly wonder what they're talking about, but a bell tinkles, a tinny voice announcing our arrival at the sixth floor.

The doors slide open and I glance around, my brow furrowing. I expected a busy gynae ward, but it's deserted. The only sign of life is more beta guards, all dressed in black, milling aimlessly around the reception. All eyes turn to me as I step out of the lift. The two next to me shift on their feet.

What's going on here?

An older nurse dressed in purple scrubs, her face pale, steps out of one of the side rooms, pulling the door closed behind her. Her brows dip down, spotting me, and she strides forward.

"Can I help you?" she asks, her voice strained.

"I'm Dr. Morgan, the locum. Reception sent me up – something about your gynae consult being out of action?"

She tenses, glancing around the corridor. The guards watch us closely, paying attention to every word. My back stiffens.

"Dr. Hale is currently on leave. I'm not sure... excuse me for a moment."

She turns on her heel and heads back to the room she just left. I lean against the wall, crossing my arms. This whole set-up is weird. My money is there's some sort of VIP in residence and they've cleared space out.

Uneasiness curls through my stomach. I need to stay

under the radar, and this definitely doesn't fit the brief. Luc would lose his shit.

I'm about to cut my losses and leave when the nurse leaves the room again. She's followed this time by a stocky older alpha. He's early fifties, salt and pepper hair, clearly ex-military from the way he holds himself. He looks me up and down with gunmetal grey eyes, expressionless.

"You're the doctor?" he asks, a hint of derision in his voice.

It's a struggle not to let my lip curl, but I'm not interested in a dominance battle with this prick. I don't like the look of him. Even his scent is off, sulphuric oil and some sort of acidic mix I can't quite identify.

I decide on the affable, nice guy approach. "I am," I say, sticking a bemused but polite smile onto my face and holding out my hand. "I'm Dr. Morgan – temporary locum support. I was told to head up to this floor. Has there been a mistake?"

He ignores my hand, pursing his lips slightly as if he's displeased. The nurse shifts uncomfortably from foot to foot, her hands fidgeting.

"What's your background?" he asks.

Shit.

"Medicine at Northwestern, specialized in general surgery, moved around a fair bit. I've just come back from Colorado so I'm on the lookout for a permanent role but picking up some locum in the meantime."

I'm trying not to sweat. If he investigates my backstory, there are some false trails, but any deeper digging and they might realise I'm not who I say I am.

"And your gynae experience?" he asks.

"A year's residency in Colorado."

Lies. I should have told him I didn't have any gynae

experience, but it's too late now. And I can't deny the spark of curiosity in my chest.

The alpha thinks it over for a moment, his stare assessing and cold. I *really* don't like the look of this guy.

"Any work with omegas?" he asks abruptly. The nurse lets out a tiny, shocked sound and he glares at her. She stares at her feet, mumbling apologies.

A grim feeling uncurls in my gut, and I try hard not to let my eyes wander to the door behind them. If I was curious before, it's nothing to how I feel now. If there's an omega in there, I need to get a look.

"Some." I don't expand.

He eyes me before turning on his heel and walking back to the private room. I stay where I am until he turns and beckons me.

"Maybe you'll be able to assist us, Dr. Morgan. The last consultant was… unhelpful."

If it's possible, the nurse turns paler. A touch of trepidation fills me as I wonder what happened to the unfortunate Dr. Hale.

What am I heading into?

Chapter Two
Max

As I enter the sterile room, the beeping of machines draws my attention to the hospital bed.

The omega's eyes are closed, tubes running from her nose and mouth, hooked up to the machines keeping her breathing. Her tanned skin is sallow with an ashy tinge, and tangled caramel hair lies in limp strands around her face.

I catch the faintest hint of vanilla in the air, tinged with burnt sugar that bites at the back of my throat.

My fists clench instinctively, nails digging in so hard I'd be surprised if my palms aren't bleeding. I unpeel my fingers with an effort, conscious of the alpha watching me with his cold stare.

I clear my throat. *Focus, Max.*

"May I take a closer look?"

He gestures impatiently and I step forward to pick up the chart at the foot of her bed. Flicking through the pages, my eyes dart up – assessing her cheekbones and elbows, so sharp they're almost cutting through her skin. Her tendons stand out on her neck, dark veins running down her arms.

Chapter Two

Despite her unconscious state, leather restraints hold down her wrists and ankles, locking her to the bed. A compound-issued collar sits around her neck. Pressing my lips together, I turn back to the chart, reigning in the disgust coursing through me.

Stopping on a particular page, I stare at the text, forcing myself to breathe calmly as I take in the scant details. There's no name listed, of course. Only a number. *864*.

Of course she'd be a compound omega. The Omega Compound legally owns all awakened omegas. Following the civil Omega War a few decades ago, all omegas were brought under government ownership to help address our decimated birth rates. Nobody really knows why betas stopped being able to give birth, but fingers were quick to be pointed at the omegas. Human rights didn't get a look in when the survival of our race was at stake.

So all omegas now belong to the compound by law, and they're carefully managed to maximise their breeding capacity – either by being allocated to alpha packs, since omegas can only become pregnant through induced heats with an alpha, or by being sent to heat nests, where any alpha who has the money and a knot can do their part and help to populate the world, any children allocated for adoption through a beta agency. The whole set-up makes me fucking sick to my soul. That's why Em—

I cut off the thought abruptly and focus again on the paperwork, blinking as I take in the contents. It doesn't add up with the battered condition of the omega in front of me.

Even the assholes at the OC don't do this to the omegas in their care. Beat them, starve them, force them into submission, even drug them, but this is another level. I've never seen an alpha, beta, or omega in this condition.

I continue flicking, trying to think through my options

before a word catches my eye. "She's been given codroctymal?"

Not just a single dose either. Use of codroctymal – also known as artificial heat hormones - is carefully managed to avoid damaging omegas by giving too much, handed out sparingly by the Omega Compound. This omega's been given so many doses of it, it makes my stomach flip. No wonder her fucking veins are protruding. Just one dose can be incredibly dangerous if administered incorrectly, and this girl – I thumb back through the pages.

Twenty-four doses of codroctymal administered over a six-month period.

I force the bile back, ignoring the anger crawling up my spine. She's been in heat more than she's been out of it during that time. It works out to a heat every single fucking week, and each heat can last from 24 hours to three days.

Now, she's lying on the bed like a broken toy.

Whoever did this to her got exactly what they wanted. The thin sheet covering her doesn't hide the swelling of her stomach. It looks obscene against her small frame.

She's pregnant.

A growl bites at the back of my throat, and I push it back as my hackles rise.

"Can we discuss this somewhere more private?" I ask, fighting to keep my voice steady.

Get yourself under control, Max. I can't be in that room with her without wanting to rip someone's head off. If my suspicion is true, that person will be him.

The alpha takes me to a small office down the corridor marked *registrar*. Two guards follow us, taking up positions on either side of the door.

He gestures to a plastic chair with superiority. "Have a seat."

Chapter Two

Ignoring the implied command, I stay standing, holding up the charts in my hand.

"What exactly do you expect from me?" I demand.

The alpha takes a seat behind the desk opposite. Leaning forward, he steeples his fingers together, eyes piercing.

"She's dying."

The words are delivered matter-of-factly, but his jaw clenches. For a moment, I wonder if there's any genuine concern there, but his next words prove my suspicions right.

"I need you to make sure she survives long enough for the children to be born."

I gape at him.

"I appreciate that this may sound cold, but a lot of time and money has been invested in this process. We have come too far to lose everything now and those children are hugely valuable."

What a fucking asshole.

My aggression rises and I push it back down. If I react badly to this, I'll be out of this room in a heartbeat. I have to stay calm.

I raise one eyebrow at him. "What if I'm able to save her?"

He pauses, calculation flickering in his eyes. "That would be appreciated, but the children are to be your main priority."

I sit back in my chair, choosing to continue reading through the notes rather than engage further. The room is silent for a few minutes while I digest everything the omega's been put through and her current condition.

She's five months pregnant with twins. Since the birth rates dropped, most omegas have only been known to carry a single child. To carry two is almost a miracle. That she's still holding on despite everything her body has been through… she's strong. Amazingly so.

But maybe not strong enough.

The alpha clears his throat and I look up.

"As I'm sure you'll understand, this case requires a certain level of discretion. You'll be asked to sign a non-disclosure agreement before leaving, and I'll also need a copy of your ID and medical license."

Shit. Bastien had better be able to wipe this shit.

Nodding, I stand up. "That's fine. I'd like to take another look at the patient."

He holds out an arm, stopping me from exiting the room. "Remember, Dr. Morgan – the children are the patients. *Not* the omega."

"Noted." My response is short and clipped.

Heading back into the room, I sidestep the guards to find the nurse hovering, hooking up a bag of fluids to the omega's tiny arm.

She's so fucking frail. I don't know if I can save her, but I'm damned well going to try.

Guilt fills me as I think of Leah.

One week, I think. I'll give it one week to try and save her – to try my damned best to save all three of them.

If my pack doesn't kill me first, that is.

Chapter Three
Lucien

"You're doing fucking *what*?" I explode.

Max's deep voice rumbles out of the speaker, his guilty tone telling me we're in the shit – again.

"She's in bad shape, Luc. I don't even know if she's going to live, but I have to try and help. I can't just walk away from this. You understand that, right?"

Next to me, my brother Bastien pushes back his dark hair to massage his fingers against his temples. Nikolai sits motionless opposite me, his face tight with tension and his blue eyes fixed to the screen of the phone on the table in front of us.

"Max," I grit, trying not to snap. "I know you're doing the right thing, but I'm worried about the timings here. We're not far off being out of Leah's insulin, and we need pretty much all the basics stocked up. We'll need to do a full stock run and I don't want us to split up any more than we already have. How long do you need?"

I'm not the kind of pack leader that demands full obedience from my pack. But goddamned if Max isn't pushing me to the very edge of my fucking sanity.

"I'm sorry, Luc," he offers, sincerity ringing in his words. "But I can't leave her, and I know you wouldn't either. If you saw her…," he audibly swallows. Nikolai shifts in his seat, tension radiating from his giant frame.

I grit my teeth. "Two weeks, and we'll need you back here. Bastien – can you sort the ID trail and background info?"

My brother nods as he straightens, his grey eyes already flickering as he thinks through options. "Yeah, I can do that. Max – how detailed do I need to be?"

"As detailed as possible," Max says. "Thanks, Bas. These guys are hardcore."

I grit my teeth. Max's savior complex has gotten us into trouble more than once, but this one feels like it could truly implode.

"Talk us through it again," Nik demands, a hint of a growl behind his words. I glance at him but he ignores me.

Max runs through what he knows about this injured omega before he pauses.

"What is it?" I snap. *What the fuck now?*

"She… she's pregnant. With twins." Max's voice is somber.

Everyone inhales sharply. My stomach twists. *Pregnant.*

"What?"

"How—"

"We can't—"

Nik and Bastien start bickering over each other, and I snap out a growl, shutting them up.

"Max," I challenge. "If she's pregnant, they'll be watching her like hawks. We're not going to be able to help her get out of this."

Not without bringing the law down on our heads. I hate having to say it, but one of us has to be reasonable. Max's silence speaks volumes. *Stubborn fucker*. Nik growls softly but doesn't speak.

"Luc, if you *saw* her – I—shit," Max's voice drops. "I gotta go. Please just fucking trust me. She *needs* us. I'll call when I can."

The line goes dead.

"Fuck!"

I pace around our kitchen, linking my hands behind my head as I try to think through the worry pounding at my skull like a sledgehammer "This is too dangerous. He's putting himself and the pack at risk."

Nik leans back in his chair, his deep blue eyes solemn as Bastien shifts, fingers no doubt itching for his keyboard already.

"He's right, though," Bastien says with a hint of excitement. "Isn't this exactly what we've talked about before? We said we wanted to help omegas who needed it—"

"Not like this, Bas. It's way too public," I snap. "What if they realize his background's a cover?"

"You know that's unlikely," Nik throws in, a soft growl underlying his words. "Bastien can cover him."

"It only takes one phone call to check, and this whole insane half-plan will fall apart. And what happens then?" I throw my hands up.

How the hell am I supposed to protect a pack that refuses to be protected?

"She needs help," Nik mutters. "Max has the right skills to do that. Seems straightforward to me." He stands as if to leave the room.

I try to make them see sense one last time. "I'm not saying he shouldn't help her. But he's putting our family at risk if he tries to do any more than that. He already sounds attached to this omega. We have no idea of her background or even her fucking name. What if this comes back on Nash, Nik?"

He curls his lips back, snapping at me in a low tone. "*I trust Max*. And we've talked about this, Luc. About helping omegas. Was that bullshit? Or are only the *easy ones* worth helping now?"

Cold clenches in my gut as regret thrums in my chest, and I stare at my packmate. His jaw is tense as he shakes his head before sitting back down.

"None of them will ever be easy to help, Luc," he says softly. "Not with the fucking OC involved."

Taking a deep breath, I swallow around the golf ball that's taken up residence in my throat and rub my hand over my face. Exhaustion fills me, the worry that's settled in my chest over the last few weeks since Max left curling fingers around my muscles, trying to physically drag me down.

I sigh. "This is way beyond anything we've done before."

"We know that," Bastien says quietly. "But Max won't put us at risk. He's only helping her get the treatment she needs. This shouldn't come back on us in any way."

Not intentionally, I know. But it only takes a moment for Max's actions to come crashing down around us and tear us all apart.

Bastien gets up from the table. "I'm going to work on his background."

Nik stays where he is, his fingers clenched on the table as I pull up a chair next to him.

"Am I being that unreasonable?" I ask, a tired sigh punctuating my words. "I just want us all to be safe, Nik. And this is the furthest thing from safe that I can think of."

My packmate watches me, his dark blue eyes seeing too much as always.

Chapter Three

"It's fine to be worried, Luc," he says quietly. "But Bastien is right. We've always said that we wanted to help people like Emery." Nik's breath hitches on her name, and I look away as he clears his throat. "This omega sounds like she needs help more than anyone I've ever met."

"And you're okay with this?" I ask.

His brow furrows. "Of course I am. How could I not be?"

My chest twists.

"When you put it like that, I feel like an asshole," I admit, my body slumping back into the chair.

He gets up, resting a hand on my shoulder. "You're not an asshole, Luc." His words are soft, but they cut into my chest like knives. "You made this house a home, you know. You kept us together – kept *me* together. I understand why you don't want to risk that. But what type of pack would we be if we stood by and let shit like this happen?"

A typical alpha pack, that's what. Rutting, snarling, misogynistic assholes who want omegas for their status, not because they give a fuck about their conditions.

Nik's right. That's not the type of pack I want to lead.

Grimacing, I nod in reluctant agreement. Nik squeezes my shoulder before he heads off, leaving me to my thoughts.

I blow out a breath, staring out of the window at the grounds behind our house. The normally green grass is starting to wilt, autumn settling in, although the temperatures are still warm for this time of year. Catching the depleted log pile, I decide to head out and chop some wood, burn off some of my anxiety. For Max, for Nash, for my pack, even for this omega.

As I leave the kitchen, heading into our large living area, my gaze is drawn to the small wooden staircase winding up in the corner. The one we never use. We all try to avoid looking at it, particularly Nikolai. An echo of pain flickers in my chest, the bond reflecting the turmoil Nik won't admit to out loud. Even the idea of having an omega here, in the space that was meant for Emery…

It makes my chest hurt, and she wasn't my mate.

That's not happening. Max is only treating her, nothing else.

Pushing away my morbid thoughts, I head to the main door, the stained glass sending shadows of lights across our wooden floors, I try to ignore the thoughts flitting through my head, focusing on the old tree trunk we've been taking in turns to cut up, giving us wood for the winter.

The wind outside is brisk, and I rub my hands on my arms, regretting the short-sleeved shirt I put on this morning. A branch rustles behind me and I pause. The rustling stops and I wander on, a smile tugging at my lips.

Three, two, one…

"Gotcha!"

Little arms wind their way around my neck as a voice shrieks into my ear. I playfully cry out and dramatically fall to the floor, careful not to squash the little boy clinging to me.

High-pitched giggles peal out as I flip Nash over and tickle him mercilessly.

"Noo!" he cries, laughing hard as I lean in to blow a raspberry on his neck. "Uncle Luuuuc!"

Letting out a bark of laughter, I take pity on him and let him scramble up. Nash pulls himself into a sitting position next to me, and I bump his little shoulder gently with mine.

"Where's Lee?" I ask. Nash is supposed to be with Max's sister in her cabin. His eyes flicker to the side with clear guilt. "She's… in her cabin?" he asks.

"Is she?" I feign surprise. "Isn't that where you're supposed to be too?"

Chapter Three

Nash pouts, his bottom lip sticking out adorably. "I don't want to do spellings today, Uncle Luc. It's too nice outside."

"Careful," I warn, grabbing his lip gently. "Leave that out and one of the birds might grab it."

Nash gasps dramatically, holding his lip and mumbling something that I don't catch. I watch him for a moment as he throws himself back into a bunch of leaves.

"Uncle Luc?"

"Yes, bud?"

"When's Uncle Max getting back?"

Nash's brow furrows in concern. Too much concern for a six-year-old.

"Soon, Nash. We just talked to him. He won't be long, but he needs to help someone first."

Nash considers this for a minute, his acorn-colored eyes reflecting the trees around us in the afternoon autumn sunshine.

"I guess that's okay," he declares seriously.

"It is?"

"Sure," he says. "Because helping people is really imprudent. Aunt Lee told me. And Papa."

"Important?"

"That's what I said!"

I bite back a laugh at his earnest expression, but it swells into sadness. Nash is so like his mom sometimes it's painful.

Nash is the reason we're all here. The reason our pack exists at all, really.

Nikolai built our house, hidden on acres of land, as part of his long-term plan to protect Emery from the reach of the Omega Creed. We'd already bought the land through a series of false identities thanks to my brother Bastien, our chief technical wizard. We wanted to do everything we could to get them somewhere safe, even though we hadn't made any decisions on the pack at that stage.

When Em died, we came here anyway. All our broken, grieving parts, a pack held together by prayers and sheer fucking stubbornness, with a newborn baby and a shattered alpha to take care of. It took months to even get Nik to eat, only Nash able to pull him out of his grief. Max haunted the hallways like a ghoul, his guilt soaking into the walls of the house until I could almost taste the tart scent on my tongue.

Bastien and I did the best we could with the help of Max's sister Leah, making sure the house was as protected as we could possibly be, and that we had the right set-up to keep Nash safe for life. But it took us years to reach any kind of normality.

My brother was right. We have talked about whether we might be able to help other omegas like Em keep out of the reach of the Omega Compound and their stupid fucking rules. Between Bastien's not-so-legal skillset for hacking, and my gift for the stock markets, we've got more than enough money and knowledge to help anyone who needs it.

This is the first omega we've come across, though. And she's in the worst possible fucking situation, the eyes of the OC undoubtedly focused firmly on her due to her pregnancy.

I understand why Max wants to save this omega. I do. Fuck, if there was a way to get her away from them without putting my pack at risk, I'd go there myself.

I just hope that we don't lose what we've built because of it.

Nash cuddles into me, hoping to avoid his schooling for the day. Affectionately, I run my hand over his downy blonde hair.

I know I can be over-protective. Our home was built on the ashes of grief and loss, and became something *more*. It's Nash's home. And anything that could put our family at risk is never going to win my vote. This situation with the omega at the hospital has trouble written all over it. What we've done is dangerous enough – and I know Max. He won't leave her there, especially if she's pregnant.

If anything goes wrong, we're all screwed.

Chapter Four
Nikolai

The dream comes out of nowhere.

"Niko, catch me!"

The impatient redhead runs full pelt down the dock and I curse as I swim towards the stone steps. "It's too shallow!" I shout, but she's yelling war cries like she's heading into battle and doesn't hear me. My heart drops into my stomach as Emery flings herself off the pier, sailing clear over my head to cannonball into the water.

"Emery!"

She doesn't come up for a second, and I continue bellowing her name as I swim over to where she jumped.

I panic as I swim around in the water, diving down for a glimpse of her.

"Em—fuck!"

The little witch grabs hold of my legs from below the

water, unbalancing me and sending me under with a splash. I come up for air with a gasp, spluttering her name.

"Little idiot," I wheeze. "You scared me, Emery!"

The smile falls from her lips and she glares at me in response. "Stop treating me like a kid, Nikolai," she hisses back at me, pushing dark red hair away from her face.

I don't get it. She's been like this all summer, since she came back from a year at boarding school. Since she changed.

I swallow hard as she treads water until she's pressed against me, the warmth of her body sinking into my chest. Desperately, I try to pull away. Max will kill me if I try anything with his little cousin.

Even if she's not so little anymore. Even if I can't stop wondering about her curves, her eyes, her damned infectious laugh.

"Don't," she pleads, grabbing my arm and pulling me back to her. I stare into her eyes, so like the oak trees at the end of my yard.

"I can't, Em," I mutter. Even as I say it, I can't resist lifting my hand up and pushing strands away from her face. The lines of Emery's face are so familiar to me – but not, at the same time. It's the feeling I get when rereading a favorite book after years and discovering something I didn't catch the first time. Except I feel like that every time I stare at her.

She only pushes closer to me. "You can," she breathes. It's so soft, like a whisper of air against my lips.

Our lips clash, awkward and fumbling and so damned right. The taste of cherries on my tongue, the sounds she makes as I wrap my arms around her, finally.

Like coming home.

A rushing sound makes me look up. Behind Emery, a hole opens up, water pouring off the sides like a waterfall.

Emery's grasp tightens around my waist and I look down into her panicked face.

"Niko," she cries. "It's pulling me!"

Desperately, I try to pull her backwards, try to swim away. But no matter how hard I try, I can't stop the power of the water, can't stop her arms being torn free of mine as she's dragged away. Can't move a step towards her as I float, frozen in place. As Em is pulled over the sides of the hole, and it closes up like nothing ever happened.

I wake to sweat-covered sheets, my chest heaving as I fight for breath.

"Shit." That *fucking* dream again.

Untangling myself from the sheets wrapped around my legs, I stagger into the small en-suite bathroom, flicking the light on and running the faucet to splash cold water onto my face. It takes a few minutes before I feel steady enough to lift my face and look in the mirror.

Would you recognize me now, Em?

It's only been ten years since that day. A drop in the ocean compared to the lifetime we should have had together. But I feel like I've lived a hundred years since that day at the dock. Alone.

A hole torn right through my soul where Emery should be.

I tug gently on my pack bond, reassured when Luc and Bastien both send a pulse back to me. Luc's has a questioning tinge to it, and I push back. I don't need a hug, I just need to make sure they're safe. Max doesn't respond. He's too far away from us.

Pushing away my unease at the reminder, I remake my bed and slide into the cool sheets. I wonder if I'll sleep at all for the rest of the night. Staring at the ceiling, my mind wanders to Max and his omega.

His pregnant omega.

Unbidden, my mind slips to Emery. Her excitement when we found out she was pregnant, our first scan with Max gently rubbing cold liquid onto her belly and making her laugh. The nursery we planned to build here, in a space where no one would ever find her and take her away from us.

The screaming. The blood. Max, face ashen, telling me we had to take her to the hospital or lose them both. The despair in his face as he fought to save his cousin.

Memories march through my mind like a wave of soldiers. I can't push them back, can't escape them no matter how much I beg. I know there's no one out there to listen to my prayers. I stopped praying six years ago.

I understand why Max wants to save this omega. Nash and I aren't the only ones who lost someone that day. He tried so fucking hard to save his cousin and it wasn't enough.

I just can't see a happy ending for this one either.

My eyes stay open until the sun creeps against my far wall.

Chapter Five
Ava

Voices creep into my mind, fading in and out like a bad radio station. Words rise and fall around me, unfamiliar and undeniably male.

A noise wheezes from my throat. I can't see. I can't move.

The voices stop. I don't want them to stop.

My brain feels like cotton wool. I can't remember my name. I can't remember who I am. All I know is that if they stop talking, then bad things will happen.

There's warmth next to me. A hand brushes down my arm.

No.

Nonononononono.

Chapter Six
Max

"She needs to come off that medication."

The dickhead alpha and I are facing each other in the office, yet another standoff. Stone crosses his arms over his chest.

"Conscious or unconscious, it doesn't matter. All I need is—"

"I *know* what you need," I snap. It comes out harsher than I intended, and Stone's mouth tightens. It's a sure sign that I'm treading on thin ice.

I force myself to calm down. Aggression is leaking from my pores, and if I keep it up, we'll have two brawling alphas tearing the office apart. And he definitely won't let me take her off the meds if that happens. I'll be lucky if I ever see her again.

My chest tightens at the thought, and I push the feelings down. I don't want to consider why saving this omega has suddenly become so important to me.

But it has. *She* has.

I've barely left the floor since signing up to be the omega's personal physician. It's clear that Stone ran some checks on my background, but they held up against Bastien's skills.

And she's no better. In fact, she's worse.

"If you continue to pump her full of sedatives to keep her asleep, she will be dead in a matter of days." My voice is dark as I lay out the facts in a way that I hope will get through to him. "She'll be dead, and those children will not survive to term. Her body is too weak to handle these constant levels of narcotics. Her heart is going to *stop*, Stone."

I hate this man more than I've ever hated anyone. He stares at me, expressionless.

"If you want to save *them*," I point out, "then we have to save *her* first."

His fist clenches on the armrest. "Fine."

I don't let my jubilation show. "Excellent," I say, turning for the door. He says my name as I'm about to leave, and I turn around.

Those gunmetal eyes are assessing. "It would not be a good idea to become too attached to my daughter, Dr. Morgan."

Asshole doesn't even deserve to use the word. I don't respond, turning and pulling the door shut behind me harder than I probably need to.

Don't I fucking know it.

Heading back into the omega's room, I stop Nicole, the nurse I met on my first day, from hooking up another bag of that shit.

"Reduce the dosage down hourly," I tell her. She shoots a look at the door and back at me.

"He's approved it. 10 milligrams less per hour."

I can't take her off all her meds straight away – the shock to her system could kill her. As it stands, if I can even wake

Chapter Six

her up, she could still have to go through withdrawal. We'll cross that bridge when we come to it.

Pulling up a chair, I settle in to catch a few hours of sleep. The dark circles under my eyes tell me I'm not getting enough of it.

I wake up some time later, yawning and rubbing sleep from my eyes in the darkened room. The ever-present monitors beep in the background, reassuring me that she's still here.

Still with me.

Leaning forward, I study her face.

Even in unconsciousness, she looks troubled. Brow furrowed, she shifts, and I check her charts. I've slept for a few hours and her dosage has reduced further in that time. It's a hopeful sign that we're seeing some movement.

My eyes slide to her swollen stomach and away, shame crawling up my throat. I'm part of the shitty world that did this to her. My mind flits to Emery, and I shake my head, clearing it of bad memories.

Another movement draws my attention back. Standing to check the monitors strapped to her body, I confirm that her vital signs are stable and so are the heart monitors connected to the twins, making a note in the chart.

The crude scent of oil winds around me as Stone enters the room, making my lip curl as he comes to stand next to me.

"Update?"

"She's stable, for now. Signs of consciousness. Heart rate is steady—"

I bite off my words as the beeping suddenly increases in frequency. "Shit."

"What is it?" Stone demands.

Ignoring him, I check her pulse, my own starting to race like it's connected to hers. Her heart rate is increasing rapidly, the peaceful rise and fall of her chest changing to a choppy, ragged pace. A quick check on the babies' vitals shows they're still stable, but the omega's heart rate is rapidly climbing to dangerous levels.

No. I am not losing you.

"Nicole!"

She comes running from the front desk with wide eyes.

"Bring the defibrillator," I snap. "We might need to restart her heart."

The omega's arms start to pull jerkily at the restraints. Pulling a flashlight from my coat pocket, I lift her eyelids to check her response. Her pupils flicker back and forth, dilating against the light.

"Come on, omega," I snarl.

"Check on the children," Stone pushes behind me.

"They're fine," I throw over my shoulder. "But they won't be if *she* isn't."

I turn back to the omega and freeze.

Dull, vacant eyes look back at me.

Chapter Seven
Ava

Flashes of light creep beneath my eyelids, pulling me back to the land of the living.

It feels like a herd of elephants have been trampling through my head. Blinking once, twice, I shake my head to try and clear the glaze across my eyes.

Fuck, that was a bad idea.

A cool breeze shivers across my skin. Lifting my arms, I try to rub them, but something tugs at my wrist. *Both* wrists.

Something nudges at my memory. *Why can't I move my arms?*

Why am I so tired?

Who am I?

My head pounds, overwhelmed by lights, pain and creeping dread. My palms tingle as my fingers close, my fist clenching. Who the fuck *am* I?

Sound burbles close by, and I twist my head as slowly as I can, seeking out the source of the noise. My bleary sight shows me the outline of someone leaning over me.

They lean closer. It's a *male*.

White-hot, incoherent terror splinters up my insides.

Chapter Eight
Max

The omega and I lock gazes, her vacant eyes gradually sharpening into clear focus.

An overwhelming scent of burnt sugar floods the room, the intensity stinging the back of my nose. Then she *whines*, a high-pitched, petrified sound that pulls me forward.

My hand reaches up to cup her face, instinctively soothing a distressed omega. "Shhhh," I murmur, but she tries to pull herself away from me. "You're safe. You're safe here, and you're in the hospital."

She doesn't respond, her face lined with fear as she pulls back as far as she can. I turn to Stone, trying not to punch him in the face. He's watching closely, his face looking a little paler than normal. Good. Let him see what he's fucking done.

"What's her name?" I demand.

"8—," he begins, but I snarl back at him. I'm done with his bullshit.

"Don't give me that shit. What's her real fucking name, Stone?"

Chapter Eight

He shakes his head in refusal, lips pressed together firmly, and I turn back around with a curse. The omega starts to thrash, her frail limbs everywhere as she pulls hard against the restraints, the veins in her neck pulsing against that fucking collar around her neck as she gasps for breath, gagging around the tube in her throat. Her body pulls away from me, and I belatedly realize how I must look, leaning over her, an unfamiliar alpha in an unfamiliar place.

You stupid prick, Max.

Forcing my feet back a step, I give her space as she weakly tries to pull herself away from me. Small, anguished noises squeeze from her throat around the tubes, each one pulling at my heartstrings. The omega wretches, the tubes kicking in and pushing against the collar, and Nicole makes a concerned noise from the doorway. The defibrillator hangs loosely from her hand, her eyes wide.

Spinning to Stone, I snarl. "Take that collar off."

He huffs derisively. "I don't think so."

"She can't breathe, Stone!"

She's going to seriously injure herself.

"Do you want them to survive this or not?"

Where the fuck is she going to go, with her arms and legs strapped to the bed like a fucking lab rat?

Stone glares at me as he pulls a set of keys from his pocket. Moving past me, he selects one from the ring and forces the omega's head to the side. Her whimpers pull me forward a step, a distress signal I can't ignore. Stone pushes the key into the lock, snapping his teeth as she tries to pull away from him. The collar unlatches with a click and Stone pulls it away roughly, squeezing his fist around the metal.

I make a split decision even as I hate myself for it. But it's better than the alternative, better than filling her with more drugs to make her sleep again.

Striding back toward her, her eyes flicker as she sees me

and she moans in distress. Her previously subtle vanilla and sugar scent is almost unrecognizable now, the acidic spikes flooding the room betraying just how terrified she is.

My arm reaches out and she renews her push to escape, the leather restraints yanking in a way that must be hurting her. She's too far gone to realize.

I curl my hand around her throat as gently as I can, mindful of the wires. A high-pitched whine reverberates through my wrist.

"Stop," I growl. When she slows but doesn't stop, I push her again, my alpha bark curling out of my throat and wrapping itself around her.

"Stop this," I bark at her, and she freezes. Her eyes clear slightly, showing me flecks of hazel and green that disappear behind a mist of tears.

She makes a pleading sound, but it's muffled behind the tube. Stone move in from behind me, but I hold up my other hand, not breaking our eye contact, and he stops. I can feel his disapproval sinking into my back, but I don't give a flying fuck what he thinks at this moment.

The sound of his shoes hitting the floor disturbs the omega. Her eyes start to flicker around the room, looking for danger, and her already rapid breathing starts to speed up even more.

"Give us the room," I bark.

Nicole makes a swift exit, but Stone stays where he is. Keeping my tone low, I turn my face away to growl at him.

"Her heart rate is elevated. If I don't calm her down, it will escalate until her heart stops. At that stage, I may need to defib her or put her back under. Either of those may mean that we lose her and the twins. Give. Us. The. Fucking. Room."

His response is low and furious. "I'd better see some improvement from this, Dr. Morgan."

Chapter Eight

The door slams behind him, and I ignore it as I turn back to her.

She watches me with wet eyes. Tears slip out and down her cheeks, soaking my wrist. When I lean in to meet her eyes, she makes another muffled plea, the restraints sliding against the railings holding her in place. The edge of a whine urges me forward.

I speak quietly, but firmly.

"My name is Dr. Morgan. You're in the hospital and you have been in an induced coma for several months. You are safe here, and nobody is going to hurt you."

She stares at my mouth, following my words. When I finish, she squeezes her eyes shut tightly and makes a noise around the tubes. I point to the ventilator next to her and release my grip, keeping my movements slow.

"The tubes in your throat are connected to a machine that's been helping you to breathe while you slept. Now that you're awake, I can take them out. Are you comfortable with that?"

She pauses, wide eyes scanning my face. Keeping my expression calm, I wait, not pushing her for a response.

I exhale in relief at her small nod. Turning, I check to make sure we have the right equipment in the room for extubation. I debate calling Nicole back in, but it should be simple enough.

And I don't want anyone else in here right now. I push down a low growl at the thought. I should not be anywhere near this protective over a patient – let alone an omega in her condition, with her level of trauma. It goes against everything I was taught at med school.

Taking measured steps across the room, I keep her in my line of sight, washing my hands in the small sink as her breathing levels out. Clearing my throat, I focus on explaining what's going to happen, preparing her for my movements. *Try and keep it fucking professional, Max.*

"Before I can take the tube out, I need to suction it to clear out anything that might stop you breathing properly when it's removed. I'll do the same in your mouth outside of the pipe. The tube is held in place by a cuff – sort of like a balloon – inside your throat, so to take out the tube I need to let it down very slowly and then I can remove it and give you a normal oxygen mask. It's pretty uncomfortable—"

I pause as an unmistakable small huff of derision comes from the bed. My lips twitch. Glancing over, horror lines her face as she stares at me warily. She's clearly waiting for a response, but I carry on.

"It's uncomfortable, and you'll probably cough a lot – that's completely normal."

Coming to a pause in front of her, I get everything I need ready, noting her breathing stop as I get closer. When I glance at her face, her eyes are squeezed closed, tears gently dripping from her eyelids and down into her hair.

My hand reaches out impulsively before I ball my fingers into a fist. She won't welcome comfort right now. She doesn't like having me so close to her.

Trauma response.

I swallow. I want to give her the space she needs, but those tubes need to come out.

"Are you ready?" I ask her gently.

Her eyes flick to the device in my hand and back to my face, wariness creeping back in.

"I'm not going to hurt you." My whisper sounds like a vow in the quiet space, dropping between us like a rock.

She nods and closes her eyes.

Chapter Nine
Ava

My body shakes as the unfamiliar alpha leans in closer to me. His scent soaks into me, a heavy dose of apple pie. Despite my fears, it's strangely soothing.

Not an alpha, I lie to myself. *A doctor. Just a normal, beta doctor.*

Focusing on my breathing, I try to keep it even as he fusses with the pipe attached to my throat. My mind still feels like cotton wool, and I can't look around because of the tube, so I push down the feelings swirling inside me and focus on the doctor.

His slightly bushy, dark eyebrows furrow as he writes something down on a clipboard. Russet hair falls over his forehead and into his eyes as he pushes it away impatiently. Earthy brown eyes lift and catch me watching him, and a slight red flush colors his cheeks.

If I were a different girl, a beta, then I'd probably call him handsome. But I'm not a different girl. All I feel is empty. The most hideous of monsters can sit behind a charming smile. I move my eyes to the ceiling and keep them there.

Just breathe. In, out, in, out. Don't go back to sleep.

His voice rumbles as he tries to distract me. When I ignore him, his voice takes on a questioning lilt, and I nod. *Whatever. Just get on with it.*

Although I don't know why I want them out. The longer they keep me here, the longer I stay away from *there*.

Memories threaten to break through, and I scrunch my eyes closed. Images flicker like a projector screen, a mixture of hands and faces and alphas and burning and—

The whimper slips out, and the doctor pauses. His brown eyes soften as he watches me.

"You still with me?" he murmurs quietly.

I don't want my concentration to break, so I ignore him again. When he pulls back, I could scream and cry with relief at the same time. I just want him to get on with it.

A hand comes to rest gently on my arm.

Nausea rises, twisting my stomach viciously. *Don't touch me.*

The restraints pull against my arms as my fists clench. I swing my eyes to him with a glare, and he takes a step back, hands raised in apology as he watches me.

Glancing away from me, he inhales deeply and blows out a breath.

"Look," he says roughly. "I know that you've been through something that nobody should have to go through. Something that I will never be able to understand. And I know that the last person you want around you right now is an alpha."

My flinch draws his eyes to mine. He takes a small step closer.

"I am *sorry*," he whispers fiercely, his voice low but

determined. "I am so fucking sorry that this has happened to you. I promise, I only want to help."

Sincerity rings through his tone.

A lump appears in my throat. Breaking our gaze, I drop my eyes down to his hand and blink.

I'm asking him to carry on with the tube removal, but he mistakes my meaning and slowly reaches for my hand, curling his warm fingers against mine. My vision blurs as tears well up. I can't remember the last time anyone touched me with any sort of gentleness, but just the feel of his skin touching mine makes my skin crawl.

I'm broken.

As I slip my hand out from his, he immediately pulls back from me, clearing his throat.

"Should I carry on with your tubes?" he asks softly, and I nod, turning back to the ceiling.

He starts his work again, gently probing the tube with a device that makes a humming noise. It barely registers as I stare at the ceiling. His words aren't so easily ignored, though.

"You've been here for four months."

Four months? I blink rapidly as his words sink in, but he's already carrying on, his voice low.

"You were admitted because you had been given too many doses of codroctymal. Artificial heat hormones." His voice breaks off as he clears his throat uncomfortably.

Burning. Burningburningburningburning.

Brown eyes appear in my line of sight, a hand pressed to my cheek as I wheeze for breath. My chest seizes from the lack of air. *Too close. He's too close.*

His growl is low but enough to capture my attention. "Breathe."

I struggle to get in enough air around the tube, and he

curses under his breath before continuing his work a little faster than before.

"You'll feel better when this is out."

He's silent whilst he works, cleaning around my mouth gently with a suction tube. Finally, he starts fiddling with the tube, and pressure releases in my throat.

"That's it. It's coming out now, I'll take it slowly. Don't worry if you need to cough."

He gradually draws the tube from my throat, making my eyes water. The cough builds up and explodes as soon as the tube is out, forcing tears from my eyes and down my face. I try to lean forward but the restraints pull me back.

Hands pull me onto my side, and I wheeze as I try to push them away.

"You need to be able to breathe, sweetheart. Turn on your side as much as you can. These fucking restraints…"

His last words are almost under his breath, but I still catch them. *What kind of doctor curses like that?*

The burning in my throat subsides when he offers me a glass of water with a straw. I slurp it down, not caring enough to be embarrassed when it drops down my chin and onto my gown. He pulls it away before I finish, my throat closing as I fight off more tears. I'm so thirsty. I need *more*.

"Steady, now. Too much will make you sick."

He holds the straw back against my lips as I sip greedily, hyper-aware of his body perched on the edge of the bed next to me. My nerves stand on end, but I want the water more. Breathing slowly, I try to push the panic back down. Exhaustion is already pulling at my bones, trying to drag me back to sleep despite apparently being unconscious for *months*.

God. What happened?

Leaning back against the hard pillow once my thirst is finally slaked, the doctor gently places the glass on the nightstand next to my bed.

Chapter Nine

I expect him to leave, but he sits perfectly still for a moment, his eyes on the door. I strain to hear his quiet words.

"My name is Dr. Morgan," he says, his honeyed brown eyes meeting mine. "But you can call me Max."

A strange expression flits over his face. I wonder if he'll get in trouble for telling me his first name. It doesn't seem like something a doctor would do. But then, he hasn't acted like I would have expected a government doctor to act. *Max*.

I wet my lips with my tongue, wondering if my sore throat will let me speak. Wondering if I dare to speak the word aloud, to trust him not to punish me.

"Ava," I rasp. It's painful and quiet, but it comes out.

I haven't heard my name out loud for a long time.

The doctor – *Max* – smiles as a machine starts to beep next to me. I turn my head to look, no longer restricted by the tubes in my throat.

Scanning the room, I take in the bland grey walls, the steel sink in the corner, the tall wooden cupboard. Artificial strip lights above us throw Max's face into sharp angles, highlighting the beginnings of a beard. There's no window, and a hint of regret flickers in my chest. I would have liked to see outside.

The machine beeps again, and I glance over to see my heartbeat on the screen. It looks fast, like a hummingbird.

If only I could fly away.

My attention is drawn to the next machine, and I look between them, confused. Why do they have two heart monitors? Three, I realize, taking in the one next to it.

Maybe they're not heart monitors? My eyes trail the wire from the first machine that caught my attention, following it from where it's plugged into the monitor, down and onto the bed and towards my stomach.

For the first time, I pay proper attention to my body. A

stab of pain hits my chest as I suck in a breath, my vision tunnelling. More beeping sounds, and then Max is there, concern in his eyes as he follows my gaze.

A whimper sounds in my throat, and his eyes swing to mine, horror filling them.

"You didn't know," he whispers, swallowing hard. "Ava, you're—"

"No," I gasp.

No. He is not going to tell me that. He can't tell me that.

But the truth is literally staring me in the fucking face.

I'm pregnant.

Chapter Ten
Nikolai

Lucien paces around my workshop again. No matter how much I try to hide away in the wooden hut on our grounds, my pack always seem to wander in when I'm trying to focus.

I give him the side-eye as he growls and throws his hands up in the air. "Talking to yourself isn't a good sign, Lucien."

"What?" he snaps, turning to me. Sighing, I point to the chair.

"Sit your ass down. You're giving me whiplash watching you strop back and forth."

Luc throws himself down, hunching his shoulders as he huffs in frustration. His raven hair stands on end from the dozens of times he's run his hands through it.

"We should have heard from him by now."

I lay down my sanding machine and take a seat next to him, crossing my arms.

"He needs to be careful," I point out. "And he doesn't need to call all the time – Bastien has been tracking his phone and it's still at the hospital."

"But it hasn't *moved* from the hospital for three days," Luc snaps. I growl lightly back at him and he waves a hand at me in apology.

"Sorry," he groans. "I just—"

"I know, Luc, but we need to trust him. If we don't hear from him by tomorrow, we'll make contact. And if he doesn't respond, we'll go and bring him home. Agreed?"

He looks across at me, guilt across his face. "I'm being an asshole, aren't I?"

I pull my shoulder up in a shrug, a smile twitching on my lips. "Nothing more than usual."

Luc shoves at me with a strained laugh, getting up to leave. As he walks past my workbench, he stops and looks down.

"What's this?" he asks, lifting one of the figures.

We both look at the scattered parade of figurines decorating my workbench, one for each of us. "Nash asked me for something new to play with."

I turn my back to Luc and move over to mess around with my paint, hating the pity I see on his face as he picks up a redheaded female figure.

A moment later, he places his hand on my back. "I'm sorry. I know this is hard. I shouldn't be making it worse."

I turn back to him, fondness creeping into my expression as I look into his forlorn green eyes. "You're not. It is hard, but Max is doing what he needs to. And if he's helping an omega, then he can take the time he needs. He knows when the meds run out, and we have time, Luc. You should put more faith in him."

Luc winces slightly. "I know. I was an asshole in the kitchen."

I raise my eyebrow at him, but I won't deny it. He was, and he knows it.

Chapter Ten

Luc knows that I would never refuse an omega in need. Not after Emery.

Familiar pain punches me in the gut.

They say that time heals all wounds. I say they're full of fucking shit. If anything, mine has festered, leaving an Emery-shaped hole in my heart. And the only one who has a chance of filling it is—

"Papa!"

A crash announces Nash's arrival and I catch my son in my hands, swooping him into my arms before he can cause any more chaos.

"Nash, you know you can't run around in here." I bop him on the nose as he cringes and slides out of my arms, a crestfallen look on his face as he rights the stool he just knocked over.

"Sorry, papa. Aunt Lee asked me to come and get you and Luc. Uncle Max is on the phone!"

Luc flies out of the room before I can do more than blink. Nash stares at the space he leaves behind, his mouth open a little.

"Papa," he whispers. "I think Uncle Luc has magic powers."

Snickering, I grab him and carry him out of the workshop, swinging him up onto my shoulders as we follow Luc's path to the pack house. Leah paces on the veranda, chewing on her lip as her hands grip her elbows. Nash waves to her enthusiastically, and she offers us a wan smile in return.

"I'll take him." She nods her head at Nash. "I think Luc's gonna blow a gasket unless you calm him down."

A frustrated bellow echoes out of the doorway behind her. Nash's eyes widen, and I nudge him toward Leah.

"Go and finish your schoolwork, Nash. I'll come and get you when we're done."

He drags his feet, glancing behind him as Leah takes his hand and they move in the direction of her cabin. My breath constricts as I watch his little legs trudge along.

We all try so hard, but he's getting to the age where it's obvious he's missing out. Social interaction, kids his own age. I wonder for a second if we did the right thing in deciding to keep him away from society completely, rather than Bastien attempting to create a false record for him.

Another shout pulls my attention back to the house. When I get to the kitchen, Luc gives me a look and points to the phone before throwing his hands up. "He's lost his damn mind!"

"Niko's here, Max," Bastien announces, leaning back in his seat and rolling his eyes at me.

Luc stares at me with a pained gaze, his face filled with trepidation. A prickle runs up my neck.

"What is it?" I demand. "What's wrong?"

Max's voice sounds strained over the speaker. "It's the omega, Nik."

I straighten at his somber tone, fists clenching on the walnut wood of our table. "How's she doing?"

I won't admit that Max's omega hasn't been far from my thoughts since our first conversation.

The silence stretches out before he speaks, his voice rough. "She's awake, but she's weak. They want to remove her from the hospital and take her to a secure location for monitoring until the twins can be removed by surgery."

Bastien's brows lower. "If she's better, isn't that a good thing?"

"Stone asked me to go, and I can't."

I can hear how torn he sounds. "Because of the meds?"

"That too." There's a note in it that I don't recognize, haven't heard before despite knowing Max since we were

Chapter Ten

children. "But I just... honestly, I don't think I can leave her, Nik. Not like this. Not with *them*."

His voice cracks on the last word, and I finally understand the tension in the kitchen. Luc unfolds himself from where he's been leaning against the counter and takes a seat next to Bastien.

"You want to bring her here." My words hang in the air, waiting for a response.

"Yes."

We all take a breath.

"Let me get this straight," Lucien rumbles. He's glaring at the phone as though he'd like to wring Max's neck through it. "You want to steal a pregnant omega and bring her here?"

Max makes a noise of affirmation. "I do."

"Max, have you thought this through? Stealing meds and supplies is hard enough. You want to take a person, too? And one who's being closely guarded?" Bastien's voice is firm, but stress lines his forehead as he glances at me.

"I have a plan," Max pleads. "It's a shot in the dark, but it could work."

"And the omega?" I ask. Everyone goes quiet. "What have you said to her?"

Panic slices through me. If he's mentioned our pack, our set-up here, we might all be at risk. We have no idea what loyalties this omega has. We're an unregistered pack with a biological child that was never handed over to the adoption agency. If the government find us, I'll lose Nash.

"Nothing," Max promises instantly, sincerity ringing in his voice and relaxing my muscles. "That's not just my decision to make. I haven't said anything to her. And I wouldn't – just in case..."

His voice trails off.

In case it doesn't work.

Bastien is deep in thought. I can almost see the cogs whirring, identifying possibilities faster than most people could even fathom.

"Tell us the plan," he says suddenly. Luc drops his face into his hands with an exasperated groan. Bastien grabs a notebook that's been left on the table and flips it open, his silver-gray eyes meeting mine across the table. "Talk us through it, Max, and we'll go from there."

Chapter Eleven
Bastien

My fingers tap against the solid wood of the table. Plates, cups and discarded bits of paper are scattered everywhere, littering the kitchen with half-baked ideas and frustration. Luc stares out through the window at the darkened sky, the tic in his jaw betraying his unease.

Max had to go, with a promise to call back this evening. Nik disappeared to grab Nash from Leah and bring him home for bed, but he slips back in as I pore over the rough notes in my hand.

Max was right. We do have a plan. It's full of enough holes to sink a ship, but it's getting there.

Nik clears his throat and I hand him the notebook, watching as he flicks through it. When he's done, he glances up at me. "Nice work."

"You say that like there was any doubt," I respond wryly. His lip twitches, but stress lines his face. I feel it too, but Nik has a lot more to lose than me.

I lean forward to catch his eye. "If we do this, you're staying here."

His jaw clenches, and he opens his mouth.

"No buts," says Luc firmly. His eyes are resolute, arms crossed as he matches Nik's glare with one of his own. We've talked through all the options.

"You need to be here, Nik," Luc say softly. "Bastien will hook up the van so you can listen in, but Nash needs you. We can't risk it."

And if anything goes wrong, Nik and I can get Nash and Leah out of here quickly and to the emergency site. My stomach flips at the thought.

Standing up, I grab the papers and start pulling them into a file.

"I'm going to my office to run some checks. I'll take the phone with me in case Max calls back."

Luc slides the mobile over to me and I slip it into my pocket.

The phone chimes an hour later, just as I'm digging through the security cameras at the hospital. I answer the call and flip him onto loudspeaker.

"It's just me. I'm in the office."

"Is it hopeless?" Max is clearly aiming for joking, but I can hear the desperation in his voice.

"Nope," I say, popping the 'p' sound in my mouth. "I think we've got it mapped out."

He goes silent for a moment. "You're serious?" he says, a thread of hopefulness coming through.

"Serious as Luc when Nik eats his Froot Loops."

Max snorts out a weary laugh. "Holy shit. Talk me through it."

I take him through the plan that he came up with but I've refined based on camera locations and the research I've done so far. When I trail off, Max picks up on my unspoken question.

"Ava is the biggest risk in this."

"She is," I acknowledge. "Can she handle it?"

Of all of us, Ava will have the most difficult job. Her body will need to be able to handle a certain level of medication, enough to suppress her hormones for a short period, enough that Max can get her through the hospital without raising alarm bells, and through a side exit where Luc will be waiting.

Max's silence speaks volumes.

"Yes," he says finally. His voice is firm. "She can. But she's not strong enough yet. I need a week."

I nod slowly, tapping my pen against the page. "We'll need the week anyway. I need to reach out and see if we can get any help with this."

"You think he'll help?" Max's tone is curious. It's a good question.

"We need him." I hesitate before saying my next words. "This omega... she means something to you."

Max sounds sharp. "She needs our help."

"Max."

We've known each other for too many years to hide our feelings from each other. He might be too far from the pack bond for us to pick anything up, but it's clear from his words and actions that this is personal.

"Fine," he growls. "Yes, I like her. She's brave, so fucking brave, Bastien. She should be in a ball, rocking back and forth, but she's not. She's sad, and she's angry, and maybe she's a bit fucking broken, but who wouldn't be, after what she's been through? And—" he stops and blows out a shaky breath. "She reminds me of Emery."

I wince. "I'm not trying to discourage you, Max."

"It's not like that," he insists. "I *need* to help her because of Emery. I *want* to help her because she's Ava. It doesn't go any further than that for me. Besides… I don't think she'll ever want another alpha near her like that."

Anger courses through my veins and I back down. He's right. Of course, he is.

"Right, then," I say, clearing my throat. "Let's go over this again."

Chapter Twelve
Ava

Vomit burns my nose as I turn my head to the side. Again. Bile trickles down the side of my face, running into my hair. Max rushes over to me but he doesn't touch me. He knows I won't let him.

It's been like this for two days. Dr. Morgan - *Max* - tells me that my body is experiencing withdrawal from the amount of medication I've been given over the last ten months.

I don't know why he's bothering.

"Why?" I whisper. He turns from placing the bowl into the sink, his brows drawing down over his face.

"Why, what?" he asks just as quietly, moving up and taking a seat next to me. He holds up a wet cloth, and I shake my head, not wanting him that close to my face. He places it to the side with a sad smile, but he doesn't push.

"Why are you making me go through this? The withdrawal?"

He holds my gaze. "If they give you any more narcotics, it's very likely that your heart will stop."

I feel a spark of hope in my chest, and his eyes sharpen on mine.

"Let them, Doc," I murmur. "You should just let them."

I know why he won't, though.

I purposefully avoid looking down at the bed. I can't look.

Looking makes it real. Looking means acknowledging what happened to me, and I can't do that right now.

Avoidance, thy name is Ava.

"Ava," Max says softly. "I know—"

"No, you don't," I retort. "You don't know anything, Doc."

I pull at the restraints locking my wrists and ankles to this god-forsaken metal bed.

"They have taken, and taken, and taken. And I have nothing left to give them. But they're going to try anyway."

He shakes his head at me and opens his mouth to argue.

"Stone already told me what's going to happen, Doc."

I won't call that man father. Never again. The alpha who walks in and out of my room, ignoring me unless it's to tell me how my body will be used, is not my father. He came to visit me this morning. Three minutes while Max was out getting food. He doesn't leave me unless he can help it.

Stone noticed that too.

"864."

My body freezes, an instinctive flinch making my restraints jingle against the bars of the trolley as the scent of sulphur and oil invades my nose.

I keep my eyes on the ceiling as he moves to stand next to me. Nausea creeps up my throat as he inspects me like a prized cow. A cold hand cups my stomach and a small noise escapes me. My vision blurs.

"Such a disappointment, 864," he murmurs. "You've been no end of trouble. But thankfully, this situation will be dealt with shortly."

I stay quiet, knowing better than to push any of the creed laws around this alpha. Don't speak. Don't make eye contact.

His hand rubs over my stomach as he speaks, and I battle not to show my revulsion.

"You're well enough to be moved. Tomorrow, you'll be transferred back to the estate until we're able to remove the children. You'll be returned to the nests after that. We'll see if we can get any more use out of you."

My breath stutters, stopping, the pain in my chest piercing. They're sending me back.

A thought strikes me, and I glance toward the door. Stone's hand abruptly grips my chin, his fingers digging in.

"Dr. Morgan will not be accompanying us," he says icily. "He is here for me, not for you, 864."

I close my eyes at the reminder. Max isn't here for me. He's here to get them what they want.

A functioning omega, still breathing, able to carry the male heir Stone desperately wants.

Stone's fingers tighten painfully. "Don't forget what you are, 864," he hisses.

A thread of anger pushes through the empty spaces in my mind.

I slide my eyes to his purposefully. There's only so much he can do with his precious heir inside my stomach. "I know what I am," I croak. "I know what you are, too."

I hold his gaze for a moment longer before my eyes drop, my body physically unable to battle for dominance with an alpha. He drops my chin abruptly, his hand moving to my thigh and gripping it tightly, nails digging in as I inhale sharply at the burning sensation. He squeezes and twists until tears spring in my eyes.

"Useless omega," he snaps as he leaves. "Just like your fucking mother."

I press my lips hard together at his parting shot, unwilling to give him the satisfaction of seeing it land.

Max's face pales as he stares at me. I stare at the ceiling, continuing to count the endless whorls in the plaster. It passes the time.

"They're taking me back," I tell him. My voice echoes slightly in the room, the emptiness in my chest making my words sound monotone, even if they're anything but.

"When?" he asks, his voice hoarse as he sits forward. His tone sounds urgent. "*When*, Ava?"

"Tomorrow," I breathe. "So, you see, Doc, you're wasting your time. You may as well put me back under now and save yourself the clean-up."

I turn to look at him, noting his pale face and his hands tight on the chair. He seems angry.

At least one of us is.

I turn back to the ceiling and lose myself in my counting.

Chapter Thirteen
Max

"When were you going to tell me?"

Stone barely looks up, his tone cutting as he inspects paperwork in the office he's taken over. "Please, do come in, Dr. Morgan."

I ignore his words. "She's not safe to be moved, Stone."

He lets out an aggravated sigh and places the paperwork back down on the desk. "You will be pleased to know that we have completed the recruitment of a specialist team to take over 864's care."

His words hit my chest like a dagger, and aggression rises in my chest. "You *what*?"

He watches me, those gunmetal eyes almost as empty as his daughters.

"You're too close to her," he says plainly. "I don't like it. I appreciate the services you have provided, Dr. Morgan, but they will no longer be needed from midday tomorrow. The new team will take over and my daughter will be transported to my estate, where the children will be delivered as soon as it is safe to do so."

His words burn like acid in my veins.

"And after that?" I challenge.

His mouth turns up at the corner in a cruel smirk.

"It seems that there is a possibility of more children, provided the rest of this process goes smoothly. Following the delivery, she will be returned to her role."

"That's a fucking death sentence," I growl. My hands clench on the chair in front of me.

"If so, then she has outlived her usefulness in any case. It makes no difference to me."

The ice in his tone shocks me, even now. "She's your *daughter*, Stone."

He stands. "She is an omega. And you would do well to remember that, Dr. Morgan. 864 is the property of the government, and I am acting on their behalf. There is no room for family in this situation. We are working to ensure the survival of our race, and her sacrifice is appreciated."

Words fail me.

Midday tomorrow. The two words rotate in my mind. Our plans are for three days' time.

I'm going to lose her. She's going to die.

Stone is watching me closely, and I school my face into a disapproving look. "As a doctor, I believe in the sanctity of human life, Stone. *All* life. That is the reason for my work here. The *only* reason."

"As do I," he responds drily. "I am especially interested in making sure it continues."

I nod, slowly. "I'll prepare for the handover." The words taste like ash on my tongue.

"Thank you, Dr. Morgan." He looks back down at his notes. The dismissal is clear, and I walk out of his room. Ignoring the urge to go back to Ava, I head to the reception desk.

"Check on her every twenty minutes," I tell Nicole.

Truthfully, Ava doesn't need that level of observation now, but her earlier words have disturbed me.

Grabbing my phone, I walk out of the hospital and across to the sandwich bar on the other side of the road. I get a bagel and drink and walk into the park, casually strolling with my hands in my pockets before ducking into a side path. I cross and turn for a few minutes until I reach a secluded area. Settling right in the middle, I lay out my food before dialing Bastien's number. From my position, I'll hear anyone coming.

"Max?" Baz answers immediately.

"We need to move it up. *Now*, Baz." My voice shakes, the emotion I couldn't show in front of Stone leaking out to my packmate.

"What? Why?" I can already hear him tapping frantically, the clunk of his phone being set down as he puts me on speaker.

"Luc and Nikolai are here," he tells me.

"What's happened?" Luc demands.

"Stone is flying in a new team and they're taking her from the hospital to his home tomorrow. Our chance will be gone. We have to move now. I have to do a handover at midday tomorrow."

There's silence on the other end of the phone.

"Max." Luc's voice is resigned, and I squeeze my eyes shut.

"No," I push out through the ache in my throat. "Don't say it, Luc."

It's Nikolai who responds, his voice grim. "It may not be possible to go with the original plan, Max."

"So we need to come up with a new one," I say desperately. We can do this. Nik is right – the original plan was to set a distraction for the guards and get Ava through the emergency exit. We're going to need something else. Something more.

"For us to pull this off we'd need to launch an all-out assault," mutters Luc.

"Not an assault." Bastien's words come slowly as his mind gets to work. "A deception."

"Sorry, Baz," Niko asks. "But who the fuck do you think we are?"

"Not *us*," Bastien sounds exasperated. "I can speak to Devlin."

"No. Too risky."

"You know what happened with their omega."

"No," Lucien insists, his voice tight. "This is too much. We don't know anything for certain, only what we saw on that video. Rogue Winter's father is the director of the fucking OC! Have you lost the fucking plot completely?"

Luc first met Devlin Winter when they went through basic training to join the Government's ranks. Devlin has his own pack, and Luc dropped out when we made the decision to help Nikolai and Em, but we suspected they may have their own omega sympathies thanks to a video that circulated the internet. The Winter pack, going into full rut over their omega at a Government-sponsored dinner made waves everywhere. The furore calmed down, but the Winter pack essentially disappeared from the public eye after that.

"Lucien," I say, my throat dry. "I'm not leaving here without her."

There are curses on the other end of the phone.

"I'm sorry," I whisper. "I'm so fucking sorry. But I will not leave her there. I'll get the meds and put them somewhere safe, one of you can collect them. I'm going to try and get her out. And if I can't…" my voice wavers.

"This is fucking suicide, Max! Nik, tell him," Lucien pleads, devastation lacing his words.

Chapter Thirteen

There's silence on the end of the phone.

"You want her," Nikolai says softly. I close my eyes.

"I just need to make sure she's safe, Nik."

For the first time, I think I fully understand the terror in Nik's voice when he told us that Emery had awakened as an omega. The fear ripping apart my insides tells me that I'll do anything, give anything, to give this omega a future that doesn't include pain, or fear, or fucking torture.

Even my own life.

"Max," Luc chokes. His harsh breathing echoes over the line before he curses.

"Bastien," he says in a low tone. "Call Devlin. Don't tell him anything unless it's absolutely essential. Use a secure line so you can't be tracked if things go south. Sound him out, and let's go from there. Max, you need to stay contactable."

I blow out a breath, plans running through my mind as a hint of hope flickers in my chest.

"Luc," I say gratefully. "Thank you."

He swears at me. "We're a damned pack, Max. That means we stick together. Nik, talk to Leah and get everything together in case we need to relocate."

I close my eyes, taking a deep breath, thinking of the bleak acceptance on Ava's face.

One way or another, we're getting you out of there.

Chapter Fourteen
Ava

Max sits quietly at the side of my bed. He's staring at the clock on the wall. My wires have been swapped to smaller, transferable machines attached to my bed. I ignore the regular beeps, my eyes focused once more on the whirls decorating the ceiling.

"A watched clock doesn't move, Doc," I say quietly.

"If only that were true."

I turn away from my counting to look at him. Carefully, I take in his tired face, his messy hair, those brown eyes that watch me so carefully.

This… this is a kind man. A kind alpha.

I force myself to think the words, even though they're conflicting for me. A kind alpha is something I have never encountered.

"How long?" I ask. I don't look at the clock.

"Thirty minutes."

I swallow. A small amount of fear manages to break past the walls I've built up.

"You could stop this," I say. There's a hint of pleading in my tone. *Please*.

Please don't make me live through this.

He blows out a breath. "Not like that, Ava."

He keeps saying my name. I drink it in, making the most of it. This moment of feeling like a little more than an empty shell.

"Thank you, Max," I whisper.

He leans forward. His hand tentatively strokes a strand of hair away from my face, and for once, I don't flinch away from it, leaning into the warmth. "I'm sorry," he murmurs.

"Me too."

And we wait.

A few minutes later, there's a commotion outside. Max stands, his face paling enough to let me know that this is it.

It's enough to break down my walls a little more.

"Max," I say quietly. "Max, *please*."

His face is agonized as he looks down at me. He leans in, closer than he normally does, and I close my eyes. His apple pie scent envelops me as he whispers directly into my ear.

"Trust me."

My eyes fly open and I stare at him as he takes a few steps back, just as the door slides open. Stone enters along with two men.

"This is Dr. Morgan," he says, introducing Max with a wave of his hand. "He stabilized 864 but unfortunately is unable to continue with her care."

Something twists in my chest. They asked him, and he said no?

One of the doctors approaches my bed, and I turn back to the ceiling, counting desperately as my breathing starts to stagger. He ignores me, instead taking my paperwork from the bottom of the bed and looking through it.

Max remains silent.

"Everything seems in order," the new doctor says. He's much older than I expected.

Another doctor, this one younger, moves forward, and a tremor slides up my limbs. Too close. They're too close.

"We can move forward with the transport now. Everything seems to be in order. Thank you, Dr. Morgan," the young one says dismissively.

I turn my head to look at Max. He stares at me before Stone moves between us, blocking him from view.

"That will be all, Dr. Morgan," he says coldly.

The wall breaks. My tremors become fully fledged shakes. Max is leaving. These men are going to take me.

"Please," I whisper. A whimper slides from my throat. There are too many scents in this room. "Please, Max. Please."

He doesn't respond, and my shaking increases. One of the doctors reaches out to me and I rip myself away from him. My restraints pull tight against my ankle, making me hiss.

"No," I say, my voice shaking. "I don't want to go."

"I'm sorry," the older doctor says quietly. "But the law is the law."

I see a flash of Max's face behind him. There's a tic in his jaw, and his eyes are fixed on the younger doctor. He looks…desperate.

"Leave, Dr. Morgan," Stone orders.

The hoarse cry travels out of my throat and bursts out before I can stop it.

"Max!"

I watch as he closes his eyes and turns away from me. He strides to the door and walks through it.

He's gone.

A keen rips from my throat.

"No!" I shriek at the alphas around my bed. "No! I don't want to go!"

I pull desperately at the restraints, but they hold firm. I pull harder and my wrist burns with pain.

"No, no, no, I won't go back there, please don't take me there—"

The two alpha doctors look grim, their gazes darting between me and Stone. The younger one turns to Stone.

"I would recommend taking her through a side entrance, to avoid too much… disruption."

Stone looks at me with disgust. "Can't you put her under?"

"The children would be at risk. She needs to remain free of sedatives until after the birth."

Stone tuts, his eyes moving over me. "I have something that may help."

He walks to the cupboard in the corner and returns with something in his hands.

At the sight of the familiar leather he's holding, my pleading disintegrates into screaming. Mindless, mindless screaming.

I scream for Max. I scream for him over and over again.

But he doesn't come.

He left me.

And as the leather closes over my face, restricting my breathing, I feel the very last, tiny piece of me shatter.

Chapter Fifteen
Max

My hands shake as I walk slowly up the corridor.
Keep it together.
Ava's screams echo down the hall, bouncing off the walls and making the handful of guards shift uncomfortably.

My breathing turns ragged, and I battle the urge to turn around. Closing my eyes, I inhale deeply. I can scent her fucking terror, her vanilla scent so acrid that it burns my nose. Nicole stares at me as I lean in to grab my phone and duffel bag from behind the reception desk.

"I'm heading out," I grunt above the screaming. The fucking effort it's taking to keep my face normal is almost more than I can take. I can feel aggression rising, tensing my shoulders.

We have one shot. One fucking shot.
Please, God.

Nicole nods at me, her eyes moving in the direction of Ava's room, and I walk to the elevator. Pushing the button, I keep my eyes turned forward as her screams turn to sobs. I can make out my name in between, her sounds sending stabbing pains through my chest. She's flaying me open.

Blood runs down my wrist from the strength of my nails digging into my hands.

Silently, I make her a promise.

Just hold on, sweetheart. Just a few minutes longer.

I hit the button for the eighth floor. Adrenaline licks at my spine as I move in the direction of the pharmacy. I lean against the wall by the bathrooms, fiddling with my phone. My white coat affords me a few smiles as staff walk past, but all I can manage is a grimace. Checking the time on my phone, I wait.

Every day, at 12.15, the pharmacist goes on break.

It's a little habit I've picked up from my lunchtime walks.

Bang on 12.15, the door swings open and the short, stocky pharmacist exits. He glances at me, and down to my coat, before he moves past me with a nod.

I wait for him to turn the corner before I move.

I walk into his pharmacy, not bothering to hide my identity. Scanning the cupboards packed full with medication, I look for Leah's insulin first. Spotting it, I pull the bag open and sweep the contents in, leaving two packs behind. I follow it up with a few other medications we might need, listening out in case the pharmacist comes back earlier than he usually does. All the while, Ava's screams ring inside my ears.

Gritting my teeth and pulling the duffel bag closed, I listen at the door for anyone walking past and ease myself out. Slinging the bag over my shoulder, I head down the corridor and open the door to the stairwell, jogging down concrete flights of steps until I hit the bustle of the ground floor reception area.

I don't bother signing out – I won't be coming back.

Instead, I move away from the main doors and head towards a corridor reaching off the main room. Checking the time, I curse and pick up the pace. I've only got a few minutes.

Reaching the set of double exit doors, I push one open slowly and check down the narrow alleyway.

A set of vehicle lights flash back at me and a large ambulance with blacked-out windows rolls down the alley, coming to a stop as I go for the rear doors. Before I can get them open, they swing out and a hand pulls me into the interior.

Chapter Sixteen
Lucien

"Fuck, I missed you," I push the words out past the lump in my throat as I wrap my arms around Max. His familiar apple pie scent wraps around me and I take a second to just breathe him in.

He holds onto me just as tightly. "Same, Luc." He sounds a little choked, and we both clear our throats as we break apart.

"Cute," A deep voice drawls from the front. "You gonna get it on back there? We don't have long, so make it quick."

Max's hackles rise at the unfamiliar alpha and I shake my head. "Ignore him."

Devlin Winter snorts. We've been in this ambulance for four hours now, and the one thing I can say without question is that this guy still embraces sarcasm as an art form.

Max eyes the hand that snakes between the seats before shaking it once. "Max," he says gruffly.

"Devlin."

"Devlin, it's Lucien Grey. I need to talk to you."

"I'll call you back."

The line goes dead, and I stare at the phone in my hand with disbelief.

"That was anticlimactic," Bastien runs his hand over his hair in frustration. We've been discussing how to approach this for the last few hours. Guess it'll be a few more.

We settle in to wait, but it only takes a few minutes for the screen to light up in my hand.

"Sorry." The voice is marginally warmer, but not exactly what I'd call friendly. "I wasn't expecting to hear from you, Luc. Thought you'd moved away."

"We need your help." I don't waste any time, and he barks a half-surprised laugh in my ear.

"Mine? How exactly do you think I can help you?"

He's curious, rather than scornful, and hope flickers to life in my chest as I look to Bastien. He's listening in and gives me the thumbs up.

"I think you're someone who can see the cruelty in the omega creed," I say quietly. "Someone who may know what it feels like to care for an omega."

His sharp inhale tells us everything I need to know.

Fucking ace, Bastien. My brother's a genius.

He grins at me knowingly. An unsufferable genius.

"There is an omega who needs help," I break the silence with a certainty I didn't feel before. "I never knew you to be the type of alpha to follow the creed, and the video that popped up recently told me that you might be the right person to help us with a…difficult situation."

Devlin clears his throat. "I'm handing you over to our pack leader."

Chapter Sixteen

I gotta admit, he came through for us. When we set out Ava's situation and he told us he'd be in touch, we only had to wait a few hours before he called back with an update.

Two doctors with fake identification set up by Bastien? Check.

An ambulance for transport? Check.

One slightly sociopathic getaway driver? Check.

I've been on edge for twenty-four hours, worrying about my pack, worrying about Nash, worrying about our home. Even worrying about this damned omega.

There's movement on the monitor mounted to the wall of the ambulance, and I turn towards it, pulling Max with me.

"They're on the move," I call to Devlin, and he nods.

I push Max towards the corner and hand him a plastic sheet. "Stay hidden. If they see you, we're fucked."

Nodding, he folds himself into the corner. As I turn away, he reaches out for my arm, grasping it.

"Luc..."

I can see the pain in his face. Whoever this omega is, she's got a hold over my packmate.

I squeeze his shoulder softly. "We're here now, Max. We won't let her go."

Relief stands out on his face as I turn away, shrugging on the white coat. We're all doctors here. Or that's what we need them to think.

Devlin's packmate, Ace, pulls the door open and stands back to let his companion climb in first. Ezra nods to me and I reach forward to help him lift the trolley behind him.

The scent hits me first, and I choke, my eyes watering.

It burns up my nostrils, pushing me back a step. I can scent the vanilla underneath, but it's twisted, soured. It smells fucking *wrong*.

I need to be professional, to play my part, but I can't stop my eyes sliding to the omega on the trolley. Whimpers crawl out of her throat, hoarse and rasping as though her throat's filled with blades.

A hand prods my back sharply as a snarl curls from the back of my throat.

I bite it back, my breathing harsh as I grip the edges of the trolley and lift her in. Ace Winter meets my eyes, his eyes acknowledging my horror with his own.

Fuck, I hope Max can't see this.

Ezra calls out to the men outside.

"Thank you, gentlemen. We'll meet you at the specified location. You have the tracker?"

A cold voice fills the small space, a stocky, gray-haired alpha shifting past the guards to stand at the front with a frown on his face. This must be Stone.

"I do. You'll be taking one of my guards with you also."

Ace and I swap wary glances. Ezra smiles.

"Unfortunately, there's no room," he says smoothly. "Only two permitted in the back and two spaces available in front. By all means, though, they can follow behind us."

The other alpha frowns, but nods as he takes a step back. Our credentials checked out. Bastien made sure of that. But we need to go now, before the real medical team turns up and our whole plan goes to shit.

"I'll meet you there."

He doesn't look back as he strides back into the hospital, his guards trailing behind him.

Ace jumps up behind the trolley and pulls the doors shut.

"Go. *Now*, Dev," he calls. "We need to get clear before they come back."

Devlin pulls out of the alley, shadows of traffic passing by the tinted windows as he picks up speed. Ezra leans over Ava, checking her pulse.

Max bursts out from his hiding place in the corner. I hold

out a hand to him, blocking him from seeing Ava, and his nostrils glare as he growls at me.

"Steady, brother," I say in a low voice. "You're not gonna lose it in here."

He pushes my arm out of the way. "Let me through, Luc."

I move to the side, awkward in the little space we have. A twinge of…something, moves through me when he blocks my view.

He stops and stares. A ripple runs through his back and he lets loose a feral growl.

"Fucking *monsters*."

Ezra looks up at him. "Take it easy, son," he warns gently. "She can hear you."

It's enough to pull Max forward. He moves to the omega's side, his eyes running over her face and to the leather across her face.

They fucking muzzled her. Like an *animal*.

A small, low whimper comes from under the restraint as Max leans into her. The pitiful sound of it damn near rips my heart in two. The other alphas look the same way, moving to the back of the ambulance to give Max space to kneel beside her.

"Ava," he whispers brokenly. "I'm sorry. I'm so sorry." He leans over, trying to unbuckle the metal keeping that thing over her face. I wordlessly move to help him and her eyes move to me, a high-pitched noise making me freeze.

Max holds up his hand to stop me, giving me a pleading look.

"Shhhhh," he murmurs, stroking his hand over her hair. "This is Lucien. He's a member of my pack. Nobody here is going to hurt you, sweetheart."

Her restraints clink against the metal rails as her body shakes.

This omega is petrified of us. With good fucking reason.

I press myself back alongside Ezra and Ace, and we watch silently as Max painstakingly works through the buckles keeping the muzzle in place. As they come away, he keeps talking to her, trying to soothe her.

The shakes continue.

He pulls the muzzle away from her face and drops it to the floor in disgust. Her sobs are louder now.

"You left me," her small voice breaks.

"I'm sorry," Max keeps his voice low, but the sound carries. "I'm so sorry, sweetheart. I had to, so we could get you out of there. Walking away from you was the hardest thing I've ever had to do."

The moment feels so intimate that I turn to stare at the wall. Beside me, Ezra does the same. His eyes look suspiciously shiny as Ace ducks through into the spare front seat. I hear him murmuring with Devlin about our route out of the city.

It hits me. "We did it," I breathe. We actually pulled this off. We got her out.

Ezra pats my arm. "You did. But now you've done it, what happens next?"

I can't help it. I cast a look back to the tiny omega shaking on the bed. Max leans over her, not touching her but staying close.

I have no idea.

Chapter Seventeen
Bastien

Nik and I are glued to the screen in my office. Thanks to the tech I rigged up this morning, we can see and hear everything going on. Nik vibrates next to me, growls ripping out of him as he tries to get himself under control.

"Take a break and go and see Nash," I urge, turning to him. "You look like shit, brother."

He snaps his teeth at me but doesn't move, his eyes not straying from the screen.

The screen displaying our soon-to-be guest.

They fucking muzzled her. Nausea climbs my throat at the thought.

She's so fucking small, too. I think I could probably lift her with one hand. It's hard to believe that she's five months pregnant, although the swelling of her belly gives it away.

An idea hits me, and I swivel in my seat to the growling hulk next to me.

"Go and check on her room," I suggest. "I don't think it's set up properly yet. I thought she'd want to do it, but she might not be well enough to sort it out straight away."

Nik snaps his head towards me with a frown.

"You didn't set it up for her?" he asks, aggravation lacing his tone. Pushing himself up from his chair, he stomps to the door. "Idiot," I hear him grumbling as he heads upstairs.

A smile pulls at my lips, but it slides off as I turn back to my camera and worry fills me. Max is still kneeling next to her. He hasn't moved for more than an hour except to check on the wires linking her to the monitors, check her vitals and give her water. Lucien keeps shifting in the corner of my screen, clearly uncomfortable in the small space.

The door opens behind me and Leah slips into Nik's vacated seat. She passes me a coffee and I curl my hands around the mug, grateful for the warmth.

"Update?" she asks.

"Trackers are off. I redirected the cameras, plus a few others in case they track them and catch on."

I turn to Lee as she stares at the screen, her face twisted in thought.

"Stone has half of the city searching for them, but they're not looking this far out. They should be clear. Especially since we swapped the plates. Should be here in around an hour."

She nods, lost in thought.

"We're not prepared for this," she says quietly.

We both stare at the screen as I consider her words. She's right.

"When has that ever stopped us, though?" I nudge her shoulder with mine, and she nudges me back with a small smile. "Never stopped you, scrap," she jokes.

"Hey!"

Leah snickers at me. I hate that nickname, and she knows it. I was scrawnier than Luc when we were kids, but the reason became obvious when he awakened as an alpha and I… didn't.

Chapter Seventeen

I'm just a plain old beta.

Pushing away the old tinge of regret, I sigh. I wouldn't even want to be an alpha now. Not with all the shit going on. When I was a kid, sure – but as soon as I saw the reality of what it means to be an alpha in this world, I was secretly glad to be me.

Plus, I can give my brother a run for his money in the muscle stakes any day.

And I'm still part of the pack. My family is all that matters to me – the family I've chosen. My pack - Luc, Max, Nik. Nash and Leah too. They're all I need.

Leah clears her throat, nodding at the screen. "My brother's attached to her."

I give her my best 'Captain Obvious' look. "You didn't pick that up sooner?"

She bites her lip. "What if… what if he leaves? With her?"

Dread rolls through me at her words before it slips away.

"Lee." I wrap my arm around her shoulders and pull her in for a hug. "Max isn't going anywhere. We're family. Besides, it wouldn't hurt to have some new blood around here. My jokes are only funny the first thousand times you hear them. I need to practice on someone new."

The tension in her frame slips away as she snorts, tossing her hair back. "They weren't funny the first time you told them."

I feign outrage. "*Lies*."

She stands up. "I'm going to check her room."

"Nik already beat you to it."

Leah rolls her eyes at me, but there's affection in her words. "Of course he did. Overprotective bear."

I shrug. That's exactly what he is.

I check on the cameras when she leaves, making sure they're all still pointing where I need them to be. The road they're currently on has three, so I've looped older footage to make sure there's still a record of the road if anyone checks.

My eyes drift to Ava on the screen. Her eyes are closed, Max still sitting beside her.

She's so goddamned small. If anyone's a scrap, it's her.

Who are you, little scrap?

Chapter Eighteen
Ava

I stare at the ceiling as Max talks to me.
You left me. You left me.
Everybody leaves me.

He tries to touch my hand, but I pull it back. I don't want to be touched.

I don't know where we're going, and I'm not going to ask. I don't know Max, not really. I could be going anywhere. Somewhere even worse than where I was heading before.

Although... as much as I don't want to feel it, my body relaxes a little more the longer Max stays with me.

Turning my head, I stare into his eyes. The honey brown depths are dark today. Angry. I don't like it.

"Don't be angry."

The words slide out of me before I can catch them, bite them back on my tongue.

He squeezes his eyes closed before he opens them again.

"I'm not angry at you," he says quietly. "I'm angry at *them*."

My leg starts to shake again, and the restraints pull at the bars. Max curses softly.

"I want to take those off, but we might have to wait until we get back."

I flex my wrists as much as I can whilst they're trapped inside the leather. At Max's words, one of the alphas moves forwards a little, but keeps his distance as much as possible in the small space we're all trapped in.

"I have a knife on me," he murmurs, his voice soft. "I could get them off."

Max looks at me, his gaze questioning. Swallowing hard, I nod. I want these off more than I want space.

The new alpha moves towards me slowly. His raven hair glints in the strip of lighting overhead. He's so *tall*.

I shrink back, and he stops, looking from me to Max with concern in his face.

"I won't hurt you," he says softly. "We can wait until we get to the house if you'd prefer to have more space."

The house?

Hesitating, I look down at the restraints. The ache is familiar, a throbbing in my wrists and ankles where I've pulled on them over my days in the hospital.

I don't want to be shackled for a second longer.

Meeting his emerald gaze, my face twists in determination. I can do this. They won't stop me from having this.

"Now, please."

His brows fly up, and a hint of something crosses his face.

"Brave omega," he says with a ghost of a smile.

I grit my teeth and hold out my wrist as he pulls up a stool next to me. On my other side, Max keeps a careful watch as the alpha pulls out a small penknife.

His warm fingers slide under the leather and against my skin as I fight to control my breathing.

Chapter Eighteen

Get yourself under control, Ava.

As if sensing my unease, the alpha begins to talk quietly, diverting my attention.

"I'm Lucien, but you can call me Luc," he murmurs. "I'm going to slide the knife underneath this cuff and move it back and forth. It'll be a little tight, but it'll work."

He glances at me, waiting for approval, and I nod. My hand quivers underneath his, and he grasps my fingers for a second before releasing them.

"You're doing well," he says quietly. "I'll be as fast as I can."

Max and I watch as he starts to move, slowly twisting the knife and sawing at the leather. I stare at his hand. He's so *gentle*.

"I think you'll like our home."

His words make me start, and he grips my hand quickly to stop my skin coming into contact with the knife, releasing me quickly.

"We're not going to the estate?"

Luc locks eyes with Max, a wordless communication passing between them.

"No, sweetheart," Max murmurs quietly. "You're not going there."

"We have a home," Luc says quietly as he continues working the knife. "Max and I live there with our family."

A family.

My mind flashes to Stone, and I push the feelings down. He's not my family.

"Along with me and Max, there are two other pack members. Bastien and Niko – Nikolai. We're the Grey pack, although we're not registered with the Government."

"My sister, Leah, lives close by to us," Max explains, but my attention snags on his previous words.

Four alphas? An alpha pack?

A tremor starts in my arm, and Luc notes it straight away, pausing.

My mind fills with images of the omegas at the compound. Pretty, broken toys. Property. The fucking omega creed.

Distaste and disappointment choke me. For a moment, I thought they were different. But they're the same as every other alpha I've met, just with a softer smile to draw you in.

Fury rises up my throat. I feel... betrayed.

Yanking my hand from Lucien's fingers, I pull my hand as far away from him as I can.

"You don't need to do that." My voice is ice cold.

They cast concerned glances over my head and Lucien looks at me, confusion swirling in his eyes.

"Why not?" he asks. He seems genuinely perplexed.

I close my eyes. "What's the point? I know the drill."

This is just another cage.

"Ava," Max says. His voice is so careful. I could kick myself for nearly falling for it.

When will you fucking learn, Ava?

"Will you tell me what's wrong?" he asks.

I laugh. It's rusty and broken.

"I thought you were different," I say dully. "But you're the same as *them*."

My tone is savage, and Max flinches away from me.

"Hey," Lucien's voice is low but firm. "We are *not* the same as them. I know that you've been through hell, but Max has turned himself inside out to get you out of there. To get you somewhere safe. I don't know what you think you know, but I won't let anyone speak to my family like that. You hear me?"

His tone is quiet, but the passion in it takes me aback. Only for a second, though.

"To get me somewhere *safe*? Where you can lock me in a cage until you want me? Make me crawl for you?"

I'm shaking again, but this time it's not fear. It's fucking fury.

"You don't own me," I hiss at this black-haired alpha who thinks he can tell me what to do, just like every fucking alpha I've ever met.

"I'm not joining your little pack to call you master and present when you want to knot. I'll kill myself before that happens. And in case you haven't noticed, I'm not currently available for *fucking breeding*!"

Lucien's eyes widen as my voice gets louder, and Max groans behind me.

"We're messing this up," he says to Luc in a frustrated tone.

"Ava." Max grabs my hand and doesn't let it go. "Listen to me. None of us are expecting that. None of us want it. We only want to help you."

Tears trickle from my eyes. "You're an alpha pack," I whisper. "How long before you make me line up like a good omega?"

This can't be real.

I can't let myself think this is real.

Lucien growls. "We will *not*—"

"We don't want that from you, Ava. Not now, not ever," Max says, shaking my hand a little. He searches my face, looking for something.

"I don't know how I managed to land in your room that day, sweetheart. But I did. And I think I knew from that first day that I wouldn't walk out of that hospital without you. I would never have left you there, love. We're taking you back to our home, but then it's your decision. What you want to do, how you want to live. We will help you in any way we can, but you are completely free to make your own decisions. We will never force you to do anything you don't want to do. You will be *free*."

My tears flow faster at his words, and I glance between them with blurry eyes, their faces swimming in and out of my vision.

"Free?" It's a whimper.

Lucien grabs my other hand. I don't even pull away this time.

"Free," he growls. The word settles into my bones.

When Lucien carefully lifts the knife again, I don't stop him.

Freedom.

Chapter Nineteen
Nikolai

My back slides down the wall of the hallway, my legs not enough to hold me up as my ass hits the ground.

I stare blankly at the wall, as the sound of Ava's tears echo through the doorway of Bastien's office.

Emery. Emery. Emery.

Her name thunders through my head like the beating of my chest. Permanent, unending.

Em.

Balling my fists, I put them to my eyes and push, hard. Trying to shove the tears out.

I didn't realise how much this omega would remind me of *her*. This is what her life might have been. If the Compound had gotten their hands on her.

Footsteps bounce down the corridor, and I wipe my face as my son appears, dragging a patient Leah by the hand. She gives me an apologetic look as Nash throws himself onto my lap, smooshing my cheeks together.

"You look sad, papa," he says quietly. "Hug it out?"

I wrap my arms around my son and bury my face into his

shoulder, blowing a raspberry and making him giggle as he wriggles away from me.

"What's Bastien doing?" he asks curiously. "He said he can't help me with the treehouse today."

Leah ruffles his hair, rolling her eyes at me where Nash can't see. "Am I not enough for you?" she asks wryly.

"'Course you are!" Nash looks contrite, and my heart swells. He's so *good*.

But his comment reminds me.

"Nash…" I start slowly, and he grins at me.

"Papaaaa…" he imitates me in a grunt, and I bite back a laugh.

"I do *not* sound like that," I scold lightly. "We have someone new coming to stay with us for a little while."

His eyes light up, and he lets out a whoop.

"We do? Who is it?" he tugs at my sleeve in his urgency.

"Her name is Ava," I say softly, and his eyes round. "It's a girl?"

"An omega," I correct him. "But she's not very well, Nash, so she's not going to be able to play for a while."

His little face crumples. "That's really sad. Can't Uncle Max make her better?"

I stand up and pull him with me. "I hope so, Nash. But you need to be very careful with her, okay?"

Bastien calls from inside the room. "ETA 5 minutes. They've just pulled through the main gates."

I look down at my son, who's pulling on my arm with the force of a stage five hurricane. "Come on, pa!" he calls. "We gotta go!"

Leah throws me a meaningful look as she sweeps Nash into the air. "Ava isn't very well, remember? Let's go back to the treehouse, and you can meet her later."

Nash pouts, but Leah distracts him with chatter about his plans for the new treehouse. I nod at her with gratitude as we

Chapter Nineteen

exit the house together, Bas and I heading in the opposite direction towards the main gate.

I glance at Bastien, and he gives me a crooked grin.

"This should be interesting."

Huffing, I speed up a little. "That's one way to put it."

"How are you doing?" Concern laces his words.

"I'm...," I blow out a breath. "I'm alright."

"If this brings back—"

"It's fine, Bas." I shrug off the words even as nerves twist in my gut.

Emery's name still beats inside my chest. The background to my life. One small omega won't change that.

We walk out into the lot, the sun shining down on us. An ambulance with blacked-out windows rolls slowly down the gravel lane.

"You're sure they can't be tracked?" I murmur to Bas.

"As sure as I can be."

I choke a little. That's not hugely reassuring.

The vehicle comes to a stop, and we wait for a sign of movement. Taking a deep breath, I let it go slowly.

The doors open, and Lucien jumps down first. Bastien's shoulders loosen, and he strides over to embrace his brother. Murmuring words I can't hear, Luc glances at my face and nods at me. He looks away and I breathe a sigh of relief. I don't want them to look too closely. This isn't about me. It's about her.

Luc heads back to the doors, and grabs hold of the metal rail of the trolley.

I've been watching the screen along with Bastien for the last few hours, but I hold my breath anyway. Waiting for... I don't know. I know what she looks like.

But my first real glimpse of Ava threatens to steal the breath from my lungs.

Chapter Twenty
Ava

"We're here," Max announces.

I stare at my newly unshackled wrists, twisting them around and feeling the lingering ache. Purple bands of deep bruising and raised welts wrap around my skin, and Luc scowls again as I catch him looking at them.

"Thank you." It's nearly silent, but he looks up anyway, a slight flush colouring his sculpted cheeks. "You're welcome."

The ambulance eases to a stop, and the older alpha behind me jerks awake. His gentle snoring's been filling the air for the last hour.

"Sorry," he murmurs sleepily when he sees me looking at him. "Early start today. Not as young as I used to be."

He smiles at me, and I look away.

Lucien opens the doors and gets out, natural light spilling into our space. I try to push myself upright, but Max reaches out and touches my shoulder softly.

"Careful," he warns. "You won't be up to walking around just yet."

My shoulders slump in disappointment, but he's right. I can't remember the last time I walked anywhere, truthfully. I'd probably just collapse like a sack of potatoes.

Max fusses around me, checking the machines and making sure the thin blanket covering me is in place. "We'll get you to your room, and I'll check you over properly," he mutters.

My room. A space of my own.

Longing swoops low in my stomach. *Freedom*.

Whatever this is, it's looking a damn sight better than my last location.

Lucien's face appears in the doorway, and his eyes sweep over me. I wait for the familiar nausea to fill my stomach, but this feels…protective. He smiles a little and opens the door wider.

"Are you ready?" he asks. Max searches my face, uncertainty lining his features.

I stare at the light. "Who's out there?"

"Just Nik and Bastien," Luc says quietly. "They'll stand back. It's just in case we need help."

Okay. Four… five, six, seven alphas, including the other three in here.

I can do this.

"Okay." At my nod, Lucien grabs the metal base of my bed, and Max moves behind me to grab the other end. Gently, they lift me out of the ambulance, and the sunshine sears my eyes. It's so *bright*, but I can't close them. It's been so long since I felt the warmth of sunshine on my face.

"Wait, please," I breathe.

They both stop, and I pull in a deep breath. It smells like… fall. A light breeze dances across my skin, lifting my sticky hair away from my face. I suddenly realize how filthy I am, and embarrassment flushes my skin a deep red.

Max gives me a questioning glance. In the sunlight, his

hair glimmers like fire. Luc's hair shines too, and I bite my lip, glancing down. I suddenly wish they weren't looking at me.

"Okay."

My voice is small, but they pick up my cue and move forwards. I catch a glimpse of two males standing behind Lucien – a tall man with dark hair a shade lighter than Luc's, and a blonde mammoth of a man. This must be Nikolai and Bastien.

They make sure to keep well back, and I don't look as Max and Luc carry my bed past them. I feel stupid, lying on a bed as they carry me across the gravel.

Clearing my throat, I draw Max's attention.

"Can I try to walk? Please?"

Max starts shaking his head, but Luc's eyes stay on my face. He must see the pleading in my expression because he interrupts whatever Max is about to say.

"You'll need help." He's blunt and matter-of-fact. A recognition that help isn't an option. I won't be going anywhere without one of them helping me.

But the idea of them getting that close... my muscles lock up, and I swallow hard. I don't know if I can cope with that. Arms wrapped around me, squeezing me, hurting me—

"Ava." Max appears in my line of sight, his hands on either side of my face. "Breathe," he orders, the edge of a bark in his voice.

I've always hated the alpha bark. Hated that a tone of voice can make my body react in ways I have no control over. But in this moment, I'm ridiculously grateful. I don't want to break down here, in front of these people I don't know.

Slowly, I move my hands up to cover Max's. His brown eyes widen until I can see the barest glimpse of my own reflection, my own face staring back at me, looking frightened and pale. His hands feel warm under mine as I grip them.

No.

"Help me, Max?" I ask quietly.

His eyes scan my face before he nods. His thumb strokes down my cheek, barely touching me, but leaving a trail of fire in my wake. I force myself to stay still. *I will do this.*

"Okay. I'm going to put my arm underneath your back and lift you up. If you want me to stop, to sit down, if you panic or need a break, if you need anything at all, you *tell me*. Deal?"

My lips twitch as his bossy tone makes a return. "Got it, Doc."

It feels good to let a little sass out.

I try to cling on to that little spark of bravado as Max carefully slides his hands under my back. His warmth sinks into my back like a brand, making me inhale sharply. He moves to pull back and I grab his other arm.

"Don't stop." It comes out as an order, and I mean it. Dragging this out won't help me.

I breathe as he carefully lifts me, his arm cradling my shoulders. As I'm pulled into a sitting position, I become much more aware of the bump in my midsection. My new reality is right there, but I just… can't. I can't think about that yet. A tsunami threatens to overcome me at the sight, and I wobble in Max's arms. He grips me a little tighter, and I lean into him despite myself.

"You're doing so well, Ava," his praise is soft, and it makes tears gather in the corner of my eyes. "I know it's hard, but you're being so damn brave."

Luc nods in agreement from where he stands a few feet away, arms folded tightly. I glance down at the ground and gradually pull one of my legs over.

"Slowly," Max warns me. "It's going to hurt."

I get both legs over and place my feet on the floor before I realize just how right he is. One of the new alphas – Nikolai? – steps forward abruptly at my groan, and the other yanks him back. He offers me an apologetic smile when I glance over at them.

Finally, I push myself up and onto my feet. I don't expect to feel so off-balance, and I overcompensate, collapsing into Max. Fucking hell.

He's hot against me as his arms wrap tightly around me, holding me close to him. "Steady," he breathes into my ear. "You're perfect."

I glance up at the afternoon sun as he holds me. It's a reminder of where I am.

You're not in the nests. You're not in the hospital. You have your own room right there, you just need to get off your ass and walk to it.

So I walk. And Max stays beside me, every step of the way.

Chapter Twenty-One
Bastien

Our new omega has fire in her blood.

Still gripping Nik, holding him back from offering the help he desperately wants to give, I pull him towards the ambulance as Ava and Max slowly make their way to the house, Luc hovering around them like a protective mama. A smile tweaks my lips upwards. My frosty brother seems to be quickly thawing towards our new addition.

Devlin and Ace Winter swing themselves down from the front of the ambulance, Ace going to the back to help his grandfather down. Devlin holds out a hand to me and I shake it firmly. We would never have pulled this off without them.

"Thank you," I say fervently, glancing between them. "I can't tell you how much we appreciate your help."

Devlin's face tightens as he glances after Ava. "It was our pleasure," he mutters. "What's happened to her…," he trails off, his face a little pale.

Ace intervenes. "Let's just say it was personal for us."

Curiosity tugs at me, and I wonder what their own story is. It's not my right to ask, though.

Ezra, the older alpha and Ace's grandfather, looks around, his eyes shining. "This is quite the location you have here."

Nikolai nods next to me, but neither of us offers a tour. "It's home," I say simply, and Ezra's eyes move to mine with an understanding glint.

"We'll get out of your hair," he says firmly.

Ace and Devlin exchange a loaded glance, and I tense. Nik pauses next to me, and I know he's noted it as well.

Devlin turns to me. "When we agreed to help, we weren't aware of her name."

I frown. "Does it matter?"

The two alphas share another look, and Ace nods.

"We met our own omega, Harper, over a year ago," Devlin continues. "She came from the OC too. I think that your omega may be a friend of hers. Someone she's been looking for."

Surprise fills me. Their omega knows Ava?

Beside me, Nik takes a protective step forward. "She's not going anywhere," he growls.

Devlin holds his hands up. "Steady. We're not suggesting that," he explains hurriedly. "But when she's feeling a little better, I'd like you to check to see if she'd like to get in touch with Harper."

Ace snorts. "If Harper thinks this is Ava, we'll probably be knocking on your door in the next few days."

I shake my head.

"No. We'll let Ava know, and she can decide if she wants to reach out. It should be her choice."

God knows she's had enough choices stripped away from her. Ezra nods approvingly from where he watches us. "Quite right. Harper will understand. Let's get going."

Ezra and Ace get back into the ambulance as Devlin lingers.

Chapter Twenty-One

"Even if it doesn't turn out to be the same omega, Harper would be thrilled to speak to her either way. She doesn't get a huge amount of contact with other omegas."

His eyes soften as he mentions their omega.

Hesitating, I ask, "She came from the compound?"

His face darkens. "She did."

Not giving any more information, he nods at me before turning and getting into the driver's seat. Ace waves from the passenger window as we watch them drive away.

Nikolai frowns. "That was unexpected."

Unexpected, indeed.

"She might need a friend." Especially with everything she's been through.

Nikolai sighs as we move back towards the house. There's no sign of Ava, Max or Luc. I hope they're okay.

"I need to check on Nash," he mutters and strides off in the direction of the treehouse. I let him go without saying anything.

Grabbing a coffee from the kitchen, I settle back into my office, monitoring the activity on the cameras and trying not to think of our new guest. My mind keeps drifting back to her no matter how much I try to focus on tracking Stone's men through the city. They spread out like little black ants, but they're nowhere near us.

I wasn't expecting to feel so drawn to her. As a beta, I don't have the same instincts as Luc and the rest of my pack. I'm not driven by my hormones in the same way, but protectiveness ripples through me at the thought of her.

She reminds me of a quote I read once.

Though she be but little, she is fierce.

This omega isn't broken. Not completely.

Chapter Twenty-Two
Ava

Max gently steers me towards a huge wooden house, and I pause to look up. I'm not sure what I was expecting – truthfully, I didn't even give it a thought. But this wasn't it.

Their home is a massive combination of dark wood and beautiful brick, floor-to-ceiling windows across the front and a double door with stained glass panes that immediately draw my eye. Large brick pillars are dotted over the veranda, with balcony space above them.

Sprawled out to the side of us is a vast lake, surrounded by trees. Sunlight shimmers across the blue water.

This is… I don't have any words. So much more than I expected.

Beautiful. Warm.

It's worlds away from Stone's cold estate. The place where I grew up is dark, built in a warped reflection of the omega compound. A prison, not a home. A shiver runs down my spine at the thought, and Max's arm tightens around me. I glance at him apologetically, realizing that he's waiting patiently for me while I gawk.

CHAPTER TWENTY-TWO

My legs buckle when I take another step. I'm starting to flag – my body is not on the same page as my mind. A frustrated growl echoes from behind me and I flinch.

"Calm down," Max hisses to Lucien.

"She's exhausted," Luc snaps back at him. "Carry her."

I shake my head. I'm not sure I'd be able to cope with that. Having Max's arm wrapped around me, his scent entwining with mine, is still too close for me to be comfortable.

Max ignores him. "It's not far now," he promises me in a low voice.

We get up the steps, and Luc brushes past me to open the front doors. I slowly move forward, taking in the vast open space, the wooden surroundings, comfortable looking couches and blankets everywhere. My fists clench. The desire to move towards them, to wrap myself up in them like a cocoon nearly overwhelms me, and I stagger slightly. Max catches me, his tone worried. "Ava?"

"I'm fine," I whisper. "Sorry."

He leads me carefully to a room just off the main living space. Pushing open the door, he reveals a small space with fresh white walls. A double bed sits against the far wall, full of pillows and blankets that look even softer than the ones in the lounge, with a wooden table next to it, a vase of fresh flowers in place. My eyes flicker from the bed to the large wooden-framed window taking up most of the wall, a comfortable-looking leather armchair next to it. Beyond it, the lake glitters, a stretch of blue beckoning me. There's a small door tucked away in the corner, and I turn to Max questioningly.

"The bathroom. It's small, I know," Max apologises. "We have more space upstairs, but I didn't think you'd be up for walking up and down them just yet. As soon as you're ready, we can get you up there, and you'll have more privacy too."

I shake my head, my words soft. "This is for me?"

Lucien's voice filters in from behind us, and I shift slightly. "All yours," he says roughly. "Nik and Leah put everything together, so you should have the necessities, but we can get you anything that's missing when we do a stock run. There's a key on your table in case you'd feel safer with the door locked."

I close my eyes at his words. A space that's just for me.

Eagerly, I take a step forward. Max rushes to my side as I stagger.

"Careful," he admonishes quietly. "You didn't get all this way just to fall at the last minute."

He carefully takes my hand, and my fingers flex in his warm grip. He helps me steady myself as I move towards the chair. Lucien stands in the doorway, his piercing green eyes assessing me as I drop into it, my fingers flexing on the soft brown leather.

It suddenly registers that we're all enclosed in a small space, and my scent spikes again. I bite my lip and both alphas drop their eyes to my mouth. Stiffening, I pull away from Max. Glancing between the two large alphas in front of me, I try not to flinch at the sight of them standing there within easy reach of a bed.

Both immediately take a step away, heeding my '*back the fuck up*' vibes without me having to spell it out for them. Lucien's handsome face tightens, and he nods to me before turning away and heading out of the door. A tiny kernel of guilt runs through me before I push it away.

Pain flickers across Max's face, and he shifts from side to side. His brown eyes search mine, seeing too much.

"Ava…we should get you checked over," he says carefully. "Just to make sure everything's as it should be."

I glance down to my stomach briefly and away again.

Chapter Twenty-Two

"Not today." It comes out more abruptly than I meant it to, and Max's eyes widen a little.

"I can't... cope with that," I admit honestly. Not right now. I need space, time to think.

"I think tomorrow will be fine." Max's voice is subdued, but he tries to smile at me. "It's been a long day."

He points at a cord dangling from the ceiling.

"If there's anything wrong, you can pull on that and one of us will come straight away. Doesn't matter what it's for, it just means that you need help. Use that until we can get you a phone."

His smile grows a little at my mystified expression.

"Why would you get me a phone?" I ask.

"So you can contact us if you need us. Or anyone else if you want to. We have to be careful, but Bastien makes sure nobody can track us."

My hand clenches on the back of the chair. "I don't have anyone else to talk to."

A hint of apology enters Max's eyes, and he steps forward. When I hold up my hand, he shuts his eyes and stops.

"Ava..."

"I'd like to be alone now, please." My words are soft, but there's a test in them.

Max sighs, but he turns to leave. "Please use the cord if you need us. You should have everything you need here at least until tomorrow, but if there's anything we haven't thought of, or something you'd like, just pull it and we'll be here in two seconds. I'll come by in the morning to check on you."

Nodding, I wait until he's moved to the doorway. Lucien's voice murmurs, and Max heads back in, setting a tray down on the small table. It's filled with a sandwich, a banana, some cheese, and a large jug of water.

"Luc thought these would be easier on your stomach," he explains. "You don't have to have it if you don't want anything, or if you want something else, we can make it for you—"

"Max," I say quietly. "That was thoughtful. Please thank Lucien for me." It must be getting later in the afternoon, and Max's hair glints with strands of gold as we watch each other carefully in the fading light. I take a deep breath, gathering the words I want to say into something coherent.

"Thank you, Max. For the room. For… everything, really." My words are fervent. This morning, I thought I was being shipped off to live out the last few weeks of my life under the eyes of my father, and now I'm here. With them.

His mouth turns down, those expressive brown eyes squeezing shut for a moment. "You don't ever need to thank us, sweetheart," he responds firmly. The vehemence in his words takes me back, but it also reassures me. I don't want them to regret it.

I'm not sure how to respond, and Max must pick up on it. He gives me one last shy smile before he turns and disappears, closing the door softly behind him.

Alone. I'm completely, utterly alone.

I stare at the key on the table. With wobbling steps, I grasp it and move slowly to the door, pushing it into the lock and turning until I hear a reassuring 'click'.

My breath leaves me in a whoosh. Turning around, I slump back against the door and slide to the ground. Pulling my knees up, I wrap my arms around them with difficulty, trying to ignore the bump in the way.

What do I do now?

CHAPTER TWENTY-THREE
LUCIEN

"*Uncle Maaaax!*"

Nash's scream of excitement echoes through the kitchen as he flings himself at Max. Max laughs and grabs him into a bear hug, lifting him off the ground and making Nash squeal as he swings him around.

"Hot damn, kid, how much have you been eating?" Max scolds him with a grin.

Nash giggles. "Lots. I ate all of your dinners while you were gone!"

"I can see that." Groaning theatrically, Max swings Nash onto his hip as Leah barrels into him with a sniffle, wrapping her arms around him.

"I missed you, little brother," she mumbles into his chest. Her voice quivers.

"Hey," Max runs a hand over her hair. "Enough of that. We all know I'm the oldest."

Leah breaks away from him with a watery laugh, wiping her hand across her eyes. "You did it, Max," she says. We all pull out chairs, Nash refusing a chair and staying on Max's lap.

"*We* did it," he says. There are lines on his face that weren't there when he left. This trip has taken a lot out of him, and I see the concern Leah tries to hide.

Nikolai and Bastien walk through the door and there's another round of greetings before we all settle down for dinner.

Max eats like a horse.

"Hospital food," he grumbles when Leah questions him on his eating. "Instant noodles just aren't the same as your cooking, Lee-Lee." He laughs as she scolds him and heaps more pasta onto his plate.

Bastien leans back in his seat when he's finished. "How's she doing?"

All our eyes flick to Max, including Nash's.

"Can I meet the omega yet?" he asks hopefully, and Max taps his nose. Nikolai grabs him and pulls him onto his lap, ignoring Nash's protests.

"Not yet. She needs a few days to get used to being here, and then we'll see." Nash pouts like a champion, but he doesn't argue.

"How was she when you left her?" I ask quietly.

I didn't want to leave her earlier. But her face when she saw us so close to the bed... I never want to see a woman look at me like that, ever again. She's so damned small, I feel every inch of my height around her. Having alphas around puts her on edge.

I try not to think about exactly how much I wish that wasn't true as I focus on Max.

His face is grim. "She wanted some space. I showed her the cord and left."

Bastien nods in satisfaction. The cord was his idea, so if anything happens she can get hold of us easily. They're coded to send an alert out to me, Bas, Nik and Max so whoever's closest can get there quickly.

"She didn't want me to check her over." Max prods at his almost-empty plate, his expression conflicted. "She doesn't want to do anything that might remind her... of *that*."

His pointed glance reminds me that there are little ears avidly listening to the discussion, and we change the subject, talking about some of the places Max visited while he was gone.

But his words play on my mind. How would it feel to look down at yourself and see something so alien? Something that was put there without your consent?

How is she still functioning?

A snapping sound draws all eyes to me, and I glance down at the crack I've left in the table.

"Sorry," I mutter. But the thought doesn't leave me.

Making my excuses, I leave the kitchen. Bastien locks eyes with me, a silent question, and I pointedly ignore him.

I linger outside her doorway. There's a soft light coming from the crack under the door, so I don't think she's asleep. I listen hard, but there's no noise.

Footsteps echo behind me, and my brother emerges with a scowl on his lips.

"What are you doing?" he hisses quietly. "She wants to be left alone!"

"I know," I hiss back. "But I'm worried about her. She doesn't know any of us."

His face softens. "We'll all help her, Luc. This isn't all on your shoulders."

I glare at him. "What's that supposed to mean?"

He grins, a crooked half-smile that makes him look like a kid again. "You're a good pack leader, but you're also the biggest mama alpha I know."

I snort. "I wouldn't have to worry if you'd all stop giving me mini heart attacks every other day."

We both stand quietly for a moment.

"Do you think she's okay?" I ask my brother, not taking my eyes off the door.

"No."

I slide my eyes to him. "You know what I mean."

He shrugs. "Honestly? I doubt it. But she's asked for space, and we should respect that."

My shoulders drop. He's right. But I still don't want to go too far, just in case.

"I'm going to stick around for a while," I say quietly. Bas frowns in the corner of my eye.

"You won't—"

"Of course I won't," I snap, trying to keep my voice down. "Jesus, Bas! I just want to be close in case she pulls the cord."

He eyes me carefully as he nods. There's understanding in his gaze.

"Message if you need me," he offers as he wraps his arm around me. I pull him in close, breathing in the subtle hint of sage. His beta scent isn't as strong as ours, but it's reassuring and familiar and wholly Bastien.

When he leaves, I take up a position on the couch in sight of the door, but not so close that Ava would see me if she looks out. I don't want to panic her.

Her light doesn't turn off.

I watch her door until dawn.

Chapter Twenty-Four
Ava

The sound of the door quietly knocking interrupts my light sleep. I finally managed to drift off around dawn, after spending hours practicing using my legs again, pacing back and forth in the tiny space whilst staring at the bed and realizing... I can't touch it.

I spent years bowing down to Stone and then another two years in intensive training at the Omega Compound. Harsh, brutal training to teach me exactly where my place is in the world.

Omegas are not permitted the use of a bed.

I could recite the creed backward in my sleep. Clearly, something has stuck with me. Every time I even try to approach the bed, my palms become sweaty, and I feel sick.

So I slept on the floor.

Exhaustion pulls at me as I prop myself upright from my small space between the bed and window. I didn't feel comfortable using the clothes that I found in the small set of drawers, so I'm still in my hospital gown.

I make my way slowly to the door before I hesitate. "Who is it?" I ask warily.

"Ava? I'm Leah. Max's sister? I just wanted to say hello and see if you need anything."

I freeze at the undoubtedly feminine tone. There's a sliver of disappointment too. I thought it would be Max, and I'm quick to shut down any thoughts about why that might be.

My throat closes as I stare at the door. When I don't respond, Leah clears her throat.

"It's okay. I get it. I brought you some breakfast from the kitchen, but I'll just leave it here in case you get hungry. I'd love to meet you properly and show you around, but I know you're probably not up for that at the moment."

She sounds a little disappointed, and it's enough for me to pull my proverbial big girl pants up and pull the door open. She's still talking, bending over to place a plate on the floor. "Anyway, I'll just leave – oh! Hello."

She's beaming at me, so I try to muster a smile back.

This girl is gorgeous.

Long red hair the same shade as Max's and deep brown eyes watch me intently. She's so like her brother I feel my breath catch, and she laughs.

"I know, right? Max 2.0," she grimaces dramatically as she gestures to her face, and a small smile tugs at the side of my lips. Leah drops her gaze to my body, and I flush, embarrassed at the way I look.

"I, um, I didn't…"

"Oh, honey," Leah says soothingly. "Shall we get you cleaned up a bit?"

Biting my lip, I glance behind me before pulling open the door. Not an alpha, I remind myself. A beta. A female beta. Safe.

My embarrassment rises as Leah takes in the untouched room. She keeps her face expressionless, but I feel the concern in her eyes as she turns to me.

"Ava?" she asks, gently. "Where did you sleep, honey?"

Fucking hell. "On the floor." I avoid her eyes. "I know it's weird, but I can't... I can't touch it." Hugging my elbows, I keep my eyes on the floor. She sucks in a breath before she turns to me.

"Oh, sweetheart. They really pulled a number on you, huh?" Tears gather in my eyes, and I quickly turn away from her.

"Can you not tell Max, please?" I force out. "He'll think he did something wrong, and it's not him. It's just..."

"Them." Leah's voice drips with derision. "Don't worry. I won't tell him anything unless you tell me it's okay. God knows you need someone to talk to who isn't an overprotective moron." I choke a little at her words, and she laughs. "Someone's got to keep them in their place, or that pack would walk all over us without even realizing they're doing it."

Somehow, she maneuvers me into the bathroom despite my protests. The bath is filled, trails of steam rising up as Leah stands in front of me with her arms crossed.

"Now, I'm not one to push, but you need a bath, Ava. You need to feel clean, and we need to get you something else to wear, and then we need to get you some food. Okay?"

My throat closes again as I nod. I do want to be clean. And I should probably eat something, although I don't feel hungry. I drank the water Lucien brought me, but I couldn't touch the food.

"Good." She smiles at me proudly. "So, I'll leave you—"

I grab her hand before I can stop myself, and rapidly drop it like it's on fire.

"Sorry. I'm sorry," I whisper. *What the hell is wrong with me?*

"Hey, it's totally fine. You want me to stay with you?" At my nod, she gestures to my nightgown.

"Let's get this off you, shall we?"

Leah efficiently divests me of my filthy hospital gown and dramatically throws it out of the small bathroom window, despite my protests.

"I'm burning it," she says fiercely. I don't argue with her. I'm quickly learning that Leah is the most alpha-like beta I've ever met. But I think I like her. She actually reminds me of someone.

I push away any thoughts of Harper. I can't think about her right now.

Or about what I did.

Swallowing hard, I push the thoughts deep down and focus on Leah. She takes a seat on the toilet as I carefully step into the hot water.

It's… pure bliss.

I let out a sigh without even meaning to as I sink beneath the water, holding my breath and letting my hair fan out. When I surface, Leah hands me a bottle of shampoo and I manage to smile at her.

"Thank you," I whisper.

She nods at me, and I get on with the mammoth task of washing my hair. It's riddled with knots, and Leah hands over a comb without me even having to open my mouth.

Twenty minutes of tussling later, I want to cry. Some of the knots are way too big for me to get out, and tears of pain and frustration prick my eyes.

"I'm going to have to cut it," I whisper. My voice wobbles at the thought.

It's so stupid, I know. It's only *hair*. What does it matter? But I've always loved my curly hair.

One more thing they're taking from me.

Leah frowns. "Can I have a look?"

At my nod, she moves across to me and starts working

her hands through my hair, feeling the knots. "I think I can get these out," she announces.

"You can?" I ask hopefully.

"Yep. I have spray and conditioner that I use. I'll go and grab it now."

She leaves the room and I lean my head back against the tub with a sigh.

Staring at the ceiling, I ignore the small tug I feel to look down. I don't *want* to see it. I don't want to be reminded of exactly how much my body doesn't belong to me anymore.

You can't hide from it forever.

Fucking watch me.

Rationally, I know that I can't put off thinking about this for much longer. But a little time is all I need. Just a small amount, enough to remember who I am.

Not *86-fucking-4*.

Not just an omega.

Not a fucking breeding mare to be strapped to a cross for faceless alphas to rut on.

Just me. Ava.

A tear plops into the bathwater. Then another.

When Leah walks back in with her arms full of products, I'm having a full-blown snot session in the bath. I try to scrub my cheeks clean, but her eyes widen and I can't hold it back. I make a sound that's between a honk and a wail, and Leah's face creases in sympathy.

"Oh, sweetheart." Ignoring my flailing, she hauls me into a hug, ignoring the water sloshing all over the floor. It takes me a minute, but I'm crying raggedly into her shoulder, covering her in bathwater and tears as I sob out my frustrations.

I'm not sure how long I cry, but Leah doesn't move, rubbing her hand over my back until I pull my head away and she steps back.

I bury my face in my hands. "I'm so sorry," I whisper. I'm fucking mortified. I just met this beta, and within twenty minutes I've fallen apart in front of her.

Leah gives me a stern look. "You listen to me," she says firmly. "I don't know all the details, and I don't need to unless *you* want to tell me. But I do know that you've been through more hell in the last two years than most people will ever see in a lifetime. And it's not even over yet." Her eyes fall to my stomach, and a fresh bout of tears threatens.

"I know I kind of steamrolled in here, but I've known you for five minutes, and I can just tell that we're going to be friends. You wanted to hide away, but you *didn't,* Ava," she continues.

"Now you've got a whole lot of shit on your plate, and we're going to help you. We're not going out of our way, you're not disturbing our lives and you are *not* an inconvenience to us in any way. So if you want to cry, scream, eat ice-cream, smash plates, I am here for *all* of that. If you just want to lie down and sleep for a week, I'm up for that too."

She finishes and takes a deep breath. "Was that too much?" she asks sheepishly. "I really do have a stack of plates we can throw, though. I saw it on a video once."

I stare up at her, bemused, before shaking my head.

"No," I say, an unexpected smile lifting the corners of my lips. "I'd say that was pretty much perfect, actually."

I'll hold off on any plate throwing for now though.

Chapter Twenty-Five
Nikolai

I'm concentrating on a piece of oak I've dragged into my workshop when Max calls out.

"In here!" I shout back. Grabbing some tarps, I try to cover it up but Max catches me in the act.

"What are you doing?" he asks, eyeballing me.

I cross my arms defensively. "Nothing."

"Is that…"

"Doesn't matter." I throw the rest of the cloth over it to stop the conversation. "What's up?"

Max gives me a look, but he lets the subject drop. "Bastien told me about the conversation you had with the Winter pack. About their omega."

I rock back on my heels cautiously. "Yeah. Devlin asked us to let Ava know."

Max inhales slowly, trepidation on his face. "Do you think we should?"

Hesitating, I turn and start fussing with my workbench. "I don't know," I say at last. "And I don't know her well enough to guess. Do you think it's legit?"

Max frowns. "They've got no reason to lie."

I turn to face him, crossing my arms. "I think it's a possibility. And I think we need to tell her. It's not our job to keep things from her. She's not a child."

Max grimaces. "I know that."

I raise an eyebrow at the light flush on his cheeks. "Something to tell me?"

The flush deepens, and he looks away. "It's nothing."

Hmmm.

"Max," I say softly, but with enough meaning that his head snaps up to face me. "You're developing feelings for her."

He swallows, hard. "I can't have feelings for her. Not like that."

"Why not?"

Max gives me an incredulous look. "Why do you think? She *hates* alphas, Nik. With good reason. She's not going to choose to stay here with us permanently. I got her out. We got her out. I need to be content with that and not ask for anything… *more*."

"Says who?"

He splutters. "You know what she's been through. And what she's got to come. There's no way in hell that this is even a possibility. And she was my patient!"

I sweep past him, ready to go rescue Luc from Nash's treehouse.

"She was never just an ordinary patient, Max," I say, turning back to face him. "Was she?"

I leave him behind to think it over. I know what he needs – time and space to think through his feelings. Max feels so passionately about everything that sometimes he has trouble taking a step back.

Ducking under the branch of a tree, I frown, making a note to come back and cut it down before anyone gets hurt.

Chapter Twenty-Five

My hands pause on the solid wood when I hear voices in the distance. *Female voices.*

I debate hiding for about a second before they both come into sight.

Ava looks a little better. Still pale, still exhausted, still covered in bruises, but there's a lightness to her expression that wasn't there yesterday. Her hair falls in damp ringlets around her face, the morning sun flashes hints of bronze and caramel. She's wearing a yellow sundress, the soft cotton fluttering around her bare legs and showing just a hint of her bump.

Her light expression drops off when she spots me, panic leeching into her face. Beside her, Leah threads their arms together and tows her forward, murmuring into her ear.

When she doesn't run away, I decide to stay where I am and let them come to me.

They come to a stop a few paces away, and there's a heartbeat of uncomfortable silence before Leah and I both speak at the same time.

"Good morning—,"

"Ava, this is—,"

We both stop, and Leah snorts a laugh.

"I'll go first." She tosses her flame-colored hair back. "Ava, this is Nikolai. I know he looks like a giant, but he's a giant marshmallow. Nik was the one who designed the house."

I flush as Ava looks at me like she's seeing me properly for the first time.

"Thank you, Nikolai," she says quietly. "The house is beautiful. And so is my room."

I shrug awkwardly, shifting on my feet. "I'm glad you like it."

We linger in silence for a few more seconds. I'm aware that I'm staring like an idiot, but I can't stop.

I've always thought that our eyes are the window to our souls. You can tell a lot from a person when you look into their eyes. Ava's eyes are the deepest I've ever seen. Pools of hazel, with glimpses of green, gold and brown. I've never seen eyes that look so *fractured*.

I want to sweep her up, hide her away so nothing can hurt her again.

As soon as the thought crosses my mind, I feel disloyal.

"I should go," I say abruptly. "It was nice to meet you, Ava."

I try to smile at her, but it feels a little flat. Careful to give her space as I move past, I stride away from them without looking back.

Chapter Twenty-Six
Ava

I turn to stare at Nikolai's retreating back.

"Is he okay?" I ask Leah. She's quiet next to me, watching the large alpha move away with sadness on her face.

"He's fine." With a small cough into her fist, she gives my arm a little tug. "Come on."

We move through the grounds as Leah explains the layout. It's huge. The house is just one part. There's also a large workshop, a cabin for Leah, storage areas and more.

I could get lost here. I think I like it.

My mind keeps drifting back to the blonde alpha, though. *Nikolai*.

Leah was right. He was a giant. But he didn't give me the same vibes I've felt from alphas in the past. No, Nikolai... he's so *sad*.

"Leah?" I ask quietly. "What's Nikolai's story?"

I regret asking as soon as Leah stiffens next to me. "I'm sorry," I blurt out. "Forget I asked. It's none of my business."

Leah elbows me gently. "You can ask whatever you

want, Ava. And you're right. Nik does have a story. But I think you should ask him."

Shame floods me. She's right.

"Sorry," I whisper.

"Don't stress it," she says warmly. "He's one of the nicest people you could ever meet, Ava. Everyone here is safe, I swear."

That's not why I asked, but I nod anyway as she leads me to yet another building.

"These are our work areas," Leah explains. She pulls the door open and tugs me through, walking down a corridor and waving her hand as she labels each room.

"Max's medical bay, Luc's office for all his financial wizardry, Bastien's tech room…"

A ruffled head pops out of the last room, and I squeak. Bastien meets my eyes with a small smile.

"Good morning, ladies," he purrs. Leah whacks him across the back of the head and I snort out a surprised laugh, flushing when they both turn to stare at me.

"Don't flirt with her," Leah warns. "I mean it, Bastien!"

He grins, unrepentant, and winks at me. I wait for disgust to fill me, but there's nothing. Then I realize… I can't smell anything. Just the smallest hint of herbs.

I try to sniff unobtrusively, and his eyes flick to mine, his smile dimming slightly.

Bastien is a *beta*. Not an alpha.

Leah misses our exchange and pulls my arm, encouraging me to move past Bastien.

"Bastien is Lucien's brother," she confides as we move along. I can feel eyes on my back, but when I turn around, he's nowhere to be seen.

"Twins?" I ask, even though they don't look exactly the same.

Leah laughs. "Nope, that's just me and Max. Bastien is

two years younger than Luc, and Luc never lets him forget it." She rolls her eyes, and I bite back a smile. Having only met Lucien for a short time yesterday, I can see it.

"Bastien is a certified genius. He's crazy smart, IQ of more than two hundred. They tried to get him into Mensa when he was a kid, but he didn't want any of that. He's better with technology than anyone I've ever met. Hacking, math – he just does it. Bastien's the one who filled out the plan to get you out."

Surprise stops me in my tracks. "Bastien did?"

Leah nods. "It was obviously Max's idea, but Bastien took it and worked on it until it was actually doable. Plus he changed all of the cameras and everything so they couldn't track you."

Track me.

Track me.

I stop short, and Leah pauses. "What is it? Ava?"

She's shaking my arm, and I turn to stare at her, my eyes widening.

"Tracking," I whisper. She looks at me, confused.

"Leah," I whisper. "Did anyone scan me for a tracking device?"

Leah goes pale.

"Bastien!"

He's there in seconds, grabbing her arm. "Leah?"

A door bangs and Lucien appears from a room down the hall, striding up the corridor as his green eyes flicker between us with concern. "What is it?"

His sandalwood scent hits me, a wave of pure alpha that combines with the fear in my stomach.

I'm vaguely aware of Leah explaining, Bastien cursing and Luc—

Luc crouches down in front of me. I don't remember being on the floor.

"Ava," he says gently. "Ava, sweetheart, we need to scan you *right now*. Can you get up?"

I stare at him blankly, and he sweeps his arms around me and scoops me up. I shudder, and he stares down at me, a tic in his jaw working.

"I'm sorry," he says softly. "But we have to check, and we have to do it now."

Bastien runs alongside us. "Depending on the type, our scanners might have scrambled it." He sounds agitated, and I want to apologize. My father, hell, the whole damn OC could be coming down on their heads right now because of me.

But Luc's arms keep me from talking. It's all I can do to breathe, to not freak out, so I stay silent. Luc looks down at me, and I give him a pleading look.

"Don't worry," he reassures me, and I want to scream. The government could be on its way to destroy his home and family *right fucking now*, and he's reassuring me?

"I'm not worried for me," I choke out. His hands tighten, and I whimper.

Luc relaxes his grip immediately. "Sorry," he apologizes quickly as he places me down on a table.

A metallic, sterile smell fills my nose, pulling me into dark memories and taking away from Luc's aromatic sandalwood scent. My hand stays clutched on his arm as I fight to control my breathing. Luc starts to move away, but he stops when I whimper, my fingers clenching in his shirt. Everyone stops.

I don't know what I want. No, that's not right.

Stay with me. My fingers curl into the soft material, a low whine slipping out.

Luc doesn't miss a beat before he scoops me back up and sits on the table with me in his arms.

"If you want me to move, squeeze my arm," he says to me. I nod.

Chapter Twenty-Six

Max runs into the room, and I burrow a little more into Lucien. The number of stressed people in the enclosed space is enough to make me anxious.

He freezes when he sees me in Luc's lap. "What's the matter?"

His demanding tone makes me shrivel a little more. Oh god. Everything he's done for me, and now I've ruined it all.

I can't stop the sob from breaking free.

"I'm sorry," I mumble into Luc's chest. "I'm so sorry, Max."

Max drops to his knees in front of me as Bastien appears with a device in his hand.

"Max, you need to shift out the way," Bastien tells him. "We might have to move."

Max rocks back on his heels. "They're coming?"

The dread in his voice breaks my heart.

"I don't know," Bastien grits out. "I need to check Ava and you're *in my way*."

Max moves away, and Bastien stops in front of me. Leaning in, he traps my eyes with his silver-gray gaze.

"Ava," he murmurs. "I need to scan you, love. Can you stand up for me?"

I nod, reluctantly sliding off Luc's lap. His arms tighten around me for a second before he lets go.

His hand trails across my back, just once. It's reassuring in the chaos around us, and I hold my breath as Bastien runs the scanner over me.

"I didn't know they used trackers at the OC," Max mutters. He's beating himself up for not knowing, but this isn't his fault. It's mine.

"They don't," I say, and everyone snaps their attention to me. I swallow, hard.

"Stone did it. Years ago."

When I was ten, to be precise. Max curses. "That asshole."

I drop my eyes to the floor as Bastien's scanner beeps over my neck, just above my right collarbone.

Bastien turns to Leah where she's hovering by the door. "Get Nash ready to leave. I haven't seen any signs of anyone heading this way, but we can't take any risks."

Leah nods and darts into the room. I inhale sharply as she throws her arms around me.

"This is *not* your fault," she whispers, and my tears start to fall again.

This is absolutely, one hundred per cent my fault. I should have told them, and I didn't.

Max grabs my hand, and I jump.

"Leah's right," he says, squeezing. "This isn't your fault, sweetheart."

Bastien nods, his fingers hovering over the location of the tracker as he hesitates. I look down and back into his face, grim determination filling me.

"Cut it out."

All three of them turn toward me. Max starts shaking his head.

I swallow. "It's not far from the surface. Cut it out now. It's quicker than waiting to do whatever you need to do. I'll be fine."

Behind me, Luc swears. "We're not doing that to you."

I turn around and hold his gaze, determination stiffening my spine. "This isn't your choice. Your family is at risk because of me. We need to act fast. So cut it out now."

I direct my last words to Max, and he starts protesting again.

"Max." My voice is flat. "You know this is nothing compared to what they did." Bastien flinches next to me. "I promise that I don't care about a little pain. So stop wasting time and *cut it out!*"

I'm breathing hard, ready to grab the damn scalpel myself if he doesn't move. Max's eyes move to Luc's behind me before he nods.

"Okay. Let's do it."

Max leaves to get what he needs as Luc squeezes my arm gently. "I'll need to hold you."

"I don't need a hug," I snap back at him. "I just need this damn thing out of me."

He raises an eyebrow at me. "To stop you from moving."

His lips twitch in a smirk, and I kind of want to hit him, even as embarrassment turns me scarlet from my head to my toes.

"Right." I clear my throat. "Of course."

Gingerly, I settle myself back against him. His arms wrap around me, and my breathing comes a little faster. His breath heats my neck as he turns my head to the side. His palm feels warm against my face, but his grip is firm. Bastien takes a step back and Max returns with a medical bag. He digs through it to pull out a scalpel and a needle and thread.

"I'll go as fast as I can," Max says to me. His brown eyes bore into mine, distress darkening them. "Just so you know, I am *not* on board with this plan."

I smile, just a little. "I'm getting that loud and clear, Doc."

He rolls his eyes at me and pulls a stool over, motioning to Bastien.

"When I cut, hold this over the wound. I'm going to move quickly so she loses as little blood as possible."

Bastien nods as he glances at me. "Anyone tell you you're too brave for your own good?" he asks wryly.

Lucien gently turns my head to the left, away from the tracker. "Can't say they have," I manage to croak out.

Luc's other arm wraps across my arms, and his breath warms my ear. "You know, there's a fine line between bravery and stupidity."

My mouth drops open as he holds me still. "Are you seriously fucking with me when Max is about to carve me open with a scalpel?"

Max groans. "It's really not that big," he says, his voice reassuring. "Around an inch."

"That explains a lot," Bastien murmurs smoothly. I bite back an unexpected laugh at their banter, and Luc glares at his brother over my shoulder, tightening his grip as my body shakes.

Max smooths something cold over my skin, and I feel the edge of the scalpel. I tense, and Luc's arm tightens.

"Steady," he murmurs as Max begins cutting. The sting is intense, but it's bearable.

Max hesitates, and I try to move my head. "What is it?"

"I can see it," he says slowly. "But I'm going to need to dig it out. It's a little deeper than I expected."

I close my eyes. Of course it is.

Fucking Stone.

"Just do it," I rasp. A white-hot pain stabs in my shoulder as Max digs out the tracker, and Luc holds me steady as I flinch.

"Son of a *bitch*," I curse, and Luc huffs a laugh.

"You have a mouth like a sailor," he tells me, and I hiss at him. "You try having a poker shoved into your shoulder—"

"What's your favorite food?" he interrupts, and the sudden change is enough to distract me.

"My – my favorite food?"

"Yep," he grits out. I feel warmth dripping down my bare shoulder. The sensation makes me sway, nausea rising up my gut.

Luc squeezes me. "Don't make me bark at you."

I snap my teeth at him. Like a dog. The asshole laughs at me.

"You're insufferable," I snarl.

"I know. And you have a hell of a temper for an omega. Now tell me what you like to eat. Or what you like to do."

"I like—," a stab of pain pulls a whine to the back of my throat, "—sitting in my cage and doing what I'm told."

He squeezes my throat, just a little, and lets loose a low growl that vibrates against my back. "Brat. That's not even funny. Be serious."

God, this pain. How is this so fucking painful? Remind me never to be heroic ever again. Next time, I'll take my chances and wait for an anaesthetic to kick in.

Max digs in a little further, and my back arches. Luc pulls me in with a curse.

"Focus, Ava," he growls at me.

"Are you freaking serious right now?" I half shriek, half moan.

"Yes, I'm serious. I want to know more about you."

"Small talk is vastly overrated."

I can feel the asshole smirking. His breath dusts my ear as he lowers his voice.

"You're nearly done. Now tell me."

He's like a dog with a fucking bone.

"Fine," I spit. "Strawberries."

I can feel his smugness. "Was that so hard?"

"Not as hard as my fist hitting your face is going to be."

Luc groans. "I think I like it when you talk sass to me."

I inhale a shocked breath at his words, just as Max pulls back triumphantly, the clink of the tracker dropping into a metal bowl. "Got it."

Bastien moves past me to peer at the tracker. "It looks old. I doubt it's working, but I'll double check it. I have scanners in place at the edge of our land that should have scrambled it anyway."

"It's tiny," I gasp. "How was it that fucking painful?"

"Sorry," Max apologizes. "You were amazing. I just need to stitch it up and you're done."

Nope. No way. Not a chance in fucking hell.

It'll just knit itself back together, right?

I try to wriggle out of Luc's arms, but he doesn't let go.

"You can let me go now," I say. "I'm done."

"Nope." He pops the 'p' sound. It's annoying as fuck.

"You said you'd let me go."

"I would if you were freaking out. You're not. You just don't want stitches, and you need them, so you're staying right there until they're done."

I huff. "I've decided that I don't like you very much. You're my least favorite."

Max leans over to catch my eye. "You have favorites?"

He sounds a little hopeful.

"Yep. Nikolai is at the top, because he's not in this room right now."

There's a quiet cough from the doorway, and Luc sniggers.

Really? I can't catch a break right now?

Chapter Twenty-Seven
Bastien

I smile to myself as I listen to Ava grumbling, Luc still holding onto her as Max finishes his stitching. She was amazing.

Placing the tracking device onto my desk, I run the scanner over it again.

"Anything?" Nik asks, coming to stand next to me.

Ava goes silent behind me.

I shake my head. "I'm pretty sure it got scrambled at the boundary lines, but I'm going to run a few tests to make sure." Turning to look at Ava, I can see the stress on her face despite her bravado.

"Don't worry," I say softly. "Now that I've seen it, I can tell it's not working. There's no sign of anyone following you here."

I'd know. I haven't slept since she arrived, watching the activity on the cameras and tracking Stone's men across the city.

She blows out a breath, her small body quivering. "Thank God. I thought…"

Nikolai rumbles next to me. "We won't let anything happen to you, little bird."

She tilts her head at his words. "Little bird?"

We all turn to look at Nik, and I watch in fascination as his neck flushes a deep red. He opens his mouth, searching for the right words.

"It... uh... it's just a saying," he fumbles, and Luc smirks where Ava can't see him.

Nik suddenly makes a dash for the door. "I need to check on Nash."

When he disappears, Ava looks after him for a moment, her brows lowering, before swinging her attention to me. "Who's Nash?" she asks hesitantly.

Now it's my turn to fumble. "Nash is... um... he's our...,"

"Nash is Nikolai's son," Max explains quietly as he packs away his supplies. He presses gauze against Ava's collarbone with an apologetic smile, and she winces.

"He has a son?" Shock rounds her eyes.

It's unusual to have a child outside of the restrictions set by the Omega Compound. There are generally only two ways to bear a child. For alphas, it requires making an application for an omega through the pack process and impregnating them through artificial heats.

The second is through the heat nests. Any children borne as a result are normally placed into an adoptive program for betas. Ava's situation was an exception. Her father must be high up in the Government ranks.

I can see Ava drawing conclusions, her mouth twisting down as she stares at her hands.

"It's not what you think," I murmur, and she looks up, her hazel eyes meeting mine.

"It's not?" There's a hint of challenge there, but this isn't the right time to talk about Emery.

I shake my head. "Do you want to come with me to look at the cameras? I've been tracking Stone across the city. I can show you what they're doing."

Luc frowns at me, and I meet his disapproving look without flinching. Our new omega is much stronger than they think. And I can still see the worry in her eyes – if she can see that Stone's men are nowhere near here, it might make her feel a little more relaxed.

She considers it for a moment, and I hold my breath, my stomach flipping when she nods at me.

Lucien slowly releases her, and she scrambles away. Her face is flushed, her breathing a little heavy.

"Thank you for doing that," she says to him, primly smoothing down the material of her dress.

"My pleasure, brat."

Her face reddens again, and she lets out a strangled sound of frustration before turning and stomping past me into the corridor. I hear grumbles of *impossible man* and *stupid alpha*, and I bite back the laugh on my tongue before I call out to her.

"Ava? It's the other way." Stopping sharply, she spins on her heel and storms past me.

Looking behind me, I catch Luc grinning.

"Dangerous game you're playing, brother," I note in a low voice.

He smirks at me. "It's good for her to remember she has a temper."

I have a feeling he might live to regret that, but I shake my head and pull the door closed.

Catching up to Ava in a few paces, I gently steer her into my office. Catching her looking over her shoulder, I make a point of leaving the door wide open, and her shoulders soften as she turns to the main desk.

"Wow."

A small burst of pride thrums through me at her surprise.

The walls are lined with dozens of screens showing various angles from the city and the area around our home. I point Ava towards my comfiest chair, and she takes a seat as I talk her through the different set-ups, keeping to the other side of the room.

"You redirected the cameras?" she asks softly.

"I did. Whichever surveillance camera they tried to track when you disappeared, I redirected in another direction. I did as many as I could, including all the ones you drove past on your way here, plus others to stop them guessing the route you took."

It must have driven Stone mad when he realized that every camera was pointing the wrong way.

I turn to Ava with a grin, but it breaks off when I see her wiping her eyes.

Shit. Well done, Bastien.

"I'm sorry. I didn't mean to upset you."

She shakes her head abruptly. "You haven't upset me. This is…" she blows out a breath, staring at the screens around us.

"I thought I was alone."

Her whispered confession drops into the room like a stone. The small words just about break my heart.

"I thought they were taking me back. Max left me, and I really thought…,"

She swallows hard, hugging her arms. I desperately want to touch her, to give her some comfort, but I know she won't welcome the contact.

Ava laughs a little. It's the saddest sound I've ever heard.

"Now I'm here. And I don't know what to do."

I stare at the screens in front of us, thinking over her words.

"Why do you have to *do* anything?" I ask her.

She slides a look at me. "I can't just sit here on my ass forever."

Her sass, even when she's upset, still makes me want to smile.

"It's okay to just take some time to rest, Ava," I say quietly. "You've been through a lot—,"

"So everyone keeps telling me." A hint of frustration colors her tone as she waves her hands in exasperation. "But I don't have time to rest, Bastien." She gestures at her stomach for the first time. "I have to face *this*."

Her voice breaks on the last word.

I scooch my chair across the room, giving her plenty of time to see me coming. She stares at me, her eyes dark as I pull the chair up next to her.

Slowly, I reach out for her hand, raising my eyebrow in a silent question. *Is this okay?*

She nods imperceptibly, and I swallow a sigh of relief as I draw her hands into mine, swallowing them up.

"You might have thought you were alone." I stare at the soft whirls in her palm, so small between my hands as I try to explain the jumble in my head. "But you weren't, Ava. You had *us*, you just didn't know it yet. And you're not alone now. You don't have to face this on your own. We're a family. And there's a space for you if you want it."

I can't explain the chaos of feelings in my chest. But Ava... staying here, with us. It feels *right*.

Her eyebrows draw down over her face as she watches me. "Why would you do all of this for me?" she asks, glancing away. Her face is open and vulnerable. "I'm going to bring trouble to your door, Bastien." She swallows hard, looking toward the screens. "If Stone finds me..."

I gently squeeze her hands in mine, but my words are forceful. I need her to *see*.

"I will *not* let that happen. Do you understand? None of us are going to let that man find you, sweetheart."

A tear trickles down her face. "And what then, Bastien?"

"Then," I say firmly, "You *live*, Ava. And we'll be here to help you."

The tears fall faster now. "Are you... are you offering to be my baby daddy?" she sniffs. A small amount of terror runs through me at the thought, but... actually, I don't mind the idea.

I open my mouth, and she snorts out a tearful laugh. Catching the twinkle in her eye, I growl lightly.

"Luc was right. You *are* a brat."

"I'm sorry. I just... I can't cope with much more right now."

Snark is her coping mechanism. We have that in common.

Giving her hands a final squeeze, I sit back.

"You know what I think you need?"

"Psychiatric help?"

"No shame in it if you do." She looks away from me, and I touch my fingers, very softly, to the side of her face.

"You haven't given yourself any time to rest." I pick up my point from earlier. She rolls her eyes at me, but I stand firm. "You need to take a little time just for you. Push the world out for a few days, Ava. There's time for that."

"I don't know...," her voice wavers.

"There *is*. We'll make time. Do whatever you want to do during those days. You want to sleep? Sleep. You want to cry? I'll bring you tissues. Just take a little bit of time for yourself. Everything else will be waiting when you're ready."

She wipes her hands over her eyes. "A little bit of time sounds good," she admits shakily.

I lean back in my chair. "Then that's what you'll get."

Chapter Twenty-Eight
Lucien

I've had enough.

"This is insane," I snarl, stalking into the kitchen. Max, Bastien and Nik look up at me where they've had their heads together.

Max leans back in his chair. "What is?" he asks, tension in his voice.

I wave my hand in the general direction of Ava's room. "It's been seven days! She can't stay in there forever!"

My brother leans forward. "She can stay there as long as she needs to," he says quietly.

I whirl on him, pointing at his face. "Don't even talk to me. This is your damned fault. I can't believe you all think that this is okay. Max, you haven't even checked her to see if the pregnancy is progressing as it should be!"

Max sighs. "I know. But she needs this time, Luc. And Leah has been in and out, checking on her."

I snort. "She was doing well," I point out. "She was coming out of her shell, and now she's right back at square one."

Nikolai stands up. "She was not doing well," he says quietly. "She was breaking on the inside."

I throw my hands up. "How do you know that?" I demand.

He takes a step toward me. "Because I have been there, and I can see it in her eyes. She was *not* okay."

I step back, blowing out a frustrated breath. I thought we'd made progress the day we took the tracker out. But then she disappeared. I find out that Bastien encouraged her to lock herself away in her room, and now she won't speak to any of us.

How is this fucking progress?

"If she hasn't come out by tomorrow," I snarl, "I'm going to—"

"What are you going to do, Lucien?"

I whirl around to see Leah standing in the doorway, her expression mutinous.

"You're going to drag her out?" she snarls, advancing on me. "You're going to force her into something she's not ready for?"

"She's not functioning, Lee," I snap back. "She needs to be pushed."

"She needs fucking time! Just because you want to see her—,"

"What is that supposed to mean?"

"You. Want. Her," Leah's fingers jab into my chest as each word hits me like a knife, and I flinch.

"I don't want her," I croak out. I *don't*.

"You do! You spend every night camped on the couch outside her room like some sort of psychopath—,"

Bastien sinks his head into his hands with a groan as Max and Nik turn to glare at me, and she turns on him. "You're not much better, Bastien. When was the last time you slept? There's no sign of them tracking her here!"

Max stays quiet as he stares at her with wide eyes, but Leah's on a roll now. "And you, little brother," she snarls. "You mope around this place like a kicked puppy waiting for a bone."

Nikolai raises his hands as she swings to him. "Shit, Leah, have mercy!"

Leah stares at us wildly for a second, her fingers slowly dropping before her face crumples. We all stare as she sinks her head in her hands and begins to sob. Crossing the kitchen, Max cradles her face before pulling her into a hug.

"Talk to us, Lee. We're all worried about Ava, and now you, too. What's going on?"

"Sorry," she whispers. "I'm just really tired."

Bastien passes Leah a coffee as she sits down, and she turns to us with a sigh.

"Luc's right," she admits. I try not to let my shock show.

"I…am?" I ask, hesitantly.

Leah nods. "Ava's… not doing so well."

The kitchen erupts with questions, everyone talking over each other until Nik bangs his cup down on the table.

"Let her speak," he snarls.

Leah closes her eyes as she leans forward. "She won't eat properly. And she's still refusing to sleep in the bed."

"What?" Max snaps.

She cringes a little. "I promised not to say anything to you, but… she won't even touch it, Max. It's like she's regressed back into her training from the compound. She sleeps on the floor and she won't even use a blanket. She won't even look at me anymore. I haven't been able to get her to talk since yesterday."

I cut her off with a curse. "Shit, Leah."

"I'm sorry," she cries. "I just didn't want to betray her trust. I thought maybe she'd come out of it, but she's getting worse, and I'm really worried about her. Max, she needs help."

Max is already up and moving. "I'm going to get my bag."

Bastien sits in his chair, his face pale. "I thought it would help," he whispers. Leah puts her hand over his.

"I think it did, at first," she says haltingly. "But after a few days, she just changed. I don't know what triggered it."

"Trauma," Nik says softly. "She finally let herself think about it."

I push to my feet. "I'm coming."

Max starts to argue with me, and I snap out a growl. "I'm coming with you, Max. Stay here or don't, but you're not going to stop me."

I'll force food down her throat if I must. I am not letting her give up. I caught a glimpse of the real Ava the other day, and I will hold onto it with both hands, tease her and pull her chain until she comes back to us. Whatever I have to do, I'll do it.

I'll crawl on my knees if that's what it takes.

Bastien starts to stand, and I snap at him. "Stay here. You've done enough."

Pain flashes over my brother's face. Nikolai shoots me a disapproving glare, but I ignore it as I leave the kitchen. Max catches up to me as I reach her door.

"Luc," Max grabs my arm as I raise it to knock. "We need to be careful here. We don't know what condition she's in. Just take it easy."

I force out a sharp nod as I rap my knuckles on the door.

"Ava?" Max calls out. "It's Max and Luc. Can we come in?"

There's no response from inside, and the worry in my chest morphs to full-blown panic.

CHAPTER TWENTY-NINE
MAX

Luc rattles the handle, but it's locked.

He doesn't miss a beat. Lifting his foot, he slams it against the door. It shudders, and a crack appears in the wood. He kicks it again and makes a gap that he puts his arm through to unlatch the door.

He disappears inside and I follow, choking on the harsh scent that fills the room.

Burnt, acrid vanilla stings my nose, making my eyes water.

Luc and I exchange a glance, the panic in his expression clear to see. He moves across the room, ignoring the empty bed. There's a twinge in my chest as I stare at the untouched covers.

How did we get this so fucking wrong?

Luc emerges from the bathroom, shaking his head.

"Not there," he says sharply.

I scan the empty room, my eyes moving to the window before—

It takes me a split second to reach the small figure

huddled in the corner of the room, lifting her into my arms. Luc drops to his knees next to me, his breathing ragged.

"Ava? Sweetheart? Can you hear me?"

Her hazel eyes are open and completely blank, the expression I saw in them just a few days ago completely gone. Her limbs hang down limply, dangling like a ragdoll. My hands tremble as I frantically check her vital signs.

"Her pulse is slower than it should be. I need to check her blood pressure."

Luc is frozen next to me. "Luc," I snap. "Sit against the wall. I need you to hold her up."

Luc scrambles to where I direct him, and we gently maneuver Ava into his lap. Her head lolls to the side, and Luc stares down at her with terror on his face.

"Max," he whispers. "What's wrong with her?"

"Shock, possibly." PTSD, Post Traumatic Stress Disorder, more likely. I pull out the blood pressure cuff and wrap it around her arm. Pumping it, I watch her face for any reaction.

Her eyes don't even flicker.

"Her blood pressure is low. I need IV fluids. Lay her on her back with her legs in the air, I'm calling Bastien."

Luc follows my instructions silently.

Bastien skids through the door less than a minute later with a drip and fluid bags in his hands. The color drains from his face when he sees Ava.

"What's the matter with her?" he rasps.

"I don't fucking know, but I'm trying to find out," I snap back at him, and he recoils. I take a deep breath.

"Sorry. Hook up the fluids here."

Luc looks up from where he's holding her legs. "There's a little more color in her face, Max."

He's right, but she's still not responding. Bastien and Luc

both look at me, and I try not to let the panic in my stomach overwhelm me.

"I don't think this is physical," I say quietly. I'm not sure if she can hear me, but I keep my voice down anyway.

"What does that mean?"

"It's inside her head." Bastien's voice is bleak as he looks down at her.

I nod when Luc looks at me, his face disturbed. "I don't know for certain, but this... she's catatonic, Luc."

He looks down at the broken omega in his arms. "Can she... can she hear us?"

"Maybe. I don't know."

"What do we do?" Nikolai's growl comes from the doorway. "How do we help her, Max?"

"Lorazepam, normally," I swallow. "But her body is still recovering from the heat drugs. To dose her again so soon..."

It could kill her.

I drop my head into my hands, trying to *think*. Everything I know about omega biology I learned from Emery, and she never experienced anything like this.

Bastien starts to rummage in his pocket, and we look at him as he holds out a crumpled card.

"Devlin Winter's number," he says, shaking it. "Call them. Ask the other doctor if he has any ideas."

Luc stares at me, his eyes full of agony.

I can't fix this.

Reaching out, I take the paper from Bastien and walk to the door, exiting the room before dialing.

"Devlin? This is Max Grey."

The phone rings again less than three minutes later.

"Hello?" My voice comes out as a croak.

"Hello, son. This is Ezra. I understand your omega's not well."

"No," I whisper. "She's not. And I can't – I don't know—,"

My voice breaks, and I swallow. "I don't know what to do," I admit.

Ezra's deep voice echoes through the phone. "Talk me through it, Doctor Grey."

He listens carefully as I describe how we found Ava, her current condition, her blood pressure.

"You're right," he concludes. "It sounds like she's experiencing some significant post-traumatic stress."

I squeeze my eyes shut. "I can't give her lorazepam," I grit out. "Her body won't cope with it."

Ezra snorts. "She doesn't need lorazepam. She's an omega."

I sit up. "What do you mean?"

He tuts down the phone at me. "What are they teaching you in medical school nowadays?"

"I can't say omega physiology was on the curriculum."

He grunts. "Can't say I'm surprised. Damned stupid laws."

"Please, Ezra," I breathe. "I need to help her."

"And you will. You have everything you need right there. How many alphas in your group? Four?"

I frown. "Three."

"More than enough. Ava is an *omega*, Max. That means her genetic makeup is different to ours, or to a beta. She doesn't need medication like that. All she needs is you, and your pack. She needs care. As long as you can give her that, you should be able to bring her around."

I squint at the phone. "Are you serious?"

This sounds like mumbo-jumbo bullshit to me.

He laughs. "As a saint. It's not a magic fix – it wouldn't help if she had something physically wrong with her. But for this... I'd say it's exactly what she needs. Ava needs to understand that she's finally in a safe environment, that you're not going to hurt her, and that you'll take care of her. It might take some time, but she'll come around. Just make sure you're giving her what she needs."

My mind races.

"And those needs are..." I say carefully. Fuck, I hope he doesn't mean –

"Not that," he says sharply. "That girl's been through hell. She needs nesting, and a safe space to recover. An enclosed space – warm, low lighting. She might respond well to your scents – used clothing, for example. Make sure there's plenty of soft materials. Stay with her, talk to her, tell her she's safe. See how she gets on in a day or so, and call me if there's no change."

I blow out a breath of relief. This, we can do. Even if it's the strangest medical advice I've ever heard.

"We'll try it. Ezra... thank you."

"No thanks needed, Max. Call if you need me."

Tentative hope fills me as I cross the room, my panic already clearing now that I have some sort of plan.

Nesting. Safe space.

We can give her that.

CHAPTER THIRTY
NIKOLAI

I stare at the limp girl in Lucien's arms. Her hazel eyes look straight past me. No longer fractured, but *empty*. So fucking empty.

Like the world has finally broken her.

Max pushes past me, his ear to his phone as he calls Devlin Winter for help.

I vaguely register that I'm shaking. Bastien appears in front of me, his mouth moving, but I can't hear the words. I just keep staring at her.

"You absolute bastard!"

Emery's screams echo down the hallway, and I grimace. Luc and Bastien glance over to me, both of them wincing with sympathy.

"Tough ride," Bas offers, and I nod absently. My whole attention is focused on the door in front of me, leading to the room my soulmate just kicked me out of.

We wait for a few minutes. I can't sit still, pacing in front of the door.

Emery, Emery, Emery.

She's having our baby.

I'm going to be a father.

Emotion claws at my lungs even as I continue to worry. We've soundproofed the house as best we can, but we weren't expecting her to go into labor early. We were supposed to move to our new home next week, where she could give birth without the risk of anyone overhearing.

Leah pulls the door open, panting. Luc and Bastien jump up as I stare at the ruby splatters covering her blue gown.

Why is she covered in blood?

"Nik," she whispers. "Nik, you need to come now."

Em isn't screaming anymore.

When I push past Leah into the room, I can't comprehend what I'm seeing.

Max turns to me, his face pale. He holds out a bundle in his arms.

I don't take it. Staring at the bed, I stagger over and drop to my knees next to my wife.

"Em," I whisper. "Em, sweetheart,"

I hear Max yelling at Leah to take the baby. I know I should look, but the only thing I can focus on is her.

Sweat dots her forehead as she stares at me. Her beautiful blue eyes, so full of life, look glassy and dull.

"Niko," she breathes. "Where is he?"

"I'm here, baby. I'm here."

I kiss her knuckles, trying not to show my panic. Looking over to Max, my heart stops.

"Max..." I choke out.

He doesn't answer me. He's too busy trying to stop the bleeding. I can see it dripping off the end of the bed.

Closing my eyes, I begin to pray.

Leah gently touches my shoulder, and I ignore her.

"The baby, Nikolai," Em rasps. It pulls me from my stupor, and I finally turn to Leah.

I lay eyes on my son for the first time. A tiny face, surrounded by dark curls, stares up at me. Wide eyes, so like his mothers, capture mine as he scrunches his face up.

A fist clenches around my heart as I carefully take him into my arms.

"Hello, little one," I whisper. Swallowing, I hold him to Em. She tries to raise her arms and fails, and Leah lets out a sob as she carefully lifts her cousins' arms so I can settle our son against his chest.

"Nash," she whispers softly. "So…beautiful…"

"Nik." Max stands beside me, his arms drenched in my wife's blood.

"We have to take her to the hospital," he forces out. I recoil.

"We can't," I hiss. "The Compound—"

"She's dying, brother," Max's voice breaks, and I stagger. He grabs my arm to hold me up, leaving a bloody handprint on my sleeve.

"She needs more help than I can give her here. We have to go now."

Leah cries out behind me, and I spin to see her sweep our son out of Emery's arms. My mates arms and legs jerk, her body twisting on the bed like a puppet.

"Em," I shout. "Emery!"

Max shouts instructions behind me as Bastien and Luc burst through the doors, their faces painted with horror. He climbs on the bed, pushing down on her chest and giving her oxygen, but it's no good.

All I can do is watch.

As the forever we were promised disappears like smoke.

As my wife's beautiful eyes turn glassy and blank.

As my Emery dies in front of me.

Chapter Thirty

"Nikolai!"

Bastien is shaking me, his gaze concerned. I push him away. "I'm all right," I say hoarsely. "What are we doing?"

Max looks at me, his expression understanding.

"Ezra agrees with me that this isn't physical. He believes – and so do I – that Ava's experiencing a severe PTSD episode. She could very well be aware of what's happening around her, but we don't know."

Luc beckons him impatiently. "So how do we help her?"

Max hesitates. "We have to build her a nest."

A nest.

My mind pulls me back to Emery, gathering blankets and shirts and taking over the basement of our house.

"A what?" Bastien asks dumbfoundedly.

"It's an omega thing." They all look at me with varying degrees of concern and confusion, and I ignore them as I focus on Ava. Turning, I take in the bare wooden walls, the open spaces, the lack of anything especially soft.

"She needs to feel cared for, by us," I whisper, and Max nods.

There's a lump of lead inside my chest. I don't know if I can do this.

Bastien looks between us, his jaw clenched. "I really fucked this up, didn't I? Telling her to have some space, away from us?"

Max shakes his head. "You didn't know, Bas. That would have been the right move for anyone else. It's not your fault."

"Right, then." Luc stands up, carefully balancing Ava in his arms. She's so still and silent. He glances down at her and pulls her closer before he looks up.

"How the fuck do we build a nest?"

I swallow. "We have one upstairs."

Three gazes swing to me with varying degrees of surprise. I've never let anyone go into the space that was meant for Em.

"Niko," Luc says softly. "We don't need to use that."

Emery's space. Emery's nest. The one she never got to make.

Ava's lifeless face stares back at me and resolve settles in my chest.

"Yes," I say firmly. "Yes, we do."

Chapter Thirty-One
Ava

I drift, endlessly.
 Sometimes, I can hear voices. They sound muted, almost as if I'm underwater.
I can't *feel* anything, though. I'm completely, utterly and blissfully numb.
And I don't want to go back.

Chapter Thirty-Two
Bastien

I linger at the door of Ava's makeshift nest.

My fist raises to knock, before I drop it and turn away, shoulders sagging.

This isn't for you.

I hate this. I hate that I can't help to fix this mess that I've created.

I can't help her because I'm not an alpha. Just a useless beta.

Heading out of the house and down to my tech room, I quietly close the door and turn to my screens.

This, I can do. I can make sure none of her father's men get anywhere near her. I can make sure she's safe and secure with us. That no one who means her any harm will ever lay a hand on her again.

Hours later, I groan and stretch out in my chair, popping my muscles. The door opens and I turn to Leah, gratefully accepting the coffee she hands me. "Nash is asleep. Thought you could do with this."

"Thanks, Lee."

I expect her to leave, but instead she slips into the chair

next to me. When I glance at her, she looks at me expectantly.

"What?" My voice is flat.

"Nothing," she remarks. "Just watching you get in your own way."

A laugh huffs out of me. "What the hell does that mean?"

Leah shrugs. "It means you're letting old feelings cloud your judgment. Nobody cares that you're a beta, but you're moping around like it makes some sort of difference."

"It does make a difference." I stare at the screens in front of me. "I can't help her, because I'm not an alpha."

A snort comes from the chair next to me. "What kind of bullshit is that?"

She waves a hand at me. "You can take care of her just as much as an alpha. What, because you're not built a certain way biologically, you can't help her?"

I drag a hand over my face. "Not like them," I insist.

"Well, you're right. You can't help her like this. You need to pull your head out of your ass and realize that you're just as important as the rest of us."

Her words hit me like a punch to my solar plexus. "When did you get all wise and shit? Did Nik put you up to this?"

Leah laughs. "No, this is all me. I know a little something about living with a group of alphas."

She points to the door. "Now get up to that house and help your girl and your pack."

My throat feels thick. "Thanks, Lee," I say quietly.

She raises her mug to me in a salute as I leave the room, heading back up to the main house. The stars flicker overhead, lighting the ground in soft shades of gray.

As I walk into the house and up the winding stairs, the combination of scents hit me like a punch to my solar plexus.

Holy shit.

Okay. Deep breath. Just go in.

Bracing myself, I push the door open and walk inside.

Luc sits up in the pile of blankets and cushions spread across the floor, his hair a mess and his forehead wrinkling.

"Where the hell have you been?" he gripes. "Get in here."

I toe my shoes off, leaving them with the others at the door, and pick my way across the soft floor.

Reaching my pack, I debate for a second. Luc and Nikolai are on either side of Ava, their arms wrapped carefully around her. Bundles of clothing are scattered haphazardly everywhere. Max sits against the wall, his expression indecipherable.

Luc scoffs and yanks me down. "Swap out with me," he says. "She'll need all of us."

I carefully move into the warm space, my eyes tracing Ava's closed eyes. "She's sleeping?" I whisper. Luc nods.

"Fell asleep around an hour ago. It feels… more natural than how she was before."

My hand lifts, gently touching her hair, stroking down the soft curls that bounce around my fingers. It feels instinctive to move my hands down, slowly stroking her arms and face until she shifts, rolling into me with a sigh. I breathe in her scent, a little softer now, and something loosens in my chest. Exhaustion threatens, the lack of sleep finally catching up to me.

Closing my eyes, I drift off with our omega in my arms.

Chapter Thirty-Three
Ava

Awareness filters in slowly.

Warmth under my cheek. Silky softness against my skin, the scent of sandalwood, sage, apple pie and gingerbread mixing in the air. It's not an unpleasant mix, and my chest flips a little. Then I register the soft rise and fall of breath against my hair.

My eyes fly open, and I come face to face with an alpha's chest pressed against me.

Letting out a small squeak, I glance up into Luc's sleeping face. His dark hair falls over his eye as he shifts slightly, and I freeze as warm arms tighten around me.

What the hell is happening here?

I wait for the inevitable freak-out. My heart pounds, but I don't feel that sense of *panic* I expect.

I feel...peaceful. My body is perfectly comfortable with this arrangement.

Slowly, I rotate myself in Luc's arms, trying my best not to wake him. I'm so *tired*. As though I've spent too long with my muscles tense, and now I'm paying for it. I wince as

I turn, and inhale sharply when a pair of gray eyes meet mine and widen.

Wetting my lips, I croak out his name. "Bastien?"

"You're awake." His face creases into a deep smile, and something inside me perks up.

"What happened?" Why is my throat so dry?

"Let me get you some water." He climbs over to a shelf and brings me back a glass. I drink it quickly and make pleading eyes for another one. Bastien laughs quietly, and once I've downed four full glasses, I feel a little more human.

"Bastien," I whisper. "What happened?"

Why can't I remember anything?

His face shutters, and he looks towards his sleeping brother hesitantly.

"Tell me." It's a demand, my eyes searching his face.

"You went into a type of shock," he murmurs quietly, settling next to me. "We couldn't wake you, couldn't get you to speak, eat, drink…"

He swallows, watching my face closely. "We thought you were dying," he whispers. "You were *empty*, Ava. Like the lights were on, but nobody was home."

Nausea twists in my stomach. "How long was I like that?"

"This is day four," he admits, and my throat closes.

Four days?

"I…" without thinking, my hand drops to my stomach. Bastien follows my movement and immediately shakes his head. "They're fine," he reassures me quickly. "Max checked."

Swallowing, I nod and look down, pushing back the relief that fills me at his words.

I realize he's not wearing a top just as he flushes a deep red. "Oh! I…um… Ezra said—"

"You needed us." Nikolai's deep voice rumbles in the small space, and I whip around to see him kneeling at the edge of the blankets they've set up. His small smile is full of relief.

"Welcome back, little bird," he says quietly. "I'm glad you're awake."

I'm in a small space with two alphas and a beta, two of whom are shirtless. Everywhere I try to look, there's naked male flesh on display. With a squeak, I stare up at the ceiling, just as Max walks in and drops the plate he's carrying.

"Ava!"

The clatter wakes Luc, and now there's four damned alphas – well, three and a beta - crammed into this space and trying to talk to me. I don't know where to look.

And a small – *very* small – part of me can admit that it's all very nicely defined.

Wait. Glancing down, I'm relieved to see that I'm in a nightgown. My eyes move from the gown to the soft floor, covered with dozens of cushions and soft blankets. My hand trails over a particularly pretty silver one before I snatch it back.

They're all silently watching me. "You can touch it," Nikolai says, his voice a little rough.

My hand sneaks out to stroke the soft silkiness again. Just once.

Okay, maybe twice.

"I'm not allowed to have a nest." I squeeze my eyes shut.

A good omega does as she's told.

A good omega follows the omega creed.

"Fuck the creed," Max says savagely. I glance at him with surprise, and he grabs the blanket and holds it out to me determinedly. "This space is yours, Ava. If you want it."

I hesitantly take the blanket from his outstretched hand. My space.

Glancing up, I see soft sheets hanging from the ceiling, creating a tent effect. Fairy lights twinkle in strands from wall to wall.

I bite my lip.

"You built me a nest?" My voice wobbles, and I swallow.

Luc's eyes are soft. "You can change whatever you want. We had to build it quickly, but we tried to think about what you might like."

I take in the jewelled tones, the cozy atmosphere – even the scents don't feel strange. This feels like heaven.

"I love it," I whisper. "I've never had a nest."

Leaning back a little, my hand brushes something cotton. Tugging it, I lift out a white shirt. It smells like… gingerbread?

Nikolai's wide eyes meet mine, and I realize my face is basically buried in his shirt as I inhale deeply. My fingers clench on it, and his eyes note the movement, a smile twitching at his lips. They gave me their clothes?

I glare at him. *This is mine,* I silently communicate through frowns and squinty eyes. *You can't have it.*

I carefully tuck it back into position before turning to them.

"I think I'd like to get up now," I decide.

As if on cue, my stomach growls.

I've never seen four grown males move so quickly.

Chapter Thirty-Four
Nikolai

Heat simmers in my chest as we follow Ava into the kitchen.

Watching her tug my shirt from the pile we gave her, seeing her fingers clench and smelling the sudden spike of her vanilla scent... it's awakened something in me that I thought was gone forever.

Guilt and desire wrestle for control, and I can't stop myself from pulling a chair out for her. She slides into it carefully, shooting me a shy smile that goes straight to my knot.

Shit.

This is not going to happen, I tell myself. *She's been through hell, asshole.*

But I can't stop myself from running my eyes over the soft curve of her neck or appreciating the way her nose wrinkles when Bastien hands her a coffee. Truthfully, there's not a part of her I'm not drawn to like a fucking beacon. And that scares the shit out of me.

"What would you like to eat?" Luc asks. He's been quiet

since Ava woke up, but he's tracking her every move with predatory stillness, drinking in every movement she makes.

She shrugs, lifting her frail shoulder. "Whatever is easiest."

Bastien tuts at her dramatically. "Luc doesn't cook for just anyone, you know. I'd make the most of it."

Luc makes a vulgar gesture at his brother, and Ava laughs quietly.

Everyone pauses, drinking that laugh in like it's the damn elixir of life.

Something has changed, I realize as we sit together in peaceful quiet. Ava feels... more relaxed. Maybe because we've spent four days with her tucked between our bodies, wrapped in our arms, entwined in our scents.

She picks at the pancakes Luc makes her, sucking strawberry juice off her fingers and making us all shift in our seats.

She has no fucking idea how tempting she actually is.

I frown as she pushes away her plate, leaning back in her chair. Most of the food has been left untouched. Glancing to Max, I see him watching Ava too, his mouth turned down at the corners, but he doesn't say anything.

"Thank you, Luc." Ava's eyes flit around the kitchen. "Where's Leah?"

"With Nash," I answer. Leah has been watching Nash for the last few days. I've managed to get out to put him to bed and do some schoolwork with him yesterday, but I know he's curious about where I've been. And truthfully, I'd like him to meet Ava. Especially if she might stay.

Ava bites her lip. "I'd like to meet him," she ventures shyly.

Warmth spreads in my stomach. "He'd love to meet you too," I say quietly. "Whenever you're ready."

When she smiles back at me, a *real* smile, I force myself

not to lean over and drop a kiss on those plump lips. This omega is well and truly under my skin. She shifts in her seat and our attention zeroes in on her, making her blush and drop her gaze to the table.

"I was thinking," she starts, her voice soft. "Will you tell me a little bit more about you? All of you?"

"I'm an open book. Ask anything you want, love," Bastien declares, but there's a hint of worry as his gaze flicks to mine before moving away.

Rubbing my suddenly clammy hands on my pants leg, I push away the empty feeling in the pit of my stomach. It's good that she's asking. It means she's interested in us, but damn if I don't want to head straight out of that door and hide somewhere until this conversation's over.

Ava wrinkles her nose at Bastien. It's a quirk I've noticed before, and it's adorable.

Deep breaths, Nikolai. This will be fine.

"Okay," she says hesitantly. "Where are you from?"

"We're all from Oregon," Bastien responds, after a quick glance at Luc. "Luc and I grew up next door to Max and Leah, and Nik was across the street."

She grins. "That's sweet. So you always knew you'd be a pack?"

This time, everyone looks at me, and I want to kick myself when Ava's smile dims a little as she picks up on the tension.

"I'm sorry," she mumbles. "I didn't mean to—,"

She falls silent as I reach out and tap her hand. "It's fine, little bird."

Shooting her a crooked smile, I take a deep breath before looking to Max. He nods, jaw tense as he stares at the table. This story isn't pleasant for either of us.

"We were all born before the war but when the birth rates

had already started to drop," I tell her. "We met when our parents moved to one of those gated neighborhoods."

Ava looks between us, confused. "Gated neighborhoods?"

"They popped up after the beta adoption process was introduced, mimicking the old-style American neighbourhoods where children played on every street corner," explains Max. "It was a way for betas to raise their adopted kids in a way that gave them social contact with other children."

Clearing my throat, I continue.

"Luc, Bastien and Max created a pack first. I joined later."

I can sense her confusion without even looking.

"I… I met someone. You know how most packs normally go through the omega application process, or they steer clear and meet a beta partner instead?"

Her confusion clears, replaced by curiosity. "So, you met a beta?"

Her tone sounds a little sorrowful, likely picking up on the undercurrents of our conversation. But her scent spikes when I shake my head. "Emery was an omega."

"An omega?" Ava's eyes widen. "How is that possible? Wasn't she in the compound?"

I pause as the familiar ragged pain rears up. My hand reaches up to my chest, an automatic reflex, and Ava's face softens as she picks up on my unease.

"Nikolai…," she says gently. "You don't need to answer that. I'm sorry."

Shaking my head, I push words out through the lump in my throat. "I'm fine, little bird. It's important for you to know, I think."

Haltingly, the words tearing free from the locked box in my chest, I explain about Emery. Sent to live with Max and

Leah when her mom and dad died in a car crash, she grabbed my attention from the moment we met.

"So Emery was your cousin?" she asks Max quietly, and he nods. "By adoption. She was younger than me."

"How old are you?" she asks curiously.

"Max is the oldest at thirty. I'm twenty-eight, Nik's twenty-seven," Luc explains. "Bastien is twenty-six."

Emery and I were the same age.

She glances back to me with a sad smile. "So, love at first sight?"

Luc snorts out a laugh. "Not exactly." Bastien sniggers, and even Max breaks out in a smile.

"She drove me mad," I confess. "From day one, we argued over everything. Movies, food, anything the group talked about, we seemed to pick a fight over. Then Max's parents sent her to a summer school, and when she came back….,"

I just *knew*. Knew from the second she waltzed back into my kitchen, her eyes locked on mine and her hips swaying. I don't go into that, though. These memories are precious, and they belong to Em. Maybe one day I'll feel ready to share them.

I wet my dry lips. "We were inseparable," I whisper. "And then she awakened, when she was twenty."

Ava's eyes slide closed. "They took her?" she asks, her voice wavering.

"No."

It's Max who answers the question, his voice grim and low.

"We weren't going to let her go. Our parents travelled a lot, and Nik had already awakened as an alpha, so we managed to hide it at first. We knew we couldn't keep it secret forever though, so Emery moved in with Nik and we looked for somewhere permanent to go."

"What about your parents?" Ava asks me, her voice small. I take her hand into mine.

"My mom died when I was sixteen, lung cancer. My dad... he didn't really want me. It was always my mom who pushed for a child, so when she died and I'd just awakened, he moved out pretty quickly. I think he's living with a beta now, outside of Denver. I don't have any contact with him."

"Oh." Ava's brow creases as she looks between us.

Luc takes up the baton for me. "I'd been playing with the stock markets for a while, and we'd built up some savings for a pack house. Bastien found this land for sale. It was secluded enough that Em wouldn't be restricted to the house, and close enough to a major city that we could do supply runs without getting too familiar with the locals. Nik was in charge of the renovations."

I see the moment the lightbulb switches on. "The nest," she whispers. Her face falls. "You designed that for Emery, Nik."

I swallow. "It wasn't meant to be, little bird. She never saw it."

"Because of me." Max interrupts us, and Ava flinches at his dark tone. "Because I failed her."

"You didn't fail her, Max." My voice is tired but I'll have this conversation as many times as Max needs me to. "There was nothing else you could have done."

Ava stays silent, her hazel eyes swiveling between us. I steady myself with a hand on the table, and her small fingers reach over, entwining with mine. She squeezes my hand, and I grip her fingers.

"Em had her first heat not long after she awakened," I explain softly. "She became pregnant, but it wasn't an easy pregnancy. Max did everything he could, but she went into labour early, and there were complications. She didn't survive."

Ava's sudden spike of fear pushes Bastien to his feet. Rounding the table, he picks her up, sitting back down with his arms around her. "That's unusual, love," he promises her, but his eyes flicker to Max. "Isn't it?"

Max pales. "It is."

But he doesn't sound convinced. Ava shivers as she glances down at her rounded stomach. She squeezes her eyes shut, and I want to kick myself.

"Ava – little bird – I didn't mean to scare you."

She shakes her head. "It's fine, Nik. I just… I'm so sorry. I'm sorry that happened to you. And Nash…," Her words trail off with a waver, and her eyes glisten as she watches me.

That's what hurts the most, some days. Watching my son, so like the mother he'll never know. Em would've been a fantastic mom. But here we are, without Em, and Nash is trapped in the place that I intended to be Emery's freedom. Unable to leave, to play with other kids. He's never even *seen* another kid. And Ava, sat in front of me with tears glistening in those fractured hazel eyes. If nothing changes and she stays with us, this place will become her prison, too.

Fuck the Omega Compound. Fuck them and their barbaric laws. And fuck them for ruining so many of our lives.

The unfairness of it all sours my stomach, and I push my chair back.

"Excuse me," I say quietly.

Ava starts, half rising from Bastien's lap, but I wave her off with a forced smile. "I'm okay, little bird. Just need to check on something."

Her nod seems equally forced, but my anger is rising, and I need to let it out somewhere that Ava and Nash can't see.

I flee the kitchen like the hounds of hell are at my heels.

Chapter Thirty-Five
Lucien

Ava stares after Nikolai, her face crestfallen.

"I didn't mean to upset him," she says, her shoulders slumped.

"You didn't, brat." My voice is firm. "Nik wouldn't have shared his story unless he wanted you to know."

Ava nods, her face still dejected, before she turns to Max. He springs to attention.

"What is it? Is something wrong?" he asks, worried.

"No, nothing like that. I… would you be able to scan me? *Them*, I mean? So I can see them?" She places an awkward hand on her stomach.

We all pause, and Max's eyes soften. "Of course I can. Whenever you want me to."

"Now?" Ava clears her throat. "I feel… well, I don't want to change my mind."

He smiles at her. "I have an ultrasound set up in my office. Come with me and we'll take a look."

She glances around at all of us uncertainly, and I wonder what's running through her mind. Slowly, she nods, and slides from Bastien's lap to follow him. Silence echoes in

Chapter Thirty-Five

their wake as they leave the kitchen, until Bastien blows out a breath.

"She's okay," he breathes, staring at the door.

I nod. "She's okay."

It's enough, for now.

Chapter Thirty-Six
Ava

My knees shake as I follow Max out of the house and down to the offices. He takes it slowly, and I seize the opportunity to tip up my face to the sun.

I don't even know what month it is.

"September," Max tells me when I ask him. We head into the space where he removed my tracking device. Embarrassment stains his cheeks as he darts around, scooping papers off chairs and trying to tidy the mess.

I smile at his flustered movements. "Organized chaos?" I ask.

"Not even a little," he admits wryly. "Just chaos, unfortunately." He gestures to an examination table in the corner. "Take a seat."

Slowly, I move over to the padded bench and pull myself up. My legs dangle over the edge as Max moves around, pulling a machine towards me.

"This is an ultrasound machine," he explains. "I'll use this rod to move over your stomach, and we'll be able to see what's happening on the screen."

Chapter Thirty-Six

Nerves swirl in my stomach. "I'll be able to see them?"

Max nods, watching me with understanding in his brown eyes.

"We'll take it slow, okay?" he whispers. "If you want to stop, we can stop."

Resolve firms my spine. I can do this. *I want to do this.*

"I don't want to hide anymore," I whisper back.

He touches my hand before glancing down to my nightgown and clearing his throat.

"I'll need to scan your abdomen."

A flush of heat tickles my neck.

"Ah... okay."

Trying not to blush, I lift the edge of the gown until it's above my underwear. Max directs me to lie back with a gentle hand on my shoulder, his cheeks stained with red as he squeezes some jelly onto the rod in his hand.

"This is going to be cold," he warns. "Are you ready?"

He leans forward on my nod, and I inhale sharply at the coolness on my skin as he reaches over me and flicks the machine on.

Max spends a minute fiddling with the buttons before a black screen pops up. I close my eyes and try to breathe.

Time to face the inevitable.

My eyes fly open at the whooshing noise. It sounds like...

"Here they are," Max smiles softly.

I stare at the screen, where an unmistakable baby-shaped blob bobs around on the screen, the sound of a heartbeat pulsing through the air. My hand slips down to gently rest on my stomach. An ache appears at the back of my throat and behind my eyes.

"Hello," I whisper. Tears begin to slide down my face, and Max's fingers grip mine, offering his silent strength. I give him a watery smile as we both watch the screen.

When he pulls his hand out of my grip, my hand shoots out to wrap around his wrist.

"Wait, please," I beg. I'm not ready to let this feeling go just yet.

He gives me a crooked grin. "Shall we look at the other one?"

Oh my god. I'm having two babies. I nod, wordlessly waiting for him to find the second heartbeat. The whoosh starts back up again, and my tears start to fall faster, the ache in my throat rippling into full-blown agony.

This is real. This is really and truly happening.

I barely register Max pulling the machine back and lifting me onto his lap. His arms come around me and he rocks me as I sob into his chest.

"I can't do this, Max,"

His hand strokes over my hair. "I think you could do anything you put your mind to," he says gently.

Shaking my head abruptly, I brush off his words.

"I don't know anything about children," I say shrilly. "I don't have anything for them. I don't even have a *home* for them."

Max's hand pauses. "You do have a home," he says roughly. "Here."

It's a beautiful offer. Just for a moment, I let myself sink into that fantasy. All of us, living happily here together. My children and I being part of this family. Part of the Grey pack.

Reality is quick to sink in, though. I can't take over their lives like that. Stone is absolutely still coming after me. How can I settle here and ask them to risk their safety? Max picks up on my feelings, and he lifts my face to his.

"Ava...," his brows lower over his eyes. "Stop thinking you're an inconvenience to us."

"But I *am* an inconvenience," I insist. He shakes his head and I hold up my hand.

"You risked everything to get me out of there," I breathe, looking into his face. "You risked your whole family for me, Max. And I'm so grateful. You saved my life." My voice breaks on a sob.

"But I can't put you at risk anymore. If they find you, if they find me *with* you, you will be arrested. All of you. What happens then, Max? What happens to Nash?"

Max shakes me lightly, startling me enough that I take a breath.

"Listen to me," he says firmly. "We saved you because it was the right thing to do, sweetheart. I couldn't leave you there. But you being here? Right now? We choose this, Ava. And we want you to choose us. Choose to be a part of our family. Choose to *stay*." His voice cracks a little.

I swallow as my heart flips, that impossible future suddenly creeping back in. Does he mean…

"Max," I say awkwardly. "I don't know if I'll ever be able to – to give you—,"

"I don't care," he says roughly. "None of us will ever ask you for more than you're willing to give. I swear it, love. Give us the chance to show you that not all alphas are the same. I promise that whatever you want to give us will *always* be more than enough."

My chest aches at his words.

I don't want to go anywhere, I realize. *I want to stay.*

"You deserve more than a broken omega, Max." The words are painful.

"Don't," he says roughly. "You're not broken. Your soul is a little scarred, but so is everyone else here. You're brave, Ava, so damned brave. And I would be proud to stand beside you, for as long as you'll have me."

I look down at my hands. "I need to take... whatever this is, slowly," I warn him.

He pushes my hair back gently. "I'd wait forever if you needed me to."

We sit in silence for a few minutes, as I curl up in Max's lap. The tart sweetness of his apple scent soaks into me, warm and comforting. As I breathe in, I realize how far I've come since we first met. I could never have gotten this close to Max when I first arrived.

A sudden thought occurs and I stir, Max's warm breaths huffing against my hair as he looks down, his eyes questioning. "What's wrong?"

I lick my lips. "When you asked about me staying, did you mean... with everyone?"

I wait for the bite of panic, for the shaking at the thought of getting involved with the whole pack... but it doesn't come.

He hesitates. "I can't speak for the pack, love. But I know that none of us want you to leave."

He doesn't say anything else, and I sit quietly as I mull over his words.

I never expected to find a pack like this. But now that I have... maybe I need to give this a real chance. Because the idea of losing them, of never seeing them again...

I think that might be the thing that truly breaks me.

Chapter Thirty-Seven
Bastien

Nash and I are working on his treehouse when Max rocks up.

Nash's face scrunches up as he carefully sets out the lengths of wood to make sure they're the same size, his tongue sticking out in concentration.

Dropping down from the branch I've been working on, I brush the sawdust off my hands as Max walks across the clearing, his hand blocking out the sun as he peers up at us.

"How's it going?" he calls as I reach him.

"Think we've got everything now, just need to put it all together." We both watch Nash for a minute as he tries to drag a branch much longer than him. Max laughs quietly. "He's growing so fast."

Nodding, I cross my arms and wait.

"I spoke to Ava," My attention swings entirely to Max as he shuffles his feet. "I asked her if she'd stay."

My pulse starts pounding as I stare at him. "With us? What did she say?"

He stares at the ground, his brows furrowed. "She's willing to consider it."

Swallowing, he looks up and holds my gaze. "I told her I have feelings for her."

Whistling, I push down the pit of jealousy that suddenly starts ripping apart my stomach.

"That's great," I say, swallowing hard.

"We agreed we'd take it as slowly as she needs to. She asked me how the rest of you felt."

The jealousy suddenly changes to something else. Something... lighter.

"And you said?" I prompt him.

"I *said*, I can't speak for you." Max raises his eyebrow. "But you're feeling it too, right?"

I nod. *Feeling it? I'm fucking obsessed with her*.

"I don't know how to do this, Max," I admit, kicking at some of the leaves on the ground. "Will she even want all of us?"

What if she wants everyone else, but not me?

Max's honey brown eyes swing to mine, understanding coloring them. "Bas, we're a *pack*," he says softly. "Alpha or beta, you're still one of us. Just as good as any one of us. Ava's choices are her own, but it's no reflection on any of us if things don't work out."

"Yeah," I say softly, glancing back to Nash. I just wish I believed him.

He nudges my arm. "We'd all be lost without you, and you know it."

Snorting, I push him back. "Well, that's definitely true."

Nash comes barrelling over as we break into a scuffle. "Uncle Max!" he yells. "Can I meet the omega yet?"

"Soon, little man," Max laughs, shoving me away and ruffling his hair until Nash pushes him off with a groan. "I gotta head back to the house, but I'll come and do your biology lesson with you later." Nash groans, but he doesn't argue.

Before Max leaves, he turns back to me. "Nearly forgot. We need to start thinking about things for the babies, when they get here. We'll need to do a decent stock run."

I nod. "We can take my truck." Max left his behind in the rescue. I have zero doubt that Stone will have been all over it like a rash, but he won't find anything. All of our vehicles are linked to false identities.

"Have you heard anything?"

I shake my head. "Not yet. I can't see him giving up that easily, though."

The silence is what concerns me. I haven't heard a whisper about Ava on any of the channels I'm monitoring. A pregnant omega goes missing? You'd expect wall-to-wall news coverage. If they're not using the public to find her, what are they doing?

Nash starts grumbling that he's hungry, abandoning his work with all the enthusiasm of a six-year-old. I swing him on my shoulders as we all walk up to the kitchens.

"Where's Ava?" I murmur to Max.

"Sleeping."

Except she's absolutely not sleeping, because when we reach the kitchen, I can hear Leah's crying apologies a mile away.

Max and I both look to Nash in a panic as his eyes light up.

"Hey, little man," I start, "Why don't we—"

He dives through the kitchen door before I can get another word out.

Fuck. Nik is going to murder me.

Max sighs, gesturing for me to go first. "This isn't a bad thing. It was always going to happen, sooner or later."

When I walk through the doors, Nash is already climbing onto Leah's lap. "Don't cry, Aunty Lee," he demands, pushing her cheeks together. She moves his hands away with a half laugh, half sob.

"I'm fine, sweetheart. I promise. Do you want to say hello to Ava?"

We all watch in amazement as the loudest six-year-old in the history of the world blushes. Nash promptly hides his face against Leah's shoulder, and she tries not to laugh. Ava glances between us all, a little wide-eyed, but her eyes keep going back to Nash.

"Hi," he mumbles. "I'm Nash."

Ava smiles. "Hello, Nash. I'm Ava."

"I know," he grumbles. "She's *pretty*, Aunty Lee," he whispers loudly into Leah's neck.

Max's shoulders start to shake, and I try not to laugh as I tug Nash away from Leah and hang him over my shoulder until he shrieks.

"I think Ava's very pretty too, Nash," I say, throwing a small smile at Ava and watching with interest as her cheeks go pink.

"Why don't you sit next to her and tell her what you've been learning about?"

It takes approximately thirty seconds for Nash to get over his first crush and start telling Ava about the schoolwork we've all been taking in turns to teach him. Ava gives him her full attention, exclaiming and asking questions, and my shoulders relax.

Nik stops sharply when he and Luc walk in a few minutes later, his eyes widening as he takes in Ava and Nash chatting animatedly at the table.

"Papa!" Nash exclaims delightedly. "Look! I met Ava!"

"I can see that," Nik grumbles, and Ava flinches.

He turns to her in a panic. "I didn't mean… he can be a lot," Nik says under his breath. "I didn't want to overwhelm you."

Ava's shoulders relax at his explanation. "I don't mind," she says with a small smile. "He's beautiful, Nikolai."

They smile at each other as Nash continues to chat non-stop, only pausing for breath when Luc pushes his plate towards him. Mumbling something around his sandwich, he swallows.

"Are you going to live with us, Ava?"

Everybody goes silent as Max flushes, and I try not to stare at Ava. She clears her throat uncomfortably, pushing her sandwich around her plate.

"Nash," Nik scolds quietly. "It's not polite to ask Ava that."

"Oh," Nash looks down. "But Max and Bastien were talking about it earlier!"

Oh, god. Please let the floor swallow me up.

Max stares at the ceiling for inspiration as Luc leans forward to glare at us.

"I, uh," I fumble for words as Ava stares down at her plate, the tips of her ears pink. "Well—"

"We'd like her to stay with us, Nash," Luc says abruptly. Ava's head jerks up as she stares at him, her eyes wide. He grins at her, unrepentant. "You need to help us persuade her," he wiggles his eyebrows at Nash, and he crows delightedly.

"I can do that!"

He starts spouting off all of the things he loves about being here as the adults swap uncomfortable glances. I frown at Lucien, and he leans back in his chair with a whistle.

"What?" he says mildly when he catches us all staring. "We do want you to stay."

His last words are soft, directly to Ava.

Max nods, clearly on board with this conversation, and Ava glances between me and Nikolai.

Nik is focusing very intently on his food, so I flounder for the right thing to say.

"Yes," I settle on. *Nice and easy, Bas. Don't blow it.* "We do."

Her small smile takes root inside my chest and twists.

Clearing my throat, I jump up, taking my plate to the sink. "I have some things to sort out, so I'll see you all later."

I collapse into my office chair with a groan, leaning back to rub my hands down my face.

Smooth, Bastien. Real fucking smooth.

A knock comes a few minutes later. "Bastien?" a female voice calls, and I jump up. "Are you busy? I can come back."

I rip the door open with a little too much enthusiasm, and Ava flinches, taking a reflexive step back.

"Sorry," I apologize, rubbing the back of my neck. "Come in. You don't need to knock, just push the door open."

Ava follows me in and takes a seat in the wide leather chair she sat in before. It almost swallows her.

"Max said you might be able to help me," she begins. Turning from the screen, I give her my full attention as she leans forward, picking a thread on her dress.

"Anything you need."

"I want to do some research." The words fall out on top of each other, a little jumbled, and I frown. "Research?"

She nods, looking away. "On…," she touches her stomach, and I suddenly get it.

"On your pregnancy?" I ask gently, and she winces. "I guess so? The whole thing, really. I just – I don't know anything, and I hate feeling so unprepared. If I know a bit more, I can start preparing, you know?"

"Hey, I get it." I hold up a hand. "You don't need to explain yourself. Let's have a look."

I set her up with an old laptop that doesn't have a track-

Chapter Thirty-Seven

able browser and show her how to use it. "This won't send up any alerts, in case anyone's tracking certain search terms," I tell her, and she stares up at me, her eyes wide.

"They could do that?"

Lifting my shoulder, I shrug. "Technically, but they won't be able to do it with this."

Clearing my throat, I sit back down in my chair and turn to my keyboard. "You mind if I have a look too?"

Those beautiful hazel eyes just blink at me, and I try to explain.

"I just thought, if you need any help or anything – I don't know that much about kids, so it would probably be good to do some research, maybe? And you can talk to me about it. If you want to, that is. You don't have to." I laugh nervously. "Never mind."

"No!" she leans forward earnestly, and our eyes meet. "It would be nice to have someone to talk to about it. Thank you."

I cough into my fist. "Okay, then."

And that's how we spent the rest of the afternoon.

Chapter Thirty-Eight
Ava

Groaning, I lean back in my chair and swivel to face Bastien.

"I'm done for today," I admit. "I don't think I can read anymore."

It still doesn't feel real.

Lights flicker across Bastien's face from the screens as he turns his silver eyes toward me.

"How are you feeling?" he asks, hesitantly.

I think it over, picking through my jumbled thoughts.

"Like we're talking about somebody else," I murmur. Placing my hands on my stomach, I cup it gently.

"I know it's not their fault," I whisper. "But it feels like my life has been stolen from me, Bastien."

He slides closer to me, a question in his eyes as he lifts his hands.

Holding my breath, I nod in permission, watching his large hands settle gently onto my stomach. The warmth of his hands penetrates the thin cloth of my nightgown, heating the skin underneath.

"I think," he says quietly, not moving his eyes. "That if

we blamed everyone for their beginnings, the world would be an unforgiving place. But I also think that everyone deserves to make choices in their own lives."

His hand comes up slowly, making sure that I can see him before he gently cups my face.

"You didn't have a choice about coming here," Bastien says quietly. "We know that. Every choice you've had since your awakening was taken from you. This is your time to think about what *you* really want, Ava."

My eyes search his as confusion twists in my chest. "I don't know what I want."

He leans back in his chair, giving me space to breathe.

"You have options," he says carefully. "Even if it doesn't feel like it."

I laugh humourlessly. "Do I, though?"

He stares at me, his eyes boring into mine. "You have several. You can decide to go your own way. I can create a paper trail that will show you're a beta, not an omega. You could decide where to go, and what you do. You'd have to be very careful, but it's a possibility."

His stilted offer hits me like a punch to my solar plexus. "You could do that?" I whisper, and he nods.

But where would I go?

"People would ask questions," I say, looking down at my stomach.

Bastien looks away from me, his shoulders tight as he hesitates. "Adoption is another option."

My eyes widen as I stare at him, and he meets my gaze with a sad glint in his eye.

He shakes his head at what he sees. "I'm not saying that you should, or you shouldn't, Ava," he says. "But you deserve to have a choice."

A shiver works up my spine as my hands move to my stomach. *Give them up?*

"I..." I don't know what to say to that.

The uncertainty spreads across my face, and Bastien notices. "This isn't something you need to think about right now, or ever, if you don't want to."

"Max asked me to stay." The words slip out, and Bastien inhales.

"I know, love," he says. His voice is rough and low, and I only see honesty in his face when he turns to face me.

"What do you want, Bastien?"

My question drops like a stone into the silence.

"I...," he rubs a hand over his face. "I want to do this right, Ava. I don't want to make you feel like you have to stay, because you don't have anywhere to go. I want you to choose us because you have options and we're what you want. I want you to know that you can say no to us and that's fine, too."

I bite my lip as a sliver of disappointment runs through me. I'm not sure what I was expecting. Slowly, I pull myself out of the chair as Bastien watches me, his clear eyes dark in the small room.

"I understand," I nod at him and try to smile, but it doesn't quite reach my face. "Thank you, Bastien. I appreciate your concern."

I turn to make my way to the door, and a hand snakes around my wrist, holding it gently.

"Wait," he says in a low voice. A small kernel of hope appears, and I try not to look too pathetic as I turn back to him.

"What do you want from me?" he asks.

As he stands up, his hand slides down to entangle with mine, our fingers lacing together.

My heart gives a thump. "I want...,"

Bastien stares at me, his grey eyes darkening. "Tell me."

Swallowing, I close my eyes and bite the bullet.

"I want to know if you *want* me, Bastien. Like... like *that*."

I keep my eyes closed as his hand tightens around mine. The faintest scent of sage – not an alpha scent, but all *Bastien* – wraps around me as I feel him step closer, the warmth of his body brushing mine.

Fingers trail across my neck, small bumps springing up on my skin as I inhale.

"Open your eyes," he whispers into my ear. Shaking my head, I keep them firmly closed. I don't want to ruin the moment.

"Please."

I slide them open a touch to see Bastien's face in front of mine. His full lips curve up at the ends as we watch each other.

"I want you," he confesses. A ragged breath falls from my lips as his hand slowly cups the back of my neck, caressing it with gentle touches that send sparks flying through my body.

"I want you so badly it hurts, Ava. You're brave, and you're beautiful, and you're so perfectly *you* that I can't imagine ever feeling this way about anybody else. And I need you to know that I'm here waiting for you, whenever you're ready."

His words burn along my veins like lightning, pushing away the darkness that hovers over me. Tilting into him, I lift up my mouth as he steps closer, his body arching protectively over mine as a hint of sage surrounds us.

"Bastien...," It's a plea. *Don't stop*.

"Stay with me, Ava," he whispers, as his mouth descends on mine.

I don't know if he means in this moment or forever, but my mind blanks as he moves his lips gently over mine. Warm and soft, Bastien savors me, taking sips from my mouth like a fine wine. I gasp as his arm curls around me, slowly pulling me until I'm pressed against him, the curve of my stomach warming from the heat of his body.

His warm, hard, very male body.

My eyes fly open as he pulls back, his eyes moving over my face in concern.

"Stay," he murmurs, curling his hand around my face and stroking my cheek with tender slowness. My hand takes on a mind of its own, wrapping around the back of Bastien's neck as I pull myself into him, lifting my mouth up to his and drawing a rough sound from low in his chest as our kiss deepens. My nipples pebble, drawing across the thin material of my gown and pulling a gasp from me.

He pulls back at the sound, his darkened eyes searching mine. I try not to squirm at his assessing gaze.

"I'm all right," I whisper. It's half statement, half plea. My hand clenches in his hair as I try to urge him back to me. "Don't stop, Bastien. Please."

Let me lose myself in you.

His mouth moves down my jawline, languidly tasting my skin in a way that makes my knees buckle underneath me. Bastien's arm tightens around me before he takes a step backward, dropping down into his chair. Startled, I blink down at him, sprawled across the leather with a smile built for sin tugging at his lips.

My hand clenches. "I want…"

"Take it," he swears roughly. "Whatever you want, love."

My hands reach out to carefully trace his face. The coarse beginnings of a beard feel rough beneath my fingers. Bastien closes his eyes with a sharp inhale as I follow a path across his cheek and down his neck to his white cotton shirt, the colour bright against his olive skin.

I tug at it gently, and his eyes flick to mine.

"Take this off, please?" Heat spreads across my cheeks.

Chapter Thirty-Eight

Bastien doesn't hesitate. His hands drop to the hem and he peels the shirt over his head, dropping it carelessly to the floor. My heart thuds as I look over his body.

A smattering of dark hair dusts his sculpted chest. He might be a technical genius, but my beta gives the rest of the pack a run for their money in the six-pack stakes. Following the trail of hair down past his waistline, my eyes fly up to his face, my cheeks burning as my stomach twists with sudden need.

He shakes his head wryly. "And you think I don't want you?"

I guess I can see his point. Literally.

Swallowing, I look down again at the bulge in his pants, and he holds his arms out to me, understanding in his eyes.

"We're playing by your rules, love. You stop when you want to."

Slowly, I step forward until his arms gently enclose my middle. He draws his thumb down my back on either side of my spine in soothing lines, softening my tense muscles as he works until I'm a purring, boneless pile of *want*.

And I want more. More of this. More of him.

Pressing my palms to his chest, my fingers smooth the coarse hairs as his hands continue their magic. My nipples chafe against soft material, sensitive and aching, and Bastien pauses when I grab his arm, drawing it forward until I can press his hand to my breast and squeeze it, aching for relief.

"*Ava.*"

Leaning forward, I trace my tongue carefully along the seam of his lips, asking for entry.

"Please, Bastien," I breathe, and his hand finally takes over and closes over the sensitive flesh, his fingers massaging my skin in just the right way.

My core clenches, each contraction of his hand sending a pulse straight to my clit as my eyes flutter closed. My scent spikes, hips twisting as my frustration leaks into the air, and Bastien picks up on it.

"I might not have a knot," he whispers. "But I can still make you feel good, love."

Curiosity thrums through me as he gently beckons me to him.

"Climb up here," he murmurs. He pats his lap, and I bite my lip at the look he gives me, his grey eyes burning.

Slowly, I lift my knee and place it next to his thigh, repeating the process until I'm hovering over him, the heat of his skin warming the inside of my thighs. His hands brush my face, my neck, my arms, soothing me until I relax. Slowly, I sink down until his hardness brushes the dampness of my underwear, and we both suck in a breath.

Wrapping my arms around his neck, I bury my face in his warm skin, breathing in the freshness of his scent as a spike of anxiety runs through me. Bastien's strong arms move to my back, and he holds me gently.

"It's okay," he whispers in my ear. "We can stop. You're incredible, Ava. Just say the word and we can take a step back."

Frustration mounts inside me, but his words give me the push I need. I don't want to take a step back from him. I *want* this.

I will not let them take another damn thing.

Staying pressed against his neck, I gingerly move my hips back and forth, brushing the solid length resting between my legs. Bastien lets out a strangled groan and pulls my mouth to his.

I keep my eyes open and so does he, pushing aside my insecurities and leaning on him as I move back and forth on his lap. Every brush of his cock against my clit sends a pulse of pleasure through me, Bastien allowing me to control the pace of our movements as we rock together.

The pulses build up to a flood of sensation, bursts of sparks and arousal combining into a ball of need as I feel my release drawing up on me, but it remains achingly out of reach. I shift restlessly, my body drawn tight as a spinning top but unable to breach that final barrier. A frustrated whine breaks free, and Bastien tips up my chin, dropping a soft kiss on my lips.

"Do you trust me?"

I do.

When I nod, his hand drops down to my leg. The feel of his fingers on my bare skin makes me pause, his other hand stroking my back as his fingers move up my thigh and under my nightgown.

"Look at me, baby," Bastien's words are firm as I move my eyes to him. A tinge of worry threatens the edge of my consciousness, but he holds my gaze firm.

"Keep your eyes on me. Remember whose cock you're rubbing that pretty pussy against."

His dirty words pull a trickle of fluid from me, soaking my already wet underwear, and my body trembles as I feel his warm hands move to the top of my abdomen, stroking the skin.

"So soft," he murmurs. "So beautiful, Ava."

"Bastien." His name stays on my lips like a prayer, and I repeat it over and over again, keeping my eyes on him as his hand drops to the top of my underwear.

"I'm here," he promises, his eyes burning into me. "I've got you, baby."

A sob slips from my mouth as his fingers slide into my underwear, through the warmth and slick of my pussy to circle my swollen nub.

He rubs his coarse thumb over my clit as I break our gazes, throwing my head back and toward the ceiling with a wordless keen.

"Fucking perfect. Such a pretty omega, Ava. I can't wait to watch you come apart on my hand, soak me with that lovely slick."

Words of praise drop from his lips as I writhe on his hand, those fingers moving and rubbing and tugging until my pleasures sweeps me away and my back arches, my mouth open as I cry out.

"Good girl," he grounds out, and I shudder at the pleasure that flickers at his praise. I can't fight the lightning raking down my spine, the scent of my own slick as it's pulled from me by his talented hands.

Burying my face in him, my hands drop to grab at his wrist, pushing him on, both of us moving together to a rhythm only we can hear until I shatter completely in his arms.

He holds me tightly as I shake, murmuring endless words as he rises from the chair, wrapping my arms and legs around him as he crosses the room and lays me down on a soft couch.

When he tries to move away, I grab his arm tightly. Tiredness, pleasure and a little worry are all battling for space inside my head, and I don't want him to leave me.

He touches my face gently before nudging me back and sliding in next to me. He lifts until I'm half on top of him, a soft blanket sliding over us.

He drops a butterfly kiss on the end of my nose. "Rest," he whispers, pushing my hair back from my face as I blink at him sleepily.

A small smile curves my lips as I drift off, his arms tight around me.

Maybe I'm not so broken after all.

Chapter Thirty-Nine
Lucien

I force my eyes down to the reports in front of me, squeezing the pen in my hands as I make a note on our accounts. Normally the stock market can keep my attention for hours, but not today.

Words blur in front of my eyes as a low, drawn-out moan filters through the wall of my brother's office. The plastic snaps in my hand and I curse as black ink spills out across the page.

Pushing myself away from the desk, I glare at it as the sweet scent of an omega's slick hits my nose.

Fuck.

I need to get out of here before I end up in there. I don't think Ava or my brother would appreciate me barging in on them.

Bursting out of the front doors, I take in a bracing breath of fresh air and try to push down the jealousy making a twisted mess of my intestines.

Nik approaches, eyeing me curiously, and I hold up a hand.

"Do *not* go in there," I warn. His brows fly up as he stares from me to the door.

"Why not?" he asks cautiously.

Swallowing hard, I gesture wildly behind me. "Bastien is with Ava."

Nik's eyes grow wide, a flush trailing across his high cheekbones.

"Is she all right?" he asks, a thread of anger in his words. "She hasn't recovered enough—,"

"Trust me," I grit out. "She's fine."

At least, judging from the sounds I heard.

Nikolai eyes me, and I roll my eyes at him, pushing down the hint of hurt in my chest.

What made you think she'd come to you for comfort anyway, asshole?

Swallowing, I walk past Nik, ignoring him when he falls into step next to me.

"You're jealous," he notes softly.

I scoff. "I'm not jealous. She can be with whoever she wants."

I mean it. I'm so fucking glad that she's exploring her own pleasure, and not letting those bastards keep her from it. I just... *I wish it was me*.

Fuck. I'm not just jealous, I'm bright green with fucking envy. My fist lifts, rubbing the space over my heart. This damn omega has me twisted up in knots. Nikolai kicks at the leaves as he walks, drawing my attention to him.

"Maybe I am a little jealous," I admit. "I like her, Nik."

He side-eyes me with a smile. "I know."

"Asshole." I push him, and he snorts with laughter.

"We're a pack, Luc," he says. "Maybe it's time we start acting like it."

I stop, turning to face him as hurt lances my chest. "You don't think we act like a pack?"

Nik shrugs. "We do, most of the time," he notes. "But the last few years...," he stops, swallowing. "I haven't helped."

I stare at my pack brother. "When I made you part of this pack, I knew what I was asking," I say roughly. "I never expected you to give us your all, Nik. Not when you didn't have it to give."

He nods. "I know. But maybe it's time for us to put the pack first."

"What do you mean?"

He swallows. "Ava. If we're going to do this... then we should offer her a real pack, Luc. All of us. All in. We already know Max is, and it sounds like Bastien's the same. I don't want her to worry about who's in, or who's out."

It sounds perfect. All of us, together. The way that a pack should be. But...

"This'll be different to before." Nik and Emery were a couple outside of the pack structure. Unusual, but it worked for them and for us, especially with her being Max's cousin. There was never even a question, the relationship too familial despite their adoption status. Having our whole pack focused on one omega... god, I want that.

He nods. "I know. I think I'm ready for it, Luc." Hesitating, he looks behind us, to the omega we've left behind with my brother. "She makes me want a future again. I think I felt it when we needed the nest. I thought it would feel wrong, like she wasn't supposed to be there, but it didn't."

Hope unfurls in my chest. "It felt like she was exactly where she was supposed to be."

Nik's shoulders tense as he nods, and I turn him to face me as our pack bond flares a little. His blue eyes are shadowed, a sheen across them telling me how close to the surface his grief is.

My mind flashes to Emery. The agony tearing through our pack bond as Nikolai lost his soulmate, the bitemark on his chest turning black. His hand comes up to rest on his shirt, directly above the mark.

"Nik," I breathe. "This doesn't mean that you loved Emery any less. And we don't need to move too quickly. Ava wouldn't be ready for that level yet, anyway."

There's a reason that most packs only share one female. Having too many outside bonds – too many strands of bitemarks - can make things complicated. Unstable. But Nik has always been a part of us, bonded or not. And whilst it was never an option for Em to be a full pack member to all of us, Ava doesn't have that restriction. There's nothing stopping any of us, all of us, from giving her a bitemark. From creating a bond between us and her that ties us together forever.

But I won't push Nikolai into more than he's comfortable with.

"Just take your time." The words come out roughly. "Take it slow, and don't let the rest of us push it to more than you're both comfortable with."

Although I've seen the looks he gives her when he thinks no one is looking. This little shattered omega could be the one Nikolai needs to bring him back to life. A real life, not just a shell, only existing for the sake of his son and avoiding anything to do with truly living.

Shadows flit across his face. "I loved Emery, Luc," he says hoarsely.

When he tries to look away, I grip his neck, pulling him back to me. "God, Nik, I know you did," I insist, my throat tight. "We know Em was your everything. You gave her everything you possibly could, brother. To find another chance at happiness… don't let this go, Nik. Grab onto it with both hands."

Shaking his head, he looks away from me. "But why are

my feelings so strong now? Why does this feel so *intense*? Do you feel it, too?"

I nod slowly. "I do. But it's an intense situation."

"What if she doesn't want us?" he asks in a low voice. "What if Nash is too much? Or we're too much?"

I shake my head. "I don't think that will happen, Nik. You saw them together. Nash already idolizes her and he's only met her once."

Nikolai grunts. "I know the feeling."

"We'll take it at her pace. Whatever she's comfortable with, whatever she asks for."

"Should we talk to her as a pack?"

A hint of nervousness thrums through me. "No, not yet. I don't want her to feel like we're pushing her into something she's not ready for."

Nik nods, and we continue walking in silence, both of us contemplating the changes our pack is facing.

"Nik," I ask gruffly. "The children—,"

"She's a package deal, Luc," Nik responds instantly. "That includes them, too."

I blow out a breath of relief. I'm glad he sees it the same way I do.

"Yeah," I agree. "I feel the same way."

Truthfully, I feel like Ava and those kids were always meant to be ours. We just need to prove it to her.

Chapter Forty
Ava

Bastien walks me to my bedroom door, retreating with a kiss to my forehead.

"Do you want me to stay?" he asks, concern pulling his face down. He glances towards my door and back to me. "You could go back to the nest."

Shaking my head, I give him a soft smile. "I'll be okay now, I think."

It's true. I feel... stronger. Like something's shifted inside me. And I wanted to come back here and think.

After Bastien leaves, I close the door and turn to face my empty room. Blowing out a breath, I put my hands on my hips.

Time to feel like me again.

Starting with a bath. I use liberal amounts of Leah's bath bubbles and soak for more than an hour, washing my hair with the scented shampoo she's left and carefully combing out the few small knots still in my hair.

I lie back in the tub and run my hands over my belly. It just pokes out through the top of the water, and I watch as the water droplets roll off the top.

CHAPTER FORTY

Clearing my throat, I stare at it, remembering my research. Apparently they can *hear* me now.

"Hello," I start cautiously.

Blowing out a breath, I squeeze my eyes shut, feeling stupid.

"I guess...I wanted to say hello." *You already said that, Ava.*

"This is weird," I admit. Lying back, I stare at the ceiling instead. It feels a little easier this way, and I run my hands over my stomach as I talk.

"I don't know how to feel about you, you know," I say quietly. "None of this is your fault, but I guess we're stuck with each other now. I'm going to be your mom."

Bastien's words on adoption spring to my mind, and I swallow hard. Even thinking about it feels...wrong. Like we'd be feeding into the twisted narrative of the Omega Creed and their archaic laws. Besides, what if Stone realized? Two babies, twins, up for adoption when they track every pregnancy. He'd get hold of them in a heartbeat.

I'm not going to let that happen. A surge of protectiveness takes me by surprise, and my eyes drop back to my bump.

"I'm going to do my best for you," I whisper, a lump in my throat. "I can't promise I'm going to be the best mom ever. But I promise to try. And I won't give up."

The pack filters into my mind. Bastien, Max, Luc, even Nikolai.

"There's this pack," I confess to my stomach. *I think I'm getting the hang of this strange, strange conversation.*

"I think that they want to help us."

Us. It's not just me anymore. My head spins slightly at the realization. I have to think of them first.

I bite my lip.

"I want to stay," I whisper to them. "But I don't want to stay because they feel obligated."

My mind flashes to Bastien, his hands on me, and my face grows warm.

Staring back to the ceiling, I try to think of boring thoughts.

No seggsy thoughts in front of the babies, Ava.

My mind wanders to the pack even as I let the water out and get dressed in a pair of shorts and a large t-shirt that smells like sandalwood. I have the soft cotton pressed to my face, inhaling the lightly spiced scent like a creeper, when the door knocks.

I drop the shirt immediately. "Coming," I call in a strangled voice.

Lucien turns to look at me when the door opens, and his eyes widen at my look of panic. *Did he somehow work out that I was perving on his shirt?*

"What's the matter?" he demands, staring around and behind me. "Ava?"

My face explodes like a tomato. "Nothing!" I say, a shrill note to my voice that has Luc squinting at me in suspicion.

"Are you sure?" he asks.

"Yep. Absolutely. One hundred per cent fine."

His eyes slide down to where my fingers are tangled in his shirt, and his nostrils flare.

"Are you... scenting me?" I ask indignantly.

A ghost of a smile plays on his lips. "Is that my shirt?" he asks casually, nodding.

I drop my hands like they're on fire. "No!"

His face turns smug. "That's definitely my shirt," he points out.

Insufferable alpha.

I sniff. "Is it? I didn't realize," I say coolly. "Do you want it back?"

I really don't want to let go of it, but I want to prod at him, something driving me to push this alpha and see what happens. My hands grip the bottom and I pull it up, revealing my bare skin. Luc makes a strangled noise, his large hands suddenly gripping mine, and I inhale sharply through the fabric.

He eases the shirt back down, and I blink at him as his face comes into view. His green eyes glitter at me.

"As much as I would have liked to see that play out," he grits. "I like you wearing my shirt."

My throat closes, and a little flutter tingles in my midriff. "You do?" I ask unsteadily around the lump in my throat.

The heat from his hands sinks into mine. He hasn't let go yet. "I do."

We watch each other.

"Fuck, you're overbearing," I breathe.

He grins at me. "Brat."

I shouldn't shiver at the nickname – *I hate that fucking nickname* – but I do.

My afternoon with Bastien comes back to me, and I wonder how it would feel to have Luc running his hands over me. His large palms squeezing my breasts, sliding beneath my shorts to cup me. My belly clenches, and I sway into him as he inhales sharply.

"Your scent, Ava," he mutters harshly.

"I…," my nose meets his chest, and I can't help but breathe him in. "I feel…"

My words come out a little garbled. Luc's hand sneaks past me and up to my hair. Gathering it in his fist, he gently tugs me back until I'm staring at his face, the light pull on my hair going straight to my cunt. I whimper, and he curses.

"Ava," he says darkly. "You're not ready for the kinds of games I like to play, sweetheart."

"Don't tell me what I can do," I choke out, and he laughs.

"Do you want to try?" he asks me. Dipping his face to my exposed neck, he nips me with his teeth. Stars scatter in my vision as my thighs clench, and he has to hold me to him or let me drop to the floor.

"Jesus fucking Christ," he grits out as his hand slips downwards. "Are you wet for me, Ava?"

His words force through the haze in my vision, and I stare up at him, my eyes wide. When I nod, he curses again and sweeps me up into his arms, stalking into my room and kicking the newly repaired door shut behind him.

He moves over to the bed and I cringe, instinctively flinching away. "Luc…"

Luc puts me down, sliding me against his body and making me twitch. His hand moves back into my hair, and I bite my lip. I don't want him to know how much I love it. I get the feeling he'll never let me forget it.

"If we're doing this," he says, his words quiet but forceful, "then I want you in a bed, brat. So you need to decide what's more pressing to you right now." He thrusts his hardness against me as he says it, and I grind against him with a whimper.

"What's it going to be?" he whispers in my ear. "Can I play with your pretty pussy, or are you going to let some ridiculous law stop you from coming all over my fingers?"

His hand slides down the back of my shorts and he cups me from behind. My vision short circuits at the feel of his fingers tracing my slit.

"Fuck, you're so hot," he groans. "Damned stubborn omega."

He rubs lightly, and I whimper, trying to push myself down on him.

"No," he tells me sternly. "Don't let them win, brat." He

rubs harder and I pant as I look at the bed. Closing my eyes, I focus on the feel of him.

"Okay," I whisper, and he pauses.

"Good girl," he purrs. I'm about to snap at him for stopping when he lifts me and deposits me gently onto the bed.

I sink into the softness and my breathing speeds up, panic freezing me. I stare at Luc pleadingly as he follows me down, lying next to me and tugging me to face him.

"Oh, baby," he sighs when he sees my face. "Come here."

He lifts me until I'm lying on top of him, my knees resting on either side of his stomach. Closing my eyes, I bury my face in his chest, inhaling his scent in as deeply as possible and trying to push the terror away. Luc slides his hands under my shirt, stroking his hands up and down my back as my skin tingles under his touch.

"Sorry," I bite my lip. "I ruined the moment."

Luc's hand pauses on my back. He places a finger under my chin and tugs it up to face him, gripping it firmly when I try to move away.

"You didn't ruin anything, brat," he says firmly. "You faced your fears, and you're on the bed. I'd say you're doing pretty damned well, all things considered."

I wriggle, and he groans as I brush against his dick. "I'm not quite on the bed."

Luc's lips curve up. "We're going to be rolling around every inch of this bed tonight, if you don't behave yourself."

His words make me shiver, but there's no way in hell I'm letting him know that. I sniff. "You sound awfully sure of yourself, alpha."

His hand slides around to my breast, kneading the flesh until I groan. "Tell me I'm wrong, brat," he goads. His fingers twist my nipple and I cry out.

"You're wrong," I gasp as I push my breast towards him, wordlessly begging for more. His chuckle is fucking filthy.

He pulls his hand out from under my shirt and a whine slips out. He raises an eyebrow at me as I clamp my mouth shut in mortification.

Stupid omega hormones.

Although I'm not sure I can blame them entirely. My reaction to these alphas is on another level.

He runs his hands up his – *my* – shirt. "Take this off," he rumbles, his green eyes piercing mine.

My hand clenches in it. *Mine.*

"Brat," he warns me. "Take the shirt off and show me those pretty nipples I've been dreaming about. I'll bring you more shirts if you do as you're told."

I'm tempted to continue our banter and hiss at him, but I'm not stupid enough to turn down the idea of more shirts.

Shuffling back, I try not to feel self-conscious about my breasts and stomach as I lift up the shirt. When I tug it off, letting my breasts fall out, Luc's eyes darken. I try to pull my hands up, instinctively covering myself, and he grips my wrists gently.

"You don't ever have to hide yourself from me," he rasps. "You're fucking beautiful, Ava."

Leaning forward, I gasp as he sucks a cherry-coloured nub into his mouth and draws hard. The sting goes directly to my pussy, and I push myself against his length. "*Luc.*"

He growls around my nipple, letting it slide from his mouth with a wet pop and moving across to the other. My thighs clamp around his hips, and he pushes up into me, making my legs shake.

My thoughts are splintered and fuzzy, and I stare at him hazily as my hands settle on either side of his head. He continues thrusting into me gently, pushing himself into my shorts until my dampness spreads, soaking us both.

CHAPTER FORTY

He slides a single finger through the dampness, and I shake for him. "Off," he demands roughly. "Take these off for me, baby."

I lift myself, and he tugs my shorts and panties down my legs, pulling them off and throwing them. I swallow hard as his eyes fall to my pussy. When I try to close my legs, his hands clamp down on my thighs and he shakes his head.

"What did I say?" he growls. Steeling myself, I slide my hands down and spread myself open for him. His gaze feels like a fucking brand.

"You are…fuck, brat, I don't even have the words." His voice shakes a little. "Get up here and let me taste you."

His hands pull on my thighs, and my eyes widen as I realize what he means.

"Luc," I hiss. "We can't—,"

"We can and we fucking will. I'm not going one more minute without tasting that pretty slit. Now *come here.*"

He easily lifts me up and positions me directly over his face. My eyes roll back as his tongue dives in, probing and licking and fucking devouring me.

"Oh, fuck," I hiss. My hands jump to the bars on the headboard and I hold on for dear life as Lucien sucks my clit into his mouth. My vision goes white.

He sucks hard before he growls straight into my cunt, sending a vibration directly through my clit. I throw my head back with a scream as my slick gushes out of me, and Luc shifts, delving his tongue into my opening and thrusting it in and out.

My hands shake on the bars as he fucks me with his tongue.

"Luc, please." My words come out on a sob, and he pulls himself away.

"Fucking delicious," He grins at me defiantly, his eyes

glittering and his chin wet, and just the look on his face makes my pussy clench.

"I'm going to roll us over now," he says gruffly. "Are you okay with that, baby?"

Wordlessly, I nod, and he pulls me down, cradling me to him as he rolls us over in the bed until I'm underneath him. His bare chest presses into mine, the hairs scraping my sensitive breasts as Luc curves himself over my stomach, and I shift restlessly.

"Luc," I beg. "I need—I want – "

He strokes my damp hair back behind my ear. "Show me what you want, Ava," he challenges. "If you want it, take it."

My eyes close as my hands wander down his body, and he slaps my breast lightly, making me cry out.

"No," he says darkly. "Keep those beautiful eyes on me, brat. I want you to remember who's making you come. You hear me?"

He slaps my breast again and I writhe against his touch. I didn't know sex could feel like this. It's raw, and messy, and so fucking far from anything I've experienced previously.

My eyes meet his, and he stares down at me, a question mark behind his green eyes. Leaning upwards, I catch his lips with mine. It's clumsy as hell, but his lips curve in a smile as he gently captures my lower lip with his teeth.

My hands move down as we explore each other until they reach the waistband of his boxers. My fingers trail over the bulge, and it jumps underneath my touch. Luc groans.

"That's all for you, baby," he says hoarsely. "You do whatever you want to do."

I stare into his eyes, trying to seize the courage. Luc watches me carefully. Leaning down, he presses gentle kisses against my face and my neck. "We can stop," he whispers. "Anytime you want."

My hands move underneath his waistband as I tremble

Chapter Forty

from the feel of his mouth on my neck. Luc groans into my heated skin as I feel him for the first time. He's hot in my hand, his cock thick and long as he thrusts gently into my palm. My fingers close around him and as I imagine him thrusting his length inside me, I moan into Luc's mouth.

"I know what I want," I breathe.

Gently, I pull him down, lifting my thighs and pulling them wide in invitation. His swollen cock brushes my entrance, and we both curse as I rub his cock against me, coating him in my slick.

"Ava," he says, his voice strained. "We don't have to—,"

"You told me to take what I want," I pant. His swollen head nudges my entrance, and my empty channel clenches for him. "I want to feel your knot inside my pussy, Luc. *Please*."

"Fuck," he swears. "I should've known your dirty mouth would come out in bed."

I whine as he brushes against me again. "Now, Luc," I demand. His hand rises up, squeezing my breast as he pushes inside me with one thick stroke.

My back arches, a cry ripping from my mouth as Luc surges inside of me, his cock filling me inch by inch until he feels like he's nudging my womb.

He stops, dropping his forehead down to mine gently. "Tell me you're okay, brat," he grits out, his teeth clenched. "Because the feel of you is about to send me fucking crazy."

I groan as my hips shift and he slides in another inch, his knot resting against the edge of my entrance. "Fucking yes. Now *move*."

Leaning forward, he bites my lip, making me yelp. "Demanding, bratty omega. I want you to scream for me."

He pulls back, making me whimper as his cock slides out of me. I gasp when his strong arms come under my knees and he lifts me until my feet are dangling in the air. He grins down at me, a dark, savage god.

"Now, I'm going to fuck you," he promises, a primal threat in his tone. "Watch me, Ava."

I follow his eyes down to where his cock sits at my entrance, his arms holding me in the air like a trophy. He pushes into me in one long thrust, and I throw my head back with a breathless moan, my arms curling against his thighs as I grip him.

"That's it," he encourages. "Hold onto me, love."

Then he starts to *move*.

The bed rocks beneath us as Luc plunges into my pussy over and over again. He doesn't enter, he fucking takes, the muscles in his back rippling with the force of each thrust.

I can't breathe. I can't think. All I can do is hold on and feel every inch of him as he brands me from the inside out.

My breathing is choppy and uneven, gasping for air as he moves inside me. Dropping my thighs, he leans forward, his cock creating friction against my pussy with each thrust. His face drops to my neck as he licks and bites, tiny, stinging nips that keep me firmly centred on him.

My release comes upon me in waves, making me cry out against Luc's demanding mouth. He captures my cries, his mouth swallowing them down as his thrusts slow and deepen. I can feel my body shifting, his knot pushing against my entrance, demanding entry.

"Lucien," I sob. Lifting my hips, I chase the promise he's keeping out of my reach. "Give it to me!"

"Demanding omega." With a final suck to my neck, he pulls back, letting me watch as his swollen knot pushes against me before sliding inside my opening. My body goes taut as I scream out my orgasm, Luc's bellow following me as his seed fills me up, his knot sealing us together.

He gently rocks against me, our breathing ragged in the

rawness of the moment as we watch each other's face. Gently, he pulls my thighs around him and rolls onto his back, keeping his knot locked deep inside me. Shivers of aftershock roll through me as I press my cheek against his chest, listening to his breathing settle. His hands stroke over my back, both of us quiet.

That was... indescribable.

His knot slowly loosens as the minutes tick by, and my hips shift, chasing the feel of him again. Luc tips my face up to look at him.

"Ava," he says, slowly.

"Brat," I correct as my face flushes. He grins a little, but concern crinkles his eyes.

"Don't," I whisper, staring at him. "I'm fine, Luc. More than fine."

His eyes soften, and he rises from the bed, holding me against him as he pads into the bathroom. I lock my arms around his neck, resting my head against him as he runs water into the bath.

"I just had a bath," I grumble. "Now you're going to wash it all off." He pinches my ass cheek playfully in response, and I squeal.

"Now," he says in a low voice. "I'm going to take care of you, and you're going to let me."

Oh. Heat rises to my face at how much I like his words.

Luc carefully places me in the bath, cleaning me from head to toe. Grumbling, he avoids my efforts to drag him in as he cleans between my legs.

"Don't move," he says sternly as he heads back into the bedroom, leaving me to relax with my head tilted back against the edge of the tub.

My hands gently rub my stomach and I try to avoid thinking about my future children overhearing their mother having sex. Luc walks back in as I'm having a small breakdown, and his brow creases as he kneels next to the tub.

"Tell me," he demands, worry in his voice. "Was I too rough? If I was—,"

The guilt shifts to embarrassment and I turn my face away, hiding it.

"Brat."

I huff. "What if the babies heard us having *s-e-x*?"

I spell it out, flicking my eyes down to my stomach. Luc follows my gaze and coughs as his cheeks redden. He glances away from me, his body trembling.

I pull myself up in the water, indignation thrumming through me. "You're *laughing* at me!"

His shoulders shake. "I'm not," he gasps out.

"You are. It's a genuine question! They could be scarred for life, Luc!"

Luc is properly laughing now. A deep, booming sound echoes around the bathroom, making me smile despite my annoyance.

"Oh, brat," he lifts me out of the bath and wraps a towel around me as I pout. "Life will never be dull with you around."

He walks me back into the bedroom that smells like us, placing me down into clean sheets and climbing in next to me. Turning my face to him, I bury it into his chest, and he chuckles as he pulls the blanket over us. His hand covers my hip possessively, and I debate whether or not to point it out.

His hand tightens, and he pulls me closer to him, hitching my leg over his hip and dropping his hand to my stomach.

Well. I swallow. *Okay, then*.

"Luc?" I ask quietly. The curtain above our heads is open, starlight filtering in through the panes of glass. His hand strokes my belly, and a lump comes to my throat.

"What, baby?"

I grimace as I try to get my thoughts in order. Luc, picking up on my uncertainty, twists until he's looking into my face. "Tell me."

Avoiding his eyes, I mumble, "Am I... yours, now?"

His growl makes me jump, and his hand soothes over my skin in apology.

"Damned straight you're mine," he grumbles. "Unless... you don't want that?"

There's a strange note in his voice, and I shake my head. "No, I do!"

"Well, thank fuck for that," he mutters. "Because I wasn't letting you go anyway, brat."

I tug his chest hair lightly with my fingers, and he snaps at them with his teeth. After a few minutes of me fidgeting restlessly, he sighs and rolls me onto my back, leaning over me.

"Talk to me," he demands. I frown at him, and he eases back. "Please," he offers begrudgingly.

"I..." I blurt it out. "What about the others?"

I can't see Luc's face properly in the shadows. "What about them?"

Oh, gods. Just say it, Ava.

"I had a – a thing, with Bastien today." I squeeze my eyes shut.

"I know," he responds wryly.

My eyes fly open. "You do? How?"

"Your scent was all over my office, love." He chuckles at my groan. Fucking omega pheromones and scents. Why can't a girl just come in peace without the whole damn world knowing?

"And you're okay with that?" I venture cautiously.

"I am." Now his voice sounds just as cautious as mine. Getting frustrated, I sit up with a huff.

"I don't know how this works," I complain to him. His hands draw patterns on my back, and I slap at them. "Stop that! I'm trying to explain a real worry!"

The hands stop. "Sorry, love." Luc sounds genuinely contrite as he sits up. "What exactly is worrying you?"

I nibble at my thumbnail. "So that's okay? If I was with him, and then with you?"

Luc's face softens in understanding as he finally understands my dilemma. "Ava...yes, love. You can be with whoever you want to be," he says gently. My frown only deepens.

"And you can be with whoever you want to be too?" I ask hesitatingly. He flinches.

"No." His voice is absolute, and I try to hide the way my whole body shrivels in relief. "I only want you," he promises in a low voice. "Only you, Ava."

My eyes drop to his hand resting on my belly. "Them, too," he adds softly. My eyes fill up, and I try to turn away from him, but he doesn't let me. He kisses the tears from my face, his soft, quiet, careful words wrapping promises around my heart until I eventually drift off in his arms.

Chapter Forty-One
Max

My fist taps against Ava's door before I lean down to pick up the tray that's been left outside. I frown at the discarded food. She's not eating properly, and it's getting to the point where I'm going to have to say something.

As a knot forms in my stomach, the door swings open and I lock eyes with a shirtless Lucien, who at least has the decency to look a little sheepish. The scents spilling out of the room explain *very* clearly what happened. He edges outside, closing the door softly behind him.

"She's sleeping," he explains quietly. Nodding, I follow his lead and take a seat on the couch. Their entwined scent hits me like a freight train, vanilla and sandalwood tangled together.

"How is she?" I ask directly. Luc winces, and when my hackles rise, he waves his hand at me. The tips of his ears have gone pink.

"Don't panic. She's...good," he says, blowing out a breath. "Really good."

He turns to me. "I wanted to talk to you, actually."

Ignoring the creeping envy sitting like a ball in my chest, I listen as he runs me through his conversation with Nik.

"You want to give her a bitemark?"

I didn't expect Nikolai to come up with the idea. But the more I think on it, the more a bitemark feels like a natural step for us, if Ava wants it. She calls to all of us in a way I didn't expect when I brought her here. To have our full pack, together, all of us connected through an unbreakable bond... it's a beautiful image.

"I want that," I admit. "As long as Ava wants it too."

Luc grins at me. It's a carefree smile, one I haven't seen for a long time, and my answering grin feels a lot more natural.

Oh, Ava. Fixing us all, one broken alpha at a time.

There's a noise from inside Ava's room, and Luc and I turn to the door. When she doesn't appear, I turn back to him.

"I came to talk to Ava. I want to tell her about what Devlin said."

Luc's face twists. "Are you sure?" he asks.

Nodding, I stand up. I spent hours thinking about this last night. "If Ava really does know their omega, we don't have any right to keep this from her."

At that moment, the door edges open, and Luc springs up beside me as Ava pokes her head out. Her caramel curls fall riotously around her face, her hazel eyes soft and sleepy as she catches Luc's eye and blushes. When her eyes move across to mine, the red flush spreads down her neck and arms, disappearing into her white shirt.

She shifts from side to side. "Morning, Max," she whispers, darting her eyes back up to me.

My chest aches. I don't want Ava to feel any sort of hesitancy around me. I stroll up to her, cupping her cheek and kissing the other one. She inhales sharply, but she doesn't pull back. "Morning, sweetheart. Will you come and talk to us in the kitchen?"

I pull back, noting the glint in her eyes as she watches me, before a small smile curves her lips. Luc holds out his arm dramatically, making her laugh as she accepts the gesture and he escorts her into the kitchen, forcing her to sit at the table while he makes coffee. As I take my own seat, I note the way her eyes follow him, the scent of vanilla rising from her skin until Luc turns to stare at her, brows raised pointedly and making her huff.

"Brat," he teases. She waves a hand at him grumpily and sniffs. "Alpha... something. I don't know. I'm still half asleep and I can't be bothered to come up with insults."

I stifle a laugh, and Ava turns to look at me, her cheeks tinging pink as Luc sets some fruit in front of her. "Eat," he demands.

"Bossy alpha," she mutters, but she does as he says and starts picking at the strawberries he's set out. I try not to stare at her, but she catches me anyway. Leaning forward, I swipe a piece of strawberry from her lips with my finger, sucking it into my mouth.

"You taste delicious, love," I grin at her, delighted when her scent jumps and her eyes dilate.

That's right. I'm not holding back anymore, baby.

If she wants me, I'm all in. She stares at me wordlessly before biting her plump lip, taking a large sip of her coffee. Noting her happy look, I make a mental note to get her some decaf. I don't think she'd thank me for cutting off her apparent caffeine addiction.

Clearing my throat, I draw Ava's attention as she finishes her breakfast. "I wanted to talk to you about something," I hedge.

Her eyes flit to Luc, a hint of nervousness entering them as she puts her cup down. "Go for it, Doc."

Pushing out a breath, I explain the message Devlin left behind for her.

She frowns at me, her brow wrinkled as she looks between me and Luc. "I don't know any other omegas."

Luc and I exchange concerned frowns. "They said her name was Harper," I offer.

Ava pales, the warm tones of her skin leeching to gray. "Harper?" she whispers.

She sways in her seat dangerously, and I get to her first, catching her as she falls. Sweeping her up, I pull her into my lap, Luc cursing behind me.

"What the fuck, Max?" he hisses, and for once I agree with him.

Ava's eyes flutter, and I check her pulse as Luc fusses around her. Her hazel eyes fly open and she tries to sit up. I steady her with a hand on her shoulder.

"Steady, love," I say grimly. "You fainted on us."

She grabs hold of my wrist, her small hand curling into me. "Max," she pleads. "I need to speak to her. I need to talk to Harper. Now, *please*." Her breathing speeds up.

"Okay," I say gently. "Okay, love. We'll call them now. But I need you to relax for me. Take deep breaths."

Ava nods, taking a glass of water from Luc as I pull my phone from my pocket and dial the number for the Winter pack.

A male voice answers. "Max?"

Pushing out a breath, I watch Ava's face as she grips Luc's hand like a lifeline.

"Ava would like to talk to Harper," I say. "Is she there?"

"Shit—,"

There's a flurry of motion on the other line, and I hit the speaker button as Ava stares at the screen, her lips trembling. She looks… devastated.

"Ava? *Ava?*"

Chapter Forty-One

A warm, husky voice calls frantically down the phone, and Ava claps her hands to her mouth with a wail as she starts to sob brokenly. Luc gathers her into his lap, soothing her quietly as the Winter omega calls her name frantically down the phone.

"*H-Harper*," Ava croaks. The line goes silent, and a muffled sob comes through.

"Oh, Ava, honey" Harper whispers. "I thought—"

"I thought you were dead," Ava interrupts. "I thought you were dead, Harper!"

"I'm not dead, honey," Harper whispers down the phone. "I'm good. I'm well, and I'm so damned happy—," her voice breaks off, and I hear soothing male murmurs on the other line. Ava stares at the screen, tears trailing down her face as Luc rocks her gently.

"I thought she was dead," she whispers vacantly, and I exchange a glance with Luc.

There's a sniffle on the line, and Harper comes through again. "Where are you?" she says urgently. "God, Ava, I have so much – *so much* – to tell you. Are you... are you safe? Are they taking care of you?"

Ava whimpers, and the sounds tugs at my heart as she drops her face into her hands. "Yes," she says. "They are. They *really* are. But Harper, I...I have a lot to tell you too."

"Okay," Harper says unsteadily. "Okay. I'm coming to you. No, *Devlin*—,"

A muttered argument breaks out on the other end of the line as I frown at Luc in question. He shrugs.

"They've been here before," he reminds me.

Eventually, Devlin persuades Harper to put their call on speaker, and we arrange for their pack to come to us tomorrow, despite Harper's arguments to come immediately. Ava stares at the screen sightlessly, her tears dripping off her chin as she hugs her legs as best she can around her bump.

"Ava? I'll see you tomorrow, honey." Harper's voice wavers. "I can't believe you're *there*."

Ava clears her throat. "I know," she murmurs quietly. "I can't... I'll see you tomorrow?"

"Promise." There's a final, choked sob before the line goes dead. We sit quietly as Ava processes the last few minutes.

"Ava?" I ask gently. "Why did you think Harper was dead?"

I feel Luc's sharp look, but I keep my eyes on Ava. She curls in on herself at my words. I can see the guilt coming off her. Clearly, Harper is very much alive.

In halting words, she tells us about their time at Omega Compound. The awful conditions, the lack of food, the fucking training, the assaults. The way she cried at night. My heart breaks a little more with every sentence.

"She was my only friend," Ava mumbles, her face pressed to Luc's chest. He stares at me, cold fury burning in his green eyes at her words.

"They took her away because of me," she continues, and we both look at her. "Because of you?" I ask. She nods, her face agonized as she recounts the lunch incident that led to Harper's removal from the OC.

"He told me she was dead," she whispers. "He came to my cell."

She starts to shake in Luc's arms. I bite back the anger in my chest. "Who, baby?" Luc asks her, menace underpinning his soft words.

"Jason. One of the guards," she starts to cry again. "He came to my cell, and he was so *angry*."

Luc strokes her hair back as she cries.

"It was my fault. My fault." She says it over and over again, and agony blazes in my chest as I read between the lines. Luc meets my eyes, a tortured look on his face as he reaches the same conclusion.

"He hurt you?" I ask her in a low voice. "Ava... did he rape you?"

She nods, and Luc groans, burying his face in her hair as she cries.

I try to push through the pain and anger in my chest. "He told you she was dead, and you thought it was your fault?"

She nods, her voice so small we have to strain to hear her. "He said... he said I owed it to him, because he couldn't have her anymore. They found me when he'd finished, and he was sacked. My father – *Stone* – picked me up and took me to the nests the next day. He said that since I wasn't any good as a pack omega anymore, he'd get more use breeding me for a male heir. He's obsessed with bloodlines. He wanted a boy."

She shudders as she looks down at her stomach bleakly, and my fury boils over. Luc meets my eyes grimly behind Ava.

He's a dead man.
They're both dead men.

Chapter Forty-Two
Nikolai

Nash chatters beside me as we pack a bag, but I'm lost in my own thoughts. Grabbing the duffel, I throw in a few towels and some sun lotion. Despite the change in season, it's still warm outside. Perfect weather for a day at the lake.

"Do you think Ava likes jam sandwiches, pa? Pa?"

I nod absently. "I'm sure she does, little man."

"And cockroaches sprinkled in sugar?"

"Yep."

Nash stops abruptly in the middle of my bedroom, and I nearly walk into him. "Nash," I exclaim. "What are you doing?"

He points at me accusingly. "You're not listening to me, papa!"

I sigh, wondering when my little boy suddenly started growing up. "I'm sorry, my mind was elsewhere."

"Where'd it go?" Nash asks curiously, giving a little squeal when I swing him up to ride on my shoulders. He kicks his legs happily as we walk down the stairs.

I tap his leg with my hand, the other clutching the picnic

basket Nash insisted on putting together. "I was thinking about your mama."

"Oh." Nash grows silent for a moment. "Why?"

I squeeze his leg gently. "Wondering if she would have liked cockroaches with sugar on them," I tease.

"Ewww!"

We fall into our own thoughts, Nash mumbling about various other disgusting concoctions as I duly make appropriate disgusted noises to make him laugh.

"Nash," I say suddenly. "How would you feel about Ava staying with us?"

My son stops kicking his legs. "Like... forever?" he asks.

Sensing the hesitancy in his voice, my heart sinks. "Maybe? How would you feel about that?"

Nash is silent.

"Would she be my mom?" he asks finally. My legs go numb at his hopeful words, and my hand shoots out to the wall. *Oh, Nash.*

"Emery was your momma, Nashy," I say, my heart hurting. "But Ava would become part of our pack."

"The Grey pack!" Nash makes a roaring sound and shakes his fist, and I have to laugh at his abrupt change in thought despite the ache in my chest. "Who taught you that?"

"Uncle Bastien," he says, abashed. "He says every pack should have their own pack roar."

I smother my smile. "Oh, absolutely."

Nash rests his head on top of mine. "Do you think Ava wants to come for a picnic?"

"I think so. She might be busy, though," I say it gently, not wanting to hurt his feelings. "But it's nice to ask, right?" I ignore the nerves drumming inside my chest as Nash excitedly agrees with me.

I mean, jam sandwiches with me and my six-year-old probably isn't the smoothest date ever.

Does it even count? I cringe a little.

"We can show Ava the lake, too," Nash mumbles into the top of my head. "She probably hasn't seen it yet."

"Probably not."

As we walk into the living area, Luc storms out of the kitchen, his face drawn into tight lines of anger.

"Uncle Luc!" Nash waves, and Luc raises his hand half-heartedly. My head swings between him and the kitchen, and I swing Nash down as he protests.

"Nash, we need some sticks to make a fire," I think quickly, and his nose wrinkles. "But it's so hot!"

"Yes, but the weather can change quickly out here, so just in case. You don't want Ava to get cold, right?"

My son gives me a disbelieving look but trudges obediently out of the door. As soon as he's out of sight, Luc lets loose a feral snarl.

"Fucking assholes," he seethes. His fist slams into the wall plaster, sending flakes of paint floating into the air. He pulls his arm back for another punch and I grab him.

"What is it?" I say urgently. "Is it Ava?"

He snarls at me, which I take as a yes, and my head swivels to the kitchen door. "Tell me," I urge Luc. The words drag from his throat, accompanied by growls and snarls until his rage seeps into my own pores.

Hasn't she fucking been through enough?

I stumble back, rubbing a hand over my face. "Jesus, Luc."

He turns his face to me. "I know."

I catch a hint of scent as he turns, and my stomach flips. "Did you two…"

He nods. "Last night." The words are guttural. "I

thought... she seemed fine." He paces around the room. "She seemed *happy*."

I stare towards our omega, wondering what's going through her mind. "And the Winter pack are coming tomorrow?"

Luc nods. "I just..." he swallows and looks away. "I fucking hate that she has to live in this world, Nik."

The words hit me in the solar plexus. I'd once said the same about Em. Luc looks up at me as his words register.

"Fuck, Nik," he shakes his head. "How did you *cope*?"

I swallow, taking a seat next to him. "It was hard," I admit. "When Em awakened..."

I'd never forget that day. The way her voice shook, and she'd retreated into herself. Her juniper berry scent bursting from her. Max and Leah's panic as we all sat around the table, desperately working out ways to keep Emery hidden from the eyes of the Omega Compound.

"You remember," I say roughly. "You were there, Luc."

He nods. "I remember. And I loved Em, Nik. She was like a sister to me. But this need inside me... it's crippling. I can't fucking cope with the idea of Ava being hurt. And she's already been hurt so many fucking times...," Luc's voice breaks and he swipes an arm over his eyes.

"I just want to keep her safe," he forces out, and I nod. "I know, Luc," I murmur quietly. "I feel the same way."

Uneasiness swirls as I say the words, and Luc stares out of the window towards the lake, his face bleak.

"She has to hide for the rest of her life," he whispers.

The realities of the omega creed are hitting home.

Luc schools his face as Nash bursts back through the door, clutching dozens of sticks. He drops them in my lap triumphantly. "Good job, little man." I smile at him sadly, taking in Emery's eyes staring back at me.

We're all legacies of the omega creed, in the end.

Nash looks between me and Luc, his mouth twisting down. "What's wrong?" he asks, his little eyes too observant for his own good.

Luc forces a smile. "Nothing, Nash. That's a good haul."

We get to our feet, and I look down at Nash, wondering how to explain that Ava won't be coming to the lake today, and forcing down the tiny seed of disappointment at not seeing her.

The kitchen door swings open behind me as Luc springs to his feet, and I turn to see Ava and Max emerging. Ava's face is pale and wan, but she manages to smile at Nash as he dashes to her side.

"Hi, buddy," she says quietly. "Where are you going?" Her keen eyes flicker to the basket and my face. Opening my mouth, I try to explain but Nash gets there first.

"We were coming to get you!" he declares proudly. "We made you a picnic, and we're going to the lake to swim!"

Heat prickles across my neck and Luc and Max turn to look at me. Ava's mouth twitches at the corner.

"Is that right?" she says to Nash. "I don't have a bathing costume, though."

Nash's face falls for a second before brightening. "You can just swim naked," he whispers loudly. "That's what my daddy does."

Despite the tension preceding their arrival, Lucien and Max snicker at my expense as my cheeks flame red. Ava coughs politely, but I catch a small smile behind her fist.

"Nash," I grit out. "I brought my trunks."

Ava's face twitches. "No skinny dipping today, then?" I cringe a little, shaking my head ruefully as I eye my angelic-looking child, who absolutely will be jumping in buck naked.

"Just Nash. Sorry," I apologize. "He's a child of the forest. Can't be tamed."

Chapter Forty-Two

Nash crows, letting loose another 'Grey pack roar' and beating his chest as I close my eyes in embarrassment. This is not going well.

A hint of vanilla reaches me, and I open my eyes to see Ava standing right in front of me, her eyes crinkled with amusement as she looks up at my face.

"I'd like to go to the lake with you," she says, her eyes on me. "Will you wait for me to change into something?" I swallow and nod as Nash cheers, a bit stunned as she heads back into her room. Lucien follows her, and Max slides a look at me before he snorts with laughter.

I swipe my hands over my face. "I swear I used to be smooth," I grumble. Max snickers at me.

"This will be good for her. She needs to relax a bit after today." His mouth tightens at the edges, a similar look to Luc's entering his eyes.

"I'll look after her," I promise. Max stares at me, his eyes sad. "I know."

Clapping me on the back, he pulls open the stained glass door and exits. I watch him out of the window as he walks down the path, hands in his pockets and shoulders slumped.

Nash dances around me with excitement as I lean against the wall. It only takes a few minutes for Ava to reappear, her small frame clothed in a t-shirt that falls almost to her knees and slightly strains against her growing belly. A possessive feeling clenches in my stomach as I eye her smooth bare legs underneath *my* t-shirt.

Lucien smirks at me, and I push the feelings back as he kisses her gently on the lips. "I'll see you later," he promises in a low voice, ruffling Nash's hair and nudging me as he walks past, following Max's path.

I look to Ava and Nash. "Shall we go?"

Nash shrieks with excitement as he grabs Ava's hand and tows her along, making her laugh as I scold him to slow down. I follow after them with the picnic basket, trying and failing to stop my gaze from wandering to her legs. She turns around and catches me, a faint blush coloring her cheeks before she turns back as I hastily snap my gaze up, silently cursing myself.

She doesn't need you making her uncomfortable, Nikolai. She's been through enough.

The thought sobers me, and I keep my eyes up for the rest of our walk.

Chapter Forty-Three
Ava

I watch from the shore as Nikolai and Nash splash in the lake. Well, Nash splashes. Nikolai is incredibly patient with him, coaxing him to use his arms properly and teaching him to swim. It's adorable to watch.

Lying back on the blanket with a sigh, I stare up at the cloudless blue sky and let my thoughts wander.

Harper is alive.

My breath leaves me in a whoosh at the memory of her voice on the phone, moisture building up behind my eyes. I'm going to see her tomorrow.

I really thought she was dead. And it was my fault.

Because of Jason.

I cringe as memories assault me.

His meaty hands curling around the bars on my cell at the compound. The small light flickering off the eyes of the omega who'd been placed in Harper's cell as she watched us with her hands over her ears, curled up in the corner as I screamed and begged.

The sound of his bark as he forced me to open my legs

for him. The burning acidic scent of lemons, scorching the back of my throat in its intensity.

The smell of his hand, stale and hot as it wrapped around my mouth, gripping my cheeks and bruising the skin. The crushing weight of his body as he lay on top of me afterwards, breathing wetly into my neck as I lay there, staring at the ceiling.

You love taking my knot, don't you? Filthy omega slut.

Tears slip from under my closed eyelids, running down the sides of my face as footsteps sound next to me.

"Ava?"

I open my eyes to a blurry Nikolai leaning over me. A whimper slides out of my mouth as I flinch back on instinct, and he freezes.

"Oh, little bird," he says softly. Stifling a sob, I rub my hands across my eyes and struggle to sit up.

"Sorry," my voice cracks. "I should probably go." I don't want Nash to see me like this.

Nikolai takes a seat next to me, leaving a respectful distance between us. "You don't have to," he offers, staring out at the water where Nash is splashing happily in the shallows. "Would it help to talk about it?"

I don't know. I shiver involuntarily, cold stealing over my bones. Nikolai reaches into the bag and pulls out a soft blue blanket. He gently wraps it around my shoulders, and I clutch the ends as I turn to meet his understanding gaze.

He watches me steadily, his deep blue eyes shadowed. "I know what it is to have trauma," he admits carefully. "My story is nowhere near yours, but it helps me to talk it through sometimes. Maybe it will help you too."

I drop my gaze to the floor, curling my fingers in the dirt. "I was thinking about my last night at the compound." Glancing back up at him, he nods patiently, not saying anything.

He doesn't push me for more, and we sit for a few minutes in peaceful quiet while I gather my scattered memories together.

Slowly, the words drag out of me as I talk about Jason and his attack. Tears slide down my face as Nik slips his hand into mine. His jaw clenches, but he just holds my hand gently, squeezing it whenever I stop.

"It sounds like...," he says cautiously when I stop talking. "When you talk about the compound, it doesn't seem like you hated it?"

There's a hint of confusion in his voice as I shake my head. He doesn't miss anything, this alpha.

"No," I say. "I mean, I did hate it. But Stone... he believed in the creed. He always thought I would be an omega, so he made me follow the laws from a pretty young age, even though I didn't awaken until I was older. I was just... used to it, I guess. They never needed to punish me much."

The perfect omega.

Niko's hand flexes in mine. "How young?" he asks, a hint of harshness in his tone. "When he made you follow the creed?"

I swallow. "Ten."

I barely remember my mother. I think she had similar hair to mine, and I remember her singing me songs in her quiet voice whenever Stone wasn't around. But when I turned ten, I wasn't allowed to see her anymore. I don't know what happened to her after that, but I have my suspicions.

I clear my throat. "This is helping," I acknowledge, tipping my hair forwards to hide from his eyes. "It feels... like I'm pushing off a dark cloud, I guess. It sounds stupid, I know."

His hand clenches around mine. "Nothing you say

sounds stupid," he says softly. "I'm here whenever you want to talk." Something twists in my chest.

I shuffle a little closer to him, and he turns his face toward me. The sun glints off his golden blonde hair, cut a little shorter than the others. Tentatively, I lay my head against his shoulder, his breath warming the top of my head as I breathe in his gingerbread scent.

"Is this okay?" I ask, and he lifts his arm, slowly wrapping it around me.

"I'm happy to be your personal pillow," he says, lips twitching, and I laugh a little as we both watch Nash. My heart twists as he turns to wave at us happily, and I lift my hand to wave back.

"He's a very special little boy," I whisper, and Nikolai nods, his cheek rubbing against my hair. "He is."

I desperately want to ask more about his mom, but I don't want to ruin the moment we're having. A yawn creeps up on me, and I force it back as Nikolai shifts.

"You're tired," he notes. "You should sleep."

"I don't want to go back to the house yet. I'm happy here."

My eyes start to flutter closed, and gentle arms slide underneath me, lifting me up. Grumbling, I clench my fingers in Nikolai's shirt until he settles me in his lap, my face against his chest.

"You can sleep comfortably this way," he says, his voice rough.

Sighing, I rub my face against his warm chest, breathing in the comforting gingerbread scent. I open my mouth to thank him, but drowsiness drags me under.

CHAPTER FORTY-FOUR
NIKOLAI

Ava sleeps peacefully in my arms, her face nuzzled into my chest.

Resting my chin gently on the top of her head, I breathe in her sweet vanilla scent, trying to ignore the way her breasts fall and rise, brushing against my arm with each inhale.

She's so *trusting*. Even after going through years of hell. My arms tighten a little and I force them to relax as she shifts, a plaintive noise falling from her lips.

Nash comes padding up, droplets running off him and his eyes widening as he spots Ava. I put my fingers to my mouth, urging him to be quiet.

"Is she okay?" he whispers loudly, and Ava stirs. I shift my head to look down at her, watching her dark lashes fluttering on her cheek as she opens her eyes slowly, rubbing her face into my scent.

My heart clenches as she inhales deeply.

"Nikolai," she murmurs sleepily. Her husky voice buries into my chest. I want to hear her say my name like that again. "Where's Nash?"

"I'm here!"

Her eyes fly open at his words, and she pushes herself to sit up. Reluctantly, I release her from my arms as she pulls herself up, glancing at me with a rose tinge on her cheeks.

"I'm sorry I fell asleep."

"Don't be. You can sleep on me anytime." My voice comes out a little deeper than I intended, and Ava's blush darkens. Nash grabs her hand.

"Do you like sandwiches?" he asks her, and she pulls her gaze from mine to smile at him. "I *love* sandwiches," she says, and Nash pulls her over to the picnic basket where he starts digging through the food.

"Careful," I warn her. "He'll eat them all."

"I will not!" he says, outraged. "I want Ava to have the best ones." Ava's eyes soften as he picks through the contents, passing her food once he's inspected it. I snort back a laugh. I have a feeling Nash will awaken as an alpha when he's older.

"Thank you, Nash," she says softly. Nash plops himself down next to her, leaning against her arm. "Do you know how to swim, Ava?"

She shakes her head, glancing toward me before swallowing down the tiniest bite of her sandwich. "No, I never learned."

"My pa will teach you!"

Ava and I share a glance. "I'd like that," she says, and my heart jumps again.

"We can start today?" I offer, and her eyes light up.

After lunch, we walk down to the edge of the water, Nash paddling in the shallow end while I take Ava out a little deeper.

"I'll need to touch you," I say suddenly with a frown, the thought only just occurring to me. "Will you be all right?"

She grins at me, her eyes sparkling. "I've just had the

best sleep ever on your lap, right? No use in being shy now," she points out. "Besides, I've always wanted to learn how to swim."

My neck prickles at her determined words, and her curls float around her shoulders as we get deeper into the water until I stop us.

"Okay," I say. "I'm going to teach you to float first."

I encourage her to lie back against me, her head on my shoulder as I slide my hands underneath her back and lift her. My hands feel huge against her, her skin warm against my palms in the cool water as her hazel eyes watch me closely.

"I've got you," I say firmly. "I won't let you fall."

Her lips turn up. "I trust you, Nikolai."

With wobbly movements, she extends her arms out. I coax her to keep her head up, gradually removing myself until just a few fingers rest underneath her back.

"I'm doing it!" she exclaims with delight. I grin at her, her excitement infectious. "You're a natural," I tease, and she laughs. Slowly, I remove my last few fingers and step back slightly, ready to catch her. She floats unaided, her arms out as she stares up at the sky. Nash cheers from the shallows, and I give him a wave.

"This feels amazing," she breathes, turning her hazel eyes to mine. "Thank you, Nik."

I smile at her. "No thanks needed."

She moves her arms a little as she tries to wave to Nash and loses her posture, dropping like a stone in the water. Quickly, I grab her and haul her up as she splutters with laughter. Breathing heavily, she winds her arms around my neck and I freeze, my hands warm on her bare legs as they wrap around my hips.

The thick length of my cock at full mast presses into her

soft heat, and I close my eyes in mortification. "Ava—" I choke out.

Shit. For God's sake, Nikolai, get a hold of yourself.

Soft, warm lips cover mine, and my eyes fly open. Ava pulls back to look at me, her cheeks flushed.

"Was that okay?" she asks, biting her lip. Worry glimmers in her hazel eyes.

Blowing out a breath, I prop her in one arm and push her wet hair back from her face. Slowly, I run my nose along her cheek, breathing in her scent as her breathing speeds up.

"That was more than okay."

Tilting up her chin, I lean in and brush my lips against hers, inhaling traces of salt and vanilla and *Ava*.

"Your taste," I ground out. Diving in, I catch her mouth with mine, taking sips of her as she moans breathlessly. I nip at her plump lower lip and she gasps, water droplets lingering in her eyelashes as her eyes turn languid.

"Open for me, little bird," I beg, and as her lips open my tongue sweeps in, exploring the softness of her mouth. Fuck, the noises she makes go straight to my cock, pulsing around my knot as it swells at my base. I break away from her, both of us breathing hard. Resting my forehead against hers, I growl.

"We're going to continue this," I promise. "Whenever you want. But we're going to be interrupted in around three seconds."

Her eyes widen just as a screech comes from the shore.

"Papa! Avaaaaaa!"

Ava buries her face in my neck with an embarrassed moan as I start wading into shore. "Oh my god," she moans.

"That's what I want to hear later."

Ava snorts out a laugh as her body tenses suddenly against mine. Her scent spikes, a wave of vanilla washing over me as I inhale deeply. "Fuck, little bird, I'm going to have to carry you home."

There's no way I can explain my very visible reaction without an awkward conversation about the birds, the bees and the omega, so carrying her it is.

"Come on," I call to Nash. "Grab the basket. Let's get back."

He dashes on ahead as I continue walking, Ava breathing raggedly into my neck.

"Nikolai," she whispers. There's an edge of a whine in her voice, and my heavy cock jerks underneath her. "Something feels off."

She groans, and I pull back to look at her face. Her skin is pale, a slight sheen of sweat dotting her brow. Ava buries her face into my neck again and I feel her body rock against me, her scent flaring.

Fuck. My eyes widen in realization, a memory nudging at me just as a gush of warmth coats the front of my swimming trunks, and she whines in distress.

"Shhhh," I soothe her, even as my own mind races and I speed up. "Your hormones are all over the place right now, little bird."

"They are?"

"Mhmm. So we're going to get you taken care of."

It's a hormone jump, caused by her pregnancy. Em went through the same thing a couple of times. Ava pulls her head back, her hazel eyes curious before a haze settles across them and she moans.

Shit. Move faster, Nikolai.

"Who do you need, little bird? Me? Luc?" I ask her. Her eyes slide shut on a whimper.

"All of you," she admits. "I want... all of you." She shifts against me again and I suck in a breath. "But if you don't want to—"

I cut her off. "Little bird, right now that's the only damn thing I want. Just wanted to make sure. We're going to get Nash taken care of, and then we'll take you somewhere quiet."

Running my tongue along her neck, I bite down gently and her back arches. "Where I can take care of you."

She whimpers, and another flood of warmth appears where our lower halves rock together as we walk. Closing my eyes for a second, I grunt and pick up the pace.

Fuck. This is going to be the longest walk ever.

Chapter Forty-Five
Ava

I cling to Nikolai as we walk through the front doors. The clenching in my lower half hasn't eased. If anything, it's worse.

What the fuck is wrong with me?

Spotting the stairs, I slur into Nikolai's shoulder. "Nest, Nikolai."

It's a plea, and he rubs my back as he walks. "I know, little bird, just give me a minute."

The whine curls from the back of my throat. I need it now. I need soft blankets and warm lights, and my pack.

Mine.

Nikolai pushes open a door and the minty freshness of sage twists around me. "Bastien," I mumble.

Hands appear at my back, gently rubbing down my spine as Bastien hisses at Nik. "What the hell?"

"It's her hormones, Bas," Nikolai grunts back. "I need you to get Nash to Leah and meet us in the nest with Max and Luc."

Bastien ducks his head to look into my face, and his eyes

widen. Another twist makes my core clench, and I bury myself into Nikolai's shoulder with a shudder.

Nik's large hand settles on my back. "Easy, omega," he soothes, a purr escaping him. The gravelly vibration drags straight down my back as his hands follow in large, soothing strokes, and I list bonelessly against him as he turns away, heading towards the stairs and up to my nest, shouldering open the door.

Nikolai sets me down on the downy blankets, and I crawl into the centre, breathing in the scent of apples as my core clenches. They smell like Max.

"Nikolai," I whisper, my voice trembling. "Is this a heat?" *How can that be possible if I'm pregnant?*

He climbs over the blankets to settle next to me, his arms open as I crawl into them. "No, little bird. Your hormones are going a little bit wild because of the pregnancy. You'll be all right soon."

I'll have to take him at his word because this aching, burning *need* inside me isn't going anywhere. Nikolai rolls me underneath him, his sapphire eyes growing hazy as he bends his head to suck at my bottom lip. The gentle tugs move straight through my body, my breasts heavy and aching.

My groan makes him move down my neck, licking and sucking and pulling sensation from everywhere. Wriggling, I pull at my damp t-shirt. "Off, Nikolai," I beg. His warm hands slide underneath and trace over my stomach as he helps me pull it off, throwing it to the other side of the room. His eyes darken as his gaze moves over my body, my nipples standing to attention at the heat of his gaze.

"Fuck, Ava," he rasps. "Fucking gorgeous."

He runs his hands over my body, caressing my aching breasts until I push up into his palm with a frustrated mewl. "More," I hiss. "I need more."

Chapter Forty-Five

His fingers rub back and forth over my nipples, tweaking and tugging on them as his hand runs down my body, petting me. I tilt my head back at the rush of sensation, my eyes closing.

A whisper of apple pie floats across us, and I turn my face to Max where he stands in the doorway, his arm over his head as he grips the frame in his hands. Desire is harsh on his handsome face.

"Max," I beckon him, whining when he doesn't step forward to take my outstretched hand.

"Ava," he forces out. "Sweetheart, your body's in control right now, not you."

My hands clench in the blankets as Nikolai leans in, flicking small licks across my belly and down towards my panties. Panting, I keep my eyes on my healer alpha. "I know what I want," I push, the words coming out as a whine. "I want you, Max."

His shoulders hunch as he stares at me. "I can't," he forces out, his face tortured. "Not like this, love. It's not fair to you."

He doesn't want me. He lied.

Someone has taken a knife to my chest. Pushing away from Nikolai, I sit up, wrapping my arms around myself, folding over. His rejection *hurts*.

"Please, Max," my voice breaks. "Stay with me?"

Nikolai sits up, aiming a furious growl at Max. "She needs you right now. Don't be an idiot, Max. If you're not going to stay and help her," he snaps, "then get out and stop upsetting her."

"*Please*," tears spill over my cheeks. The thought of him walking away from me now is agonizing. "I'll beg if I have to."

Max's face creases as his voice drops. "I don't want our

first time to be because your body's taken the choice from you."

"This isn't a heat, Max," Nik grunts. "She needs care and attention. The sex is secondary to that."

Outrage fills me as I turn to glare at him. "No, it's not!"

Max stumbles forward as Luc nudges past him in the doorway, choking on the cloying scent of vanilla as his face swings to mine.

"Brat," he breathes, dropping down next to me. "What trouble are you making now?"

I tug him down into a kiss, my hands moving into his hair. Luc kisses me like a starving man, his mouth devouring me until I break free from him with a moan. Bastien kneels next to me, his hands tentative until I grab his palm, drawing it directly to my heavy breast.

Having them here settles me slightly, but something is missing. *Someone*.

Apple pie, honey brown eyes and gentle hands.

"Max," I whisper. "Where's Max?"

Nikolai and Luc share a look, Luc shaking his head with a frustrated growl. "He's not thinking clearly, sweetheart. He'd be here if he was."

"He... left?" My breathing starts to speed up as my chest tightens and I cover my face with my hands. Nikolai pries them away, his large hand covering my cheek as panic creeps into the edge of my consciousness. "Shhh, little bird. You're alright."

"You don't have to do this," I force the words out, my body shaking at the thought of them walking away from me. *I need them. I need them to stay*. Max's absence feels like a weight in my chest. But I don't want to force them into being here.

"You're not forcing us into anything, little bird," Nik

reassures me. "We want to be here. And so does Max. He's only staying away because he's worried you'll regret it."

My tears flow faster, and Nik rubs them away, his face distressed.

"Ava," he murmurs. "If this wasn't happening, would you still want us?"

My body might be in the driving seat, but I'm aware enough to know my own mind. And I *would* choose them, this group of kind alphas who saved my life and didn't ask for anything in return.

"Yes," I breathe in realization. "Yes, I want you. All of you."

Nik's full lips twist up into a smile. Luc leans in to run his tongue down my neck, making me gasp. "And we intend to make it very, very clear to you how much we want you, brat."

Nikolai nudges me down onto my back, his hands tracing over my body as Luc and Bastien follow his lead. Touching, petting, stroking, until I'm a shaking, trembling mess for them.

"Need more," I whine, trying to tug Nik forward. Sinking my fingers beneath my shorts, I drag them down my hips, hands brushing mine out of the way and taking over as Nik leans over me. "Are you sure, little bird?"

His clothes are off, the delicious warmth of his length brushing my empty, aching core, soaking his tip.

"Yes!" I cry. I'm done with them asking for permission. Now, I just need them to take.

Nik lines himself up, his hand wrapping around his swollen length as he rubs himself up and down my slit. His heat teases me, and I groan. "Now, Nikolai!"

He doesn't pause, pushing himself into me as I hold my breath. Luc lifts my leg, moving it open as he watches Nikolai sinking into me, his green eyes dilated. Nik doesn't stop until he's bottomed out, his full, thick cock stretching my channel. He's wider than the others, his girth pushing at me and making my eyes widen as he settles within my body, his hand reaching up to stroke my face.

"Little bird," he rumbles. "You feel like heaven on my cock."

He lifts himself, dragging himself back and pushing back in as he settles into a rhythmic rocking, each slow thrust dragging against me. Our low groans and whimpers float in the air, Bastien and Luc staying back to give us space, their hands entangled with mine as they hold me still for Nik to rut into me, his eyes steady and reassuring on mine as I toss my head, lost to desire and the feel of him filling me.

His thrusts start to deepen, becoming more choppy as he curls his hands around my hips, pulling me into him as he leans back on his knees.

"Come for me, sweetheart," he rumbles. Nik's hand moves down, his fingers toying with my clit as I writhe on him, his thick knot nudging at my entrance.

"Knot," I whine, my muscles clenching around him. "Knot, Nikolai."

He shakes his head, his blond hair damp as he leans over me. "Come, and you can have my knot. Let me fill you up, love."

He tilts my hips against him, reaching just the right spot, and I scream out as I convulse against him. His knot pushes, demanding entry as I open up for him and it locks into place, Nik roaring as his seed jets out, filling me up as we lock together.

The aching inside me subsides, replaced by a warm glow of completeness. I clutch Luc and Bastien's hands tightly as I gasp for breath, Nik leaning down until our damp foreheads touch.

"Perfect," he swears. "You're perfect, little bird."

Chapter Forty-Five

As the haze clears a little, my head turns, seeking out my missing alpha. My chest flutters, a hollow sensation taking root. He's not here.

He really didn't want to stay.

My eyes grow hot as I squeeze them shut. I shouldn't be greedy. I have three fantastic men here.

So why does it feel like my chest is caving in?

Luc wipes away a solitary tear. "Sweetheart," he soothes, picking up immediately on my distress. "He wanted to be here. He just wants it to be your choice."

My lip trembles, but I nod as they gather around me, trying to push away the feelings of rejection.

I'm not sure I believe him.

Chapter Forty-Six
Ava

Clinging to Bastien's side, I try not to flinch as the SUV appears in the distance, making its way toward us down the gravel driveway. His arm wraps around me as he holds me to him securely.

"How are you doing, love?"

Taking a fortifying inhale of his sage scent, I keep my face where it is.

"I'm fine, Bastien," I mumble.

I'm not one hundred percent sure about that, though.

My eyes catch Luc's gaze as he gives me a reassuring smile. I try to smile back, but it slides off my face as I move on to Max. His eyes are firmly planted on the vehicle winding our way, arms crossed as he stands apart from us. Hurt flickers in my chest.

We haven't spoken since my baby-induced hormone meltdown.

His shoulders stiffen as he feels my eyes on him and looks across, his brown eyes staring into mine as he opens his mouth. Biting my lip, I turn my face away, not willing to take another rejection. I press myself into Bastien, wishing

Nikolai was here too, but we decided that it would be best if he kept Nash away from this meeting.

Pushing back the lingering pain at Max's distance, adrenaline kicks in, accompanied by a healthy dose of trepidation as the SUV rolls to a stop in front of us. Luc comes to stand next to me, his fingers entwining with mine as he grips my hand. His thumb rubs over my skin, and I straighten as the passenger door is thrown open.

A familiar, muscular olive-skinned alpha gets out first, and I take an instinctive step back as memories of our journey here rush over me.

Get a hold of yourself, Ava.

Swallowing, I force myself to stay where I am. Ace Winter flicks his eyes to mine and gives me an acknowledging nod before moving over to shake Max's hand.

"Max," he says, nodding. "Lucien. Hello, Ava."

His words are gentle, a small smile tugging at his lips that I return. "Hi," I whisper, leaning into Bastien again. Nobody else has gotten out of the car yet, and I tilt my head a little to look past Ace. Following my gaze, he laughs.

"They're having a bit of a moment," he confides, leaning forward a little. "Our pack leader is a little twitchy when it comes to Harper."

Confused, I look back at the car as an undoubtedly female shout of frustration reaches us.

"Let me out of this damned car, Rogue!"

"Harper?" I whisper, taking a step forward. Luc and Bastien move with me as I take a few hesitant steps forward.

The back doors fly open, and an unfamiliar, taller alpha emerges. His hawkish face is twisted in a frown, but it's more worried than unpleasant. Dark green eyes scan over us and he grimaces. "Sorry," he says, nodding his head at us in greeting. "I'm Rogue Winter."

My pack introduces themselves around me, but my

vision narrows down to the slim figure sliding out of the door on Rogue's other side. Two other alphas exit after her, their gazes scanning the clearing, but my eyes are glued to the omega they keep between them. Vibrant red hair dangles across her face, and as she pushes it away with an annoyed huff, amber eyes turn to me and freeze.

"Harper," I breathe. Her face crumples as she stares back at me.

Then she's running, and I'm running, tearing free of Bastien and Luc as we collide in a mess of tears and cries. Her arms wrap around me as much as she can, given the bump in the way.

"Ava," she says my name disbelievingly. "Ava, it's really you!" Her words crack. I'm already gone, crying hard as I pull her to me.

"He told me you were dead," I sob, breathing in her cinnamon scent. She shakes her head against me. "Not dead," she hiccups, and I cough out a watery laugh. "So I can see!"

Our alphas linger around us, keeping a respectful distance. Her hands brush my stomach and she jumps back, glancing down and looking back at me with her eyes wide.

"Are you—,"

My hands drop to cover my bump. "I think we have a lot to talk about," I say with a wince.

Harper nods, pulling her eyes from my midsection to glance around as she wipes at her eyes. Her alphas immediately move to her side as Bastien and Luc do the same, Luc retaking my hand in his and squeezing my fingers.

"Shall we go to the kitchen?" I ask, and Luc smiles at Harper in greeting before he turns to me with a nod.

We start walking up to the house as Harper's other alphas introduce themselves to me, keeping their distance. Devlin sounds familiar, and I think he may have been driving the ambulance that brought me here. Gabe is a handsome, smaller alpha, and I note the affectionate look between him and Ace as they walk together, their hands brushing.

Max walks on ahead of us, pulling open the stained-glass doors and gesturing us toward the kitchen. Everyone takes up a chair around the large table, Harper and I facing each other with Gabe and Luc next to us. Max keeps back as he leans against the doorframe. I can feel his gaze on the back of my head as Harper and I stare at each other across the dark wood.

She shakes her head ruefully. "I don't know where to begin," she admits. I let out a watery laugh. "Me neither. What *happened* to you, Harper? Where did you go?"

Gabe takes her hand as Harper starts explaining the events that took her away from the compound. She hesitates at some points, and I know she's skirting over details she doesn't want me or my pack to hear, but tears still drip down my face as she talks about her time with Jason.

My breathing speeds up as I stare down at the wooden table, the dark grains blurring as tears build up behind my eyes. Harper pauses as Luc pulls me into him, looking at my face.

"Rogue," she says quietly, not moving her piercing eyes from mine. "Everyone. Could we have a minute, please?"

Rogue stirs, a grumble slipping out. I can understand why he's not happy to leave her in a strange place. Leaning down, he whispers into her ear as he brushes her hair back. I glance at Luc and Bastien, ignoring Max. They give me a questioning glance, and I nod.

There are things we need to say that aren't for our alphas to hear.

"Do you want to go into the nest?" Bastien asks me, but I shake my head in refusal. The nest is just for us.

"Here is fine." My voice is soft. "We'll call you when

we're ready?"

Luc presses a kiss to my shoulder as he gets up, Bastien touching my arm as he follows. Max takes a step forward, his fist clenching before he spins and leaves, the Winter alphas following.

"We'll be just outside," Devlin says to Harper. He cups her face in his palm and she nods.

When the door closes, we both take a breath. There are a whole lot of different scents packed into the kitchen right now, and my knee jumps with agitation.

Harper leans over, taking my hand. "Talk to me," she pleads.

"Tell me what happened to you, Ava. *Please*."

My fingers trace the dark whorls decorating the table. "There's so much, Harper." Squeezing my eyes shut, I swallow hard. "It's not… it's not *good*."

My friend watches me, her amber eyes dimming with a level of understanding even the pack can't reach. "I know."

My words come in stilted sentences, my eyes fixed to the table, as I tell her about Jason.

"He just… took what he wanted," my mouth is dry, my voice shaking as I close my eyes. "And he made *me* want it."

There it is. The words I can't admit to my pack. Shame hits me like a wave, rolling down my back and covering me like oil as I sink my face into my hands, unable to face Harper. Her chair creaks, and I hear footsteps padding around the table before she slips into a seat next to me, her hand nudging my shoulder.

"Ava, we're *omegas*," she whispers. "We don't have any control over what our body does when an alpha is in charge, honey. That doesn't mean you wanted it. It just means that he used biology to force you to respond to him. *That's not your fault*."

I know that. Theoretically, I understand how little control

I have thanks to my own biological make-up. But it doesn't stop the shame I feel when I think about it.

Harper stares across the kitchen, her eyes vacant.

"When he took me from the pack," she murmurs, "he injected me with those heat hormones, and I begged for it too, Ava. I *begged* them to knot me."

Her cheeks grow pale. "I would have done anything," she admits, her face ashen. "I was just lucky that the pack arrived before the worst happened."

I close my eyes. It's useless to wish to change the past. But fuck, do I wish that someone had arrived for me.

We sit in silence for a few minutes, catching our breath, before Harper speaks again.

"So, the baby…" she murmurs carefully. "It's his?"

"I think you mean *babies*," I correct her with a small smile, and her eyes widen as she sits up. "You're having twins?" she cries.

I nod. "But they're not his."

Shock pulls her shoulders back as she stares at me. "What?"

Grimacing, I brace myself for the rest of the story.

"I wish that Jason had been the last of it."

Harper pales. "Oh, god, Ava," she breathes, her tone anguished. Waving her off, I sigh.

"I don't remember a lot of it, thankfully," I admit. "But they called my father after Jason's attack. He arranged for me to be taken to the heat nests. He wanted a male heir and figured that would be the fastest way to get one."

Heat nests. If someone asked me to draw evil, that's the sketch I'd create. The absolute soulless, sterile environment. The screaming, the crying, the whining and moans. A hundred different scents, mixing together. And the sensation of waking up, over and over again, smelling different scents on yourself and feeling so fucking full of them that you lose sight of your own being. Even if I don't remember the alphas themselves, I remember the aftermath well enough.

I'll never forget it.

"They gave me too many hormone doses," I conclude. "I was admitted to the hospital, and Max was the doctor. The rest... well, that's where your pack came in."

A green tinge lines Harper's cheeks. "Jesus, Ava," she says in horror. "One dose of those drugs was the worst thing I've ever felt. And you had..."

"A lot, I guess." Even I'm not sure how many, although Max probably knows. I consider asking him but dismiss it. There are some things I just don't need to know right now.

"And now... here I am," I shrug, although I don't feel nearly as light as my tone suggests.

The sudden pull to call for one of my pack hits me hard, and my glance at the door doesn't go unnoticed by Harper.

"So..." she says, a lighter tone to her voice that I grasp onto with relief. "Tell me about your pack."

I blush. "I'm not sure they're completely my pack just yet."

Harper raises her eyebrow at me. "It sure looked that way to me."

My smile fades as I think of Max. I explain about the way he left me during my hormone fritz, and Harper throws her hands up.

"God save us from protective alphas," she grumbles. "He thinks he's doing the right thing, Ava. You need to show him that you're making the decision for *you*, and not because of your horny omega baby hormones. Are any of the others doing the same?"

"Er – no." *Is it hot in here, or is it me?* Harper grins at my bright red face.

"Okay," she whispers conspiratorially. "Here's what you need to do."

Chapter Forty-Seven
Luc

I wake up in the nest the next morning to Ava snuggled into my side, her leg tossed over my waist. The sweetness of vanilla hangs in the air, and I breathe her in, my hands stroking down her warm back.

Fuck, Lucien, you're a lucky bastard.

A sleepy mewl draws my attention down to a pair of hazel eyes. "Morning, brat," I murmur. Her eyes flutter closed and she buries her head against me with a grumble as I chuckle. "Not a morning person?"

She shakes her head, her hand blindly reaching out and pulling at a blanket. I tug it up and over us, making sure she's wrapped up, and her soft huffs sound in my ear as she drifts back off to sleep.

My phone beeps and I lazily flick my thumb over the screen to read the text that's come through.

We need to talk.

The phone beeps again, and another message comes through.

It's about the OC.

Staring at the words, I reread them as unease stirs. Why does Rogue Winter want to talk about the OC?

Slipping my arm out from underneath Ava, she rolls over to Bastien, burrowing into him as he wraps his arm around her and pulls her close with his eyes still shut. Throwing on a shirt, I quietly make my way to the door.

Voices rumble from the kitchen, and I stick my head in to see Leah, Nikolai and Max chatting quietly around the table. Bags sit underneath Max's eyes, and I give him a look. I don't have much sympathy for his self-imposed pity party.

"I've had a message from Rogue Winter," I announce abruptly, dropping into a seat and pouring myself a coffee. Everybody pauses.

"What kind of message?" Nik asks. I slide the phone across the table, his brows dipping as he reads the message aloud.

Max frowns. "He didn't say anything else?"

When I shake my head, he leans back in his seat.

"I'm not sure that's a good idea. We have no idea what he wants, and I don't want to put Ava at risk—,"

"At risk of what?"

Our heads whip around to where Ava hugs the doorway, looking between us with a frown on her face. "What's going on, Max?"

Max looks to me for help, and I press my lips closed. He needs to sort his shit out, and part of that is not running from conversations with our omega.

Half rising from his chair, he gestures to a seat. "Why don't you sit down, love?"

"Why?" Ava asks wearily. "To have another conversation where you tell me what's best for me?" Fuck. She sounds... desolate.

"Ava," Max stares at her in shock. "You *know* it's not

like that." Ava shakes her head at him. "No," she says forcefully, "I *don't*, Max."

She takes a seat next to me, and Leah glances around before she gets up. "I'll give you some space," she says delicately, pausing to kiss Ava on the cheek and whispering something into her ear that makes Ava's shoulders sag as she nods.

Her body tenses as she turns to Max. "Tell me what's happening."

Max rests his arms on the table, his eyes not straying from Ava's face. "Rogue Winter messaged Luc this morning. He wants to talk about the Omega Compound."

Ava flinches. "Why?"

I shake my head as she looks at me for an explanation. "We don't know, love."

Hating the uncertainty on her face, I reach out and lift her into my arms, ignoring her huff of disapproval. Stroking my hands down her spine, I pet her until her muscles soften and she rests against me. Max watches us with clear longing in his eyes, but Ava doesn't meet his gaze as she looks around.

"It's something to do with me, isn't it? So we should call him back?" she asks plainly. Max recoils, and she turns to him with a glare. "I'm not a helpless child, Max," she snaps. "I don't have to hide away from every conversation."

"I don't think you're helpless," he pushes out. "God, Ava. I know you're not. I just think that we need to think this through. We need to be careful about this."

Everyone winces as Ava draws herself up. "Because I'm so *unreasonable*?" she hisses. "So incapable of making choices?"

"I never said you were incapable!" Max defends himself weakly.

"You didn't have to!" Ava shouts. She pulls herself away from me and stalks towards Max, pointing her finger at him.

"It's your actions, Max. You told me you wanted me to stay, and then you showed me that my opinion means nothing compared to yours." Her voice shakes.

Max looks like someone's taken a knife to his insides. "I don't think that," he says hoarsely. "Of course I don't."

She shakes her head. "There's no *of course* about it, Max. Not when you treat me like I have no idea how to make my own decisions. Just because I had my choices stolen from me does not mean that I'm incapable of making them now!"

"I don't want to push you into something you're not ready for," he whispers. "That's it, love. I told you that I wanted you to choose us, and I meant it—,"

"But I *did*, Max," Ava cries. "I did choose you. I begged you, and you walked away from me."

She swipes angrily at the tears on her cheeks. Max looks like someone's taken a cleaver to his insides, his face stricken.

"It wasn't like that," he croaks. Ava turns away from him.

"It was exactly like that, and it *hurt*," she says. "I've chosen, Max. I chose you, and you said no. Now it's your turn."

She climbs onto Nikolai's lap, and he wraps his arms around her as she tugs at her nails with her teeth. Max sinks back in his seat, his face white. Leaning in, I draw out Ava's abused finger, noting the shaking in her hand.

"Hey," I say quietly. "It's going to be okay."

She nods but stays silent as she leans her head on Nik's shoulder. He runs a hand down her arm and gently over her midsection. "They're growing," he notes. Ava looks down at his hands, lifting her hand to cover his as her expression softens. "They are."

The sudden clanging of footsteps clattering down the stairs in a hurry draws our attention to the door.

Bastien bursts into the kitchen, his face pale and eyes moving straight to Ava as we all stiffen.

"What?" I snap out.

Ava straightens in Nik's lap as Bastien moves to her, cupping her face in his hands.

"Remember what I said," he murmurs. "I will not let anything happen to you. Do you understand?"

She swallows. "Tell me?" she asks. A tremor shakes her arms, mirroring the heartbeat racing in my chest as I stare at my brother.

"The scanners," my brother spits out. "They've picked up… well. You're everywhere, love. You too, Max. Come and see."

Max swears. My pulse speeds up as I scoop Ava out of Nikolai's lap and into my arms. She looks back at me, her hazel eyes dark. Lifting her hand, she runs it through my hair. "I'm safe with you," she whispers, despite her pale face. My heart clenches.

"You are," I swear. "We'll keep you safe."

I guess we know why Rogue messaged me this morning now.

CHAPTER FORTY-EIGHT
MAX

We're all gathered in Bastien's office, watching the screens flashing up the same images over and over again.

A headshot of Ava peers at us, her hazel eyes staring blankly out through her curls in a standard-issue Omega Compound ID photo.

An artist's impression of me sits next to her, the drawing an exact replica of what I see looking in the mirror.

I swallow as Bastien leans over, turning up the sound.

"… kidnapped from the Austin Memorial Hospital two weeks ago. The omega is considered extremely dangerous, with substantial influence over alphas. She is reported to be pregnant and should not be approached by members of the public. The alpha pictured, we understand, is a doctor from the hospital and helped the omega escape. He was using the name Daniel Morgan, but this has been found to be a false identity. A $1 million dollar reward is offered for information leading to the capture of the missing omega."

The growl builds up, my lips curling back from my teeth and releasing into the silent room. Ava jerks back, her eyes wide on the screen. "I have to leave," she turns abruptly, sending the chair next to her spinning. "I have to get away from here. If they come—,"

"No!"

All four of us immediately protest. I'm closest to her, and mindful of our previous conversation, I draw her into my arms. She doesn't struggle as I wrap my arms around her, the tang of her scent acrid with fear. "I promised you." I run my hand through her hair, gently tugging the strands back until she looks up at me.

"I choose you. I choose this. You're not going anywhere because you think it's going to protect us, love."

She glances up at me with doubt on her face. My heart breaks knowing that I'm the one who put it there.

No more doubts. No more hiding.

"I will not lose you," I say firmly. "Do you understand?"

The pack echo my words, surrounding us both as we enclose Ava between us. Closing her eyes, she buries her face into my chest. "They twisted it," she whispers. "They twisted everything, Max."

"I know." My voice is grim.

"We need to make a plan." Luc's voice rumbles behind me, fury underlying his words. "I need to call Rogue Winter back and find out what he wanted."

Pulling out the phone, he hits the speaker as Bastien turns down the hateful words coming out of the monitors.

"Lucien," Rogue's voice is dark. "You've seen it?"

Luc growls. "We have. We're coming up with a plan now."

Rogue is silent for a moment. "What if we already have one?"

Everyone pauses. Ava straightens against me as our eyes fall on her, and she nods at Luc.

He grinds his teeth before he responds. "We're listening."

"Not like this. This would be better in person. Can we come to you? Today?"

Nik straightens, the worry on his face clear. "Give me a minute," Luc says into the phone.

"Call me back."

When the screen goes dark, Luc straightens, his fists clenching at his side. "What if this is a trap?"

Ava shakes her head. "It's not. Harper wouldn't do that."

Bastien hesitates. "How certain are you, love?" he asks quietly.

Staring down at the caramel curls, I swallow down a lump in my throat. "I agree with Ava."

Having seen the Winter pack with their own omega, I don't believe they'll do anything to put Ava at risk.

"Rogue's father is the Director of the Omega Compound," I point out when Luc looks incredulous. "He might have information that could help us."

Ava begins to tremble. "His father… is the Director?"

I run my hands up and down her arms, hoping to warm her chilled skin. "Do you know him, sweetheart?" She nods. "He was there the night that Jason attacked me."

Four matching growls ring through the room.

"Call him back," I tell Luc. "Set up the meeting. I want to hear what they have to say."

When I glance down at Ava, she nods, but her mind is clearly elsewhere. I lift her up, and she squeaks. "What are you doing?"

"I'm stealing you for an hour." Ava needs some distraction whilst we wait for the Winter pack to come. There are also things we need to resolve, and I can't wait anymore, her words from this morning burrowing into my head. Turning to Luc, I ask, "You'll let us know if anything changes?"

He nods, and I carry my omega out of the office and through the main doors. She leans into me with a sigh as I stride towards the house. "This feels familiar," she grumbles.

I can't help but smile down at her, remembering her first day. "As I recall, you wanted to walk," I tease. The corners of her mouth tilt. "A lot has changed since then."

I hold her a little closer, unable to help myself. "It has."

Carrying Ava into the house, I head straight for her nest, taking the stairs two at a time, and she turns her face to me in surprise. "Max—,"

Shaking my head, I cut her off. "Let me take care of you," I plead. "Let me block the world out, just for a little while. It'll still be there when we leave, love. I just…"

I just need to make up for being a stubborn asshole.

Chapter Forty-Nine
Ava

My heartbeat sings in my chest as Max toes his shoes off. He turns to face me, his hands cupping my cheeks.

"I'm sorry I left when you needed me," he says fervently. "I'm sorry I hurt you."

Moisture builds behind my eyes as he lays me down on the soft blankets.

His honey-brown eyes search mine. "I'll never give you a reason to doubt me again," he swears. "Forgive me, Ava. Please."

"I didn't doubt you, Max," I say hoarsely. "I just wanted you to want me as much as I want you."

He closes his eyes, regret standing out in stark lines on his face. "Never doubt that I want you. Never doubt that you are the *only* one that I want. Even before I knew your name, I knew that my heart would never beat for anyone else the way that it does for you."

Tears slide down my cheeks as he leans in, kissing them away.

"No more," he whispers. "You're ours, Ava. Lucien, Nik, Bastien. But right now, you're *mine*."

My whimper is unexpected, Max's eyes flaring as he scents my arousal in the air. He slides his hand underneath my top, encouraging me to sit up as he strips me, his hands never stopping their exploration of my body as I push myself towards him. I need him to be closer.

"You're wearing too many clothes," I mutter, displeased. I want to feel his skin against mine.

He gives me a heart-stoppingly boyish grin as he scoots back, shucking off his shirt and jeans. When I move to do the same, Max stops me, his hands gently pressing my wrists into the soft blankets below us.

"No," he growls. "I'm going to strip you naked, Ava. I'm going to savour every inch of your body, piece by piece, until you fall apart in my arms."

My body shivers, eyes dilating as he leans in, his breath warming my ear.

"And then," he whispers huskily. "I'm going to sit you on my knot and fill you up, until you understand exactly how much you mean to me. Do you understand?"

"Yes, Sir," I whisper, my lips twitching. Max raises an eyebrow at me.

"I like that," he admits, a hint of color on his cheeks. "Let's see if I can make you say it again."

Chapter Fifty
Lucien

A high-pitched buzzing sounds in my ears, my vision narrowing until all I can see are Ava and Max's faces on the screen. Ava's too-thin face stares at me mournfully, her perfect hazel eyes dull and faintly accusing.

Bastien clears his throat. "Brother—,"

"Why can't they *see* it?" The rage swimming in my stomach finds its way out through my mouth. Cursing, I throw my hands up. "Why can't they all see how fucked up this is, Bastien?"

Bastien runs his hands through his hair, his face desolate. "I don't know, Luc. I wish I knew. If they did, then maybe...,"

"What?" I scoff. "They all realize the error of their ways? Shit like that only happens in books, Bas. There's no happy ending here."

We're not going to get a happy ending.

Bastien and Nikolai stare at me, their faces pale. "Fuck!"

I slump into a chair and drop my face, pushing my palms

Chapter Fifty

into my eyes like I can erase the last thirty minutes from my fucking memory.

"I'm scared," I croak. "I'm so fucking scared that we're going to lose her."

A hint of gingerbread reaches me, and I lift up my face to meet Nikolai's solemn gaze as he kneels in front of me. His eyes are dark, assessing.

"Lucien," he says quietly. "This isn't the time to give up."

I flinch. "I'm not giving up," I snap. "But *fuck*, Nik – how can we win against that?" Pointing at the screen, Nik follows my gaze to the dozens of news reports scrolling across the screen, various iterations of the same headline taunting us.

Reward offered for missing omega
Considered dangerous - do not approach
Have you seen this omega?

"I'm not going to let you give up now. Not when we've come so far," he insists. I bark out a laugh. "I haven't done anything, Nik. And I can't do anything. I can't fix this."

"Will you shut up?" Bastien snaps, and both Nik and I startle. Bastien is normally the calmest of us, but now he stands in the middle of the room, his fists clenched.

"Get the fuck over yourself, Luc. Are you telling me you're not going to do everything you fucking can to keep her safe?"

"Of course I am! I just… worried that nothing we do can make a difference. How the fuck can the four of us protect Ava from the whole fucking world?"

Bastien throws something at me and I catch it by reflex, staring down at the phone in my hand.

"Call the Winter pack," says Bastien. He's not asking, his tone the closest to an alpha bark as I've ever heard from him, and I bite back my own growl in response. Now isn't the time to let our hormones get us into a pissing match.

Rogue answers on the second ring. "Luc."

"Let's meet. Can you still come today?"

He hesitates. "If we can make it tomorrow, I'll be able to bring something with me that might help."

"What?" I demand.

"I can't say now. But we'll see you tomorrow?"

We hash out the details before I hang up the phone and stare at the screen, half-baked ideas flickering through my head.

We can't fight this on our own. But the Winter pack have their own contacts. It hasn't escaped my attention that they escaped the consequences of going into a full-blown alpha rut at a government event with hardly a slap on the wrist. None of us could expect the same treatment.

But if we worked together... maybe there's a way that we can get Ava out of this safely. Without losing her to the bastards at the compound and her own fucking father.

Chapter Fifty-One
Ava

Warm lips press against my neck, soft kisses dropping down my chest, over my breasts, and down to my belly. My breath hitches, lips curving up in a smile as Max gently presses his mouth to my growing stomach.

"Hello," he murmurs.

Lifting my hand, I run my fingers through his russet hair. He glances up at me and smiles, his brown eyes soft on mine. "I'm sorry," he begins again, and I hold up my hand.

"It's done," I say softly. "I trust you, Max."

I trust you not to break my heart again.

He drops his forehead down to my stomach. "How are you feeling?" he asks. "Any tiredness?"

"If I am, it's because I've been thoroughly fucked by you."

His eyes widen, a flush rising on his cheeks at my brash words. "Luc was right. You have got a dirty mouth."

My grin stretches across my face. "You haven't seen anything yet," I warn him lightly, and he traces his fingers across my ribs, tickling my skin and making me yelp.

"I meant, how are you feeling about the pregnancy?" He refuses to budge as I breathe heavily.

We both look down at my rapidly expanding stomach, and I rub my hands across it gently. "I think I'm starting to feel... a little excited," I admit.

Max nods, his eyes still on my skin. "Me too. I... I always wanted to be a dad. And I've had a small part of that with Nash, but this... I want to experience all of this, with you."

My eyes burn, moisture building up and blurring Max's face. "I'd like that."

My stomach flutters and Max jumps as my bump ripples, a small lump appearing before it disappears again. I laugh at the amazement on his face.

"Look at that," he breathes. "You think they like my voice?" My heart flips at his crooked grin.

"How could they not?"

He leans down to kiss me, his smile curving against my lips. Pulling me into his arms, we lie quietly for a few minutes, not willing to interrupt the moment with the drama outside our door.

"We need to find out what's happening," he says reluctantly, tracing patterns on my arm. "Even though I want to keep you here, with me."

My throat closes. "I know," I whisper. "Just a few more minutes."

His arms tighten around me.

We finally emerge an hour later, and find Luc, Bastien, Nik, Nash and Leah squeezed onto chairs and couches in the living room, animatedly debating movie choices. Everyone stops as I step through the doorway. Luc's eyes drop to Max's hand wrapped around mine, and he smiles.

"Come here, baby." He opens his arms and I willingly climb into them as he presses a kiss to my hair. "They're coming tomorrow," he murmurs. "So just try to relax for today, okay?"

Nodding, I smile at Nash, and he pushes out his bottom lip from the sofa he's sharing with Nikolai. "Will you sit with me, Ava? Please?"

Laughing, I disentangle myself from a grumbling Luc, and Nikolai tugs me down between them both. Nash jumps up, grabbing a soft, green blanket from a basket and carefully draping it over us. His fussing makes my chest twist, and when he curls into my side, his head on my shoulder, I have to swallow back the lump in my throat. I lift up my arm in tentative invitation and he snuggles into me, his small hand reaching out and drawing circles on my stomach.

Nikolai and I trade glances over his head.

"When will they be here?" Nash asks. My stomach ripples again against his hand and he giggles.

I clear my throat. "Maybe another two months?" Max nods from the sofa, all of us watching Nash closely.

He nods, cupping his hands together and pressing his mouth into my stomach. "I'm going to be a good big brother," he whispers loudly.

Emotion clogs my throat as Nikolai's breath hitches next to me. Glancing around, Leah catches my eye, her brown eyes glistening with tears as she forces back a sniffle.

I stroke Nash's hair softly, Nik clasping my left hand and squeezing.

"You'll be an amazing big brother, Nash," I squeeze out, and he grins at me, before snuggling back under my arm.

My heart feels too big for my chest.

"Can we watch the turtles?" he says brightly, changing track in a way only a six-year-old can manage. Bastien gets up, ruffling his hair as he goes to the DVD collection. "I think we can manage that."

Instead of heading back to the sofa, Bastien plops

himself onto the floor in front of me, drawing my legs into his lap and pressing his thumb to the arch of my foot.

My back arches a little. "God, that feels amazing," I groan. Nikolai shifts in his seat as Luc grabs a cushion, pulling it over his lap and raising a sardonic eyebrow at me. "I think I'm in the wrong place," he grumbles.

"You snooze, you lose, brother," Bastien quips, and my shoulders shake at Luc's disgruntled expression. I blow him an apologetic kiss and he catches it as Leah retches dramatically.

"Eww. I can't cope with Luc being all sweet."

Luc gives her his middle finger. "You don't have anything to worry about on that score, Lee-Lee."

She throws a pillow at him and we all try to hide our laughs as Nash shushes us.

I close my eyes in bliss as Bastien works his magic on my feet, Nikolai's arm warm behind me as I breathe in his gingerbread scent.

This is something worth fighting for.

Chapter Fifty-Two
Ava

Picking at my nails, I stiffen at the sound of doors slamming in the distance. Max rubs my back soothingly.

"It's going to be okay," he promises.

I nod half-heartedly, staring at the wooden floor of the living room. It's bigger in here, so this is where we're meeting. Us, and the Winter pack. As much as I'm looking forward to seeing Harper again, I really don't want to have this particular conversation.

If only I could hit the pause button. Keep us all here, where nobody can find us. But the news reports are still running my face as a main story, and it doesn't look like it's going away any time soon.

Time to suck it up.

Max and I turn as the main doors open. Luc enters first and comes straight to me, his keen eyes running over my face.

He cups my face in mine, and I look up at him, my lip trembling. "It's going to be fine, baby," he murmurs. Max gives my hand a gentle squeeze. The rumbling of voices follows Luc, and Harper bursts into the room, her gaze swinging around until it lands on me.

"Ava!" she cries. My alphas take a step back as Harper wraps her arms around me, careful of the large bump in the way.

"You've grown," she hiccups into my shoulder, and I can't help but laugh. "You only saw me a few days ago!"

She shakes her head. "Doesn't matter. You've definitely grown."

Maybe she's right. I glance down, realizing for the first time that I can't see my feet anymore. A hint of self-consciousness colors my cheeks, and Max squeezes me. "You're glowing," he murmurs into my hair.

Oblivious, Harper nods. "You are," she says with a smile. "I still can't believe it."

My eyes move to behind her as the Winter pack trail in. The blonde one, Gabe, shoots me a smile, but Devlin and Ace still keep their distance, Ace turning and dropping a bag against the far wall. I return their nods gratefully, appreciating the consideration. Having this many alphas around makes my palms sweat, the comfort I've found within my own pack not extending outside of it.

Gabe tugs Harper back gently, and we all take seats at the table. "Where's Bastien?" I ask Max. His brow furrows as he looks towards the door. "I don't know."

Rogue Winter isn't here either, I realize. "Didn't Rogue come with you?" I ask Harper.

She bites her lip, and I feel Luc tense next to me before he wraps his arm around my shoulder. "He's outside," Luc says softly, before Harper can answer. "He's brought somebody with him, sweetheart. And I'm not sure you're going to want to see them."

My spine stiffens. "Who?" I ask tightly, my gaze moving

from Harper to Luc. I settle on Harper. "Who's outside, Harper?"

"Ava," she whispers. "Sweetie—,"

I sit back, crossing my arms above my stomach. "Tell me," I demand.

"Hello, Ava."

Our gazes swing to the door, and I meet a pair of pale green eyes. My chair tumbles to the ground as I stand up, and Luc swears. "I told you to give us time!"

"I'm sorry," the alpha murmurs. "But I don't think we have much time to waste. And from what I've seen, Ava is more than strong enough to manage this."

My breathing speeds up as we stare at each other.

Christian Winter. Rogue's father. And Director of the Omega Compound.

My head spins, bile rising up my throat as I spin wildly, my breathing harsh. Max pushes in front of me, his jaw tight with anger.

"Why are you here?" he demands.

Black spots start to dance in front of my eyes, and I gasp. Luc tries to grab my arm but I pull free, the motion making me stumble as I back toward the wall.

I can't breathe.

The last time I saw this alpha, he had me carried out of my cell, half-conscious and broken from Jason's attack. He *saw* me.

And he could take me back.

Luc stays close to me, his hand out as I slide down the wall and onto the floor. The Winter pack remain quiet, Devlin with his arm around Harper as she stares at me, her lip trembling. Seeing her here, standing next to the OC director gives me a little extra strength, and I pull myself up, holding onto Luc's arm tightly.

"Are you taking me back?" I ask him numbly. The Director's eyes widen.

"No," he says vehemently. "Ava – I'm here to help. Not to take you back."

"Ava," Harper starts, pale and shaking. "I would never have brought him here if he wasn't on our side. *Never*."

I don't understand.

Rogue Winter steps into the room, Bastien following him with a scowl as he strides over to us. "Perhaps we should take a seat," Rogue suggests. "We have some things that you should hear, Ava."

Bastien murmurs into Luc's ear, and he nods. My beta strokes my cheek before he leaves the room to check the cameras and make sure nobody's followed them.

I keep Luc's hand in mine as I cross slowly to the couch, dropping down into it as I keep my eyes on the Director. Luc follows my lead as Max growls, a rippling sound that rumbles deep in his chest.

"Max," I say quietly. "Sit by me?"

Max doesn't take his eyes off Christian Winter as he sits down, his arm falling across my shoulders and tugging me into him. Rogue clears his throat, but Luc leans forward, his green gaze cutting.

"The second she gives the word," he promises. "I want you all gone. You understand me?"

Devlin Winter shifts a little as Harper nods, her face ashen. "Ava, I'm so sorry," she whispers. "It's just… we had this idea, and I don't think we have much time."

My body goes cold. "Because of the news reports?"

Harper looks at Christian, and I flinch as he turns toward me. His eyes glimmer with a hint of apology. "Your father is throwing every resource he has into searching for you, Ava. He has now correctly identified Max Grey as the doctor who took you from the hospital."

Max turns to stone next to me and my hand clenches on his thigh.

This is it. This is exactly what I was scared of.

"They don't know we're here," Luc says in a furious voice. "Nobody does, outside of our pack and Leah."

Christian nods. "That's true, but it's only a matter of time before your faces are on display alongside Max's. When that happens, how easy will it be to get supplies? To go anywhere outside of this house?"

My legs start to shake. Max won't be able to get Leah's insulin supplies. "This is my fault," I whisper. "I did this."

Luc and Max both turn to me with a snarl. "You've done nothing," Max emphasizes. "They are the ones who did this. Not you."

He turns to Christian. "Why are you here? What's your role in this?"

The alpha sighs, a hint of weariness entering his face. "May I sit down?"

Luc points him to a seat as far away from me as he can get. "Be my guest."

Rogue takes a stand behind his father, the rest of the pack settling into seats around him. Harper sits close to Devlin, her amber eyes not leaving my face, but I can't look at her right now. I need to understand how my friend is sitting in front of me, next to the man responsible for so much of our trauma, without batting an eyelid.

"I need to start with the creed," the Director begins. Rogue glances down at his father, a slight frown on his face, but he doesn't move.

"The day the Government announced the introduction of the Omega Creed, all omegas were required to present themselves immediately to the Omega Compound for processing. Anyone who didn't was rounded up by soldiers. The pain of all those families, ripped apart...," he breathes a little heavier. "It was agony."

Clearing his throat, he looks up, meeting my gaze.

"My wife and I saw the soldiers coming. We lived in a street with a lot of alpha-omega pairs, and a few packs. Rogue had just started school, and she was supposed to pick him up. We'd discussed running, but she didn't want that. Alicia was convinced that the creed wouldn't pass, that people would realize how wrong it was. But we watched the soldiers kicking down the doors, dragging women out and beating the alphas who tried to protect them."

His throat bobs. "We realized that we had miscalculated. Badly. We fought, but she walked out and handed herself over. She was too worried that something would happen, and Rogue wouldn't have anyone left."

I glance up at Rogue as Harper slips off Devlin's lap. She rounds the couch, coming to a stop beside him. He draws her into his side, pressing his lips against her hair as he closes his eyes and listens to his father.

"I was working for the Government already, and I'd started climbing the ranks. And I was convinced that I could get her out. So I went to my superiors, and they said no. No exceptions. That was that, and we were expected to just carry on and forget that our mates were locked up somewhere that we couldn't reach."

Christian's fists clench. "I realized that there wouldn't be any success trying to protest. Anyone who did was put down – sometimes killed. So I told myself I'd be smart. I'd become the perfect Government lackey, parrot anything they needed me to – whatever I needed to do, I would do it, until I was in the position to get Alicia out."

You could hear a pin drop in our silence as we digest his words. "So you lied?" I ask.

He nods. "I'm not a good man, Ava," he says in a low

voice. "I did whatever I needed to do, said whatever I need to say. I stood by and watched atrocities you can't imagine. I just wanted Alicia back."

I hold back the question on my tongue.

"When they offered me the Directors position, it was everything I'd been working towards. I thought – now, I'll *finally* be in a position to help her. It took me seven years."

My heart twists, a little pity breaking through.

"On my first day, I checked the files. She had been transferred to the heat nests two months before. They found her hanging in her cell one week before I was offered the job."

Horror ripples through me. "I'm sorry," I breathe, glancing between Christian and Rogue.

Rogue only nods. Harper buries her face into his chest.

"I should have known," Christian said quietly. "They never would have offered me that job if Alicia had been alive."

Max leans forward, his voice rough. "But you stayed."

He looks at us. "I did. I thought... better it was me, than someone who believed in their bullshit. Better to have someone who could try to restrain some of the activities happening, minimize some of the damage. At every step, I have done whatever I can to help. Some of the ideas the board have come up with...,"

Harper flinches, and he inclines his head. "As Harper knows."

My head spins with this information. "How could you stand by and watch that, every day?" I ask him quietly. "How could you sign off on what they did?"

He faces me, his chin up. "The alternative would have been worse. And I tried to help, wherever I could. There are still good packs out there, good alphas. I put word out, quietly, and sent as many omegas as I could to packs who I knew would look after them behind closed doors. When I met Harper, I matched her with my son and his pack, hoping that they would do the same. Thankfully, it worked out."

Harper smiles sadly. "It did," she says softly.

Christian turns to me. "I have an apology to make to you, Ava." I start. "To me?"

My soul unravels with his next words. "The night you left the compound, I was called to an emergency by one of the guards. I didn't realize that it was a ploy until I got there. By the time I realized that the cameras had been adjusted, and I got to your cell, it was too late."

My breathing speeds up, remembering his face appearing that night.

"You carried me," I say numbly. Luc and Max turn to me in surprise.

Christian closes his eyes. "I contacted Stone thinking that he would relish the opportunity to remove you from the compound. For Stone to *choose* to put you in the nests – I am more sorry than I can say, Ava. If I could do that night over again, I would have kept you in the compound and not contacted him."

I push myself up, stumbling a little from the weight of my stomach as I press my hands to the small of my back and move toward him. He glances down at my stomach and away.

"Have you been to the heat nests, Director?" I ask him boldly, and his green eyes meet mine with a touch of uncertainty.

"Several times," he says. "It's a hellish place. I requested several times to be given charge of the nests too, but I was always pushed back."

My lips part, and I stop, frowning in surprise. "You're not in charge of the nests?"

He shakes his head. "No, Ava," he says gently. "Only the

Omega Compound. Jonathan Stone is in charge of the heat nests."

My knees buckle, and I barely feel Max's arms surround me.

My father is in charge of the heat nests.

"We need a minute," he barks, sweeping me into his arms.

I bury my face in him as he pushes open a door and kicks it closed behind him.

"Ava, love," he smooths my hair back from my face. "Talk to me."

Shuddering, I try to suck in a breath and vocalize the thoughts racing through my head. "I thought... I thought it was only me," I confess. "But to know that he's responsible for all of that pain, Max... that's my *father*."

My father wilfully strapped me to a table, injected me with drugs, and let alpha after alpha use me. The screaming, the cries, the scents... all because of him.

His eyes are dark. "That man," he spits, "is not your father, sweetheart. And you are not responsible for his actions in any way."

I close my eyes, resting against his strength. "I don't know why this even surprises me, but it does."

"It doesn't surprise me." I pull back and look at him as his hands flex on my back. "But I am sorry."

I blow out a breath. "We should go back in there. I want to hear what else he has to say."

When I walk back in, Max close behind me, Christian stands.

"I'm sorry," he says sincerely. "I didn't mean to upset you. I thought you knew."

I shake my head. "It's fine."

Taking a seat, I direct a wobbly smile to Luc, who's watching me with concern. His fingers brush over my knuckles questioningly, and I nod, letting him know I'm okay.

"So," I begin. "Why are you here?"

He jerks a little, and his lip twists up at the corner. "Very direct," he comments, and I lift my shoulder. "The whole world seems to be looking for me right now. I don't have time to waste if I want to keep my pack safe."

Both Max and Luc shift. I can sense the protest forming on their tongues, and I squeeze their hands. This isn't something they can protect me from.

Rather than answer, Christian looks to Harper. She nods, and crosses over to me, kneeling and pulling my hands away from my alphas, folding them into hers as she looks at me, her amber eyes intent.

"Ava," she murmurs. "I think the Omega Creed needs to go. And I think that we might be the ones who can bring it down."

I glance around at the alphas watching us closely.

"Not them. *Us.*"

I blink, waiting for the punchline. "Harper, we're two omegas. We have no legal rights. *None*. What can we do?"

She takes a deep breath. "We can speak up. Tell our stories. Make people hear us. Maybe if they realized how bad things are… most betas just go about their lives unless they're involved in the adoption process. If people knew…,"

I scoff. "They wouldn't care, Harper. They didn't care then, when the laws were passed. Why would they care now?"

"A lot of time has passed. We won't know unless we try."

"How would we even go about it?" I ask, my brow furrowed. "Shout it from a loudspeaker? Nobody is going to interview us on the main news, Harper. We'd be locked up as soon as we tried."

"They won't interview you," says Christian. His green eyes watch me carefully, gauging my response. "But they will interview me."

My stomach twists, and I think I might be sick. "You're serious?"

Harper nods determinedly. "I want a life, Ava. A real life. One where I don't have to crawl when we're in public, or wear a chain around my neck. We deserve to *live*. And so do our children."

She points at my stomach. "What if your daughter awakens as an omega? What then?"

I flinch. It's a thought that I return to often.

I promised to do my best for them. Maybe... maybe this is what that looks like.

Harper shifts. "What is it?" I ask.

Wetting her lips, she glances back at Ace, who gives her an encouraging nod and a sad smile. "Go on, little omega," he encourages.

Harper turns back to me, her shoulders tense. "There are... videos."

I recoil, bile burning the back of my throat. "What videos?"

Christian leans forward. "There are many, many cameras at the compound. I have collected a lot of footage that we can use, hard evidence that people won't be able to hide behind with twisted words or lies."

Harper closes her eyes. "There are also videos from Jason. We found them when... when my pack came for me. My attack, and others."

I take a deep breath, bracing myself. I can see the answer to my unspoken question in her eyes, but I ask anyway. "Am I on there?"

When she nods, the nausea becomes too much to bear,

and I bolt for the bathroom. Luc follows me, pulling my hair back as I retch into the porcelain bowl.

"I'm so sorry, sweetheart," he says, rinsing off a cloth and pressing it against my face.

I cover my mouth with my hands as a sob breaks free, then another.

He filmed me. Filmed the worst moment of my life and kept it as some sort of sick trophy.

I curl up on the floor and Luc lifts me onto his lap.

"I need a minute," I say numbly.

"You have all the time you need," he says. I take a deep breath as he strokes my hair softly, a purr rumbling against my cheek and softening my muscles.

"That's some freaky magic," I mumble, and his chest ripples underneath me.

"Only for you, brat." Luc tips my chin up with the tip of his finger. "Tell me what's in your head right now."

I sigh. "I don't know, Luc. I'm just… so tired. Of all of it."

Examining my face, he nods. "And how do you feel about their plan?"

My pulse jumps as I consider Harper's words.

"It's insane," I whisper sadly. "It won't work, Luc."

He presses his lips together, and my eyebrows fly up to my hairline.

"You think it will?"

He fixes his eyes on the far wall. "I think that I don't want you anywhere near a camera. I don't want you on display like that. But…"

My breath hitches. "We don't have another plan."

Shaking his head, he drops his nose to my hair and breathes in deeply. "I think we're at the edge of something, brat. We would – we *will* - fight for you. I'll fight for you until the last breath leaves my body. But this isn't a battle we can fight with fists and weapons. And I'm fucking petrified of how this might turn out, but I'm more petrified of doing nothing."

The door knocks, and we both look up as Max slips inside. He takes us in on the floor and sits, his arms open as I untangle myself from Luc and crawl over to him awkwardly. His arms wrap around me, and he sighs.

"I called Bastien and Nikolai here. They're coming now."

My body twitches in anxiety, and Max picks up on it. "Ava?"

"I can't ask this of you," I confess. "I can't. This is Nash's home. If anything goes wrong, I can't be responsible for him losing his family."

I can't face Nikolai and ask this of him.

Max lifts me up. "You keep saying that you can't ask this of us, but you're not asking, sweetheart. We will do whatever it takes to get you and the babies away from them. Whatever it takes. And we have our own back-up plans to keep Nash safe, you know. We always have in case anyone tracked us down here. He's not registered. The government would put him up for adoption if they realized."

"We're all trapped, in different ways," I whisper.

Maybe... maybe it's time to break free.

I think about Nash, how his whole life is squeezed into a few acres of forest because he's not registered with the Government. I think of my pack, trapped in a never-ending web of hiding to keep him safe. Leah, choosing her family over the chance for love and a real life of her own.

Emery, losing her life because she had to choose between going to hospital and losing her freedom. Harper, crawling on the floor in public because she can't let anyone know that her pack cares about her.

I swallow, looking down. And me.

All the omegas, thousands of them, bagged and tagged like animals, tortured and starved, beaten and abused, raped and forced into slavery because the world turns a blind eye.

No more. Resolve straightens my spine. Not my daughter.

No fucking more.

I scramble up, and Luc and Max look up at me, faces a little mystified.

"I want a better world." The words tremble on my tongue, tasting dangerously like hope. "I want our children to have a better world. I want Nash to be able to go to school, and play with other kids. I don't want my daughter to go through what we went through. I want to do it."

My words are firm, and both alpha's eyes widen a little. "Are you sure, love?" Luc asks.

Nodding, I reach for his hand. "Nobody ever changed the world by doing nothing, Luc."

It sounds impressive, but fear still licks at my spine, pushing me to curl into a ball and hide away. But hiding won't fix this.

"I want Bastien and Nik," I say, and Max pushes himself up from the floor. "I'll get them, love."

Exiting the small room, I stop as the eyes of the Winter pack swing to me. Christian straightens and Harper jumps to her feet as the main door swings open and Nikolai and Bastien walk through.

"Excuse me," I say. "I need a little more time to talk to my pack."

Bastien smiles at me. "Your pack. It has a nice ring to it," he whispers as he reaches me, his mouth dipping to catch mine in a brief kiss. Nikolai follows behind him, cupping my face as he searches my eyes.

My resolve falters a little. My bear alpha has the most to lose in this.

"Don't do that," he admonishes me. "Whatever you need, little bird."

My chest feels like stone as we step into the kitchen. Taking a seat at the table, I look around at my pack. My pack. Lucien, Max, Nikolai and Bastien.

With faltering words, I explain to Nik and Bastien the conversation we had with the Winter pack. Nikolai snarls when I get to the videos, but he falls silent when I set out the proposal to go on camera.

"What do you think?" The words are awkward.

Bastien sits back in his seat, a stunned look on his face. "I think... this could work." I can almost see my brilliant beta pulling ideas together in his mind as he taps his fingers on the table.

"Ava, are you sure about this?" Leaning forward, he grips my hand in his, his gray eyes darker than I've ever seen them. "I will do whatever we need to do to make sure you're safe. But are you certain you want to do this?"

"I'm sure," I whisper. "I don't want to be a prisoner anymore, Bastien."

Swallowing hard, I stare down at the table. "Nik...,"

His voice rumbles from opposite me. "Look at me, little bird."

Gradually, I lift up my face until his sapphire blues come into view. A sad smile plays on his face. "You think I don't want you to be safe? You, and our children?"

Our. My heart clenches.

"I—,"

He shakes his head, cutting me off, and stands. My heart clenches but he circles around the table and kneels down on one leg next to my chair. His hand covers mine.

"Listen to me, little bird. I will do *anything* to keep my family safe," he grounds out, his eyes daring me to look away. "My family. Our pack, Nash, *you*. I want to give our son and kids a future. One where they don't have to hide who they are."

"If something goes wrong—," I start.

"This was never going to be easy," he shakes his head, his eyes emotional. "We have never had the chance to fight, little bird. Never even come close to it. But now...," he inhales softly. "Now, this is our chance. I would have given anything for Emery to have lived a free life. And I will do anything, *be* anything, to give you that opportunity."

My tears fall freely. "For Emery," I promise him softly. "For Nash."

He shakes his head. "For you, little bird. For all of you."

I throw my arms around his neck, swallowing around the lump in my throat. "I love you."

The words are choked, but Nikolai freezes anyway. They all do.

Wiping my eyes, I pull back. "I do. I love you. All of you."

This pack who saved me, protected me, cherished me, and are willing to put everything they hold dear on the line for me. Who see past my scars and carefully patch up the cracks in my battered heart over and over again.

I thought that I was broken. But the truth is that we are all perfectly imperfect, and I realize, glancing around at them, that there is *nothing* that I will not do to keep our family together.

"Okay," I breathe. "Let's do this."

CHAPTER FIFTY-THREE
BASTIEN

The plan comes together in my mind, jigsaw pieces sliding into place with perfect clarity.

We're all slouched in various positions across the living room, Ava curled up on Nikolai's lap as I outline my thoughts, trying to keep up with the racing in my mind as I make notes on the large sheets of paper I've tacked to the wall.

"Christian should go first," I propose, pointing at him. "It'll blow a huge hole in their narrative immediately, and they won't be expecting it."

Christian nods back at me. "I'm comfortable with that."

"Don't you think revealing our biggest weapon straight off the bat is premature?" Ace Winter challenges, his eyebrows raised.

I shake my head in response. "Christian isn't our biggest weapon."

When they turn to look at me, I grimace. "Christian will make them question everything they think they know. He'll put them off-kilter and make them more susceptible to believing whatever comes next. If the omegas go first, the government could easily twist it. But they can't argue with the OC Director. Not as easily."

Luc nods in understanding. "He's right."

"I'm always right," I say with a smirk, and dodge the pen my brother throws at my head as Ava laughs a little.

Her face looks lighter, even with the risk we're taking. In contrast, I can see the strain on my pack's face, and on the Winter pack too. Not for us. I don't give a flying fuck about myself, and I know Nik, Luc and Max don't either. But if we fuck this up, and we lose Ava or Nash as a result... a fist grips my heart, and my mouth dries.

This plan needs to be the best I've ever come up with. We can't hold anything back.

Clearing my throat, I continue. "We push Christian's message out first. A live broadcast over every channel."

All conversation stops as they turn to me. "A live broadcast?" Devlin asks, his dark brows raised. "We don't have the resources—,"

"You may not," Luc says drily. "But my brother does." He smiles proudly at me as the Winter pack erupts with questions.

Holding up my hand, I explain. "I can hack the security systems they have on the main channels. I won't be able to hold it forever, but ten minutes should be more than long enough to get the message out. Just uploading it to the internet won't have the same impact. It'll get lost on the fringes and dismissed as conspiracy. But pushing it into the main news – nobody will be able to bury it."

Gabe whistles. "Go big or go home?"

Nodding, I watch Ace whisper something into his ear that brings a flush to his face.

"What then?" Nik asks, his hand gently rubbing Ava's arm as she watches me silently.

"I'd like to follow up with a longer broadcast. One where people can hear your stories."

"Mine and Ava's?" Harper asks, and I nod. Luc narrows his eyes. "What else?"

"We all have stories," I swallow. "Not just Harper and Ava. Nikolai?"

"You want me to talk about Emery." His jaw clenches and Ava puts her hand on his chest. Nik stares down at her, his eyes unblinking.

"It's your decision, and I'll support you whatever you decide. But she deserves to have her story told," Ava says softly. It's an intimate moment, and the Winter pack and Christian look away politely.

"Em deserved more than this world gave her, Nik." Max's words drop into the quiet. "She died because she couldn't access the help she needed without losing her freedom, and I wasn't enough to hold her together." Luc starts to protest, and he holds up his hand.

"I know. It wasn't my fault," he acknowledges, *finally*. His throat bobs. "But it doesn't change the fact that if she'd been able to go to the hospital without ending up in a collar, she might have survived."

Ava nods. "I think you should, Nikolai," she murmurs. "For Nash. But it's your decision."

Nik flinches, taking a deep breath. "Okay."

Rogue sits forward. "Where are we going to film? Here?"

Luc immediately shakes his head. "I don't want anyone able to trace the broadcast back to this location. I know Bastien can stop that from happening, but it's a risk that I'd rather not take. Where else can we go?"

Christian stirs. "I know a place. It's a warehouse outside of the city. About an hour's drive from here and abandoned."

Luc's forehead wrinkles when I glance at him, his fingers flexing on the chair as he hesitates.

I understand his reticence. If we've gotten this wrong, if Christian isn't who he says he is, then this could be a huge mistake. One that could cost us everything.

It's Ava who sits forward, her caramel curls falling haphazardly around her face. "If we're going to do this," she says firmly. "Then we have to trust each other."

She's right, but Luc still looks uncomfortable, although he nods in acknowledgment.

"The warehouse it is, then," Rogue says, looking around. "Let's take it from the top."

Chapter Fifty-Four
Nikolai

Rogue Winter shakes my hand firmly, his green eyes shadowed.

"I'm sorry about your mate." The words are genuine, and I nod. "I'm sorry about your mother."

We pause, the heaviness of the task in front of us settling across our shoulders. Rogue gives me a firm look, his lips tightening. "We'll end this."

Fuck, I hope we can keep that promise.

Ava and Harper embrace, whispering words into each other's ears. Both of our packs have angled themselves around their omega, like points on a compass.

Ava is our north.

Their strength humbles me. More so as Ava breaks away and turns with a sigh, rubbing at her lower back. Stepping forward, worry wrinkles my brow as I note the dark circles under her eyes. Today has been difficult for everyone, but not everyone is carrying around two nearly full-term children. Max is by her side in a flash, the healer in him not missing a trick.

"Your back hurting, sweetheart?"

"I'm a little sore," she admits wanly. "I think I need to walk it off."

Holding out my hand, I offer, "Walk with me to get Nash?" That way, I can keep an eye on her. Max nods at me in appreciation as we turn to wave off the Winter pack.

Ava's smile softens some of my concern. "That sounds like heaven, actually. I've missed him today."

"Me too."

Her hand wrapped securely in mine, we make our way slowly down to Leah's cabin.

"We'll need to explain the plan to Leah."

Ava cringes. "How do you think she'll take it?" she worries.

Badly.

I cough into my fist. "She'll be fine."

My voice is a little high, and Ava turns to me, her eyebrow raised. "Somehow, I don't quite believe that."

"Well, we do call her hurricane Leah for a reason," I tease lightly, rewarded with her gentle laugh, before she sighs.

"I understand if she's angry."

"She won't be angry at you, little bird. She'll worry, though. For all of us." Including Ava.

The early evening air starts to chill as we arrive at the cabin, and Ava rubs her arms. I draw her close to me and she curls into my warmth as I knock the door.

It flies open and I'm nearly bowled over by my son. "Ava!"

Raising my eyes, I glance past him to Leah, and she smirks at me. "Think Nash has a new favorite, sorry Nik."

Nash mumbles from where he's buried his face into Ava's belly. "The babies are my favorite."

Ava closes her eyes, her arms wrapped around my son.

She runs her fingers through his hair. "They like you, Nash. Can you feel them?"

Wide-eyed, Nash pulls back and Ava places his small hand on her stomach to feel a kick. He turns to me in astonishment as he feels the ripple. "Papa!"

"I know," I laugh. "Isn't it amazing?"

It's a brief moment, but my heart clenches at the thought of all the memories I want to make with our family. I want it all.

As we walk Nash back to the house for bed, his small hand in mine and Ava tucked carefully beneath my arm, I cast my eyes up to the sky and pray, for the first time in six years.

Please. Please help me keep them safe.
Please don't let us lose this.

Chapter Fifty-Five
Bastien

Pouncing, I sweep our omega away from Nikolai as soon as they walk through the door. He scowls at me as I tug her into my arms.

Unrepentant, I shrug. "I'm claiming her tonight. I have plans."

Ava's shiver runs straight to my cock, but I push the thoughts back down. I can see the exhaustion she's trying to deny, the weight of our task and the toll of her pregnancy heavy on her frail shoulders.

"Where are we going?" she laughs as I tug her towards the stairs.

"My room."

I wipe my suddenly sweaty palm on my trousers. I hope I don't fuck this up.

Before her foot touches the bottom stair, I bend and lift her, swinging her into my arms and carrying my precious cargo up the wooden staircase. Ava tilts her head to look at me, a glint in her hazel eyes. "Are you stealing me?" she whispers dramatically. Stopping in the middle of the stairs, I drop my lips to hers in a brief kiss.

"I am." I'm unapologetic. "You need some pampering, baby. And I'm going to make sure you get it."

Surprise and anticipation brightens her tired eyes. "Pampering?"

"Mmmm."

Shouldering open the door to my room, I gently place her feet down on to the rug, and she looks around curiously. Between her old room and the nest, she hasn't spent much time in this side of the house, and tonight, I want her in my space. Wearing my scent, mild as it is compared to my pack.

Mine.

Ava spins slowly, taking in the prints hanging on the cream walls, black and white movie posters giving a nod to some of my favorite films. The rest of the room is small but neat, a double bed taking up most of the space with clean white cotton sheets. I don't spend a huge amount of time in here, but whilst I can cope with chaos in my office, I hate it where I'm sleeping. Ava turns to me with a grin. "I didn't realize you were so tidy," she nudges me, and I laugh.

The sound of the faucet running next door draws her attention and she looks at the wooden door longingly. "Is that a bath I can hear?"

"It is." I gently nudge her to sit down on the bed and drop to untie her laces. Pulling off her shoes, I tickle the bottom of her feet, and she gasps out a laugh. "Bastien! What are you doing?"

I sit back up, cupping her face between mine. "You've had a busy few days, and I can see how tired you are, sweetheart. Let me take care of you tonight, okay?"

My omega stares at me, her mouth parted slightly with confusion.

Oh, baby. So used to nobody caring that you stopped paying attention to yourself.

Next, I urge her to lie back, and I peel off her soft

trousers, dropping them next to us. Her breathing comes a little faster, and I tap her knee, scolding. "None of that, love. Spoiling first."

She throws a hand over her eyes, grumbling a little as I pull down her underwear. Her slick scents the room in a delicious burst of sugar, and I can't resist bringing the soft material to my nose and inhaling deeply. Ava gapes at me, her cheeks rosy.

"Bastien," she groans, wriggling her hips for emphasis. "You're not helping."

"Later," I promise, pulling her back up and sliding her top over her head. Her breasts are heavy and swollen, and she winces as I brush my hands across the lace covering them. I pause, frowning. "Are you sore?"

She looks away, and I grasp her chin. "Tell me," I command.

She snarks at me. "Are you sure you're not an alpha? Because you're giving me the vibes right now."

Folding my arms, I wait for her to answer the question and she throws her arms up. "Fine! Yes, they're sore," she admits. "But it's fine, Bastien."

It is not fine.

I reach behind her, unhooking the clasp of her bra and drawing the straps down her arms, revealing the creamy softness of her skin.

My eyes go straight to her reddened, cracked nipples. "Ava."

She tries to pull her hands up to cover them, the hitch in her voice telling me she's embarrassed. "They're fine, Bastien."

Shaking my head, I duck into the bathroom and emerge with a basket of toiletries. It's a little overloaded, and her eyes round with curiosity. "What's that?"

Chapter Fifty-Five

I carefully set the wicker basket next to her. "This is for you."

We both survey the vast array of lotions and potions on display. There are bubble baths, soaps, and various other soft squishy things that Leah assured me Ava would love.

Ava bites her lip. "You got this for me?"

Rubbing the back of my neck, I self-consciously gesture. "Yep. I wasn't sure what you'd like, so I picked out a variety."

I search the basket until I see what I'm looking for. "Here it is," I swallow, showing her the tube of cream. "It should help with your nipples."

I'm not sure who's redder right now, me or Ava. But I won't let her sit there in pain if I can do something about it.

"Bastien," her voice shakes. "This is...,"

"If you don't like it, don't worry," The lump in my throat threatens to choke me. "I can pack it away. You don't have to use it."

Fuck. What if she doesn't like those scents? I didn't have a clue what I was doing on the supply run, just trying to remember what I could from what Leah had told me and my research.

Her hand shoots out and grabs my arm. "Don't you dare take it away." Her voice cracks. "I love it, Bastien. No-one's ever done *anything* like this for me."

Pulling herself up, she wraps her arms around my chest, and I enclose her, breathing in the warmth of her scent as the knot in my throat finally loosens in relief. "Better get used to it, sweetheart," I whisper in her ear. "We have many, many plans to spoil you."

She wriggles. "I think I may be okay with that."

"Ready for your bath?"

"Hell, yes."

I lift her again, and she grins at me as I carry her through the door. Nerves twist my intestines into knots as Ava stares at the setup.

Warm light dances across her face, dozens of candles scattered across the room on every available surface. The bathtub is full, copious amount of bubbles floating as steam rises in lazy curls, and I lean in to turn off the water. Ava gapes at me, her hazel eyes shimmering.

"Bastien, this is…,"

"Exactly what you deserve," I interrupt her. "Every damned day."

And it's what you'll get if I have any say in it, love.

I never thought I'd get so much pleasure from caring for another person. But it thrills me when Ava sinks into the hot water, a groan spilling from her lips as she relaxes against the porcelain tub.

Picking up the soft washcloth, I lift her arms and start smoothing down her skin with long, sure strokes. She watches me, her eyes flickering with the flames around us.

"Don't talk," I coax her. "Just enjoy it, baby."

I stroke the cloth carefully over the taut steel of her belly. She's a goddamned miracle, carrying two lives inside her.

"I can't wait to meet them," I admit, and her eyes meet mine, lips lifting in a smile. "Me neither."

I continue my slow exploration of her body, washing her legs and feet before moving up to her chest, carefully avoiding her sensitive areas as she closes her eyes with a sigh. I pay particular attention to the noises she makes as I learn the soft curves and contours of her body, the soft murmurs and hitches in her breath telling me what she likes.

I try to ignore the growing hardness in my pants as her little pants and mewls slowly drive me fucking wild.

Shit, I did not think this through. I'm so hard I think I might actually burst.

When I dip the cloth to wash her sex, her legs part for me and she lets out the sexiest whine I've ever heard.

"Fuck, baby," I croak. "You're not making this easy on me."

She grabs my hand and pulls the washcloth away, pulling my hands to the hot slick I can feel even with the water floating around her. I squeeze my eyes shut with a groan.

"Touch me," she implores. "Please, Bastien. I feel *empty*."

This definitely wasn't my intention, but I'm helpless to resist her pleading.

My fingers slide through her slippery folds, and I dip a finger into her heat, testing how wet she is. We both hiss as my finger slides in easily, and I add another, sliding them in and out as her back arches.

"So wet for me," I coax her. "Aren't you, baby? Do you need to come?"

"Oh, god." Whimpering, she tries to close her legs, but my hand shoots out. "You wanted to play," I murmur, holding her legs open. "You're not leaving this bath until you come all over my hand, sweetness."

She keens, throwing her head back as I add my thumb to the mix, sinking my fingers to the hilt and pressing my thumb directly against her clit, circling it lightly before pressing down and rubbing it. "Fuck, Bastien!"

"That's it," I encourage her. "Moan for me, Ava. Show me those beautiful sounds you make when you're riding my fingers."

Her sounds rise, her ragged breath and moans growing louder. Satisfaction runs through me at her cries. I want her breathless, boneless, shaking underneath me as I sink into her.

I scrape the edge of my nail over her clit and she sits up, her hands flying to my arm as her cunt clamps around my fingers. "Such a good girl," I praise her, and she clenches again, fluttering around me.

My voice is dark with satisfaction. If I was an alpha, I'd be fucking purring right now at the way my omega shatters on my hand, screaming her release. When my fingers slide free, I trace them up her body, petting her damp skin as she catches her breath.

"I think I'm clean now," she pants. "Time for bed?"

I bite back a smirk at the hope in her tone, and lean over to lift her out, grabbing a white fluffy towel from the stock I've prepared just for her.

I spread it out on the bed and lay her down, peeling off my wet shirt and throwing it aside. Her eyes sit at half-mast as she scans my body, and damn if her look isn't the sexiest thing I've ever seen. My chest puffs out at her appreciation, a peacock preening for its mate.

"You look so proud," she teases, and I grin back at her. "I'm not finished yet."

Ava squeals with laughter as I straddle her legs, careful to keep my weight off her as I lean over and grab the lotion. When she spots it, she throws a hand over her face and grumbles.

"I can't believe you're going to rub cream on my sore nipples. This is *not* sexy, Bastien!"

"Baby, anything to do with me touching your body is going to make me hard as a rock." Proving my point, my erection nudges her thigh and she tries to open her legs.

"Not yet," I tut playfully. "Hands above your head, love. If you move them, I'll stop."

Breathing hard, she raises her arms above her head, the movement pushing her breasts toward me. They've definitely grown, thanks to the babies. My mouth goes dry.

"You're so damn beautiful," I croak out, and she shivers. "Don't say things like that and make me cry."

"I need to say them more, then, so you get used to it."

"I'll never get used to it."

I hope not, not if it puts that light in her eyes.

I pop the lid and squeeze some of the lotion onto my fingers before I reach down and stroke it against her left nipple. She gasps at the coldness, and her nub hardens under my hands as my finger smooths back and forth, gently rubbing in the cream.

Fuck, the way her nipples rise under my fingers makes my mouth hunger for a taste. I want to wrap my lips around them and *suck*.

There'll be plenty of time for that, I remind myself.

I press gentle kisses around her cherry-coloured aureole, and she pushes against me. "I want to touch you."

"Not yet, baby." She huffs in frustration, and my smile grows against her skin. I can't taste her nipples, but there's something else I fully intend to feast on.

My mouth trails downwards, kissing over her stomach and down, until I'm pressing my lips to the thatch of caramel curls above her pussy. Her hips twist, and I gently hold them still. "Bastien, please," she begs, the edge of a whine in her voice.

Her scent teases me, the rich, warm scent of vanilla filling the room.

Cupcakes and frosting. Fucking delicious.

"Fuck, Ava," I groan as my hands spread her wide and I look at her soft, pink slit, wet and inviting. "Fucking perfect."

She moans, and I watch in fascination as a trail of slick trickles from her opening. Lifting her legs, I prop them over my shoulders and her thighs quiver with the strain of holding herself back. Her hands slide down, grasping the bedding in her fists, and I grab her hands, curling our fingers together as I go in for dessert.

Her hips lift off the mattress with my first long, slow lick. *"Bastien!"*

I pull my head back. "Tell me this is okay," I grunt. "Or tell me to stop."

"Don't you dare," she gasps, and I surge back in, taking luxurious licks of her weeping pussy as she mewls and twists, my hands holding her steady as I feast. Ava cries out, my name on her lips as I thrust my tongue into her opening, savouring every last drop of her as I move it in and out, pushing my face as close I can get. And it's still not enough. My every sense is fucking consumed with the omega above me.

I pull back. "Mine, cupcake. Tell me you're mine."

It's possessive as fuck, but I don't care. She's mine, but I'm hers too. She owns me, heart, body and fucking soul, and I don't ever want her to let go.

"Yours," she cries out. "Yours, Bastien!"

Her cries grow louder as I pick up the pace, licking and sucking at her until she shakes around me, slick flowing onto my tongue in an echo of her release.

"Let it go," I snarl. "Now, baby. Come for me."

Her body tenses, her hands gripping mine as the sweetest fucking gush of vanilla flows onto my tongue. I push my tongue inside, letting go of her hands and wrapping my arms around the tops of her thighs, seeking every last drop of her as she quivers and falls apart beneath me.

I pull back, her juices covering the lower half of my face.

"Ava," I climb onto the bed, tugging her to face me and smoothing her hair back. "Are you okay?"

She blinks at me, her caramel skin flushed. "I can't feel my legs," she mumbles, and I smile in savage satisfaction.

"I want to spend the rest of my life with that taste on my tongue," I tell her, watching in fascination as her flushed color spreads down her body. "Taste?"

CHAPTER FIFTY-FIVE

I lean in, giving her a chance to pull away, but she meets me halfway, her tongue sliding into mine. Knowing she can taste her own slick on my tongue, my erection decides to make itself known again and she breaks free, glancing down.

"Don't worry about that," I murmur, trying to pull her back to me, but she sits up.

"Ava?" My mouth dries as she throws her leg over me, straddling my chest and shifting down. The fluid still seeping between her thighs dampens the material between us, and the heat from her pussy presses against my cock, making me hiss as she leans down to undo my pants.

"Off," she demands, and my cock twitches at her impervious tone. *Yes, ma'am.*

Lifting her hips so I can push my trousers down, she settles back against me. Her soft hands wrap around my length and I jerk as she lowers herself down my body, my crown disappearing as her soft mouth closes over my head.

I throw my head back with a curse as Ava licks and sucks, my cock swelling even further until she shifts forward and lifts herself, guiding my head up and down her slit, slathering my cock in her juices.

"Fuuuck." I think my eyes have crossed. "Baby, we don't have to—,"

We both cry out as she sinks down, my cock disappearing inch by inch into her tight heat.

"Shit," I grunt. "Cupcake, you're killing me."

She tries to lean forward for a kiss, but her belly gets in the way. Carefully, I sit up, hooking her legs around mine and wrapping my arms around her waist. She shifts, pressing even deeper, and a throaty moan slides out of her mouth.

I carefully grasp her hips. "Look at me, baby."

Her eyes slide open, watching me dazedly as I rock my hips into her, both of us settling into a rhythm. Her head drops back as she pants, our sweat-slicked bodies undulating.

Her slick coats us, dripping out of her around my cock as I thrust, one hand wrapped carefully around her and the other winding into her hair, holding her to me.

"I'll never let you go." My words are guttural. "Nobody will ever take you away from us. You understand?"

She moans into my skin. "Never leaving you."

"Never." I pick up the pace as the sound of our bodies slapping together echoes through the room, Ava's soft cries growing higher as she moves toward her crest. I tip her head back, sucking at the sensitive skin. Fuck, I wish I could brand her with my bite, mark her as mine for the whole world to see. She shudders against me, her rocking a little off-pace as she searches for her orgasm.

I close my eyes. I can't make her finish internally, only an alphas knot can do that, but I drop my fingers from her hair, moving to her clit and rubbing it between my fingers. She clamps down around my dick with a scream and I bury my face in her neck with a bellow as my seed erupts from me, filling her up until it spills past our joining, our scents musky in the small room.

We stay there, my hands stroking down her back as she slumps against me. Words fucking fail me. I lift her off me and onto the bed, heading to the bathroom and bringing back a washcloth. She shares a sleepy smile with me as I clean her up, her earlier embarrassment gone. Pulling back the covers, I tuck her into my bed, a possessive fist clenching my heart as she curls up in *my* sheets. I slip in behind her, and she rolls into me, her eyes already closed as she reaches for me and I wrap my arms around her.

My eyes close on one final thought.

I am never letting this go. Ever.

Chapter Fifty-Six
Ava

I stare out of the window as the SUV travels down the dusty road.

"It's secluded," Max assures me in a low tone. Sensing my unease, he winds our fingers together, and I give him my best shot at a smile, but it slides from my face as I stare out of the window again.

Luc slows the SUV as he twists in his seat, his eyes scanning over me. "You doing okay, brat?"

I nod briefly, wishing Nikolai and Bastien were here too. But Bastien is travelling with Ace and Gabe Winter, transporting the equipment we need to record Christian's speech and broadcast it live to the whole world. And Nikolai is at home with Nash. Luc wouldn't let him come, and I agreed. Let's just say that Nik was *not* happy with the arrangement.

My hand shakes in Max's grasp. Fear has a tight grip on my throat. Once we do this… the avalanche begins. There's no going back.

Max rubs my cold hand between his. "We don't have to do this, sweetheart. We can turn around right now and go home."

My eyes slide to his. "No, we can't, Max," I say sadly, my voice small. No matter how much I want to demand that our whole pack goes back home and hides. "This isn't going away."

Max nods in agreement, although his jaw is tight, lips pressed together. None of us are hugely enthusiastic about this plan, not even Bastien, but it's our best shot at getting our story out there.

Luc pulls into a bland parking lot, two other vehicles already parked up. Bastien looks up, his dark hair glinting in the light as we pull up next to him. I scrabble to undo my seatbelt, but my door is already open, his hands gently pushing mine away.

He lifts me out and into an embrace, his hands running down my spine soothingly as my shakes overspill into full body trembles.

"I'm sorry," I sniffle. "I'm a mess."

"You're not a mess, brat," Luc says quietly from next to me. "All things considered, you're being pretty damn brave here."

Murmuring a sound of agreement, Bastien drops a soft kiss on my lips. "I need to set up," he whispers. "I won't be far."

Giving him a nod, I watch as he heads back over, diving into a deep discussion with Ace. Soft footsteps come up behind me, and Harper's cinnamon scent fills my nose. She comes to a stop and we watch the unloading for a few minutes in silence.

"I'm sorry, Ava," she whispers. I turn to her in surprise. "What for?"

"For this," she grimaces, waving a hand at the scene in front of us. "I know it's not what you want."

"None of us want this," I point out. "But that's not your fault, Harper. It's *theirs*."

Chapter Fifty-Six

Devlin nods in the corner of my eye, close to Harper on her other side. Max squeezes my hand in agreement.

Christian and Rogue walk out of the warehouse, their heads close together. My body still tenses at the sight of the Omega Compound director. Some memories aren't so easily forgotten, but I push them down until I can hear the conversation around me without the ringing in my ears drowning it out.

"Let's go," says Devlin, and we walk down together to meet them. Christian nods at me as I move closer, keeping his distance as he smiles at Harper.

"How are you feeling?" I ask him, and his eyes swing to mine. He blows out a breath.

"I feel... like it's time. Past time, truthfully."

Harper fidgets next to me. "I can't believe we're doing this," she mutters. "God, I hope this works."

Devlin wraps his arm around her. "Either way, we tried, right?"

Everyone nods somberly. Bastien calls out for Max, and we turn to them.

"We're good. Time to set up."

My nerves twist into knots as Harper and I take a seat on some old crates. Max stays close, his eyes tracking the flurry of movement in front of us with a slight frown.

Bastien clips a microphone to the collar of Christian's crisp white shirt. He looks formal and handsome, every inch the media darling of the Omega Creed in his dark suit. His face is expressionless as he stares straight ahead.

"Are you ready?" Bastien asks him, and he nods. They test the sound, Ace monitoring the volume as Bastien switches between several laptops, his fingers dancing across the keys as his brows dip in concentration.

"Okay...," he says at last. "We're all set."

The bustle around the room falls silent, the enormity of

the task in front of us settling in. Harper and I glance at each other, and she curls her hand over mine, her amber eyes darker than I've ever seen them as she chews on her lip.

Christian squares his shoulders as he strides out to stand on the square Bastien has carefully marked on the floor with black tape. Bastien follows him, wheeling a camera that wouldn't look out of place on a film set.

A hand settles on my neck, and I jump a split-second before the scent of sandalwood sinks in. Luc pulls back immediately, and I swivel awkwardly to face him, my face full of regret.

"Sorry," I say with a shake of my head. "I'm a little on edge." His eyes soften as he strokes my cheek in understanding. "It's a stressful situation."

Max makes a beeline for me as Harper is gently pulled away by Devlin and Gabe. Ace remains where he is, his head down and focusing on the instructions Bastien throws at him. Rogue and Christian talk quietly, Rogue reaching out and gripping Christian's arm tightly before he turns to us. His face is strained, and Harper jumps up as he reaches for her, burying his face in her neck.

My eyes prick. This day will change everything for them. Plans have been made, the Winter pack planning to go to ground with Christian until we know which way the wind is blowing, whether Christian's words today have made a single iota of difference in the judgemental minds of our society.

Bastien motions us to be quiet.

"On my count," he says tightly. Christian squares himself, his eyes on the camera.

Crossing my fingers, I close my eyes. Max and Luc are barely breathing on either side of me.

"Five, four, three, two, one…"

Please.

Chapter Fifty-Six

I open my eyes as the red camera light clicks on. At Bastien's nod, Christian takes a deep breath, pale green eyes focused on the camera.

"My name is Christian Winter, and I am the director of the Omega Compound."

Chapter Fifty-Seven
Max

We sprawl across the couches in the living area, watching the news play shot after shot of Christian's broadcast.

"All mainstream news channels were interrupted this afternoon by a live broadcast from the Director of the Omega Compound..."

"Winter made some shocking allegations relating to the treatment of omegas under the laws of the Omega Creed..."

"This afternoon, we received video evidence which seems to confirm Winter's allegations of abuse..."

Nikolai flicks to another station, where two beta broadcasters are in deep discussion.

"Is this really such a surprise, John?" the blonde female beta asks with a challenging expression. "You just have to look at the rules of the creed to know that actually, this whole approach to addressing the issues we're seeing with birth rates is inhumane. My only question right now is - why has this taken so long to reach public discourse?"

The rules of the omega creed roll across the ticker at the bottom of the screen, and I glance toward Ava. She's curled up in Bastien's lap, her bright eyes not moving as she listens intently.

"Look, Julia," responds the smarmy-looking beta presenter, his tone condescending. "It's easy to reach a snap judgement, but I don't believe we have the full picture. By all accounts, omegas actually desire this kind of treatment. Who are we to say otherwise?"

"Well, I'd love to confirm that with one of them, John – except that they all appear to be locked up behind the walls of the omega compound. And these allegations of sexual abuse within the heat nests... this is not what the general public understood to be happening, John. We have received thousands of messages from our viewers, some of whom are highly distressed that this activity appears to be not only sanctioned, but encouraged by our own government, and that the children they adopted in good faith may actually be a result of *rape*—,"

Ava flinches as her hands drop to her stomach, and Luc turns off the television, standing and holding out his hand.

"That's enough," he growls, his tone furious. "Enough for tonight, love. We've been watching this for hours. The message has gotten through."

Ava frowns up at him. "Luc... next time we sit here, it's going to be my words they're discussing. Nothing they can say to me is going to hurt any more than what I've already been through. I want to prepare myself as much as I can."

Luc's nostrils flare and he runs a hand through his black curls. "I don't think you need to record another video. This is enough, Ava."

Ava's mouth drops open, before she squares her shoulders and pulls herself up to face him. "I'm not leaving Harper alone in this," she insists. She plants her hands on her hips, the tiny omega facing off against the huge alpha, and Luc groans as he drops his forehead to hers.

"You've given so much already," he says hoarsely. "Everything, Ava. And those vultures will rip you apart just for daring to make them uncomfortable. I don't think I can stand behind you and watch you go through that. For fuck's sake, you're heavily pregnant. Do you realize what they're going to say?"

Ava's eyes flash with heat as she meets him head on. "What? That I'm an omega slut? That I begged for it? That I wanted it? *Let them*, Luc. The only people who will be mad at me for telling the truth are those that are living a lie. And I don't want our children to grow up in a world built on lies."

Luc tries to interrupt, but Ava holds her hand up, her voice shaking.

"I'm going to hold up a mirror, and let them see what sort of world they've created. Let them look, Luc. I will peel myself open and share my worst memories with them. I will not hold back. I will not hide away. Because I want my children to know that I fought for them. I want Nash to know that I did every *fucking* thing I could to give him a real future."

She turns to look at Nikolai. "I want *Emery* to know that I did everything I could."

Nikolai stares at her, his eyes glistening. "She knows, little bird."

I sit forward. "Sweetheart, none of us would ever think that you're hiding away from this. You have suffered more at their hands than just about anyone. Nobody would blame you for putting yourself first for once."

Ava draws herself up, her chin tilting up defiantly.

"I would," she says fiercely. "I'm putting *them* first, Max."

Her hands stroke over her swollen stomach. "I've been thinking a lot," she says, turning to look at us all. Her brow creases. "About what it means to be a mother. What I think it means."

She turns back to Luc. "I am *choosing*, Luc. I didn't choose to become pregnant, but I am choosing to be the best mom that I can be. That means putting their health and happiness first. It means doing the right thing, even when it's the hardest thing imaginable."

Her voice shakes. "I may be an omega, and I may have been bent, but I am *not broken*. And if I want my children to live in a world where they can choose the life they want to lead, then I have to speak up. And when I do it, I want you to stand next to me. Not behind me."

Luc's face falls, and he sighs in resignation. "I will stand wherever you want me to be," he promises, drawing Ava into his arms. She goes willingly, winding her arms around his neck.

"I love you," he whispers. "So damned much, brat. The only thing that scares me in all of this is the possibility of you getting hurt."

Ava strokes a hand over his brow. "I love you too. But if I don't do this, then there might not be a future for any of us."

Luc drops his face to inhale the crook of her neck. "I know," he rasps. "God, I know. I just wish this wasn't on your shoulders."

"I'm strong enough." She smiles a little. "As long as you'll be there to hold me up."

"Always."

The affirmation rolls around the room, all of us watching the omega that swept into our lives and now might be the key to bringing down the laws that have controlled our lives for decades. My chest aches. I would do anything – *anything* – to keep her safe.

But what do we do when our best chance for a future puts her directly in the line of fire?

Ava turns, her hazel eyes falling on me before moving to Nikolai and Bastien.

"I'm tired," she whispers. "Can we go to bed? All of us? Just to sleep, though."

I get to my feet and scan her face anxiously. "Are you feeling okay? Do you need anything?"

She shakes her head. "I'm fine. Just tired."

She gives me a wobbly smile that just about rips my heart out. "Then let's go to bed," I say gently, holding out my hand. Nik and Bastien are already moving, flicking off the lamps around the room as Luc and I inspect Ava. She looks paler than I've seen her since she arrived, and worry grasps my throat in a tight grip. Luc shares an anxious glance with me over her head.

She takes my hand and follows me up the stairs as Luc hovers behind us. Toeing off my shoes at the door, I pad across the nest, inspecting the pillows and blankets. Ava doesn't even bother getting undressed as she drops down and crawls into position.

The piles of material swallow her up as she burrows into the blankets with a sigh. I barely pause to peel off my shirt as I climb in next to her, the others following as we settle into an unspoken arrangement, Luc and I on either side of Ava. Bastien clambers in behind me with Nik settling behind Lucien.

Ava curls into me, her soft huffs of breath already slowing down as I stroke her hair away from her face. "Sleep, love," I breathe, leaning in to kiss her gently on the forehead and pulling a downy blanket over us. The stress lines in her forehead gradually smooth away until she's gently snoring, and I close my own eyes.

Sleep doesn't come easily.

Chapter Fifty-Eight
Ava

When I wake up, exhaustion already weighs down my bones.

I make the mistake of complaining to Luc, and he whisks me into Max's office before I can so much as blink.

"This really isn't necessary," I grumble, but Max hushes me. "You're getting closer to giving birth to two little humans," he says gently. "Excuse us if we want to make sure you're cared for."

It's a funny feeling, being cared for when you've never had anybody who asked if you were cold, or hungry, or even if you were alright. It makes my shoulders tight, makes me want to turn away from the care in their faces. Sometimes, I even bite their heads off.

Like now.

"I'm fine," I hiss. "Stop fussing over me like I'm a child!"

"You're not a child, brat," Luc challenges, his eyes gleaming. "But you're sure as hell acting like one right now."

I suck in a breath as hurt laces through me, even though our cross words are my fault. Sagging onto the trolley, I bury my face in my hands, eyes burning.

"I'm sorry. I don't know what's *wrong* with me."

"Are you kidding?" Max's words are incredulous, and I peek through my fingers at him. "Sweetheart, look at everything going on. Everything with the compound, and the pregnancy, and even us." I start to protest and he holds up a hand. "Stop," he insists, just enough of an edge to his voice that I fall silent. "You've been to hell and back. On top of that, you've got our whole pack to contend with. That alone is enough to exhaust anyone, without anything else coming into it. The trauma you've been through isn't going to go away overnight."

Flinching, I turn away. "I don't know what you mean."

"Really?" Max lifts my chin up. "You think we don't hear it when you wake up in the night? When you hide away in the bathroom and cry?"

My chin wobbles as my stomach drops. "I didn't think you knew about that."

Max brushes his nose across mine. "It kills me," he says roughly. "It fucking kills me to know that I can't fix this for you, Ava. I would walk through the seven circles of hell for you, love. I would fight any battle, tear down anybody who tried to hurt you."

He presses his finger softly against my chest as my breathing stutters. "But I can't heal what's hurting in here."

A tear falls out of my eye, and he leans in to kiss it away.

"Lean on me. On *us*," he pleads, and Luc nods silently behind him, his arms crossed over his chest. "I promise that we are strong enough to carry some of your worries for you. If you want to talk, to cry, to sit in silence and stare at the wall, to laugh. I just want you to come to one of us when you're feeling down and let us take a little of that weight for you."

My eyes slide between Max and Luc, and they both watch me with determined expressions.

"I... I don't like relying on you," I admit. "It makes me feel weak."

Luc sits beside me, and I rest my head against his arm with a sigh. "It's not weak to lean on the ones you love, brat," he says gently. "To reach out your hand when you need help is one of the strongest things you can do."

Biting my lip, I consider his words. It's true that I've been holding back from them. Not completely – but enough that they've noticed. Nerves flicker in my stomach as I gather my words.

"I feel nervous when you watch me eat," I whisper. Both of them swing their heads to me, but I keep my head down. I want to get this out before I lose my nerve.

"It doesn't feel right. Like it did with the bed," I continue, and Luc closes his hand over mine with a soft squeeze. "I have bad dreams every night. About the compound, Jason, something happening to us, to Nash... it feels like when I close my eyes a reel of the worst moments of my life play on a loop." My voice cracks. "And I'm scared of giving birth."

I glance up at Max. Those words were the hardest to say. "Max, I know... things with Emery didn't go well." I swallow. "And I don't want you to feel responsible if – if something goes wrong—,"

Max is on his knees, his arms wrapped around me in a split second.

"God, Ava," he chokes. "You don't need to worry about me."

Frowning at him, I lift up my chin and hold his gaze.

"Yes, I do. This isn't a one-way road, Max. Holding out a hand goes both ways."

He swallows, and I smile a little sadly. "It's hard," I murmur. "Isn't it?"

Max's face clears, and he holds out his hand to me. When I take it, he moves forward until his face rests on the curve of my stomach.

"I failed her," he whispers. "I did everything I could, and it wasn't enough. I didn't have the right equipment, and she was losing so much blood. Sometimes I wash and wash my hands, but I can still feel it."

There's a sound in the doorway, and I lift my head up. Nikolai looks back at me before his eyes drop to Max, his blue eyes dark as he watches his friend with a hopeless expression. Bastien stands behind him, his hand on Nik's shoulder.

"I wanted to save them both," Max's voice shakes. "God help me, I would have given anything to save her. I loved her like she was my own sister and I couldn't – I couldn't--,"

Nikolai strides into the room as I cup Max's face, moving my thumb softly up and down his jawline. "You did the best with what you had, Max," I murmur.

Nik kneels beside Max, and he flinches as they stare at each other. "I'm sorry," says Max hoarsely. "I'm so sorry that it wasn't enough, Nik."

My blue-eyed alpha watches Max with damp eyes. "You did your best, brother," he says gruffly. "You nearly broke yourself trying to save her, and my son is alive today because of you. You all gave up your entire lives to keep him safe. I have never blamed you because this was not your fault."

Max's breath hitches. "Thank you. But, Ava," he turns to me, his face imploring. "I promise you that we have everything we need here to make sure you can deliver those babies safely. I've been preparing for this since you first arrived. Most births happen without any issues, and if anything did go wrong, I promise we have everything we need to deal with it here. Do you understand?"

Closing my eyes, I press my forehead against his. "I do, Max. I'm still scared, but I'm not scared about you. You're the only part that gives me any reassurance about the whole thing."

Max's hand reaches up, and he strokes my hair. "I'll be there at every stage," he promises. "I won't leave you."

"I know."

We share a smile, before I look around at the others. Nik's watching me with his hands crossed over his chest.

"Little bird," he says in a chastising tone. "What's this I hear about you being scared of food?"

I flush, shifting in my seat as they all turn back to me, Max included. "I'm not *scared* of food. But... every time I eat around you, it feels wrong. Like I'm breaking one of their stupid laws. It makes me nauseous."

Bastien's jaw tenses. "I didn't think you were eating properly, sweetheart. But I thought it was the pregnancy."

I shake my head. "It's not," I admit. "I'm actually hungry pretty much all of the time."

My shoulders lighten as I share my worries with them. This has been playing on my mind for weeks. Hunger pains, combined with worry that the babies aren't getting what they need, makes for a cranky, tired Ava.

I shrug a little. "I'm not sure how to fix it, to be honest. Maybe time will make it better."

Luc turns to me. "Trust me?" he says carefully. There's a glint in his eyes, and my stomach flips.

"Always." I say it jokingly, but an undercurrent of truth runs through my words.

Without another word, he grabs my hand and waits for

me to slide off the trolley before tugging me out of the door. My curiosity wars with trepidation as the others follow us. "What are you planning?" I ask Luc, and he shakes his head, a smile playing at his lips.

"We're fixing your food worries. Right now."

My eyebrows raise. "Why do I feel like I'm missing something here?"

Snorting, he pulls me into the kitchen before he abruptly stops. "Nik, where's Nash?"

"With Leah," Nik answers, leaning against the edge of the doorframe and watching with curiosity. "Why?"

"Close the door."

With the door shut, all four of them feel impossibly large in the small space. Their scents battle – Luc's sandalwood is the most prominent, but I can smell traces of apple pie and gingerbread, with Bastien's sage aroma underneath. Closing my eyes, I take a deep breath. Fuck, they smell good. A murmur of appreciation slips out, and my eyes flash open as a growl thrums through the air. Nikolai, Max and Bastien all take a step closer to me, their eyes burning.

Luc turns from the counter and slides a platter in front of me. I glance down at the plate, my heart beating a little faster. Sliced strawberries, dark cherries and grapes sit on one side, separated from a selection of small cuts of meat by some soft-looking bread. My heart sinks as my stomach threatens to revolt.

"Luc…," I say pleadingly. "I'm not sure…,"

He takes my face in his hands and leans in. "You said you trusted me, sweetheart," he whispers, resting his forehead against mine. "I won't sit back and watch you suffer when we can do something about it. This, I can help with."

My heart pulses. "What are you going to do?"

He pulls back. "You associate food with bad memories."

He gives me a small smile. "So we're going to replace them with good ones."

My mouth dries up at the look he gives me. His green eyes darken as they trace my body, and I can't stop myself squirming a little. "Like the bed?"

"Exactly." Luc turns to look at the others, and Nikolai steps forward. "I volunteer as tribute," he says with a wink, and I can't help but laugh. "Okay. I'm game."

Taking a seat on one of the wooden chairs, Nik pats his knees. "Over here, baby."

I move towards him, glancing at Luc for confirmation as he nods. Gingerly, I set myself down on Nik's knee, gasping as he turns me in his lap until my back is pressed against his chest. His hard thighs move under me, nudging my legs apart as he slides his feet between mine to hold my legs open. At the same time, he draws my hair to the side and presses a deep, lingering kiss to my neck.

I flush scarlet from head to toe, dampness soaking my cotton underwear. "Nikolai...,"

It's a whine, and my wiggling only gets worse when Max and Bastien come to stand on either side of me, their nostrils flaring.

"Fuck the food," Nik growls with a lick. "I vote we eat you instead."

His words pull a gush of slick from my channel, and I shift restlessly. Nik continues to drop soft kisses on my skin, making me squirm until he wraps his hands gently around my arms, holding me in place. Holding me open for them.

A flash of fear makes me pause, and Nikolai lets go immediately. "Shit, little bird, I'm sorry."

"No." Shaking my head, I settle back against him. "I know where I am, Nik. It's okay."

His hands settle against my skin once more, and I breathe

deeply, inhaling the scents rising in the room, so deep that I can almost taste them on my tongue.

"I might have some issues with food," I lick my lips, "but I'd have no issues with deep-throating some apple pie right now."

Max growls as I slide a look at him from under my lashes. "I won't say that didn't make me hard as a rock, love, but no pie for you until you've eaten some real food."

My stomach gurgles at that exact moment, and Luc comes to stand in front of me with a knowing smirk.

"We're going to play a game, brat." He traces his fingers down the softness of my dress, grazing my breasts. I try to push myself into his hand, but Nikolai's grip is firm, and I hiss in displeasure. *I already don't like this game.*

"I'm going to feed you." Luc lifts a strawberry to my mouth and carefully applies the juice to my lips like he's painting them. I lick my lips, gathering the sweet tartness on my tongue. "And if you do as you're told, then you'll get a treat."

Oh. *Maybe I might like this game.*

I wriggle my hips. "I can be good."

Nik groans behind me, and I bite my lip as his cock swells underneath my ass. "Fighting dirty, little bird."

His voice sounds strained, and I shift my face to him, grinning as I grind down over his length and he swears. "Well, I'm glad I'm not the only one suffering here."

My smugness lasts for approximately ten seconds, right up to the second that I hear a snip and swivel my head to see Luc on his knees, cutting up my dress with a pair of scissors. "*Luc!*"

Mortified, I'm helpless to do anything but watch as he cuts up the full length of my dress, gradually revealing my naked skin to the heated eyes of my pack. Luc sets the scissors aside and gives me a savage grin, before he takes the sides of my dress and yanks, tearing the rest until it flutters either side of me. My nipples peak at the cool bite of the air, and my head falls back to Nikolai's shoulder as he nuzzles my hair. Just having their eyes on me, knowing that my body is completely in their hands...*fuck*. I have zero issues with that. Heat travels through my body, sparking my nerve endings until my hips shift, already seeking relief.

"Get on with it," I moan to Luc, and he holds up a small piece of chicken. "Open wide, brat."

Glaring at him, I obediently open my mouth and he pops the small piece past my lips, making sure to graze his fingers along them as he withdraws. I narrow my eyes as I chew and swallow. I wait for the nausea, the itching that comes with eating any sort of food that isn't OC-approved, but nothing happens. I suck in a breath and look up at Luc.

"You doing okay?" His eyes are soft, and I nod. "More," I breathe, and a satisfied smile stretches across his face. "Not yet. First, your reward."

"My reward?" I can't take my eyes off my dark alpha as he takes some strawberry off the plate. "Turns out I'm quite hungry too," he offers nonchalantly, and I gasp when he presses the cold fruit to my nipple. He rubs the fruit back and forth across it, encouraging them into hard pebbles that sting with sensitivity. The cream Bastien gave me has helped, and when Luc presses his mouth to my breast, the only thing I feel is pleasure. Tipping my head back, I squirm desperately as he sucks on one, before switching to the other and abruptly pulling back.

Fuck. They're going to kill me.

"Luc" I whine, but he only holds up a grape, his eyebrow raised. Dutifully, I open my mouth and he slides in the sweet fruit, waiting until I open my mouth to show him I've finished.

"Good girl," Max purrs, and my eyes practically roll

back in my head. He takes a step forward, swiping another piece of chicken from the plate. "You like being our good girl, don't you, sweetheart?" Max murmurs, as I chew down the meat. Any hesitation on my part has vanished, my mind focused only on getting them to ease the yearning in my body. My core clenches again at his words, and I nod, my eyes wide as he slides his hand down to my curls, his fingers tugging at them until I twist, nearly knocking Nikolai off balance.

"Eat the rest," Max purrs, "And we'll show you how good girls get rewarded."

I wriggle and pant my way through the rest of the food without complaint until Luc lifts it up, showing me the empty plate triumphantly.

"Look at that, brat," he smirks, his green eyes glittering. "You get full marks."

I bare my teeth at him. "Reward now, please." Fuck the food. I'm going to implode if they don't touch me *right fucking now*.

Max lifts my chin up as Nik holds my arms in his gentle grasp. "You're going to eat," he demands. "And we'll play this game as many times as we need to, but you are going to eat at least three square meals a day. Promise me."

"I promise!" In desperation, I try to rub myself over Nikolai, but the angle isn't right and I let out a frustrated cry. "*Please!*"

"Tell me what you'd like as your reward, sweetheart," Max strokes my hair back from my face, and I glare at him in frustration. "Apple pie!"

He grins darkly at me. "Here?" he asks, tracing his finger over my mouth. "Or here?" His hand swoops down, fingers sliding straight through my slick, the barest brush of my pussy as I buck. "There," I beg. "Please, Max. It hurts."

Max unbuckles his pants, releasing his long, curved cock as I sag back against Nikolai. *Finally*.

Nik moves me forward on his lap until he's holding me up, his strong arms gripping the underside of my knees and holding me up to Max like an offering. I can't move, can't do anything but breathe heavily as Max slides his dick up and down my slit.

"Shit," he breathes, his face dark. "You're drenched, baby."

Without another word, he surges inside me, pushing me back against Nikolai as I clamp down on him with a scream. He pulls out and pushes into me again, his cock filling me over and over until the kitchen is filled with the scent of us.

Luc pulls my face to him from Nikolai's shoulder, and I stare at him wildly. "Suck, brat." He slides two of his fingers into my mouth, and I wrap my tongue around them, sucking in the rhythm that Max and I have found. Luc groans as he slides them out, leaning in to kiss me deeply.

"Hold her still," he tells Nik, and I lose sight of him as he moves away. Max shifts a little, and I cry out at the feel of something circling underneath where Max is still thrusting. Luc's finger breaches the edge of my rim, testing my resistance before he slides his finger in as far as it'll go.

I moan raggedly, my face turned into Nikolai's shoulder, and he murmurs into my ear. "Let me hear you scream, little bird."

I feel so *full*. When Bastien steps forward, his fingers tugging gently at my breasts, I clench around Max's hips. Bastien's fingers move down to where Max and I are joined, Luc's fingers still pushing and pulling gently inside my back entrance as my beta leans in and gently rubs against my clit before squeezing it between his fingers.

My vision goes white as Max bellows, his knot locking

us together as every muscle in my body clenches, sparks setting my body alight in waves as I contract against him.

I barely feel Max leaning in, his arms wrapping around me tightly as he lifts me from Nik's lap, careful to keep my body from pulling against his knot as he slides down against the wall. Burying my face in his shoulder, I move my body in small undulations, chasing the last of the sparks before they fade away and I'm left a trembling, exhausted omega held firmly on her alpha's knot.

Heavy breathing fills the kitchen as we all take a moment to catch our breath. Max reaches up and strokes the back of my head. "How are you feeling?"

"I'm done," I grumble. "You've finished me off."

His body shakes with laughter underneath me, and I stay where I am as I feel his knot loosen.

Behind me, Bastien groans. "We need to clean up. Leah just messaged, they're coming up in a minute."

Max groans. Carefully, he pulls us up, wrapping my legs around his waist as I cling to him. I'm not sure I can walk on my own just yet. "I'm cleaning Ava up. You guys can get the kitchen, right?"

I shift my face slightly when lips press against my cheek, and Luc's green gaze watches me carefully. "I'm good," I promise him. "I don't think I can go through that every meal, though."

He snickers. "Just remember what's waiting for you in bed if you eat like a good girl, brat. I'm more than happy to remind you if you forget."

I hide my smile in Max's shoulder as he carries me upstairs.

I'm more than happy to be reminded.

Chapter Fifty-Nine
Ava

When I finally surface, feeling a little more human after the best nap in the world, I find Leah and Nash in the kitchen. Nash dashes over to me immediately, mumbling out a greeting as he presses his ear against my belly. "How long before they're here?"

I laugh. "Not long, I promise."

Leah ushers me into a chair, dropping a steaming cup of red tea in front of me.

"Raspberry leaf," she says confidently when I look at her askance. "It's supposed to be good in your last trimester. We need to look after my niece and nephew."

I run my hand absently over my stomach, her words sinking in and reminding me of the family I've discovered. "Aunty Lee-Lee," I tease, and she wrinkles her nose. "Absolutely not. Cool Aunt Leah, please."

I snort a laugh at her pose and take a sip of the tea. It's not as good as coffee, but it'll do. Leah settles in opposite me with her own cup as Nash turns on the telly in the main room, the sound of his favorite turtles coming through the doorway.

"Where is everyone?" I ask, and she waves her hand. "They had some things to do for the house, so they're down in the workshop. They wanted to get it done, before…,"

I swallow, putting down my cup. Before I risk all of us by putting my face on the news.

Glancing at Leah, I see her chin wobble before she drops her head, hiding her face behind her red hair. Guilt twists in my gut. "Leah?"

She looks back up with a watery smile. "I'm fine, Ava. I'm just worried about all of you."

The guilt gets worse. I've been so wrapped up with the pack and our plan that I haven't even talked to her properly about it. And this affects Leah just as much as it does us.

Because if it goes wrong, Leah and Nash are going to run.

"Are you okay?" I ask her. "I'm sorry that I haven't been around much." Leah shakes her head. "You've had enough going on. I think… it's just sinking in, y'know? Like, we have a real shot at doing this, Ava. At taking it all down. As much as I'm absolutely petrified, this is the first time I've felt any sort of hope that things might change."

I stare at her, this beta who gave us everything for her family. Leah stays on the sidelines, not part of the pack, caring for Nash and the rest of us, helping Bastien to pick out lotions and not making a murmur about how she might be affected. Reaching out, I grab her hand. "Thank you. For everything you've done for me since I got here, Leah."

Her cheeks flush. "Don't make me cry," she warns. "It's not a pretty sight."

Hesitating, I look into my cup. "What do you want, Leah?" I ask quietly. "If this insane plan actually works, and we can leave here. What would you want to do?"

Her brown eyes soften, and she looks toward the window. "I'd like to go back to teaching. I didn't have chance to pass my final exams before... everything happened."

I nod. "You're a born teacher. You're so patient with Nash."

She grins. "I love that kid. He's got Em's sass and Nikolai's heart. He's gonna be a heartbreaker when he's older." She side-eyes me. "He loves you, you know."

A lump appears in my throat. "I know. And having these two won't change that, Leah. I'm doing this for them, but I'm doing it for Nash too. I want him to have a life free of all of this."

She pats my hand. "You're going to be a great mom, Ava."

I can't stop the sob. "Great. Now I'm crying!"

Both of us smile at each other with watery eyes, until a commotion outside makes our head swing around. Leah dashes to the door and sticks her head out, briefly murmuring something before coming back in and pushing the door shut. I raise my eyes as she leans against it, doing the worst impression of nonchalant I've ever seen.

"It's fine," she says breezily. "They just need us to stay out of the way."

"Out of the way of what?"

"Er... they're fixing some of the railings on the stairs. Some of them are a bit loose, and they're worried about you falling."

She shifts from foot to foot, avoiding my eyes, and I raise a brow at her but leave it be.

The odd thumping noise draws my attention, footsteps banging over our heads as Leah maintains a determined stream of chatter.

Finally, the door swings open, and four very pleased men pile through with swagger in their steps. Nikolai is first, his blue eyes lit up with anticipation as he pulls me out of my chair and sweeps me into a kiss that leaves me dizzy.

"What's going on?" I ask with a breathless laugh. "I've heard all sorts of noises, and Leah wouldn't tell me anything."

Leah curtseys dramatically. "Just as we planned!"

Nik laughs, his normally serious face alight. "We have a surprise for you, little bird."

My stomach twists as I look between them. "For me?"

Even Luc's normal smirk is absent, a hint of boyish excitement in his green eyes that leaves me a little weak at the knees. He leans forward and bops me on the nose.

"We're not going to tell you," Max interjects with a grin. "You'll have to come and see."

Before I can move, darkness drops over my face. When I gasp, Bastien's voice sounds in my ear. "Trust us, love. We don't want to ruin the surprise."

Rather than carry me as they like to do, they carefully guide me out of the door and over the wooden floor, my steps creaking as we reach the stairs and slowly climb up. I can't stop smiling at the excitement radiating from them – whatever this is, it was worth it to see them like this. Carefree and happy.

When we reach the top of the stairs, I hesitate. I'm not overly familiar with this part of the house, used to going the other way up to my nest, so I wait for them to nudge me before I move. Several scents intertwine in the air, not giving me a clue.

"Are we going to a bedroom?" I ask lightly. "Because you know you don't have to blindfold me for that, right?"

Luc swats me on the ass and I squeal. "I have a feeling you'd enjoy it though, brat."

I shiver. *He's not wrong*.

We slow to a stop, Max and Nik letting go of my hands. I

can almost taste the shift on my tongue as excitement turns to nervousness in the air. I can't see much through the blindfold no matter how much I strain my eyes.

"Okay." I'm getting a little nervous. "What now?"

Hands gently settle on my hips and turn me, and a hint of warm gingerbread curls around me as hands lift up and remove the blindfold. Blinking, I look up at Nikolai. We're in a doorway, and I can see the hallway behind him.

He stares at me, his jaw working nervously. Reaching up, I brush through his hair, and something like dust falls out. Rubbing it between my fingers, it feels like... sawdust?

Taking my hands, he gently kisses the knuckles on my left hand, then the other. "I know you were worried about not having things in place for the twins, little bird. So, we made you something."

"Technically, Nik did most of the work," Bastien jokes, but his voice is a little unsteady. "We just helped with the heavy lifting."

A hand brushes my shoulder "Turn around, love," Max coaxes me, and Nik nods.

Slowly, I spin in place before stopping still, my breath leaving me in a whoosh as I look around the room.

Two large windows are adorned with simple white muslin curtains, the breeze outside making them flutter invitingly. Cream walls surround the room with a matching rug on the wall. And against the far corner, there's—

I bring my hands to my mouth on a sob.

"Oh," I whisper. "This is...,"

Two wooden cribs sit against the wall with fresh white blankets draped over them. Behind them, a painted willow tree decorates the wall in pale green. There's a chair in the corner of the room that looks comfortable enough to sleep on, and a small matching wooden table opposite with a chest of drawers packed full of *things*.

"I made a list," Bastien says carefully as I take a step forward. "When we did the research. It took a while to get hold of everything, but if there's anything missing, we can grab that too. We've got a whole store cupboard full of diapers and everything."

I smile tearfully at him. "Of course you did," I tease, and he grins at me. My organized beta.

Luc and Max stay quiet, giving me small smiles when I turn to them. But it's Nikolai, lingering in the doorway, that I grab by the hand.

"You made all of this? For them?" I ask. He settles his hands on my stomach as his eyes search mine. "I figured that our children deserved their own nursery. Do you like it?"

My heart feels too full for my chest. "I love it," I whisper. "Nik, this is… incredible."

His shy smile settles into me like warm sunlight, and I spin back around with a laugh. Tugging Nik into the room, I trail my fingers over the reddish wood of the cribs, admiring the smoothness and the intricate whirls he's engraved.

"I left a space for their names," he rumbles as his arms close around me, his chin settling atop my head. "When we know."

I twist to blink up at him as Luc steps forward. "Have you thought about names, love?"

I shift a little on my feet. I have been thinking about names, but I haven't spoken to them about it yet. I take Nik's hand in mine and wind our fingers together.

"Emery," I breathe. "I want to call her Emery. But only if it's okay with you, and Nash."

Nik's mouth opens, his eyes misting as he swallows hard and tilts his head up to the ceiling. His hands grip mine tightly. Around me, the pack shifts, moving a little closer until I'm surrounded by their warmth.

Nik finally looks back at me, a sheen of moisture across

his eyes. "I think," he says hoarsely, "Em would have been honored, sweetheart."

"Emery Grey," Max says, with a smile. "It's got a ring to it."

Luc nudges me. "What about our little man?"

I chew on my lip. "I can't decide. Maybe Nash would like to have a say?"

Nik groans, dashing his hand over his eyes. "Unless you want our son to be named after a ninja turtle, I'd suggest keeping Nash far away from any baby-naming."

Later, at dinner, I tentatively broach the subject with Nash despite Nik's concern. He looks up at me, his mouth dropping open in excitement. "I can name him?"

"We-e-ll," I say. Belatedly, nerves hit me at the thought of my son being named after a large green TV character with a penchant for bandanas and sewers. Luc smothers his laugh with a cough when I glare at him. "Why don't you come up with a name that you like and we can see if it fits?"

Nash nods determinedly, and I send a brief prayer skywards that I don't end up with a son called Donatello. He's silent all through the rest of dinner, and I even manage to finish a small second helping of chicken and rice. Luc scoops it onto my plate, his eyes gleaming, and I nearly choke when he leans down and purrs into my ear. "Such a good girl."

Oooh. I wonder if my face is as scarlet as it feels. And if we might be able to repeat some of the fun from the kitchen in bed tonight.

Nash climbs over Bastien and snuggles into my side as we settle on the couches after dinner, Max and Luc arguing good-naturedly over a games console as Leah demands a film. "Ava?" he whispers. "I thought of a name."

"You did?" I say with surprise, giving him a big grin. "What is it?"

He stretches up, putting his little face close to mine, so close that I can see the flecks in his eye color. "Are you ready?" he asks seriously, and I bite my lip, not wanting to laugh. "I am."

Leaning in close to my ear, he whispers the name. My eyes round with surprise, and he pulls back to grin at me. "Did I do good? Does it fit?"

We've got everyone's attention now, the pack and Leah watching my face. I'm careful to school my reaction as I look around with wide eyes, and back to Nash.

"I think," I say, drawing the words out. "That it's a brilliant name, Nash."

"Well?" Luc demands impatiently. "What is it?"

I ruffle Nash's hair. "Tell them, sweetheart."

He bounces to his feet excitedly, settling his hands on his hips. "Leo Grey," he announces.

Leo Grey. Emery Grey.

Leo and Emery.

Bastien throws his arm around my shoulders, pulling me close. "Best names ever," he breathes into my hair, and I have to agree with him.

CHAPTER SIXTY
AVA

My feet shift from side to side as I stretch to massage my lower back, hoping to ease the aching. A pair of hands replace my fingers, and Luc's voice rumbles in my ear. "You're hurting."

Shaking my head, I look up at him with a small smile. "I'm fine. I'm just feeling it a little more now."

Luc watches my face with a crease between his brows. "Ava," he hesitates. "We can still wait and do this afterwards."

After I've given birth to the two giant-size babies currently kicking each other in my stomach.

"No." My voice is firm, not wanting to hash out the argument again. "We can't wait any longer, Luc. It's been two weeks since Christian's video, and if we don't do it now, we'll lose the momentum."

"I still don't like it," he groans.

You and me both.

Turning, I look around at the hive of activity around us. Bastien is setting up his gear, Max and Nikolai helping him as we wait for the Winter pack to arrive. Lifting my finger, I chew on my thumbnail nervously. "When did we last hear from them?"

"Yesterday." Luc hits a particularly sore spot on my back, and I can't stop my groan from slipping out. He pauses, and I push myself into him. "Don't stop. It feels amazing."

He resumes his massage, and I tilt into him a little. "I hope they're okay."

We agreed to maintain as much silence as possible, given that Christian is currently a wanted man. The government haven't come out and said it, but there have been whispers.

And my father is now in command of the Omega Compound and the heat nests. My throat closes up as I think of all the omegas now under his control, and my hands start to shake.

"Hey," Luc turns my face to his, his thumbs stroking my cheekbones. "We'll get this done, and then we'll go home, okay?"

"Are you sure it's safe?" I ask, and he presses his lips together. "I trust Bastien," he offers. "And he's certain that nobody can track us to the house. It's different for the Winter pack. We've never shared our location with anyone."

We're interrupted by the sound of vehicles crunching over gravel, and everyone stops. Nik strides to the doorway of the warehouse and pokes his head outside.

"It's them," he calls back, raising a hand in welcome.

The tension in the room releases, everyone letting out a breath of relief as doors slam. Slowly, I lumber over to the doorway. Since I can't see my feet anymore, walking has become a high-intensity exercise. Luc stays close to me, clearly remembering my stumble down the last stair yesterday. I roll my eyes.

"I'm not going to fall on my ass just walking across a floor," I snipe, and he pinches my ass lightly. "If you think

I'm letting you out of my sight today, brat, you're gravely mistaken."

When I stop and face him, he gives me a tiny smile that doesn't reach his eyes. Sighing, I take a step forward, and his arms fold around me as I lay my head on his chest, listening to his pounding heartbeat.

"Sorry," I mumble into his shirt. "I know this is hard for you. I shouldn't be making it worse."

Gathering my hair into his fist, he gently tugs my head back. "I love you," he tells me, and I immediately soften. "I love you, too."

He kisses me deeply, cradling my face in his hands and I soften into him until he's holding me up. A whistle sounds in the background and we break apart, my cheeks a furious shade of scarlet as I spot Ace Winter grinning in the doorway.

He waves at me cheerfully, and Devlin elbows him as he walks past, nodding to me and Luc as he heads over to Bastien. Harper appears, tucking herself under Ace's arm as they move towards us.

"How are you feeling?" are the first words out of Harper's mouth as she pulls away from Ace and steps forward. Her eyes drop to my belly and widen.

"I know," I say ruefully. "It's got to be quads. Max clearly made a mistake."

Harper laughs and encloses me into a gentle hug. "How are you really feeling?" she whispers.

How am I really feeling?

"Petrified," I admit. The bags under my eyes show just how little sleep I've been getting the last few nights.

She squeezes me in unspoken agreement.

"I can't believe we're doing this," she says as we turn to watch the preparations. "Have you decided what you're going to say?"

The butterflies in my stomach explode into full-blown anxiety. I don't know what to say. I don't even know where to begin. The attempts I've made to scribble down some sort of script are currently littering the floor of Bastien's office, scrunched up into little balls of failure.

Clearing my throat, I mutter, "I'm going to wing it."

Harper nods, and I follow her gaze to where Rogue and Christian stand to the side in deep conversation. Harper smiles sadly. "They've had a lot of time to talk through things, the last few weeks. It's good to see them getting closer."

"They weren't close before?" I ask.

Harper shakes her head. "Christian never told Rogue anything when he was growing up," she says quietly. "It was only after they saved me from Jason that he finally told him what happened to his mother."

My eyebrows raise as I look at the ex-Director. Sharply dressed in a crisp grey suit with a white shirt, he looks perfectly at ease as he talks to Rogue. To keep that kind of secret to yourself for so many years... what would that do to someone?

The hairs on the back of my neck raise, and I turn to the doorway behind us. My stomach squeezes as I glance around, but I can't put my finger on what drew my attention.

"What is it?" Harper turns with me and scans the same area, her brows drawn. "Did you hear something?"

"No." Pausing, I take a final look around. "I'm a little on edge, I think."

I shrug, but the prickling sensation doesn't go away. Instinctively, I move closer to Nikolai, and he glances up at me, his blond hair ruffled. "What's wrong, little bird?"

"Nothing. I'm just nervous."

Nik unfolds himself from the speaker he's been working on and pulls me into a hug. I breathe in the familiar gingerbread scent, closing my eyes as he rubs a hand soothingly up and down my back. "We're nearly done," he reassures me. "I know it's hard to sit and wait."

"We are done," Bastien interjects, and we turn to face him. He's surveying the set-up with his hands on his hips, his gray eyes the darkest I've ever seen them. "Are you ready, sweetheart?"

Nope. I'm definitely not ready.

I take a step back and jump when I bump into Nikolai. His heavy hands settle on my shoulders, and he rubs them carefully. "You can still change your mind," he says softly. "Everyone would understand if you don't want to do this right now."

Fear clamps down on me like a vice, dizziness making my head spin. The black box marked out on the floor stands out like a pulsing beacon, making me want to curl up into a ball and hide until all of this goes away.

I am not brave. I am nobody.

Just one omega. How the hell did I think I could do this?

"Ava." I jump, my eyes moving to Harper where she stands in front of me, her amber eyes dark with understanding.

"I can do this," she says with conviction. "You don't have to get up there."

At her words, a small thread of fire burns through the fear wracking my body.

I have to do this. For my children. For Emery.

For Harper, and every omega who's currently under the control of my sadistic father.

I owe it to them to try.

Wetting my trembling lips, I offer Harper a shaky smile. "Nobody changed the world by doing nothing, right?"

Nik squeezes my hand, and I squeeze it back before dropping it and walking over to the black square. Bastien moves with me, his hand gripping mine tightly as he shows Harper and I where to stand.

Max and Luc close in on me, and Max takes my face in his hands.

"I'm so damn proud of you, baby," he breathes, his honey brown eyes scanning my face. "Whatever happens."

My heart feels too full for words as I stare at Max. Without him, I would never have had the chance to fight. My children would have been taken from me, and I would be back in the heat nests, pushed to the brink before my body gave up.

"Look at what you did, Max," I whisper back. "You made this possible."

His eyes glitter, and he shakes his head. "*You* are what made this possible, love."

He takes a step back and swipes his arm over his eyes as Luc steps forward, anxiously running his eyes over my face and body. Of all of my pack, Luc was the hardest to convince that this should happen, and I can still see the worry in his eyes as he presses his forehead against mine.

"Next to you," he breathes. "Not behind you."

I can't stop the sniffle, and he closes his eyes before he lifts his mouth and presses a soft kiss to my forehead.

"Whatever happens," he whispers. "You are not alone."

I am not alone.

I have friends, a pack. A family.

And it's time the world learned that omegas have a voice too.

Harper takes her position next to me, and her hand drops, her fingers linking with mine.

"Who would have thought?" she breathes, as Bastien switches the bright lights on. I blink at his shadow, the light too bright to see properly.

Chapter Sixty

Squeezing Harper's hand, I manage a strangled laugh. "I know. Just look at us now."

Bastien looks between us. "I'm going to start the countdown, and when the red light goes on here – we're live. Harper, you're still okay to go first?"

When Harper nods, Bastien looks to me and I smile.

"I love you," I mouth, and he blows me a kiss, pressing his hand against his heart as he steps back.

"On my count," he calls, and everyone stills.

Harper and I face the camera, both of us barely breathing. My hand drops to my stomach.

"Five…"

"Four…"

"Three…"

"Two…"

Leo and Emery Grey. This one's for you.

"One…"

Chapter Sixty-One
Luc

The red light blinks on.

Harper and Ava share a final glance before Harper turns to the camera and begins to speak.

I should be listening, but I can't take my eyes off my omega.

Ava stands proudly, her shoulders back as she stares directly into the camera. Her hazel eyes are bright, her expression fierce and her hands wrapped firmly around her bump.

She looks so small, especially next to Harper given she only reaches her shoulders, but she's never looked so fierce, or beautiful.

A lump appears in my throat as I watch her, and I have to glance away, clenching my fists to fight off the urge to sweep in and pull her away from the millions of eyes watching her.

Beside me, Max and Nikolai look equally struck. Nik's eyes flicker between Ava and Harper, his jaw clenched as he listens to Harper's story, but Max's sole focus is on Ava, every shift she makes mirrored in his body language.

Bastien darts from camera to camera, fiddling with his

laptop, but his eyes keep sliding back to Ava too. I wonder if the reality of his plan is sinking in.

What happens after this?

This is the part that we have no control over. After this, it's up to the public, and if they see enough in Harper, Ava and Nikolai's story to change their beliefs. It's a Hail Mary, at best, but it's the only chance we have.

Nikolai flinches, and I follow his gaze to Harper. Her face is just as fierce as Ava's, the emotional toll this is taking on her clear in the lines of stress on her face as she speaks.

Across from me, Devlin Winter shifts on his feet, mirroring the urges we all have to jump in front of our omegas and protect them from this.

As Harper talks about the heat hormones she was given by Jason, bile burns the back of my throat. The burning need, the begging that Harper describes in clear tones – Ava experienced that twenty times over. I'm not sure that I can listen to it without losing my shit.

Beside you, not behind you.

I promised Ava that I would be with her, and I'm not going to look away. Even if it breaks me.

Harper finishes speaking, and she turns to Ava, squeezing her hand. For the first time, I see her shake, her hand trembling where it rests on her stomach.

"Come on, baby," Max murmurs, taking a step closer. "You can do this."

My breathing comes a little faster as I watch her panic, her eyes darting from side to side.

Bastien takes a step forward before he hesitates. None of us wanted to diminish her story in the eyes of the public by standing next to her, and Ava explicitly told us that she wanted to film on her own. But I can see the panic in her posture, the fierce expression melting away. She looks petrified.

It's Nikolai who makes the call for us, striding out into the light and taking Ava's other hand in his.

"Together, little bird," he reminds her, and she blinks up at him, gratitude in her face. Steeling her shoulders, she takes a deep breath.

And then she tells them everything.

Chapter Sixty-Two
Ava

I take a deep breath.

"My name is 864. I am an omega, and I have no rights.

"When I first awakened, I was sent to the Omega Compound. I stayed there for two years, and just like Harper, I experienced the degradation and humiliation that passes for omega training.

"Once, I tried to stand up but couldn't, and I realized that I hadn't stood on two feet for more than a week. I still experience pain in my legs to this day.

"The omega creed dictates every movement that an omega can make. We're not allowed to look alphas in the eye, or to choose our own food. At the compound, food was used as a punishment by the guards. If you didn't do as you were told, or if they didn't like you, you didn't eat. If you passed out, you received a whipping.

"Instead of a bed, I slept on a stone floor in a cell that

wasn't big enough for me to walk in. We were kept weak, malnourished, and tortured physically and mentally.

"I would often wonder why this was happening to me. What had I done? What had omegas done, to be judged so harshly? It must be something horrendous, right? Must be something awful. You wouldn't treat a dog the way that we were treated.

"The night that I left the compound, a guard came to my cell. He pinned me down while others watched and raped me. He recorded himself doing it, and used the biology that we are born with to force my body to receive him. I did not consent. I did not want it, and he didn't care. He took something from me that night. The last bit of innocence I had left.

"After my rape, I was immediately taken to the heat nests, and kept there for more than six months.

"During that six-month period, I was kept sedated and injected more than twenty times with a heat serum. Over and over again, sometimes twice within the same week. Every time, I was given to alphas to rut on.

"Heat serum is unbearable, for omegas. It is an artificial stimulant that pushes our bodies into readying for pregnancy, stimulating a natural heat. Omegas only have a natural heat every year or so, because of the toll it takes on us. To go through so many... I nearly died.

"Heat nests are breeding factories. Those of you who have adopted a child... this is how their life began. With a woman tied to a bench, forcibly injected and raped over and over again. When we give birth, we're put back in within weeks or even days. There is no sense of time, no care, no privacy. You lose track of everything. I'd wake up knowing that my body had been used, covered in scents and fluids that weren't mine. I don't know how many times that happened to me.

"You have seen my face on the news over the past few

weeks. It's been reported that I escaped from a hospital with the help of an alpha, Max Grey.

"Max saved my life. He found me in a coma, five months pregnant and on the edge of death because of the treatment I received in the heat nests. At this very moment, dozens of omegas are being forcibly impregnated and their children taken from them. Whilst I was in hospital, I was restrained with a metal collar around my neck and leather restraints on my wrists and ankles. Because I was apparently such a *threat* to society.

"Is this the kind of world we want to live in? Is this the kind of world you want your children to live in? Those of you who have adopted children, are you comfortable looking into their faces and knowing what their biological mother went through, and what she may still be going through?"

I drop a hand to my stomach.

"I didn't choose to become pregnant. But now that I am, I don't want my children to be ripped away from me," I say, my voice breaking. "I don't want my daughter to wake up one day and be dragged to the compound, locked away and forced to breed in another hopeless cycle. But that's what's going to happen if nothing changes."

"The omega creed is wrong, and it needs to end. I am sorry – I am so sorry that betas aren't able to have children. But to persecute another race the way that omegas have been is *wrong*."

"I am not saying this to incite hysteria, or to drag people into another Omega War. We are trying to save the ones we love from going through what we have gone through for the last two decades. What I have gone through. What Harper has gone through."

"We have been locked away with no voice for too long." My throat closes.

"I have found my voice, and I am speaking out."

"I am asking you to look around. Look in the mirror. Look at your wives, your daughters, your sisters, your mothers. Ask yourself what you would do if someone took them away and forced them to give up their bodies, their lives for something that wasn't their fault."

"I don't have all of the answers. I don't know how to fix the birth issues. But I know that I deserve to live freely. And if nothing changes, I will end up back in those nests. I would choose death before I let them take me again."

"Look into my face," I challenge them. "Look into my face and tell me that I deserve to die. The omega creed is a death sentence, and it needs to be repealed. Omegas deserve to be free. My children deserve to be free."

"My name is Ava Stone. I am an omega, and I deserve to be free."

"Please, speak up for us."

Heaviness in my limbs drags me down as I finish speaking, silence a weight in the air. The ache in my back starts back up again with a vengeance, and I sag against Nikolai in exhaustion.

It's his turn to talk about Emery, but when I look up at his face, he's frowning, lifting his hand to his eyes to peer out, past the blinking red light to the warehouse.

"What's wrong?" I whisper. "Nik?"

He takes a step forward, his face paling as he lifts up his hand. "Stop!"

It all happens so *fast*.

An unfamiliar male voice shouts, his tone furious. A dark silhouette appears against the lights as I lift my hand to try and see. It's too wide and stocky to be one of my pack. I freeze, unable to move as Harper screams, her cry piercing my ears.

Rat-tat-tat-tat.

A heavy weight tackles me to the ground, and I cry out as

Chapter Sixty-Two

I land awkwardly, a shooting pain running up my stomach. I can't breathe, my face pressed against the damp ground, small stones digging into my cheeks as I whimper.

My head feels foggy as the shouting and snarling grows louder.

They've found us. This is it.

The weight suddenly vanishes, and I squeeze my eyes shut, readying myself for harsh hands. My mind races as I try to think.

Where are they? Where are my pack? Have they been hurt?

I flinch, a petrified whine tearing from my chest as I'm lifted from the ground. My arms thrash as I scrabble to pull myself free. But the arms are familiar, sandalwood twisting around me. *Luc.*

"Ava," he croaks out. "It's alright, sweetheart. Talk to me. Are you okay?"

The relief is all-consuming, but the pain in my stomach only grows.

"Luc. It hurts," I whimper. "The babies."

He shouts for Max, and the sound of sobbing reaches my ears.

"What's going on?" My voice sounds funny.

"Don't worry," Nik appears at my side, his face distraught as he cups my cheek. "You're going to be all right, little bird."

"I'm fine," I mumble. "Don't worry."

I can smell iron, and I look woozily down at my stomach as Nikolai runs his hands over me frantically. He pulls back, his face full of relief. "It's not hers."

My mind starts to clear as Nikolai shouts for Max again. Panicked voices sound around us, but they're not focused *on* us.

If it's not mine... then where did the blood come from?

"What's going on?" I grab Luc's sleeve, struggling to lift up my head where he holds me. "Bastien! Max!"

Is this theirs? Blind terror splinters up my insides as I look down at the blood.

He looks down at me, his skin pale and eyes wide as he shakes his head. "They're fine, baby," he chokes out. "It's Christian."

Christian?

"There was a man with a gun, and he was aiming for you." His eyes close. "I thought – but Christian moved so fast. He was in front of you before any of us even realized."

Christian. Christian is hurt.

"Where is he?" I ask Luc. "Can I see him?"

Luc hesitates, but he carries me over to where the Winter pack are gathered around the floor. Harper is crying, her eyes red as Devlin wraps her in his arms. Rogue bends over his father, his face ashen and eyes wet as he leans in, whispering something I can't hear as he cradles Christian's head on his lap.

An expanding patch of crimson stains Christian's white shirt, his smart crisp suit rumpled and ripped. Max is on his knees next to them, his face tight as he and Ace murmur in worried tones.

I push at Luc's arms. Christian *saved* me. Again.

He saved me, and now…

"Let me down, Luc. *Please*."

Reluctantly, he places my feet gently on the ground, wrapping his arm around my waist when I nearly stagger. Pain blossoms in my abdomen, and I suck in a shaky breath as his arms tighten. "I'm all right," I insist, my throat tight as I push it down. "Let me see him."

Luc helps me to kneel next to Max. Christian turns unfocused green eyes towards me, lifting his hand. I take it without hesitation, his fingers icy cold around mine.

He manages a pained smile. "You're all right."

I swallow hard. "Thanks to you," I whisper. "Thank you, Christian."

It doesn't escape me that the last time we were this close, Christian carried me out of my cell and away from Jason. As we watch each other, another memory surfaces, Christian's face full of fury and his hands around Jason's neck as he pulls him off me.

His green eyes flicker, and he coughs, a drop of blood tricking down his chin. Leaning in, I wipe it away with my finger. "I'm sorry," he wheezes. "That I didn't stop it."

I shake my head slowly. "You did stop it."

Max leans back on his haunches next to me, his hand tangling in his hair. "There's no exit wound," he says quietly, "and he's bleeding heavily from his lower back. it's not looking good, Rogue."

It's easy to read between the lines.

Rogue takes a deep breath, his face shadowed in grief as he turns back to his father.

"Dad," he croaks. "Help is coming. You just need to hold on."

Christian smiles, his tone chiding. "Rogue. I know that I'm not walking out of here."

Rogue flinches, his eyes locked on his father. "Dad…,"

"I'm sorry I wasn't a better father," Christian whispers. "These past weeks… I wish we'd had more time together."

Rogue closes his eyes. "You were," he says roughly. "When it counted, you were."

Christian's head lolls to the side. "I'm glad you have Harper," he mumbles. "Hold onto her, son. Don't ever let her go."

Harper wipes her face as she tries to smile. "I won't let him go, Christian," she promises tearfully, and he snorts out a laugh. A spray of blood. Max wipes it away, his expression tense. "Atta girl."

His eyes move slowly to Rogue. "Don't grieve for me, Rogue. I'm a little sad not to see how this turns out, but I'll be with your mother soon."

Rogue nods jerkily, wiping his hand over his eyes. "Say hi to mom for me?" he whispers.

I can't stop the tears coursing down my face.

Christian smiles widely. "I will." His breathing slows, rattling in his chest before stuttering to a stop.

Rogue gently closes his father's eyes with a choked sob.

"I'm so sorry, Rogue," I whisper. Tears soak the top of my dress. He nods as he stares down at his father, and Max gets to his feet, helping me up as we turn away from the pack to give them some privacy as they grieve.

I hope that you've found your peace, Christian, wherever you may be.

As I turn away, Max and Luc close to my side, another pinch drags down in my abdomen and I stumble. Max grabs hold of me, worry tightening his voice. "Ava?"

Shaking my head, I lean my head against his arm.

"I'm fine, Max" I say tiredly. "Where's Bastien?"

"Here, love," he says, walking out from behind a camera with tension lining his shoulders. He opens his arms and I collapse gratefully into them, burying my nose in his throat for a hit of his scent.

"Where were you?" I whisper, and he clears his throat. I pull back at his sheepish expression. "I was… taking out the trash."

"You what?" Belatedly, realization hits me and my eyes widen. "What actually happened? Who was he?"

Bastien shakes his head. "Some crazy beta. I think he lived up around here, must have seen the vehicles and gotten suspicious. There's no sign of anyone else around, I've checked."

I hold in my shudder at the thought of a strange man watching me bare my soul, getting angrier and angrier until he hated me enough to lift a shotgun to my chest.

He probably won't be the only one.

"What about the video?" I ask quietly, and Bastien stiffens. "It was still on," he mutters, "When it happened. It caught everything."

I bite my lip, not sure how I feel about such private moments being broadcast to the world. But I guess it was easy to forget in the chaos.

Another pinch feels like my stomach is being yanked downwards with a pair of pliers, and I double over. This one takes a few seconds to disappear, the frantic tones of my pack registering. Max's voice appears in my eyeline, his face stern.

"You're having contractions," he growls. "Ava. Why didn't you say anything?"

Wait.

"I'm having contractions?" I blink at Max, a hint of panic ticking at my neck. "It's too early!"

He presses his hand to my bump, feeling around with his hand. "I won't know for certain until I examine you," he mutters, "But the sooner we can get you home, the better. Bas, let the Winters know we're leaving. The kit can stay, right?"

Bastien nods. "Nothing to trace it back to us, and we can always come back and get it. It'll take too long to pack."

My breathing sounds harsh and noisy in the confined space, and I bite back a whine as reality trickles in. This could be it. I could give birth today.

I stare at Max with pleading eyes. "I'm not ready for this, Max."

He cups my cheek. "Remember what I said? I am with you. You are not alone. And I'm going to be there every step of the way."

Luc's hand settles on my shoulder. "We're all in, brat. Remember?"

I am not alone.
I have my pack.
I can do this.

Chapter Sixty-Three
Ava

"I can't fucking do this," I gasp out in furious tones as my back bows with the strength of another contraction. "Fuck!"

Sagging as it eases, I collapse back against Luc's chest. He's on the bed behind me, his body cradling mine. Nikolai and Bastien have both had a turn too. Max wipes at his brow as he stands up, pursing his lips.

"You're nearly there, love," he reassures me in a calm voice. "Nearly time to push."

"Fucking finally," I gasp, and Luc presses a kiss to my neck, damp with sweat. "Filthy," he mutters. "Mouth like a sailor."

I curse at him with every bad word I can think of until my body gets ripped apart again.

Motherfucker.

And people used to do this shit more than once?

"No more," I force out, panting. "This is it. I hope you're happy with three, because my legs are closed during any and all future heats."

Luc squeezes my fingers in his. "Sure, brat. Whatever you say."

I can't even give him the stink-eye because another contraction is coming, my stomach twisting and ripping itself apart until I throw my head back against Luc's shoulder and scream.

"Push," Max barks. "Push, Ava!"

"I can't," I sob. "I'm so tired, Max."

"You can," he says firmly. "You're so close, baby. So close to having those babies safe with us. I just need you to *push*."

My body is already responding to his bark, my fingers white as I squeeze Bastien and Nik's hands with everything I have and push down.

Something shifts and Max shouts triumphantly as I limply fall back, Luc holding me up.

A tiny cry breaks the air, and my heart stops. I stare at Max as he stands up, a cloth-wrapped bundle in his arms. "Hello, Leo," he says, smiling down. "Come and meet your mama."

My tears fall freely as I reach out weakly for my son. Max carefully places him in my arms, Luc helping me hold him as we all gaze down in amazement.

Leo Grey stares up at me with a wrinkled brow and blazing blue eyes. A soft tuft of dark hair shifts as he squirms a little, his little mouth opening and closing.

"Hi, Leo," I whisper unsteadily. "I'm your mom."

"Ava," Bastien whispers unsteadily. "He's amazing."

Smiling, I look up at my pack. Bastien and Nik have wide eyes as they crowd around us, and Luc kisses my shoulder gently. "One down, brat."

"One more to go," Max coaxes me, and I reluctantly hand Leo over to Bastien. He almost disappears in his arms, my beta staring down with a hint of panic and a whole lot of love as he carefully strokes a finger down his cheek.

My heart twists at the sight of Bastien cradling him so gently, and I sniff as I turn back to Max. "Okay, I'm ready."

Nik nudges Luc, and he shifts out from behind me, Nik sliding into his place, his warmth soaking into my back as he breathes into my ear. "Nearly there, little bird. I'm so proud of you."

Turning my face into his arm, I rest my forehead against it, soaking up some of his calming vibes. Luc moves into position next to me, Bastien cradling Leo as he watches with a smile on his face.

Luc presses a kiss to my knuckles fervently. "I'm calling Daddy, by the way," he says, eyeballing Bastien. Bastien pulls a face at Leo.

"No way," he coos. "I'm going to be Daddy, aren't I, Leo? Lucien can be Father. He's way too uptight to be daddy."

Luc bristles, and I level them both with a glare as the pain in my stomach returns. "If you don't mind," I gasp, "Can you hash this one out later?"

Luc looks down at me, immediately contrite. "Sorry, baby."

Max calls out, his face a picture of concentration. "Get ready, love. She's coming."

The cramping in my abdomen intensifies again, and I cry out, pushing back against Nik as he braces me firmly.

"You can do it, little bird," he coaxes. His low voice vibrates against my back. "You're so close."

I'm so tired. Exhaustion weighs down my limbs as the rippling in my abdomen blossoms into full-blown agony.

Luc squeezes my hand in his grip, his green eyes focused entirely on me. "Breathe, Ava," he barks. "Eyes on me, okay?"

I stare into his face as the pain increases, until the pressure in my stomach becomes unbearable, and my eyes slide shut on a cry. "I need to push, Max!"

"Push," he commands. His hands squeeze my thighs gently. "Push, love!"

The dragging down sensation in my lower back intensifies until I have no choice but to push, every tendon in my body strained to its absolute maximum as I struggle, pained grunts accompanying every push.

"I'm done," I moan. "I can't. She's not coming."

Nik wipes my damp forehead. "She is, little bird. I promise. We just need you to do one more for us. Just one, and then it's over."

"Over," I breathe. "Never again."

Luc snorts, and I grimace at him. "I mean it, Lucien Grey. Never, ever again."

Luc catches Nik's gaze above my head and quickly nods. "Never again."

I can't even call him out on his blatant lie because the urge to push is intensifying. Shoving myself back against Nik, I push with every fiber of my being until the pressure in my body suddenly releases with a snap.

"Is she here?" I rasp, sagging back. Max is silent at the end of the bed, only the top of his head visible, and panic tightens my throat. "Max?"

There's no crying, no triumphant call. The ice in my chest grows stronger.

"Luc," I ask him desperately. "Where is she?"

Luc glances back at me, his eyes worried. "Max is taking a look at her, baby. Don't worry, it's just taking her a little longer to adjust to being outside."

Oh my god. I bite back a sob, Nikolai's arms wrapping around me. Bastien watches Max, his face pale as he holds Leo gently against his chest.

Chapter Sixty-Three

"Please," I beg, although I'm not sure who I'm praying to. "Please, Emery—"

The cry from tiny lungs is a powerful one, and relief softens my bones as I collapse back into Nikolai, my hands tearing from Luc's to cover my eyes as I shake.

"She's okay," I sob. "Max?"

"She is. I promise, sweetheart. She's just fine. We've got a beautiful daughter."

His voice comes from right next to me, and I blink my eyes open, searching briefly until they come to rest on her.

My daughter is the polar opposite of her brother, downy white hair tickling my cheek as Max passes her into my arms and I breathe her in. "Thank you," I breathe. "Max—,"

He leans in and kisses me gently. "I'm so proud of you, love. Two beautiful babies."

Two healthy babies.

"Emery," I murmur. "She's beautiful, Max."

Her scrunched-up face relaxes a little, the cries settling down to tiny whimpers as her eyes crack open, and I suck in a breath. Her eyes are the brightest shade of amethyst as she stares at me.

"Nik," I whisper. "Look at her."

He presses a damp kiss into my shoulder, his voice shaking. "A miracle. They both are."

Bastien steps forward, and they carefully position me until I have both babies resting against my chest. The cries stop as soon as they're close to each other, each facing the other. I can't stop staring at them, my eyes moving slowly between them in case they vanish before my eyes.

"It doesn't seem real," I murmur. "That they're both here."

Love fills my heart, overflowing into every part of my body. "Where's Nash?" I ask. "And Leah?"

"Leah is probably outside," Max laughs. "And Nash won't be far behind."

Bastien pulls his phone out and shoots off a text. "I give it three minutes."

"Thirty seconds," Luc says gruffly. He's leaning over Emery, her tiny fingers wrapped around his thumb as he watches her, enraptured.

Leo starts to make little smacking noises, his mouth pursing, and I glance at Max in a panic. "He's hungry?"

Max grins at me. "He is. Are you ready?"

I wanted to try breastfeeding, but Max warned me that it might be difficult with the two of them. But as Nik helps me out of my gown and Max carefully positions each twin to a breast, they latch on easily, and I suck in a breath at the feeling of relief. I didn't realize how strange it would feel.

Bastien leans over me, his eyebrows waggling. "Can I try some of that?"

I can't stop the snort that comes out, and I press my lips together firmly. "Bastien!"

Although…

There's a banging at the door, and Nash's voice comes through clearly. "Ava!"

I twist my head to grin at Nik. "Go get our boy." Smiling, he presses one last kiss to my cheek, swapping out with Max, who settles behind me with a contented sigh. "As much as I loved delivering our kids, I wish I'd been able to hold you," he admits quietly, pressing his forehead to my shoulder. I lean back into him, carefully adjusting the babies in my arms as they pull away from me, their tiny bellies full.

"You can hold us now," I say with a smile. "All of us."

His arms sneak around me to gently touch a finger to Leo's cheek. Leo turns his head a little with a coo, and my heart melts.

"Am I biased, or are these the most beautiful babies

you've ever seen?" I ask, and Max laughs against me. "They are, just like their mother."

"Smooth," I grin. "Nicely done, Doc."

Bastien and Luc gently scoop up the twins, and Max pulls my gown back into place as the door opens, Nash's excitement sweeping into the room.

"Ava," he babbles, rushing to the bed. "Where are—,"

He skids to a stop, his eyes rounding as they move from Leo to Emery and back again. He swallows. "Wow," he whispers, moving his eyes to mine. "They're so small!"

He looks a little uncertain as he glances round, and my heart squeezes.

"Can you get me a pillow?" I murmur to Max. When he passes me one, I place it on the bed and motion Nash up. "Come on, sweetheart. Do you want to meet them properly?"

He nods, and Nik helps him up, carefully positioning him. "Just like this, Nashy."

Luc carefully places Leo into Nash's arms, and he blinks as a grin spreads across his face. "Hi, Leo," he whispers. "I'm your brother. Do you like your name? I picked it for you. Leonardo is the best turtle."

Hormones are clearly riding me hard right now because I can't stop the tears from coming as Nash continues to explain his favorite ninja turtles to Leo. Max wipes them away as I sniffle.

Leo stares up at Nash, his blue eyes unwavering as he gurgles, and Nash laughs. "He's talking to me!"

Nash is entranced, and Bastien kneels next to him and carefully adds Emery to the mix. "This is Emery," he explains, and Nash nods. "Just like my mom," he says, his voice wondering as he looks down at her. My throat tightens as I watch the three of them together for the first time. Nash bends down and gently kisses Emery's forehead. "I'm gonna look after you," he promises sweetly.

There isn't a dry eye in the room. Leah edges into view, her face crumpled with emotion. "I need hugs," she announces. "All the baby hugs."

Reluctantly, Nash relinquishes Leo and then Emery to Luc. "Careful, Uncle Luc," he scolds. "They're only tiny." Luc's lip twitches as we all bite back our laughter. "You're a good big brother, Nash," I reassure him, and he grins widely up at me. "I know," he says smugly, and the laughter spills out into the room as Leah takes Emery in her arms.

"She would have loved this," Leah says. Her chin quivers as she bites her lip, staring down at the baby. "You're gonna be a heartbreaker, Em."

Four staunch denials echo through the room, all four of my pack protesting that our daughter will never, ever be allowed to take a single step in the direction of any male, *ever*.

Luc's growl is particularly passionate, and I raise an eyebrow at him. "It's probably gonna happen someday," I warn with a smile, and he grimaces at me.

"Someday. Hopefully when I'm not around to break their legs."

Chapter Sixty-Four
Bastien

These fucking feelings.

Leo stares at me, his blue gaze faintly accusing like he knows that I have absolutely no idea what I'm doing here.

This isn't my first rodeo. I was around for Nash, for the feedings, the playing, even the diaper changes. But as I stare into Leo's eyes, for the first time I feel absolutely fucking terrified.

Is this what being a dad feels like?

A litany of all the things lying around the house that could be dangerous to a child runs through my mind. Every sharp edge needs to be blunted, every socket covered, every surface fucking padded because I don't think my heart could cope with seeing one of these two hurt.

Leo tenses and panic ices over my chest as his skin turns a funny shade of purple.

Is he choking?

A small trumpet noise erupts from his butt, and he relaxes. I sag in relief. Thank fuck it's just gas.

I'm going to be grey-haired in the next two weeks at this rate. Carefully, I position him against my shoulder, cradling his delicate head as I rub at his back. The swaying motion feels natural, but then I start stressing that it's going to make him ill. Can babies get seasick?

Luc appears next to me, his brows raised. "You okay? Looking a little pale there, brother."

"We have to baby-proof everything," I hiss. "Today, Luc."

He gapes at me. "Bas, they can't even walk yet. I'm pretty sure we've got a good few months before we need to worry about it."

Okay. That's good.

Luc's hand grips my shoulder. "What's in your head?"

Word vomit tumbles out of me like a confession at church. "Just thinking of all the shit that can go wrong. Luc, I don't think I can cope with this. I thought he was choking, but he farted, and now I'm worried he's gonna be seasick."

Luc gawks at me, before he wheezes out a laugh. I turn to him in disbelief. "Why are you not freaking out right now?"

Taking a deep breath, Luc smothers his snickers. "What makes you think I'm not? This is scary shit, Bas. We're now responsible for two tiny twins and a very small but vocal omega. I'm petrified."

Eyeballing him accusingly, I point out the obvious. "You don't look petrified."

In fact, he looks remarkably peaceful. He shrugs. "All right. Maybe I'm not as petrified as you, right now. But am I worried about keeping them safe? Yes. Am I panicking that we haven't got everything we need? Also yes."

My brother wraps his arm around me as we both look down to Leo, now peacefully sleeping against my chest.

"Welcome to being a father, Bas," Luc murmurs. "We're going to stress like this for the next few decades at least. Try not to let it all out on the first day."

His voice is wry, and I grumble at him. Leah passes Emery to Nik, and walks over to us, making grabby hands as she coos toward Leo. I huddle away protectively. "Have you washed your hands?" I demand, and she stops to stare at me before shaking her head.

"Huh," she mutters. "I didn't have you pegged for the neurotic one. I thought that'd be Luc."

"Hey!" Luc objects, and Leo is abruptly seized while I'm distracted. I scowl at a smug-looking Leah, already itching to take him back. "Have fun, *Aunty Lee-Lee*."

Her grin is immediately wiped off her face. "Take that back," she demands, and I smirk at her. "No way. Aunty Lee-Lee is easier for them to say anyway. Better get used to it, *Lee-Lee*."

Turning away, I make a beeline for Nikolai and Emery, but he sees me coming and hustles to the other side of the bed before I can get to him.

"Not a chance," he says on a snarl, shaking his head. "I'm having at least ten minutes."

Pouting, I flop down into a chair next to Ava. She blinks at me drowsily, her face set with a peaceful smile. "Hey, you."

Leaning forward, I brush a soft kiss against her lips. "Hey, you. Everyone is being a baby hog."

Her smile widens. "I can't actually remember what they look like," she says mildly, widening her eyes comically. "Think I might be able to get them back at some point?"

Max chuckles, his arm gently wrapped around Ava as they lie together on the bed. "Maybe this time next month, sweetheart."

She shifts a little. "Do you think we might be able to move to the nest?" she asks hesitantly. "There's a lot of scents in here, and it feels a little much. Plus I want everyone close, and there's not enough room here."

Max pulls back immediately. "Of course, we can. Do you want a quick bath before you lie down?"

Ava nods gratefully. "I feel icky. I don't want to mess up the sheets."

Everyone moves into action. Nik and Luc bundle up the babies, buttoning them into adorable clean white matching baby grows. Max does a few final checks on Ava, satisfying himself before he agrees that we can move over to the main house. Ava raises her arms to me, and I gently lift her up as she winces.

"Sore?" I ask her worriedly, and she nods. "It's normal," she assures me. "Remember the research?"

I do remember, but I hate the idea of her being in pain. I guess there's no getting around it after giving birth to two children, but I don't have to like it.

Holding her close, I carry her up to the main house, everyone else following behind. Max runs on ahead to get a bath started, and as I carry Ava through the doors, she lays her head against my chest with a contented sigh. "It's good to be home."

I smile down at her. "Bath, then rest, okay?"

She nods amiably. "Sounds good to me."

Luc and Nik take care of the babies whilst Max and I bathe Ava as gently and as quickly as we can, tipping back her head to wash her hair at her insistence.

When we get to the nest, Luc and Nik are already stretched out, cooing at the babies as they wave their arms on the blanket, space in the middle for Ava to settle. She gathers them into her immediately, sighing with relief as she lays her head back on the soft surface with a yawn.

"Nash should be here," she says softly. "With us."

Nik tilts his head uncertainly. "Want me to get him?"

Ava nods. "Sorry," she says, biting at her lip. "I'd just feel better if he was here too. I feel a little on edge."

"Totally normal," Max reassures her. "Your hormones will be a bit wild for a while, sweetheart. Omegas can become very protective and territorial after giving birth."

Nash appears with Nik, his eyes wide as he surveys the space. "Sleepover?" he asks, and Ava laughs. "It is. We need your help to watch Leo and Emery."

Nash puffs up proudly as he crawls over to Ava, snuggling carefully into her side in his flannel pyjamas and holding out his finger to Leo.

The lines on Ava's forehead finally ease, and she glances at the door. When I push it shut, she offers me a tired smile. "I feel better now."

Soft gurgles fill the air as we all prop ourselves up to watch Leo and Emery. I settle next to Luc alongside Leo, Ava next to Emery with Nash cuddled up against her. Nik is wrapped around her back with Max next to him.

Max falls asleep first, his deep breathing filling the room. "Don't wake him up," Ava whispers. "He's exhausted."

"You need to rest too," I press her. "We'll watch these two." Gently, I press my thumb to the bottom of Emery's feet, fascinated by the way she kicks.

"We all need to sleep," Ava says drowsily. Her eyes are already sliding closed. "There's a lot to do tomorrow."

Nik presses a kiss to her hair. "Tomorrow is another day, little bird. Just rest."

Ava's soft huffs of breath join Max's rumble. Nash is already fast asleep, curled against Ava. Blinking, I lean over to Nik and Luc. "I'll watch them," I offer. "Get some rest."

They nod. "Wake me up in an hour or two," Luc says firmly. "Don't stay awake all night."

"I won't."

Settling in for my watch, I can't help but smile at the tiny bundles, protectiveness a tight fist on my heart.

"Nothing is going to happen to you two," I whisper.

I swear it.

Chapter Sixty-Five
Lucien

I definitely blocked out how high-pitched an angry baby can be.

"Bas," I hiss as Ava stirs. "What are you doing?"

He jiggles Emery frantically, but the kid has lungs like her mother's and screams, her little face scrunched up and red as she waves her fists angrily.

"I don't know!" he hisses. "I think she might be hungry?"

"Pass her here." He hands her over, his face disappointed, and I shake my head at him, amused. "Don't stress it, she still loves you. You just don't have what she needs. Get some sleep."

He grimaces at me, but nods and shuffles up to sprawl down next to Max.

"Ava? Love?" I touch her shoulder gently, and she stirs, her hazel eyes blinking open and widening with horror as Emery's screeching registers. It's saying something that nobody else stirs, not even Nash. It's been a long few days.

"Sorry," I whisper, "but I think she needs to feed."

Ava nods, tiredly pulling herself up and tucking the

blanket around Nash. She unbuttons her shirt – one of mine if I'm not mistaken – and I help her position Emery against her breast until she latches on, her whimpers quickly dying off to small suckling sounds.

Ava strokes her soft head as she feeds, a sweet smile on her face as she watches her daughter. She shakes her head. "I can't believe I made her." Her voice is quiet, full of awe.

"I can," I murmur. "She's incredible. Just like you."

My heart beats a touch harder as I watch them together. Something about Ava's softness in this moment is calling to me. It's nothing to do with sex, but the urge to care for her, to hold her close is almost more than I can take.

"Come here?" I ask quietly, and she looks up at me in surprise. "I need... I need to hold you."

Her whole face softens, and she nods, keeping Emery latched on as she shuffles gingerly down the bed and over to me. As soon as she's within reach I lift her and settle her and Emery in my lap, the urgency I felt lessening as I enclose them in my arms. Ava rests her head on my shoulder with a contented sigh, and I run my hands through her hair, teasing the curls straight before they spring back up again.

"I could stay like this forever," she murmurs.

"Mmm." I drop my mouth to her shoulder, almost tasting the changes in her scent as I inhale. Her vanilla scent has softened, a little sweeter, and there's a hint of musk underneath that I think might be her milk.

I swallow back a groan. She needs to heal, but fuck if I don't want to eat her up right now. I never thought breast milk would do it for me – but then again, anything Ava-related does it for me, so I guess I shouldn't be surprised.

Emery pulls her face away, and Ava gingerly lifts her up. I grab a cloth from the basket I put in here earlier, and help her position Emery over her shoulder. Her little face watches me, her violet eyes almost inquisitive, and I grin as Ava lightly taps her back until she lets out an adorable little belch.

Ava laughs lightly. "That's cute. I didn't think it would be."

It really is. Ava lays her down carefully in her moses basket, and we watch her eyes close as she drifts off, full of milk.

"God, Luc," Ava mutters, returning to curl up in my lap. "What are we going to do?"

Her heartbeat thuds against my chest, mirroring my own. I hold her a little closer, because I don't have an answer to give her, and that scares the shit out of me.

Come morning, our tentative peace will be well and truly broken. We need to find out what's happening out there, and how the public are responding to Ava's words. God, we need to contact the Winter pack and find out how they're doing.

"Tomorrow," I murmur instead, brushing her hair back. "Rest tonight, brat. It'll all be there in the morning."

Ava moves to get off my lap, but my grip tightens. "Stay with me?"

I can't let her go right now. She settles in, her head against my shoulder as she dozes off.

Leaning back against the wall, I watch over my family until the dawn breaks.

Chapter Sixty-Six
Ava

Bracing myself, I stare at the blank television screen as everyone gathers in the living area. I'm ensconced on the couch, my feet resting on Nikolai's lap, Leo in my arms and Max's arms around me. Bastien sits at my feet, Emery dozing in the moses basket next to him, and Luc paces around us. Nervous energy vibrates from him as he runs a hand through his hair agitatedly.

"Ready, little bird?" Nik asks. Sucking in my breath, I glance down at my son, letting his face give me the courage I need to face this. When I nod, Nik switches on the screen, flicking to the news channels.

The blonde beta presenter I watched before talks animatedly, her hands moving. Nik turns up the volume and her words pour into the room.

"Marches are taking place around the country as protests continue to advocate for the repealing of the omega creed laws."

I bolt upright as everyone freezes, and Leo lets out a scolding mewl. Jiggling him, my eyes remain glued to the screen, the unbelievable sight of the images changing, flicking from city to city to city. Crowds of people line the streets, some protesting outside government buildings, some walking. But all of them carry signs calling for the creed to be abolished.

Luc's head swivels towards me, his mouth falling open. "Ava."

"I – I don't—,"

I don't understand.

This can't be real.

Turning to Max, who's staring at the screen intently, I tug his sleeve, my voice panicked. "*Max*."

I need my healer to tell me that this is real. That it's not just some sick joke. I don't know what I expected to happen. Maybe some mumblings, some public discussion. But not... not this.

Max turns to me, his brown eyes damp. "This is happening, sweetheart," he breathes, pressing his lips to my forehead with a ragged inhale. "You did this."

His confirmation breaks the dam in my chest, and I lean over Leo, holding him to me as the sobs fall out, wracking my body. In a flurry of movement, Max encourages me to hand Leo to Bastien before he pulls me onto his lap. I press my hands to my stomach, struggling to find the words I need to say. Blearily, I scrub my eyes, turning back to the screen.

"In the last 48 hours, the country has erupted into tensions over the revelations shared by omegas from the Omega Compound and the shooting of previous Compound Director Christian Winter. Protests have been focused particularly on the OC headquarters, where newly instated Director Jonathan Stone is facing significant criticism over the incidents shared by his own daughter, omega Ava Stone."

Ice shoots down my spine as my father appears on the

screen. He looks more unkempt than I've ever seen him, his normally pristine suit rumpled as he fights to be heard, standing at the gates of the Omega Compound.

"Director, how do you respond to the accusations made by your daughter, Ava Stone?"

He levels a glare on the reporter. "My daughter is and remains the property of the US Government. 864 is gravely unwell and I would urge anyone with information to contact—"

He flinches back as something hits his chest, staring down as broken yolk oozes down his shirt from an egg thrown by a protestor.

"Was your daughter unwell before or after she was impregnated by gang rape at your command, Director?" The reporter calls caustically, and Stone snaps his head back. I can see his jaw ticking, the absolute fury in his glare as he turns his back on the reporters and walks back inside.

The crowds outside the gates swell, cameras panning to show some of the signs being waved.

Omegas are not a number.
Say their names.
Heat nests = gang rape
Omegas are people too

My eyes catch on one in particular, and I suck in a breath, my eyes filling.

My name is Ava Stone, and I am not a number.

"Oh my god," I gasp, my hands over my mouth. Lost, I look around wildly. "What do we *do*?"

Bastien lets out a whoop, disturbing Emery and Leo as they start to cry. Squeezing his eyes shut, he mumbles an apology, scooping one into each arm and gently swaying them until they settle again. His eyes shine brighter than I've ever seen them when he looks at me. "They see you, sweetheart. They see you."

Chapter Sixty-Six

Nikolai kneels in front of me, his blue eyes searching mine with tentative hope. "We see how this plays out, little bird," he proposes. "This is more than we hoped for, and we don't need to do anything right now but wait this out. We'll speak to the Winter pack and see if anyone has reached out to them."

My throat dries. "Has anyone reached out to us?"

Bastien shakes his head. "Not yet, but it's likely the media is trying to track us down. They won't," he adds hurriedly, clearly picking up on my panic. "We're well hidden, love. But they may put messages out for us to pick up and get in touch."

I wipe my palms on my dress. "Okay."

Luc takes a seat next to me, his fingers caressing my knuckles. "Breathe, brat," he says simply, just a hint of a bark present. It's enough for my breathing to slow, the flickers of darkness receding, and I swallow, leaning against him.

"I never thought this would happen," I rasp. "I thought it was a lost cause."

It's only now that I realize how little hope I had. But seeing all those people, fighting for us, makes me understand how close we are to achieving everything I've never dared to want.

"It takes a single person to throw a snowball," Luc says. "But enough people together can start an avalanche. You threw the ball, love. And now it's gathering pace."

Blowing out a breath, I watch the many faces on the screen. *Gathering pace, indeed.*

Luc pulls out his phone. "Do you want to talk to Harper?"

My hand hovers over the phone. "They lost Christian," I whisper. "How can I be happy over this when Rogue has lost his father because of it? Because of me?"

Guilt swamps me in a wave of grief. I've barely thought about Christian the last day or two. What does that say about me?

"Christian knew what he was risking, little bird," Nik rumbles. "He made a choice to step forward, and he made a choice to save you. And I'm incredibly grateful to him that he did."

The others nod, but I can't take my eyes off the phone. What if they hate me? What if they blame me for Christian's death?

What if Harper hates me?

"You can't change what happened," Max whispers. "Christian's actions were his own."

It doesn't make it any easier, but I turn to Luc, straightening my shoulders. "Call them, please."

He hits a few buttons, putting the call on speaker as I brace myself, gripping my elbows.

Devlin answers nearly instantly. "How's Ava?" he asks. "You a dad yet?"

Luc lets out a strangled laugh. "Father of two very healthy twins."

"No shit," Devlin says, impressed. "Ava doing okay?"

Before Luc can answer, there's a grapple on the line and Harper shouts my name.

"Harper," I snort-laugh tearfully, "I'm here. I'm fine."

She sniffs tearfully. "And the babies?"

Smiling, I look down at them. The sight of them still hits me like a punch to the stomach, unable to believe they're really here. "Healthy and here."

"Oh, honey," Harper breathes. "I'm so pleased for you all."

A thought hits me, and I stare hard at them before responding. "Want to hear their names?"

Harper laughs, a little subdued but still undeniably Harper. "Is that a trick question? Of course!"

"Okay." Swallowing, I grab Max's hand, and he glances at me uncertainly. "Emery Harper Grey."

Max starts, but smiles at me. Bastien gives me the thumbs up, and I'm relieved to see they don't mind my throwing a middle name in there. But it feels right.

Harper is silent. "Oh, Ava," she whispers unsteadily, her voice quivering with unshed tears. "That's...I don't even have words. Thank you."

Clearing my throat, I ask, "Could you put Rogue on for me?"

"Rogue? Sure. He's right here."

The line rustles before Rogue's deep voice echoes through the phone. "Congratulations, Ava. I hope you're well?"

"I am, thank you. Rogue... I'm so sorry about your dad."

He coughs, but his voice is heavy when he responds. "Thank you, Ava. I appreciate that."

"I wanted to share my son's name with you." I sense his surprise, so I hustle out the words before I lose my nerve. "Leo Christian Grey."

Rogue inhales sharply, a whistle through the phone line. "I—I think dad would have liked that."

Smiling at my son, I offer, "I think so too. You'll have to come by sometime and meet him."

Rogue swallows audibly. "I'd like that. You'll let us know if you need anything?"

"We're fine, but thank you."

"You're welcome." His voice breaks a little, and I'm not surprised when Harper comes back on the line. "I need to go," her voice hitches, "but I'll call you later?"

"Of course, Harper," I whisper.

Handing the phone back to Luc, I turn away as he starts to speak into the phone. Max wraps a cautious arm around me, and I sink into him with a sigh.

"Leo Christian Grey. I like it," he says, testing out the words.

"It felt right." Moisture burns the back of my eyes as I stare blankly at the muted television, still showing images of omega rights protests from across the country. "It seems so unfair," I blurt out. "That he doesn't get to see this."

Christian Winter was not a good man, or a white knight in shining armour. He was a patchwork of light and dark. Imperfectly flawed, making questionable decisions to do what he thought was best.

When you have to turn a blind eye to darkness to prevent something worse from happening, where is the line?

I can't judge him for the choices he made. He made his stand, and he lost his life for it, saving mine in the process. All I can do is fight to make sure nobody else is put in the same position. I know with certainty that my father does not have the same moral code as Christian, and bile burns my throat as the gates of the Compound appear on the screen. God knows what's happening to the omegas under his care.

Luc puts the phone down, and I turn my attention back to him. "Devlin agreed with us," he explains. "They're holding on to see what happens too. He thinks it'll either die off, or it might grow into something that the government can't ignore."

"They can ignore this?" I watch the screen in disbelief.

"You'd be surprised how much it takes for people to see the evil in their actions," Bastien says softly, watching the screen with me. "They'll either bury their heads in the sand and hope this goes away, or it'll get too big for them to brush off. It's just a waiting game now, love."

A gurgling snaps all of our attention to the moses basket, where Leo blinks up at me, his face screwed up. Bastien whips him out and hands him to me so I don't have to reach for him, and I laugh lightly at my son's unhappy expression, disgruntled lines forming between his eyes as he opens his mouth and lets out a squawk.

"Hey, little one," I coo. "Are you hungry? Do you need some milk?"

"I shouldn't be turned on by that, right?" Bastien mutters as I undo my shirt, and I pause, blinking up at him. "Seriously?"

Luc makes a rough sound of agreement. "I get it."

I stare at Nik and Max, and they both glance at each other sheepishly. "I can't believe you're all turned on by me breastfeeding, you weirdos," I mutter, as Leo latches on happily. "What is wrong with you?"

Bastien clears his throat. "It's not you breastfeeding the twins that does it for me, love. It's more like... I wouldn't mind a taste?"

My skin flushes a furious shade of scarlet as my face burns. *Is that a thing?*

"O-oh. I see."

Why am I not completely repulsed by the thought of it?

Bastien is almost as red as me, and he quickly disappears with the excuse of checking on Leah, Nikolai following him to relieve Leah of Nash duties as Max switches the telly off so he doesn't see anything.

Leaning back, I sigh as Max steals Leo from me for winding, patting his back until he lets out a cute burp before he passes him back to me with a soft kiss on my lips.

"Maybe this isn't the worst thing in the world," I admit. "I could use a few days to adjust."

"And rest," Max points out sternly. "You've just given

birth, Ava. Twice. Omega or not, your body still needs to heal, sweetheart."

Grumbling, I pout at Leo, and he coos up at me, making me smile.

"All right, Leo," I say as he waves his little hands at me. "Rest and relaxation, okay?"

Chapter Sixty-Seven
Ava

My eyes fly open as the crying begins again.
That's not possible. It's only been… thirty minutes.

Groaning, I sit up as a rumpled Nik lifts Emery out of her moses basket. We haven't decamped them to the nursery yet, since they wake up approximately seventy-five times a night for feeding.

Leo's voice joins Emery's, and I lie back as Nik positions them until they're both suckling happily.

"Well, I'm glad someone's getting what they want," I yawn, stroking my hand over Leo's head. "How long until they sleep through the night again?" I ask Nik pleadingly. He grimaces. "I don't want to lie to you. It could be months."

My eyes fly open where they're starting to droop. "Months?" I'm slightly hysterical at the thought, and Nik holds up his arms placatingly. "We can try the bottles again," He soothes. "That way everyone can take turns and you can get some more rest."

I shake my head stubbornly. "I want them to feed from me."

I may have become a touch over-protective. Yesterday, I shouted at Luc for taking Emery out of the room while I was sleeping, and Bastien had a telling-off for not telling me Leo needed a diaper change and doing it himself. Sighing, I rub my eyes. "I think I'm losing it," I admit, my voice shaking. "I don't know what's wrong with me, Nik."

My bear alpha kneels down beside me, his hand reaching up to cup my cheek. "You are exhausted, little bird," he tells me gently, and I frown. He holds up a finger to stop me interrupting him. "You're barely sleeping, not eating properly, and you're so worried about something happening that you're overcompensating, and it's starting to hurt you."

His voice deepens, becoming a little firmer. "It needs to stop. You need sleep, and food, and a break, Ava."

"I don't need a break from them," I protest. *What kind of mother am I if I need a break from my own kids?*

"Yes, you do," he tells me gently. "Every parent does, sweetheart. You can't do it all alone, but you're trying to. It takes a village to raise a child, and you've got your village right here, aching to help you. Let us *help*, little bird."

I'm so tired that I can barely see straight. I might be able to admit that he's right.

Maybe.

"Okay," I concede. "I'll try and rest more."

Nik raises an eyebrow at me. "And?"

"And I'll eat more," I grumble. "And I'll let you help. Pushy alpha."

He nudges me gently, mindful of the twins. "Stubborn omega."

Leo pulls his head away, starting to squirm, and Nikolai scoops him up and lays him over his shoulder, gently patting his back. As I watch him carefully cradle Leo, his huge hand covering his whole back, the tension leaks out of my spine. He's right. They all need to be involved too.

Chapter Sixty-Seven

Nik settles himself down next to me, bringing Leo down to lay on his chest as he kicks his legs. Watching them, I can't help but smile. Something about these large men carrying precious cargo just hits me straight in the ovaries.

"Nik," I hesitate, not wanting to break the moment. He turns his blue gaze to me, scanning my face. "Little bird?"

"Do you know if Bastien has found any trace of Stone?" I ask in a whisper.

My head turns, scanning the dark corners of the room as if my father might suddenly jump out at me. Whilst the past few weeks have been a chaotic whirlwind of feedings, sleeping, diaper changes, and getting used to parenthood, Stone feels like the boogeyman, a constant threat in the back of my head. Any sudden movement makes me jump, unexpected sounds sending my pulse skyrocketing.

I can't blame Nik for calling me out. I feel as though I'm on the edge of a breakdown. My hands tighten on Emery, and she gives me an indignant grunt.

Nik's other hand searches for mine, and he grasps it tightly. "No trace," he confirms. "As far as we know, he's still hiding out at his estate."

My breath rushes out of me, although the tightness in my limbs doesn't loosen. We don't know for certain if he's still there. I know Stone will be furious at the turn in public opinion. The continued protests show no signs of abating, crowds growing every day. The call to change has been picked up by family members of omegas who have been taken into OC custody – adopted fathers, brothers, friends.

Maybe it's guilt, that they didn't act sooner. Or fear, that they'll be judged in the harsh eyes of the US public if they don't add their own voices to the clamour. Either way, it's looking positive. Whilst the Government haven't confirmed anything, they have put out a statement to say they're taking the concerns raised seriously and will respond following their own investigations.

It's a joke, but we'll take any crumbs we can right now.

Nik gets to his feet. As he holds out his hand, my eyes trace up his arm to his face, creased with sleep. His grey sweatpants sit low around his waist, hugging his hips, and my mouth dries up at the sight of him, our son nestled in the crook of his neck.

How many weeks does it take before I can have sex again?

"How did I get so lucky?" I ask. Nik shakes his head, a smile tugging at the corners of his mouth. "We're the lucky ones, little bird. Come on. Let's try them in the nursery."

Dread steels up my spine at the thought of it. But I did promise Nik that I'd try, so I grasp his hand and he pulls me up, keeping my hand locked in his as he tows me toward the nursery.

"I'm not going to run away," I can't help but laugh a little, and he glances at me over his baby-free shoulder. "I know. I just like holding your hand."

My heart thumps happily inside my chest at his sweet words.

Steering us into the nursery, Nik leans away from me, bending down to flick a switch. As he straightens, my mouth opens in silent awe as I take in the shapes swirling around the room.

Silhouettes of scattered stars dance across the walls as they move around the room, accompanied by a low, sweet melody. Nik clears his throat uncomfortably as I stare.

"They didn't... we couldn't get much," he blurts out. "That's obviously for babies. But I found an old lampshade and cut some shapes into it. Wasn't too hard to dig out the music box Nash used to have and link it up."

Taking a deep breath, my nose prickles as I try to hold

back my tears. "I love it, Nik." Giving him a tremulous smile, his shoulders relax, and he steps into the room, gently placing Leo down into one of the cots. Following him, I do the same for Emery, watching her legs kick out as she wriggles on the mattress. My hands tighten on the wooden bars as Nik turns around, holding something out to me.

"A camera," he explains. "With a microphone, so you can still keep an eye on them."

My breathing loosens, anxiety leeching from me. I should've known. He doesn't miss a trick.

"Thank you," I mumble, and he wraps his arm around my waist. "We want them to be safe, too, you know." It's a gentle chiding, and I bury my face into his arm. "I'd fight to my last breath for our family, little bird."

Nodding, I pull back with damp eyes as Nik turns to me, dropping his face to mine as he pauses, his eyes scanning mine with careful precision before he leans down to catch my lower lip in a soft kiss.

I open my mouth, breathing in the spice of his scent as he growls softly, pressing himself into me. The swelling in his pants presses against me just right, and I tip my head back in a gasp at the sensation.

He pulls his head away, shaking his head. "Sorry, little bird," he murmurs. "Ignore me. Didn't mean for that to get out of hand."

Stepping back, I press myself against him, soft omega against hard alpha muscle, and he snaps in a shocked breath. "Ava?"

My hand reaches up to curl around his neck, and I press a kiss to the edges of his mouth, working my way down his neck. "Where's your room?" I ask, blinking as I realize I haven't actually seen it before. *I definitely need a tour of this house at some point.*

Nikolai's eyes widen, and he swallows, his throat

bobbing as he glances around, a touch uncertain. "It's right next to Nash. Little bird…,"

Taking the camera from his hand, I wiggle it in front of his face. "I'm feeling a little tense," I breathe, delighting in the way his pupils expand, blackness spreading across the blue depths. "I think I need you to help me relax, alpha."

The rumble starts deep in Nikolai's chest, vibrating against my skin and making me shiver. I'm more than ready to reconnect with them, to wrap myself up in their scent until we're as close as two people can be. Nik thrusts, just barely, his length pressing between my legs. It's enough to draw a needy whine from my throat, the high-pitched sound echoing into the room. *Yep, definitely ready*.

Nik wraps his arms around me and lifts me from the ground. Clapping my hand over my mouth, I manage to stifle the loud squeak that slips out as he lays me over his shoulder and heads swiftly out of the nursery, turning to gently pull the door closed behind him before he strides down the hall. I barely notice which door he goes through, my attention drawn by the delicious angle of his ass in those grey sweatpants. I run my hand down and over the globes of his cheeks, biting back a grin as he growls beneath me.

"Ah!" I gasp as he drops me onto the bed, bouncing on the mattress as I blink up at him innocently.

"Minx," he grits, and I scooch back playfully on the bed, yelping when his hands hook around my ankles and he slides me towards him. As he moves upwards, his hands exploring my skin, my laughter dies off as my breathing speeds up. "Nikolai," I breathe, his hands disappearing under the silky softness of my skin. "Touch me here."

My hands move to cup my heavy breasts, but he bats them away. "You wanted to play," Nik rumbles, "so let's play, little bird. Keep your arms here."

Shivering, I do as he says and lie back, my eyes sliding

shut as he runs his hands everywhere except where I need him to be. Wriggling, I gasp when a light pinch lands on my right nipple.

"Sore?" he asks, stopping and smoothing over the small sting with the pad of his finger.

I shake my head furiously. I'm not sore. I'm on fucking fire, my body burning for him.

"Good." He smirks, before moving over and repeating the pinch on my other nipple, and I cry out. His hand moves up to cover my mouth, and my eyes widen before I remember Nash is in the other room.

"Can you stay quiet for me, omega?" Nik murmurs. His hands move up, tracing my neck before they slide into my hair, his weight settling on me as he holds my face still. I try to nod, my head movements restricted, and he grins at me.

"Good girl." Dropping his face, his lips close over mine. Nik doesn't taste, he conquers, his tongue surging into my mouth, licking and sucking at my lower lip, the pulling movement sending a pulse directly to my clit. I try to move but his weight prevents me, and I'm held open for him. I can feel his length swelling against me, the bulbous fist of his knot growing, and my slick starts to reappear, my whole body heating as Nikolai holds me open.

When he pulls away, I whimper. "Alpha, please."

He moves my head to the side, kissing down my neck. When his teeth close, mimicking a bite, I nearly come off the bed, bucking in his grasp.

"Bite?" I ask hopefully. I've heard about the mating bite from them, and they know how much I want it. But instead of biting down, Nik drags his tongue directly over the sensitive spot, making me groan in frustration. I can feel his damned smug smile against my skin, and I whine for him again. "Nikolai!"

"You want my bite, little omega?" he asks darkly. "Want

me to sink my teeth into that pretty neck, mark you up so everyone knows you're mine?"

"Yes," I beg. "Please, Nik."

"Not yet." He kisses my neck one last time before his hands move downwards, out of my hair and back to my silky top. My eyes widen as he tugs it, the pull of the material lifting me before it rips, Nik tossing the discarded pieces behind him as I fall back to the bed, my heavy tits bouncing as Nik's predatory gaze lands on them. When he licks his lips, my spine bows from the shivers climbing it.

I feel like his prey, the omega held for the alpha's pleasure, and I freaking love every second of it.

His darkened eyes trace my tits, his tongue sliding out to lick over his lips as he surveys me. Bowing my back, I lift myself up for him, remembering our conversation. His nostrils flare and he leans in, lapping over my tight, hard nipple as he pulls back his hips before grinding into me, his hardness a promise that leaves my core weeping for him. The slight rasp of his tongue is enough to make my eyes roll back as he growls against my breast.

"Your taste has changed, little bird."

"How?" I ask on a gasp.

He takes a final, slow lick before pulling back to look at me. "Like I'm going to die if I don't get a taste," he purrs. "Can I suck on those pretty tits?"

Flushing, I glance down at my engorged breasts, heavy with milk despite the feeding I've just given the twins. I can almost scent what Nikolai means, a muskiness in the air as a single bead of milk leaks from me. Nik traces the path it makes down the side of my breast, a feral growl shaking him as he leans back.

He rises up on his knees, hair mussed and smile savage, and I gaze up at him. Spreading my arms, I push my breasts toward him in silent offering. My body shakes as he lunges, one arm sweeping underneath me as he lifts me to him, my clit coming to rest directly over one grey-clad knee as he holds me upright, his palm spreading over the back of my neck.

His other hand captures both of mine, loosely gripping them behind my back as I'm splayed out for him. My sex pulses, slick pouring from me as his eyes dilate.

"I can scent you," Nik groans. "Fuck, little bird."

From my position, I can only move my hips, rubbing them frantically up and down over his leg. I can feel my fluids soaking us both, my head held in place by Nik as he finally lowers his mouth to my breast. His lips close over my nipple, the first strong pull of his sucking mouth making me cry out, my hips moving faster as I chase my release.

"Fuck, Nikolai," I gasp. He only growls around my nipple, the vibration sinking through my bones as he pulls my milk from me in thick, pulsing draws.

A sound next to us makes me gasp, my hair tugged in Nik's fingers as I turn my face to the side. Bastien stands in the doorway, his face shadowed and lined with fierce desire as he watches me, helpless to do anything but submit to Nikolai's branding hot mouth on my body.

"Bastien," I moan. He takes a step forward, his eyes moving to Nikolai, but my alpha doesn't react to his presence. Bastien's hands clench at his sides. "Fuck, cupcake," he rasps. "Look at you, all spread out for us like a buffet."

My answering whimper is needy, my core clenching in empty frustration as I buck against Nik's leg wildly. Nik takes a final pull from my breast before he pulls his head back, his mouth shiny as he turns to grin at Bastien.

"Our little bird tastes like heaven," his words are almost a taunt. "Care for a taste, Bastien?"

Bastien slides onto the bed, his head dipping as he seizes my other nipple in his mouth, continuing the tortuous pleasure as I mewl, trying frantically to keep my voice down.

Nik lets go of my hands and they rise to rest in Bastien's hair as Nik leans a hand down to free himself from his sweatpants. His cock rises up, thick and heavy, his knot a pulsing, bulbous fist at the base. His scent deepens, spice and musk settling around me like a blanket as he lifts my leg and slides me over his hips. His cock nudges my entrance through the silk of my bottoms and we both groan.

"So wet for me, sweetheart," Nik rasps as he rocks against me. "She tastes good, doesn't she?"

Bastien makes a sound of agreement from my breast, his fingers sliding down beneath the wet silk and pressing directly against my clit. Bucking, I throw my head back in wordless pleasure, my hips moving faster.

"Hold her up, brother," Nik instructs Bastien, and he slides behind me to drop kisses down my neck, my back resting against his sculpted chest as Nik divests me of my shorts, yanking at them until the seams split and I'm completely, utterly bared to him.

A tinge of embarrassment tints the air, and Nik flashes his eyes up to me. "I'm not...," I clear my throat nervously. I had two babies. I know I don't look the same.

"You're fucking perfect," Nik shoots back. His hand reaches up to curl around my throat, and he holds my gaze. "Perfect, little bird," he repeats.

Bastien's tongue traces down my neck. "Ours," he grunts.

"Yours." It's a whisper, but Nik's eyes soften as he traces his finger down my wet folds, circling my entrance just enough to hint at what's to come.

"What do you want, cupcake?" Bastien murmurs, brushing my damp hair away from my neck. "Tell us."

I hold Nik's eyes. "I want you to fill me up," I choke out, licking my lips. "I want you to stuff me so full that I can't breathe, Nik."

Bastien hums into my neck. "And what about me, sweetheart?" His hand slides down my front, gliding past my slit and going further. My breath stutters and stops as he traces his finger lightly over my back entrance, the tip pushing in just lightly as my back arches.

The feeling of both of them teasing me, their talented hands dipping inside me, is almost unbearable. My breath chokes on a ragged sob. "Please," I beg. "Please touch me. Anywhere you want. Just *do it*."

My words snap off with a ragged cry as Nikolai sinks his cock into me, achingly slow, inch by inch of his steely length disappearing inside me. He stops at the base and Bastien covers my mouth just in time, my frustrated shout muted against the heat of his palm.

They're killing me. This is how I'm going to die, tortured to death by the slowness of my alpha's cock.

Nik holds me still, his hands splayed over my thighs as his fingers tap against my skin. "Patience," he snaps, the tendons in his neck strained. I open my mouth, ready to ask him what the hell he's waiting for when Bastien's finger prods at me again.

"So wet," he murmurs huskily. "Look at all this mess you're making, cupcake."

He gathers up some of my wetness, his fingers brushing at me before they move back to my ass, and he slowly works a finger in. My eyes flutter shut, the fullness almost too much sensation. When he adds a second finger, I start to squirm, my hips twisting as Nik pins me in place. Finally, he slides his cock out before working it back in, and they fall into a rhythm, Bastien's fingers and his cock sliding in and out until I'm a feverish, writhing mass of sensation, our breathing echoing harshly in the darkened room. Bastien's fingers disappear, replaced by something thicker, and Nik pauses the flexing of his cock as they lock eyes.

"Show me you want this, cupcake," Bastien grunts, his head pushing in just lightly. "Let me hear you whine."

Nik leans forward and pinches my clit, the small bite of pain electric on my senses as I twist and beg. "Please," I ask, my voice trembling. "Please, Bastien."

"Like this?" he pushes in a little further, the head of his cock pushing past tense muscle to sit inside me. My whimpers fall from my lips, my head thrashing as they both sink into me at the same time, working together to create a push and pull inside me that draws my release up in a rush. Crying out, I clench my muscles and both Nik and Bastien curse. "Bite," I moan. "Please, Nikolai!"

"Holding us so tightly, little bird," Nik rasps. "I can feel your cunt pulling at me."

He yanks me onto him, his swollen knot pushing at my sex, demanding entry as it slides inside my entrance, my eyes rolling back at the completeness. Bastien steadies me, his cock thick and hot inside me as Nik bellows. His cock soaks me with his seed, his knot locking us together as he comes in a wave, his teeth snapping down to land squarely on the side of my neck in a deep bite.

My breathing stops as his teeth break my skin and something snaps into place inside me. Fierce protectiveness and a deep, pure *love* soak into my bones as Nikolai pulls back to scan my face worriedly. "Ava? Sweetheart?"

I sag back against Bastien, blinking at him wordlessly. "I can sense you," I whisper. "I wasn't expecting it to feel so… so…,"

All consuming. Overwhelming.

Fucking *wonderful*.

Nik's hand comes up to cup my face worriedly. "If you regret it—,"

"No," I rasp, my hand coming up to cover his. "God, Nikolai, I can *feel* you inside me. It's incredible."

Bastien shifts and I bite my lip, a pang of regret echoing through me that I'll never have this with my beta. He clearly picks up on my sudden tension as he curves himself around me to whisper in my ear.

"We don't need a fancy bond, cupcake," he whispers. "I'll tell you how much you mean to me every day for the rest of our lives."

My eyes dampen, and I lean back against him with a sniffle. "Gonna hold you to that."

His body shakes a little against my back. "Also, since I don't get a bitemark, can I tattoo my name on your ass?"

I slap weakly at his arm as his laughter shakes the bed. Nik shakes his head at Bastien, a playful glint in his eye. "Say yes, little bird," he murmurs. "Then you can do the same to him."

Bastien lets out a surprised laugh. "I'd wear it proudly," he teases. "You'd all get sick of my ass prancing around."

"Mmmm," I make a considering sound as Nik opens his arms and carefully lifts me, his knot still nestled inside me as I sink my face into his neck, breathing in his skin. "I think I'd like to see my name on all of you, actually. Property of Ava Stone."

Nik stills. "Ava *Grey*," he snarls. "You're ours, little bird. Not theirs. Especially now that you're bitemarked."

Bastien grunts in agreement. "Damn straight."

I look between them wonderingly. "Ava Grey it is, then."

God knows I've never had any attachment to my family surname. Taking their surname feels permanent. Binding, just like Nik's mark on my neck. My fingers lift up to trace it, and I look into Nik's eyes.

"No regrets?" I smile teasingly, and he mock growls, nuzzling at the mark with his stubble.

"None."

CHAPTER SIXTY-EIGHT
AVA

Four very determined men stand in front of me, arms crossed in identical frustrated poses as we square off. Leah sits on the couch, her eyes swiveling between us as she tucks her hands into her lap.

I try again. "Luc, this is *huge*. They're asking me to give evidence in a televised court appearance to support a vote to remove the Omega Creed. To *get rid of it!* How can I not go?"

Luc's chest heaves as he takes an angry breath. "It could be a trap."

Throwing up my hands, I look to Nik, then Max and Bastien, all of them mirroring Luc's expression. "This is not a trap, Luc. They've invited us on national television and promised a seven-day amnesty to attend. If anything goes wrong, the public will rip them apart. Look!"

I throw my hand out to the screen behind them, scenes of the growing protests front and center of every news channel. In the six weeks since Leo and Emery arrived, the number of people and the number of angry voices have only grown.

"We finally have a chance," I plead. Dampness pricks at my eyes. "I can do something to help, Luc!"

Now Max steps forward, his face tight. "Sweetheart," he says firmly. "Your father will not pay attention to any government amnesty. You might be safe from the compound, but you will not be safe from *him*."

His voice gentles. "I know you want to do this. But this isn't just about you." He points to Leo and Emery, asleep in tiny rocking chairs on the other side of the room. Nash sits between them, using his feet to carefully bounce the chairs as he watches his turtles on a screen, his mouth open in concentration and a pair of headphones slipped over his ears.

My anger spikes. "I'm doing this *for* them, Max."

"You can't have it both ways, love, no matter how much we wish that wasn't the case." Even Bastien's voice is hard, my normally open-minded beta firmly alongside the alphas in this debate. "We're not going to sit on our asses and let you put yourself at risk."

My shoulders drop, and I turn away from them, unable to hide the shaking of my shoulders as I clasp my elbows tightly. "This is my choice," I whisper, my throat burning. "You can't just decide that I'm going to stay out of it. That's not how this works."

A hand cups my elbow, Luc drawing me around to face him. His green eyes watch me carefully as he steps forward, tugging me into his arms until my face is pressed against his chest, my arms closing as I breathe in the musk of his sandalwood scent, letting it calm me.

He rocks me slightly. "You're right," he admits, his voice gruff. "We can't decide for you. But, sweetheart, we're a family. We need to talk it through together. We know why you want to go, of course we do. But you need to understand where we're coming from too."

Sagging, I mumble into his chest. "I hate it when you make sense."

He kisses the top of my head. "I'll try not to do it too often, then."

Everyone takes a seat, and I climb into Max's lap, making myself comfortable before I turn to face my pack. "All right," I grumble. "Let's hear it."

Max strokes his hand down my back. "If you go," he starts, his voice measured, "What happens if something goes wrong? Maybe it's not a trap. But tensions will be high, and your father will know you're there and likely plan accordingly. If you're taken, we might not be able to find you, love."

His hand tenses on my back as his voice drops. "We would also be hinging all of our hopes on a government that hasn't exactly been on the right side of history."

I know he's right. I know this is risky. But if this is our only chance, how can I not take it?

"They haven't asked the Winter pack?" I ask, turning to Luc, and he shakes his head. "Just you," he says flatly. "I checked with Devlin. Which also doesn't make me inclined to trust them, brat."

I turn to Nikolai next. He's silent, his eyes hooded as he watches us. The mating bond thrums in my chest, churning with frustration, anger and sadness.

"And you?" I ask him, rubbing at where the bond seems to originate, right over my heart. "What do you think, Nic?"

The anger inside my chest pulses, a strange reflection of the feelings stirring in the alpha staring at my face. He traces me with his eyes. "I don't want you within ten miles of any of them, little bird."

"But if we don't go," I counter, "They might use it as an excuse to reject the laws being repealed."

And then all of this will be for nothing. I need them to trust in me.

"And they might not," Luc's voice is still hard. "You don't owe them a single second more of your pain, Ava. Fuck knows they've had enough of it already."

I fight back the flinch that threatens. "Then it's all the more reason to go and let them hear what their laws have done!"

Bastien tugs at his hair. "Ava, please. We can offer them a video connection instead—,"

I shake my head, my jaw determined. "*No*, Bastien. I want to do this. I want to look into their faces and let them see me. I need to be there, not a two-dimensional voice on a screen!"

Luc's eyes blaze. "Damned stubborn omega," he says furiously. I square my shoulders back, facing him head-on.

"Infuriating, overprotective alpha!" I snap the words back at him, pausing at the flicker of hurt in his eyes.

He takes a step closer to me. "Is it so bad," he grits. "That we want to protect you from them? That we don't want them to breathe the same air as you? God fucking *damn* it, Ava. You have no sense of self-preservation!"

"You say that like I don't want to live," I throw back at him. "That's all I want, Luc. To live a free life with you, with our pack, our family. For our daughter to live life on her terms."

I swallow. "I can't give her that," I challenge. "Neither can you, Luc. But they can."

Luc curses. "I didn't want you to do the video," he says, but there's a defeated tone to his voice. "And now you're going to stroll into a courtroom full of government heavyweights and expect to just walk back out again?"

I kneel in front of him as he sinks down into a chair,

laying my head on his thigh. "Trust me," I plead. "Just trust me, Luc."

He lifts some of my hair, rubbing it between his fingers. "It's them I don't trust. Not you. Although I'm definitely going grey thanks to you, brat. I thought omegas were supposed to have a sense of self-preservation."

I stick out my tongue, picking up the slight change to his tone with relief. I don't want to fight with him, not when there's a bigger battle to win. "I don't need one," I tease him. "Not with you around."

With a yelp, I find myself deposited unceremoniously onto his lap, and I scramble to face him. He stares at me imperviously, and I blink. "What's wrong?"

When he stands up, my legs lock around his waist, hands winding into his hair. "Luc?"

"I'd like a word," he says silkily before he stalks towards the stairs. I catch Max's eye over Luc's shoulder and he winks at me, although worry still lurks on his face as he watches us leave.

Luc shoulders open a door, his scent wrapping around us like a Christmas bow. Bracing myself, I expect to land on the soft mattress of his bed, but instead he takes a seat on the edge, keeping me on his lap with his feet settled on the floor. I glance around a little uncertainly. "Are you okay?"

It's only when I look closer that I pick up the tic in his jaw, the tension in his frame.

"Luc," I murmur, lifting my hand to his face, "I know —ack!"

My words choke off into garbled shock as Luc flips me. One moment, I'm staring at his face, the next I'm facing the floor, blinking in confusion as my body lies across Luc's lap.

"Um. Luc?" I ask weakly. When I wriggle experimentally, his hand lands squarely in the small of my back, holding me in place.

Well, now. My face flames crimson as his hand starts to move down my neck, stroking over my ass, encased in jeans now that winter is finally settling in.

"Do you realize" he asks silkily, "how much I love you, brat?"

Sucking in a breath, I try to concentrate on his words as his hand continues to explore. "Uh – yes?"

"See, I'm not sure that you do," he says in a conversational tone. His finger dips quickly between my legs and scratches up my denim-covered slit, the sensation making me catch my breath. "Because if you did, I don't think you'd push me quite as far as you seem to like doing."

His finger slides underneath the denim, and he starts working it down, gradually revealing my bare skin as he continues talking.

"I think you need to learn how a naughty omega who doesn't listen to her alpha gets punished," he continues softly, and my breath turns ragged as I stare at the floor, my cheeks pink as I realize his game. My ass pushes up in the air, just enough to make the invitation clear, and Lucien laughs darkly.

Cool air brushes my skin as he tugs my jeans down just enough to reveal my cheeks, bare to the room. He hums in satisfaction. "No panties today, I see."

"Well, I wasn't expecting to be put on the naughty step," I breathe, rewarded with a sharp slap to my ass that curves my back with pleasure.

"Luc." His name tumbles from my lips on a low moan.

"Fuck, I love your sass, baby," he groans. "Keep it going, and you get a longer spanking. Your choice."

Decisions, decisions.

"And when we're done, brat," my alpha tells me, his voice thick, "you're going to be knotted, and then you're going to be bitten. I'm not going one more day without my mark branding you."

His words pierce me, tiny stabs hitting me directly in my sex as I groan. My scent, full and lush, seeps into the air, perfuming with rich vanilla.

"You like that?" he muses, and I nod vigorously, my hair tumbling over my head and obscuring my vision. "I *love* that," I breathe, and he laughs.

"Good." Without another word, he pulls back his hand and smacks my ass sharply, the bright sting blossoming along the crease between my thigh and cheek. My cry echoes sharply at the sensation as Luc continues, interspersing his spanking with soft traces up and down my slit until I'm a mewling broken mess, writhing underneath his touch.

"Luc, please," I beg. "Finish it. Please!"

He plunges two fingers into my cunt, and I convulse around him, my eyes rolling back in my head before he pulls back and I choke off a frustrated sob. His hand strokes softly over my skin.

"Such a pretty color," he coos. "Are you ready to be fucked now, brat?"

Fuck, *yes*. My answering groan is enough, and he hauls me upright, briefly pausing to kiss me before he nudges me toward the bed.

"Ladies' choice," he says when I look to him for guidance. A small smile curls at my lips as I climb onto the bed, settling into the position I've been holding back on offering.

Luc pauses as I crawl into position, placing my cheek down against the soft comforter and lifting my ass in the air, presenting to him. My core throbs and I feel fluid drip down the inside of my thigh, my cunt fluttering with the need for Luc's knot to fill me up. My hands settle, palm down on either side of my head as I breathe heavily, aware of every shift of material as he strips, his breathing harsh around me.

I wait patiently, not moving from my spot and smiling into the bed as Luc's hands settle on my hips, his thumbs digging in a little to my hips,

"No more teasing," I murmur, pushing back against the heat of his length. His hand strokes down my back. "No more," he promises.

His hands on my hips, he fucks his cock into me, my knees sliding up the mattress as I scream his name into the bedding. Growls ripple through him as his hand settles on my neck, pinning me as his knot pushes against my entrance with every stroke. I'm soaking us both, my fluids pooling beneath us as we gasp out for breath, Luc not pausing as he continues to slam into me. My toes curl as his arm slides around my thigh, pulling my legs impossibly wider to accommodate his thrusting.

"Yes," I grunt. "Yes, alpha, yes."

He snaps his hips, his knot pushing at me. My eyes cross as the thick bulge of his knot presses into my body, Luc holding me still as he works himself into me with a roar, his cock jerking and pulsing, filling me up as I shudder beneath his weight. He curves himself over me, his breathing misting my neck as my release crests, my cunt sucking him in greedily as his lips brush my shoulder, almost apologetically before he bites down, hard.

His teeth in my neck send me spiraling straight into my second release, continuing waves of pleasure flowing over me until my knees will no longer hold me up, and I collapse into the mattress. Luc follows me, his knot still deep inside as he settles his elbows on each side to keep his weight off. His mouth brushes down my spine, soft, gentle kisses that I soak up as I lie there.

Soaked, spent, and well and truly knotted.

Sucking in deep breaths, I search out the thread of Luc's bond. I can feel his satisfaction, male and predatory, a lion more than satisfied with his mate. His nuzzles at my damp hair, and I grumble. "Mate," Luc pushes, and I bat his hand away lazily.

"Nope," I mumble. "I'm done. Knotted and bitten and sleepy."

Luc laughs, shaking both of our bodies. "We're only half-done. You need to mark me too."

My tired eyes fly open. "Where?" I ask eagerly.

"Anywhere you want. I'd like it somewhere visible, though. Somewhere everyone can see that I'm yours," he breathes. Luc turns us until I lie on my side, my legs tucked up to accommodate his knot as it softens inside me, inch by inch.

"Your wrist," I propose. I want to mark everyone in the same place, so they can look down at any point and remember that they're *mine*.

He hums as he lifts his wrist to me, and I waste no time, sinking my teeth into his skin, holding him to me as I bond us together.

Luc curses. "Fuck, baby. I can feel you inside me."

I wriggle against him. "Can you tell how much I enjoyed that?" I ask lightly.

"Was it too much?" he asks worriedly, and I smirk into his arm. "No, sir." Luc swats my ass lightly, and I giggle.

I have a feeling I'll be in need of Luc's brand of punishment on a *very* regular basis.

Chapter Sixty-Nine
Ava

I take Emery in my arms, kissing her chubby cheek as she burbles happily before I hand her over to Bastien, my lips pulling into a frown as he leans in to kiss me goodbye.

"I don't like this," he mutters, and I'm inclined to agree. I wanted my whole pack with me, but leaving Leo, Emery, Nash and Leah without a member of the pack here was out of the question, so Bastien is staying with them. His tech-savvy means he can keep an eye on what's happening through his screens, whilst also making sure nothing creeps up on our family while we're distracted.

"It'll be fine." Max appears at my side, a sleepy Leo tucked against his grey suit. I survey him, my eyes moving over the way the white shirt covers his chest, and he grins at me.

"Like what you see?" he asks lightly. My lips press together in amusement, but I'm too tense to respond fully. A head butts into my side, and I turn around, exaggerating. "Who could that be?" I ask loudly, and a giggle buries against my skirt as Nash tucks himself close to me.

"Are you sure I can't come?" he asks, and my heart twinges. "I wish this was the kind of trip where you could, Nash," I tell him truthfully. "Next time, okay?"

He nods and moulds himself to Bastien, who places a hand on his shoulder. Nik comes to stop next to them, kneeling and murmuring words to Nash quietly as he nods.

Leah comes to me next, the sheen of moisture in her eyes threatening my own as she sniffs. "Ava," she whispers. "Good luck."

She wraps her arms around me, hugging me tightly as we both clear our throat. When I step back, Luc is holding the car door open, his hand stretched out for mine. The sleek black estate car idles, doors open as we mill around it, none of us willing to actually step inside.

Stepping inside makes what's happening very real.

We're going to the Department of Justice to give evidence against the US Government. To try to persuade them to dissolve the archaic Omega Creed for good. I'm trying very fucking hard not to think about the fact that I might see Stone there today.

Nerves pluck at my stomach, nausea threatening to make me throw up over my neat and sensible navy-blue skirt suit, borrowed from Leah.

"Not too sexy," she'd said firmly. "You need to look non-threatening, but respectable enough to be taken seriously."

My hair is tied back, my wild curls tamed into a sleek updo.

I don't feel like myself, but that's good. My clothes feel like armour, a shield between the scrutiny I'll face today and the *real* me.

I take a last look at my children, at Bastien, my eyes tracing the familiar contours of his face as he takes a deep breath, Emery held firmly in his arms. Leah wipes her face as she waves Leo's chubby little fist at me, and tears threaten. I duck into the back of the car before I lose my nerve, Max sliding in beside me as Nik and Luc take the front. Luc starts the engine, his fists flexing on the steering wheel as his eyes lock with mine in the mirror.

"Sweetheart," he says gravely. "Are you ready?"

My mouth dries up. I want to shake my head, to get back out of the car and curl up with them in my nest, hide away from all the bad shit in the world and tell everyone to go fuck themselves.

But I don't have that option. Instead, I lift my chin at Luc, and he pulls off.

I don't look back.

The ride to the city is quiet. Max keeps my hand in his, his thumb stroking soothingly over my skin, but he allows me the space I need to get my head together and prepare myself.

I need to push aside my emotions. I need to show them that I'm not a master manipulator and that omegas are not the evil they've been painted to be. I need them to see the truth, to hear it from my lips.

I cannot fail. Pressure bows my shoulders, and Max gravitates across the seat until his arm wraps around me, his chest vibrating with a soothing purr that softens my aching muscles.

"I'm scared," I confess. Max traces a pattern on my leg, his face somber.

"We'll be there," he assures me. "We won't leave you alone for a second, love."

"And if you want to leave," Nik rumbles. "You just let us know, little bird, and we'll get you out of there."

I nod hesitantly, even though I'm not sure it'll be that easy.

The tension grows as we move closer, crowds starting to appear as we inch through the city traffic towards the court building. People line the streets, many of them women, chanting and holding up placards as we pass them.

We stand with Ava.
Omegas have rights.
Ban the Omega Creed.

My eyes catch on one sign in particular, and I turn to scowl at Max. He leans past me and snorts as a particularly enthusiastic beta protestor waves a sign toward the car.

Max Grey can save me any day.

"She'd probably combust if she knew you were actually in here," I murmur, and Max clears his throat, quickly looking away from me as his shoulders shake.

The crowds grow denser as we pull into the street where the justice building stands, a tall high-rise structure looming above the apartment blocks on either side of it. Government guards stand on either side of a makeshift barrier, holding back the crowds.

I press myself back in my seat, trying to get my breathing under control as Luc pulls the car up and turns to me, his hand reaching out to grip my leg.

"Together," he says firmly. His eyes scan my face as our bond jumps in my chest, a wave of protectiveness washing over me. My limbs loosen a little and I nod at him. Nik twists in his seat, a grimace on his lips.

"I'll get out first. Stay close to me, little bird."

Apprehension builds at the base of my spine as he opens the car door, a thousand different noises and scents spilling into the quiet in a sensory overload. Flinching, I instinctively draw back, huddling into the backseat as the door closes behind Nik.

"Breathe, sweetheart," Max coaxes, and I grab his hand again, gripping it for strength.

Luc slides out of the driver's seat as Nikolai opens my

door. I take a final, fortifying breath, bracing myself for the circus we're about to dive into and step out of the car.

If the car was bad, being outside is a million times worse. The noise increases as the protestors catch sight of us, screams erupting as Max and I are recognized.

"It's Ava Stone!"

People cry out my old name, and I stay close to my pack as they guide me through the crowd. It swells into a shouting, faceless mass, and my breathing speeds up as I glance around. My panicked eyes fall on one lone protestor. She stands at the front of the crowd, a still and silent figure amongst the chaos with a sheet of dark hair. Her eyes are steady on mine as she holds her placard up.

I am an Ava too.

My breath catches. She's an *omega*. Young, too. She must be barely awakened.

Here, just… standing amongst the crowd. I don't know how nobody's noticed. Maybe she's managed to get hold of scent blockers?

She stiffens as my eyes widen, and I shake my head slightly. I won't single her out or draw attention to her.

Instead, I slide my eyes away, but hold up my fist and place it across my chest. When I glance back, she repeats the gesture.

I see you.

I see you too.

The fear clawing up my spine settles into a low awareness. This is bigger than me.

This day is for every omega who has suffered under the hands of our government.

And I will not show them my throat.

Chapter Seventy
Max

The shouts and screams only grow as we hustle Ava towards the concrete steps leading up to the justice building. Most seem positive, but I've spotted a few signs that definitely suggest they're Creed supporters. They stand silently for the most part, watching us with narrowed eyes and angry faces.

It's a reminder that not everyone is an ally. Not that we needed it.

We reach the steps, climbing up them and passing government guards until we're met by a pinch-faced beta with coiffed blonde hair.

"Ava Stone?" she asks, her gaze moving up and down Ava before briefly scanning us. She looks unimpressed.

Ava's shoulders stiffen, her back straightening as she draws herself up. "It's Ava Grey, actually. I'm mated now."

The beta purses her lips but doesn't respond, turning on her heel and beckoning us as she walks towards the justice building. I swap a glance with Luc, his mouth turned down in displeasure. Ava glares at the beta's back before grabbing my hand. We start to follow, Luc and Nik falling into step behind us, tension in the air as the double doors are held open for us to enter by two guards.

Here we go.

We walk into an opulent lobby, a wide, open space with marbled pillars stationed at intervals around the room. Ornate wooden doors are scattered between them, the hushed silence broken by footsteps as official-looking men in suits move from place to place. All activity stops as we follow the beta to one of the doors, everyone pausing to look over at us. Ava's steps remain steady even as her hand shakes in mine. I squeeze it gently.

You are not alone.

The blonde beta raps her knuckles against the door, a scant moment passing before a low, female voice responds. We file into an office, my eyes scanning our vicinity as a familiar beta female rises from behind a desk, this one older and wearing a much warmer expression.

"Ava Stone," she says with a small smile. "Thank you so much for coming."

Ava reaches out for her outstretched hand with hesitation, lightly shaking it. "It's actually Ava Grey," she corrects. The beta glances between us with a nod. "My apologies. Samantha, could you get us some drinks please?"

The blonde beta huffs a little before she stalks out of the room, and the older beta purses her lips in disapproval. "I'm sorry about that. Please, take a seat."

We settle into chairs around her desk, although Luc remains upright, taking up position behind Ava's chair, his fingers brushing her neck.

The beta female clears her throat. "I'm Senator Erica Denver."

Ava leans forward. "You're the senator who put forward the motion to repeal the law."

Denver nods, pushing her tortoiseshell glasses up her

face. "I am. I had actually been gathering my own evidence to bring this discussion to the table, but your videos and the impact they've had on the public was an opportunity to bring my work forward."

"Why?" Luc's voice is hard, his expression glacial as he stares at the senator. "What's your motive?"

The senator doesn't flinch, staring straight back at him. "My sister awakened as an omega. I haven't seen her for ten years. You are not the only ones affected by the Creed, Mr. Grey."

Luc pauses at the bleakness in her words, his head dipping in a small nod of respect. "You'll forgive me for asking, I hope. We don't live in a world where we can take people on face value."

Denver's blue eyes soften. "I understand that."

Clearing her throat, she looks back to Ava. "Today will be difficult. The debate has already been running for a number of days, and those supporting the Creed have put forward various individuals to give evidence to support their case."

Ava's fists clench on the chair as she picks up the Senator's loaded meaning.

"Stone is here."

Anger bites at the back of my throat and I swallow it down. Denver inclines her head as matching growls rumble from Luc and Nik. "He was. It's likely he'll be in the courtroom. I'm sorry."

Ava waves a shaky hand. "We expected him to be here. I just – I just hoped we'd be wrong."

Shifting forward, I catch Denver's' attention, giving Ava a moment. "Can you tell us about the structure? Who are we working to convince?"

Denver picks up the change easily. "There are five Supreme Court Justices. At the end of the debate, each will vote, and the majority rules. It then goes through a final motion in the Senate, but that will be more of a formality than anything else. The Senate will follow the decision of the Justices."

"So we need to convince these five? Do we know anything about their loyalties?"

Denver shrugs. "Justice Evans is an alpha, and I'm pretty sure he's on our side. His daughter awakened as an omega, and he didn't take it well."

Ava's snort of derision rings out. "I wish that meant something to Stone."

Denver continues. "Justices Garcia and Miller are both female betas, and I'm fairly certain they'll vote against abolishing the creed. Both have been very vocal about the declining birth rates, and Miller was instrumental in shaping the original Creed laws."

Wonderful.

"And the other two?" Nikolai asks, his brow furrowed.

Denver looks down, shuffling some papers. "Undecided. Johnson and Imler are both notorious for keeping their cards close to their chest. We won't know with them until it comes to the voting."

The door opens and we remain silent as Samantha wheels in a tray of coffees. Her face tight, she clatters around with the tray until Denver snaps at her. "Leave it, Samantha."

The blonde beta sniffs, her nose in the air as she trots out, pulling the door closed with a bang. Denver rubs at her temples. "Sorry. I can't see her lasting much longer."

Nik moves over to the tray, pouring coffees and handing one to Ava, his hand cupping her cheek. "So what now?" he asks. "We wait to be called in?"

Denver nods. "When they're ready, we'll receive a

summons for Ava's testimony. You can enter together, but you'll need to sit in the public gallery during the session."

I snap my head back in denial. "That's not happening."

Like hell are we moving more than a step away from our omega in a setting like that.

Denver holds up her hands placatingly. "I know, and I'm sorry. But this is how it works. It's not personal."

Ava's spike of worry echoes in my chest, the bond humming with the tension she's trying to keep off her face. "It's fine."

When we begin to protest, she holds up her hand. "We've come this far. I'm not pulling out now. You'll be in the same room and you can get to me in seconds if you need to."

Denver lets out a relieved sigh. "Thank you. I truly appreciate you coming here. I know that it must be unsettling."

Ava rubs a hand over her face. "I keep expecting guards to rush in and handcuff me," she admits. "It feels wrong to just be walking around like the Creed doesn't apply to me."

Denver smiles a little. "Hopefully, it won't apply to anyone soon. And your amnesty is in place for seven days, starting today. You cannot be punished or prosecuted for your role in this debate."

"Crazy to need an amnesty to be able to stand up," Luc grumbles.

Denver nods in agreement. "I'll give you some time alone," she says, placing her hands on the desk and standing. "I'm not sure when exactly you'll be called in, but it won't be long."

Ava stands too, the rest of us following her lead. She leans over and takes Denver's hand, shaking it more firmly this time.

"Thank you, Senator Denver. I wouldn't have this opportunity if it wasn't for you."

The words are heartfelt, and Denver blinks before returning her shake with a smile. "I wouldn't be so sure, Ava. Your voice is powerful. It takes a great amount of courage to speak up when all around you remain silent. Whatever happens, you should be proud of what you've achieved."

"Thank you." Ava's fervent whisper wobbles as she leans into me, and I wrap my arm around her.

Denver exits the office, pulling the door closed behind her, and I immediately pull Ava to me, wrapping her in my arms. I force back the fear that threatens to choke me. Ava needs me to be strong, but all I want to do is grab her and carry her out of here, make sure she never has to face these assholes and be forced to fight for the basic rights she should have without question.

"I'm alright," she murmurs. "I'm okay, Max."

But I'm not.

I stay silent. Ava doesn't need my worries in her head. She has more than enough of her own to contend with.

Luc taps my shoulder, and he gives me an understanding look as Ava moves into his embrace. He sinks down, burying his face against her neck and inhaling deeply.

"You ready, brat?" he whispers, pulling back and tucking a stray flyaway back into her bun.

Ava takes a step back, her breathing unsteady as she wipes her hands down her skirt. "I have to be ready."

"We can still go," Nikolai offers. "This doesn't have to be your fight, little bird."

But I can see Ava's determination. The set in her shoulders, the way her head holds high as she turns to Nik.

"This *is* my fight, Nikolai," she says gently. "It's all of ours. And if I turn around and go home, then we're not going to win."

She moves to him, and he wraps her up in his arms,

whispering into her ear as she nods. My hands clench and unclench at my sides as I battle the urge to seize her again, keep her close to me. My alpha instincts are riding me unusually hard today, clamoring at me to protect our omega. The itch crawls under my skin, leaving me agitated and twitchy. Next to me, Luc looks like he's going through something similar, his jaw twitching as he watches Ava cuddle into Nik.

The door knocks, and Ava flinches. The room suddenly feels too full, our scents erupting from our skin as we fight to get ourselves under control.

Maybe Bastien should have come, and I should have stayed behind. I won't be any good to her if I let my instincts take control.

The thought sobers me, the slight haziness in my vision clearing as I reach out for the door. Denver is on the other side, and she takes a step back, making me aware of how much energy I'm giving off. Clearing my throat, I offer her a tight, apologetic smile. "It's time?"

"Yes."

Ava ducks under my arm, her fingers briefly tangling with mine as she passes me in the doorway. "I'm ready."

Resolve fills me as I fall into step behind her, Nikolai and Luc on either side of me. If she can push back her fears to do this, then I'll be damned if I don't do the same.

I push back any thoughts of seeing Stone. I'm not sure if I'll be able to breathe the same air as him without going for his throat.

One step at a time.

We can do this.

Chapter Seventy-One
Ava

My kitten heels click noisily on the marble floor as we walk in silence. The presence of my alphas warms my back, although Bastien's absence rubs at my senses like a cut.

I focus on my breathing. Deep breaths, in and out. I can't lose control here, despite the overwhelming scents battering at me.

So many alphas. So many different scents. They claw at my spine, threatening to pull me into a dark cloud of bad memories, but I hold firm and push them back.

Today, my memories will not define me.

Today, my memories become a weapon.

I stop behind Denver as she pauses before vast wooden doors, climbing almost to the ceiling. Engraved in them are words.

In veritate speramus.

"In truth we trust," says Denver, following my gaze. Behind me, Luc scoffs.

My lips tighten. I can only hope the Supreme Justices agree with those sentiments.

Chapter Seventy-One

The guards standing on either side turn and pull the massive iron handles, opening up the doors for us to enter.

"Courage, love."

Max's words are quiet behind me, and I nod.

I will not fail.

I focus on putting one foot in front of the other, keeping my head held high as I stride after Senator Denver into the cavernous chamber. Voices rise in shocked murmurs around me.

"That's the omega who—,"

"The impertinence of it—,"

"…should be on her knees."

At the last words, Luc snaps out a growl, and a shocked noise comes from the benches. But the whispering stops.

Denver comes to a stop, and I lift my head, taking in my surroundings.

Five large wooden chairs are evenly spaced across the marble, a Supreme Justice in each. My eyes scan over them briefly before taking in the benches lined against the walls, each filled with various alpha and beta watchers. No omegas, of course.

The watchers stare at us, faces varying from fascinated to angry. Some are carefully blank, but only a few give me a smile when I catch their eyes.

A chair sits empty in front of the Justices, and Denver beckons me to take a seat. I take a final glance at Max, Luc and Nik, drinking them in for courage as they look around, before settling on a bench directly in my line of sight. A small smile tugs at my lips, especially when Nikolai snaps at an alpha who's clearly reluctant to move. They settle in, their eyes focused firmly on me as I take a seat in the uncomfortable wooden chair, my back upright. Denver takes up a position next to me, her posture alert.

"State your name and purpose for the court," a nasally

voice calls out. My eyes flicker to the beta sitting at a small desk to the right of the Justices, her hands busy typing.

"Senator Erica Denver, presenting Ava Grey, mated omega of the Grey pack, to provide evidence to support the repealing of the Omega Creed."

A stir runs through the people watching. One of the Justices, handsome and impeccably dressed in a black suit and matching shirt, raises an eyebrow.

"Ava Grey," he murmurs, his voice dry. "How… interesting."

Denver inclines her head, her voice measured. "Justice Imler."

Imler. This is one of the undecided ones. I take in the set of his mouth, the way he purses his lips. He doesn't look undecided to me.

Another Justice waves her hand. "Let's get started, shall we? We don't have all day."

She turns to me, her smile a little too cutting. I dislike her immediately.

Denver nods her head, a little lower this time. "Justice Miller."

So this is the woman involved in shaping the creed. I stare at her a little too long, my lip curling, and she narrows her eyes at me.

Game on, bitch.

"Your name is 864, correct?"

Her voice rings through the courtroom, and I fight back the flinch at her opening remark.

"My name is Ava Grey, your Justice."

My voice is clear and even, exactly the way Bastien coached me.

Be respectful, but don't give them an inch, love.

Luc nods in approval as Miller pulls her head back.

"According to our laws, your name remains 864. Despite

your... *adventures*, the law has not been overturned, to my knowledge. Therefore, you will be addressed as 864 by the court."

Whispers break out in the court, and I hide my smile. She may not realize it, but her posturing is a point in our favour.

The Justice sitting on the far right glances around the room before he takes over, clearly realizing the same.

"Ms. Grey," he says smoothly, and Justice Miller shoots him a furious glare, which he ignores. "Thank you for coming to us today. I understand that this is not likely to be an easy situation."

His tone is kind. "Thank you. I'm... very glad to be here."

"Why is that?" he asks, and I blink at him.

"Anything that may help to improve the situation of omegas is something that I am happy to support, even if it's difficult."

The alpha male is older, in his sixties, with liberal amounts of grey scattered through his dark hair. He smiles at me, reaffirming my suspicion that this is Justice Evans.

"I understand. Having seen your video – as I think most of the country now has – we have some questions to ask you. If you need to take a break, please let us know."

My hands twist in my lap, nerves springing to life in my stomach, but I nod.

Justice Evans looks to his left. "Justice Johnson, if you please."

The female beta clears her throat, glancing down at some papers before she looks up at me. Around the same age as Justice Evans, her eyes are a piercing shade of blue.

"Ms. Grey," she begins. Next to her, Justice Miller flushes a furious scarlet. "I understand that you were removed from the Omega Compound due to issues with a guard there. Can you tell me if this was sanctioned by the Compound Director?"

My stomach threatens to revolt, and I push the nausea down, wetting my dry lips. "Um, no. The Director wasn't aware it was happening. When he found out, he came to my cell and got Jason away from me. Then he contacted my - Jonathan Stone. Stone collected me the same night."

Johnson's mouth twists. "I see. Would it be reasonable to say that the Director did not endorse this behaviour, and that sexual abuse was not tolerated at the compound?"

My mouth tightens. "No. Sexual abuse was not tolerated. But physical and mental abuse was very much encouraged."

Johnson's lips part in surprise. "I… see. Could you expand on that, please?"

My eyes drop to the marble floor as I gather my thoughts. "I can give you some examples of my own experiences. Other omegas will have more."

"We're not here to listen to what might have happened," Miller interjects abruptly. "Your own experiences only."

I glance at Max, and he nods at me, his face tight. We prepared for this too.

"We were forced to kneel for most of the day, every day. On one occasion, when we were made to stand up, I'd been kneeling for more than six hours and my legs collapsed. I was taken to an isolation cell and kept there for more than a day as punishment. No food or water was provided to me during that time."

A muffled gasp sounds from behind me, and Johnson leans forward. "Can you describe the isolation cell, please?"

My voice quiets. "It's a pitch-black hole in the ground. There are no steps in and out, and you're lowered in and lifted out by your wrists. There is no space to sit down, so you're forced to stand. It was never cleaned, so I had to stand in waste from omegas who had been in there previously. You're not allowed out to visit the bathroom."

I glance at the Justices. Both Johnson and Evans look a little pale. Miller narrows her eyes at me. "There is no mention of any isolation cell in the reports we have been given."

I stare back at her. "I'd be happy to show you where it is on the grounds, although it's easy to find. You just need to follow the smell."

Miller bares her teeth at me. "I will not have impertinence in this court."

My fists clench. "Or honesty, apparently."

Johnson lifts her hand. "Enough. I appreciate this is difficult for you, Ms. Grey, but please try to keep your responses factual."

I suck in a breath. Her words aren't unkind, but they're a much-needed reminder to keep my shit together.

The last Justice sits forward. This must be Garcia. Her pinched face looks down at me as though I'm something she's stepped in.

"At the time you describe, the Omega Compound was under the control of Christian Winter. We have no evidence to suggest that this evidence is anything more than a reflection of the previous Director. Now that a new Director is in place, changes have been made."

My flinch is instinctive. I can only imagine what kind of changes my father has made.

Evans steeples his fingers in front of him, his eyes on me. "That is not quite accurate, Justice Garcia. Ms. Grey, can you explain what happened after you left the Omega Compound, please?"

My knee begins to shake.

"I—," my throat dries, and I cough. Imler frowns and

looks down to the clerk with the nasally voice. "Get her some water, please."

We wait in silence as the beta pours me a glass from the jug on the desk, carrying it over and nearly dropping it as she tries to avoid touching my skin. I think Justice Imler rolls his eyes, but I can't be sure.

I take a sip, keeping my hands wrapped around it as I brace myself.

"I was taken from the compound by my father the night that I was raped by Jason."

"Speak up," Justice Garcia barks, and I square my shoulders, looking into her face and holding her eyes as I speak.

"I was injected with something to make me sleep, and when I woke up, I was in the heat nests."

Imler speaks next. "Can you describe your environment at the nests?"

I catch his gaze next. "I can. An omega is contained in each cell, which is very small. There is no furniture in the cells as there's not enough room."

"But there was a bed," Miller prompts, and I stare back at her. "No. Omegas are not permitted the use of a bed. It's rule four of the Creed, Justice."

Which you know damned well, since you helped to write it.

Hushed murmurs break out, and Miller's cheeks flush. Evans leans forward. "Forgetting your own rules, Justice Miller?"

He turns to me. "Please continue when you're ready, Ms. Grey."

"The cells have no soft furnishings. The walls and floors are tiled, it makes them easier to clean. Lights are kept on constantly, and there are cameras in each cell."

My hands shake, the water in my hands spilling over the

Chapter Seventy-One

edge of the glass. I try to blot the dampness on my skirt clumsily. "Sorry."

Johnson responds, her voice a little softer. "Take your time."

I close my eyes.

"When I woke up, the first time, I was shackled. They sent someone in to hose me down, and gave me underwear to put on. A doctor came to examine me as I had some injuries from my attack. He told my father I was fit for a heat, and I was injected that night."

Luc's growl makes my head rise. He's staring at me, half-risen in his seat. I shake my head at him. "I'm okay," I mouth. Touching my hand to my chest, I rub at where the bond pulls at me, his anger echoing inside my chest.

"Injected?" Imler leans forward. "With what?"

"Heat hormones. They make you mindless. It's agony to be injected, and only an alpha can stop the pain through knotting." I swallow. "It makes you beg. For it to stop, I mean. You'd do anything."

Imler's face twists in disgust. "And you experienced a heat this way?"

"I experienced many. I was injected over and over again until I became pregnant."

The hushed murmurs in the room explode into full-blown discussions, some of them heated. Justice Garcia stands, shouting for everyone to be quiet. Max, Luc and Nik jump to their feet but stay where they are. Max's face is especially grim, but he forces a smile for me.

When the furore settles, Garcia takes her seat and turns to me.

"Now, 864. You have mentioned your pregnancy, and you were clearly heavily pregnant in the recordings you illegally released. Where are your children now?"

They don't know about the twins. Why hasn't Stone told them?

My body tenses, my voice cold. "Not here."

Now Miller joins in, her painted lips twisting into a smirk. "Your children are the property of the government, 864."

My pack erupt into snarls, and Miller's face loses a touch of her smugness as she glances at them. "Settle down, or I will have you removed," she hisses.

I stand. "My children are not property. And you will *never* get your hands on them."

Garcia hisses. "Insolence. This is a clear breach of the law."

"The law is inhuman," I shout, my body shaking. "It is evil. And if the evidence you have heard isn't enough, then there is nothing that I can say to change your mind."

Evans stands, gesturing for quiet.

"I believe Ms. Grey is right," he says softly. "We have heard enough to make a decision. I don't believe there is anything more to be gained by forcing her to relive any more of her experiences. Does anyone disagree?"

The Justices shake their head. I remain on my feet, my eyes finding Luc. He nods at my silent plea.

I'm ready to leave now.

Garcia holds up her hand. "Wait. There is something to consider. 864 was offered an amnesty by Senator Denver. Senator Denver does not have the legal authority to offer this, and so the amnesty does not stand."

She smiles at me smugly. "864 should be taken into custody until the vote is concluded."

Panic fills me, my body vibrating with terror as a whine slips out. *No*.

Denver steps forward, her face outraged. "This was

discussed and agreed with Justices Johnson and Evans before being offered. No law has been broken!"

"The full Supreme Court must agree," Miller shoots back smugly. "And we did not."

Evans turns to her with a frown. "Justice Miller, we have not upheld that law in the past."

"Then we should have," Garcia says crisply. "Regardless, we are within our rights to take the omega into custody."

"Like fuck you will!" Luc snarls. Max and Nik are right behind him as they jump over the wooden benches, moving to my side. Luc's lips curl back as he growls at Senator Garcia, who pales. "Nobody is taking her anywhere. We came today in good faith."

Max's hand entwines with mine, and I grasp it gratefully.

"Max," I whisper shakily, and he squeezes my hand. "You're not going with them," he promises. "I swear it, love."

Justice Johnston stands. "Everybody needs to calm down. Garcia, Miller, this is not a reasonable course of action."

"I disagree." Garcia's face is cold. "We stand in danger of our laws being seen as optional. Regardless of discussions here today, the law is the law. This omega cannot be seen to flout the authority of the government as though our laws can be followed by choice. We risk anarchy if we allow this ridiculous behavior to continue."

"And we risk anarchy if we do not." Imler's voice is low, and even Garcia pauses. "You are being watched, Maria. Tread carefully."

Garcia swallows as her gaze follows Imler's to the cameras streaming our discussion to the crowds outside, realization flickering in her eyes.

"The law is harsh," she protests, "but it is the law."

Her voice is a little weaker now, and even Miller doesn't speak up. Imler looks around, his eyes settling on my face.

"We will not break an amnesty made in good faith," he says quietly. My shoulders sag, my knees buckling beneath me as Max wraps his arm around me.

"But," he continues, "we need to resolve this. I move to an immediate vote on the repealing of the Omega Creed. Justices, are we agreed?"

Evans and Johnson nod immediately. Garcia and Miller look mutinous but follow their lead.

Imler gestures. "Everybody, please retake your seats. You too, Ms. Grey. Your pack will need to return —,"

"We're not leaving her," Luc says, his voice firm. "We stay here, or she comes with us."

Imler considers for a moment, before inclining his head. "Very well. Remain where you are."

He takes a seat as the other Justices do the same. Evans remains standing alone.

"We call upon the Supreme Court to vote on the abolition of the Omega Creed laws," he says steadily. "Should the vote be in favor of abolition, a motion will be made to formally approve the dissolvement in the Senate. Should the vote be against abolition, the Creed will continue as before."

He sits, and Garcia stands, her pinched face twisted as she glares at me.

"I vote against the abolition of the Omega Creed."

It's not exactly unexpected, but it still sends a spike of fear flickering through me. My bones feel so tense they could snap.

It's all happening so fast. My breathing speeds up, my grip on Max so tight I have to force myself to relax. Nik's hand settles on the back of my neck. His grip is light but soothing, the hold just enough to stop me from breaking down altogether.

Chapter Seventy-One

Johnson is next to stand, her eyes assessing as they slide from me to my pack.

"I vote in favor of the abolition of the Omega Creed."

She nods to me as I suck in a hopeful breath, before taking her seat.

Miller stands, her face sour.

"I vote against the abolition of the Omega Creed."

Two against, one for. Evans speaks up next, a small smile on his face.

"I vote in favor of the abolition of the Omega Creed."

An even split. Luc takes my other hand in his.

"Please," I whisper. *Please end it.*

Imler takes his time getting to his feet and brushing at some non-existent link on his suit sleeve. The whole room drops to silence, everyone holding their breath as he looks up, his face almost nonchalant as he waves a hand.

"I vote in favor of the abolition of the omega creed."

It takes a second for his words to sink in. Luc shouts out as the courtroom erupts into a mixture of cheers and anger.

My body folds, Max not quick enough to catch me before my knees hit the floor. He drops next to me, his hands cradling my face as I cover it with my hands, sobs breaking out of me.

"Ava, sweetheart, you did it," he whispers disbelievingly. "You did it, love!"

Luc is right behind him, laughing joyously as he lifts me easily, his hand wiping away tears from my cheeks. "You," he presses a hard kiss to my mouth, "are a fucking miracle, brat."

I just gape at him, and he throws his head back with laughter.

"Where's Nikolai?" I mumble, and Luc sets me down, squeezing my shoulders. I spin around, and spot my bear alpha. He's frozen, his eyes wet, and I throw my arms around him.

"Nik," I murmur, my voice hitching. "Nikolai."

"Little bird." His arms come up to wrap around me before he pulls me in, damned near crushing me as I finally break out in a watery laugh. "Emery will be safe," he breathes.

No more creed. No more compound.

Senator Denver steps forward, her mouth moving, but I can barely hear her through my light-headedness. I sink back down into the uncomfortable wooden seat, dropping my face into my hands as I gulp in breaths.

Her words finally sink in, and I snap my head up. "What did you say?"

Luc, Max and Nik instantly go on the alert.

She grins widely at me. "I said, there'll be an investigation into your father as part of the next steps. He was supposed to be here today, but he must have left."

Her smile falters as she picks up on our tension. "What's the matter? Ava?"

Fear tastes like ashes on my tongue. "Luc," I rasp. "Have you heard from Bastien?"

Luc pulls his phone out of his pocket. "Nothing."

I stagger upright. "We need to go. Right now."

Luc turns to Denver. "Can you have our car brought around? Right now, please."

"I- of course." She walks over to a guard, muttering instructions.

I press at my chest, wishing more than anything that I had Bastien's bitemark and he had mine. Luc stabs at the phone, holding it up to his ear and cursing. "It's ringing out."

Nikolai and Max close in, their faces tight as I swallow down my panic.

Chapter Seventy-One

"He could be with Emery and Leo," I offer weakly. Luc nods, but he doesn't look convinced.

There's no way Bastien wouldn't be tracking every second of this. There's no way he wouldn't pick up the phone.

Unless he can't.

"The twins," I breathe. "Nash."

Bastien. Leah.

Nikolai's face pales. I start moving towards the door in a daze as Luc clears a path. People crowd in, offering congratulations, but I can't focus on them. My heart is thrumming, my pulse beating heavily.

The joy I felt just a few moments ago has vanished, smothered by a wave of sheer panic.

We emerge into pandemonium. The crowd has swelled into a baying mass, hysterical shouting hitting my ears painfully as we push through the throng with the help of a few guards. Luc slides into the driver's seat as I dive into the back, Max and Nik following me as he hits the gas and pulls off.

My vision goes black as I struggle to pull in a breath. Max places his hand on my back. "Breathe, love," he begs. "We'll be there soon. They're probably fine."

But I know my father.

Stone wouldn't miss out on a chance to get at me.

Not unless he could get to *them*.

CHAPTER SEVENTY-TWO
AVA

The gates at the edge of our land are wide open. Nikolai lets loose a furious growl.

Nash. Leo. Emery. Bastien. Leah.

Their names echo inside my head, a vicious pounding inside my chest. My lips curl back as a snarl ripples from my throat. Luc darts a look at me over his shoulder as he hits the gas.

"Ava," he barks. "You need to stay in the car while we check things out."

I ignore him, my eyes narrowing on the path ahead.

Like fuck am I staying in the car.

My head doesn't feel right. The anger and terror I've felt for the last hour has narrowed into razor-edged focus. My breathing speeds up as I grab for the car door.

"Ava!" One of my alphas has hold of my shoulders, his face concerned as he talks to me, his face urgent.

Mine.

His words slide past me, none of them breaking through the haze. The vehicle slows, and they're too slow to stop me as I jump out and run straight for the main house.

"Ava!"

Footsteps pound on the gravel, but they can't keep up with me. I burst through the main doors and stop.

The room looks undisturbed at first glance. I inhale, tasting the taint of oil in the air, sulphuric and rotten. Underneath is the unmistakable iron tang of blood. Breathing it in, my eyes scan the room again, this time stopping on a familiar shape on the floor.

Leah.

My vision clears a little. Max bursts through the door behind me, Nik and Luc behind him as he grabs my arms.

"Ava," he snaps. "You can't just run off—,"

"Leah," I rasp, shaking him off. "Max, help her!"

Max turns, his face paling as he spots her. "Lee."

I drop down on her other side as Max rolls her over. Her red hair sticks together in a clump of dried blood, her eyes barely focusing on me as she blinks heavily.

"The babies," she slurs. "He's here. Nash is at the cabin."

My head snaps to the stairs, Luc and Nik already pounding up them as I follow, leaving Max to look after his sister.

Luc throws out his arm as I come up behind them, turning and pinning me with a fierce glare. "You stay behind us," he snaps quietly. "We will not be able to concentrate if you're in danger, brat. Do you understand?"

Pressing my lips together, I dip my chin in acknowledgment. But I can't promise him to stay out of danger.

Emery. Leo. Bastien. Where are they?

A pained groan sounds as we reach the top of the chairs. I bite back my cry as my eyes fall to the trail of blood along the floor, following it to Bastien as he limps down the hall, his hand over his side as he hugs the wall for support.

Luc is next to him in a flash, his hand landing over

Bastien's mouth as he sucks in a shocked cry. "Shh, brother," Luc says quietly. "We're here now. Where are they?"

Bastien nods, sinking back against the wall as he lifts his hand towards the nursery. Red glitters in the afternoon light, and he forces a smile as he spots me, held back by Nikolai. My eyes zero in on the darkened scarlet covering his white t-shirt.

"I'm alright," he grunts. "He's still here. He caught me outside with a bat over the head – stupid. I didn't see him coming."

Bastien stares at me, his eyes full of apologies.

Ducking under Nik's arm, I run my hands over his body, suppressing a gasp as my hands come away stained with red. "Bastien," I mutter. "He *shot* you!"

The haze descends over my vision again.

Stone is here. In our home. He's attacked Leah, and shot Bastien. My head swivels to the nursery, the lamp Nik made casting its twirling shadows out into the hallway.

"Why is he still here?" Nik mutters. "Why hasn't he tried to take them?"

My lips tighten.

I know why.

Because he's waiting for me.

I swallow. "He wants to win," I whisper. Everyone turns to me. "He wants me to know that he's won. That's how he's always been."

I take another step, and Luc blocks my way. Indecision mars his handsome features. "You're not going anywhere near that room, love," he says hoarsely. "If that's true, then he's waiting for you."

I wet my mouth. "If you go, he'll kill you, Luc. Any of you. He won't kill me."

Nik's hands land on my shoulders. "You're *not* going in there, little bird."

CHAPTER SEVENTY-TWO

Bastien grunts his agreement. He sways, and Luc grabs hold of his arm, his face torn.

I brace myself, my eyes tracing their faces. "Luc... I wasn't asking for permission."

And then I *move*.

Nik's hands grab for me desperately and miss. "Ava – stop!"

Darting to the door of the nursery, I throw myself in, spinning to slam the door shut and pushing the lock. Nik's fist pounds against it a scant second later as he roars my name.

Breathing heavily, I press my face against the wood, bracing myself to turn and face my father. Movement shifts behind me.

"864. It's so kind of you to join our little gathering." Stone's voice is cold. "Turn around."

Gritting my teeth, I force back my panic and turn slowly, my eyes scanning the room.

My heart stops as I lay eyes on my father.

"Nash," I gasp. "Sweetheart."

Tear tracks line Nash's small face, his lip trembling as Stone pushes the muzzle of a gun under his chin.

"I'm glad you came in first," he says mildly. "I would have shot the boy otherwise."

Nash's little face scrunches up, and I take a step forward.

"Ah, now." Stone holds up his other hand. "Stay where you are."

Leo and Emery are sleeping peacefully in their cots. My eyes flicker between them and Nash, desperately trying to think of a way to get them out of here.

"Let them go," I try. "We can leave. They won't stop us."

Stone cocks an eyebrow at me. "And if I believed that, I'd be dead within a minute."

He glances down at the cots. "Besides, I have what I need. And I have no further use for you."

His hand lifts to grip Nash by the neck as he lifts the gun towards me, his face twisting into rage.

"Do you even know what you've done?" he spits. "You've ruined everything, you little bitch. Just like your mother."

My sight zeroes in at the end of the gun pointing directly at me. "What about my mother?"

"She was the same as you. Didn't know her place. Thought she could do better." He cackles. "She learned, though."

Nash whimpers as Stone's fingers flex against his neck. Swallowing, I take a step to the side, flinching as the door behind me shakes on its hinges as Nikolai and Luc throw themselves against it.

Stone straightens. "I've lost everything because of you, you know."

The gun stays steady in his hand. "I'm wanted by the courts for questioning over the conditions of the heat nests." He barks a laugh. "As if you animals matter."

"I'm not an animal," I whisper through dry lips. "I'm your daughter."

He sneers at me. "A useless runt. The only useful thing you ever did was pop out these two."

He glances down at the cots, and Nash's eyes flick to mine. "It's okay," I whisper. "It's gonna be okay, Nash."

Stone grunts. "A liar to your last breath. You're going to die today, daughter. You, and your pack, and this little runt." Nash rasps out a cry as he squeezes again, and I snarl. "Get your fucking hands off him!"

"You're going to die, and your children are coming with me." Stone grins manically. "Maybe I'll have better luck with these two than I did with you."

Nash stiffens. "They're not going with you," he whispers. Stone looks down at him consideringly. "I like your spark, kid. Maybe I'll take you too."

Nash's little face scrunches up into a snarl. "You're not taking me anywhere. I'm a *Grey*."

Twisting, he sinks his teeth into Stone's hand. Stone yelps as his attention is diverted, and I throw myself at him, pushing his arm up and making him drop the gun as we struggle. Nash gets knocked aside, and I scream at him. "Run, Nash! Open the door!"

The commotion wakes Emery and Leo, both of them starting to wail as Stone pulls back his fist and hits me in the side of the face, jarring me loose as blinding pain rips through the right side of my skull. I throw myself back at him, my nails ripping and scratching at his face as he brings back his fist to hit me again.

"You will never," I spit, "touch my children again."

He snarls at me as he lands another punch, my ears ringing from the force of it, but I don't let go of his face, digging in as hard as I can.

"You will never touch *me* again."

Even if I have to die for it.

Wetness drips down onto my neck as we grapple, Stone getting a grip on my neck as he laughs, bloody gouges in his skin as he lifts me from the floor, my hands scrabbling at my neck. Behind him, Nash works frantically to try and reach the lock on the door as cracks appear in the wood. My pack are coming.

"Stupid omega bitch," he gasps. "You can't win against a fucking alpha."

I grin at him, my lips bloody as I force the words out, my voice hoarse as my throat screams for air. "I don't have to win. I just have to *wait*."

Stone's eyes widen as a rippling, feral snarl fills the air. "You—,"

I keep my eyes open as Lucien, his face twisted in fury, takes my father's head between his hands and twists, his neck snapping beneath the force. I collapse to the floor as Luc kicks Stone's body out of the way and drops to his knees, the haze in his eyes clearing as he runs frantic hands over my body. "Ava – where are you hurt?"

I choke out a raspy laugh. "Took you long enough."

"Don't start with me, brat," he snaps. "Do you even realize how many years you took off our life when you locked us out of the fucking room?"

I swallow. "A lot?"

"Damned right," he growls. "You bet your ass is getting a spanking for this."

"Nash," I breathe. "Where's Nash?"

"Nik has him. Everyone's safe, love. Everyone but *you*. What did he do to you?"

Everyone is safe.

My family are safe.

Stone is dead.

"Good," I murmur. "That's good, Luc."

My eyes start to close. Everyone is safe.

"Ava?" his voice is panicked. "I need you to stay awake for me, love. Your head – Ava!"

But I'm already gone.

Chapter Seventy-Three
NIKOLAI

I bolt upright in the armchair as the door creaks.

"It's just me," Max says in a low voice. He crosses the room and leans in to check on Ava's bandage, pulling a light from his pocket and opening up her eyelids to check her pupils. She grumbles, her hand reaching up to swat him away. Next to her, Nash snores lightly, his hand wrapped tightly around hers.

My heart hurts just watching them.

"We nearly lost them both, Max." Running my hands over my face, I blow out a breath, trying to push back the exhaustion. I can't sleep until I know Ava's all right, and she's been unconscious for hours.

"She's doing well," Max murmurs. "Her reactions are fine, Nik. She's just sleeping it off now."

We both stare down at her, at the bruises ringing her neck like some sort of fucked-up necklace. Dark bruising is already appearing around her eyes and cheeks where Stone hit her, traces of blood still clinging to her hairline despite us washing it off.

"How's Leah?" I ask, and Max snorts.

"Fine. Just furious that he got the drop on her. She's got a nice egg on her head to match the bruising to her ego."

I shake my head. Max's voice wavers despite his bravado.

We came so close to losing all of them today.

My head turns to the doorway as Bastien hobbles through it, his arm around Luc's neck as Luc fusses. "You should be in bed, not wandering around the house."

Bastien rolls his eyes. "There's a bed right here. Plenty of space for little old me, brother."

He grins at me. "Make way, we have a gunshot victim," he says lightly, and Luc swats him.

"Hey! Do the words *gunshot victim* mean nothing to you?"

"Not where you're concerned," Luc grumbles, but he ruffles Bastien's hair as he helps him settle in on Nash's other side.

Max and Luc settle into chairs around the room, and we settle into a contemplative silence.

"What happens now?" Bastien asks sleepily.

Luc blinks. "I'm not sure."

Leaning forward, I stroke my hand gently over Ava's cheek. She nuzzles into my hand as she continues to sleep, her other arm tightening on Nash.

"Wherever she wants to go," I say softly. Everyone stops and looks at me, and I glance around. "We'll follow her. Wherever she wants to go."

Bastien's face tightens. "She can go wherever she wants."

She could leave us.

"Have a little faith," Luc murmurs, his eyes on our little bird.

"Easy for you to say," huffs Bastien. "You can feel her through the bond."

Chapter Seventy-Three

"What happened to tattooing my name on your ass?"

The hoarse mumble takes us all by surprise as our attention snaps to the bed. Ava blinks up at us sleepily.

"You're so damned loud," she grumbles. Max perches next to her with a soft smile. "Sorry, love."

He checks her vitals again. "Doesn't look like you have a concussion, but we'll keep an eye on you just in case."

Ava nods, before wincing. "Bad idea."

She lays her head back with a soft huff. "Where is he?"

Luc glares at her, holding onto his grudge for locking us out of the damn nursery. "Far away from here."

I cough into my fist. To be precise, he's about six miles east, buried in wasteland and unlikely to be discovered for a very long time.

Rest in hell, asshole.

"How are you doing?" Max asks her. "Today was a lot."

Ava grimaces. "Understatement." Blowing out a breath, she stares at the ceiling. "I'm not sure," she admits. "I think I need some time to process."

"We have time," Max reminds her. "As much as you need, now."

"Now all the demons are vanquished?" she quips, her eyes tired. "Luc, what are you going to do now you don't have to worry about me anymore?"

Luc takes her hand, pressing a kiss to her knuckle. "I have a feeling I'll never stop worrying about you, brat."

"What would you like to do?" I ask, and her hazel eyes move to mine hesitantly. "To do?"

"If you had the choice, right now. What would you like to do?"

She considers for a moment, worrying her lips with her teeth.

"I think I might want to help other omegas," she whispers. "Ones like me, I mean."

"Like a support center?" Max asks, surprised, and she nods. "They'll need one, and I don't trust our government to do it."

"I think that's a wonderful idea." My hands itch for my sketchpad. I can already imagine the center layout in my mind, the different spaces we're likely to need.

Ava hesitates. "It's a lot of work. And money."

Luc smirks. "We have enough money to create anything you want to do, brat. Trust me."

"Safe space," I murmur. Ava twists her head slowly to look at me, a spark appearing in her eyes. "Safe space," she whispers. "That's exactly what it should be, Nik."

It'll need to be somewhere central. My eyes flick to Nash.

"I'd like Nash to go to a real school," I admit. "Make some friends his own age."

We're not there yet. Whilst the Creed is all but abolished, there are other laws that will need formal removal. But for the first time, I have hope. Hope that my son can have a future. That our children can choose their own path.

And it's all because of Ava. The tiny omega who dared to take on the government and won.

My eyes mist, and I swallow back the emotion.

"I love you," I blurt, and she stares at me, her lips curling into a shy smile. "I love you too," she murmurs. Nash stirs, and she strokes a hand through his hair until he settles down.

In unison, a cry rings out from the monitor clipped to my hip.

I hop up. "I'll get them."

When I enter the nursery, Emery hiccups from her cot, her little face streaked with tears.

"Hey, now," I soothe, reaching in and lifting her out, cradling her against my chest. "Are you hungry, sweetheart?"

CHAPTER SEVENTY-THREE

Her violet eyes cross, her face squishing as something rumbles under my hands, before an odour reaches my nose and I wrinkle my face back at her.

"Oh, it's like that, is it?" I ask her, and she blinks at me innocently.

My shoulders shaking, I pop her down on the changing mat and reach for a diaper.

If this is what normal looks like, I'll volunteer every damn time.

Epilogue – Ava

Senator Denver greets me at the top of the steps of the Justice building, a broad smile on her face.

"No crowds this time," she grins. I grin back at her. "Better this way."

She laughs, linking my arm in hers as we walk towards her office. "How are you feeling?"

"Excited. Nervous."

Butterflies flutter in my stomach, matching the ones on my long dress. My hair loosely falls down my back. I'm not dressing up for anyone today.

Today, I am unashamedly and unapologetically Ava Grey.

Mated omega, Safe Space founder, and signatory of the Omega Rights Bill.

"More than two years of work," Erica sighs. "I can't believe it."

I shake my head in agreement.

"It feels like ten years," I joke, but I'm not entirely joking. Our win at the Supreme Court was only the beginning. It's taken two long years to unravel the various wrongdoings of the Omega Creed, to dissolve the adoption system and to create a new Bill setting out the rights of omegas.

Equal to any alpha or beta. Property of no one.

When Erica asked me to stand in as an advisor, I'd been hesitant. It was Max who talked me into it, his brown eyes earnest on mine.

"You know better than anyone what they've done," he told me. "This is your chance to undo it, sweetheart. Build a world to be proud of."

And we have.

Emotion tightens my throat as we stand at the doors to the court. Erica squeezes my hand, and I smile at her, remembering the last time I stood in this position.

"How long do you think this will take?" I ask her in a whisper.

She grimaces. "Maybe an hour. Depends how much posturing they want to do."

Checking my watch, I nod. "Somewhere to be?" she asks me wryly.

I grin. "Yep, but I've got time for this first."

"Mom!"

I wave frantically as Nash dashes through the small gathering of kids, shouting out his goodbyes and waving to his friends enthusiastically. He hits my middle and I let out an oomph.

"How was your day?" I ask, and he grins at me excitedly. "It was so good!"

Nash links our hands together as we stroll down the street to our favourite ice-cream parlour. It's owned by an older beta couple who fuss over Nash every time we go in, and today is no exception.

"Nash!" Berta exclaims delightedly. He waves at her, happily climbing onto a stool and chatting about his day as I watch him with a smile.

Hank, Berta's husband, sidles up to me. He was a little standoffish at first, but he warmed up to me eventually.

"Saw you on the telly today," he says gruffly, nodding at the old set that plays above the counter. "Bit of a big thing, this bill?"

"It is," I say quietly. "You know, today is the first day I've been legally allowed to walk in here without an alpha?"

Hank's bushy white brows rise under his cap. "Never realized that."

There's a hint of respect in his voice, and I give him a nod and a smile as Nash calls for me. I settle down into my chair next to him as Berta slides my favorite sundae over to me. Raspberry ripple with cream and a cherry on top.

Hank whispers in her ear, and she nods.

"On the house, Ava," she calls, her face breaking into a smile. "I hear we're celebrating."

Hank smiles at me behind her.

I raise my sundae to them in thanks as Nash laughs, clinking his glass against mine. Movement outside catches my eye, and I swivel on my seat, grinning at the sight of my pack.

Nash jumps down from his chair and runs to the door, hollering with excitement. Max is first, Emery tucked tightly against his neck, her face buried in her favorite place.

"Emmy," I coax. "Hug?"

Max laughs as he swoops in for a kiss, his finger stroking over the bitemark on my throat, a hint of male alpha satisfaction purring through our bond.

My daughter side-eyes me before shaking her head and hiding in Max's neck again.

I can't even blame her. I love Max's neck too.

Leo's grizzling rises above the rest, and Bastien rocks him on his hip as he grumbles. Bastien points to his mouth. "We have new teeth!"

Leo turns his unhappy face to me, his arms reaching out, and I take him happily, snuggling him into my side as he opens his mouth to reveal an additional two new teeth to add to his set. I lean in to rub his nose with mine as Luc's hand settles on my neck.

"Brat," he murmurs, a smile tugging at his lips. "You were brilliant today."

"You watched it?"

"Of course we did," Nik interrupts, offended. "We wouldn't miss it, little bird."

I beam at them. "How was the build today?"

Nik pulls out the latest floorplans for our expansion of Safe Space. Our small idea has turned into a huge success. I just wish there weren't so many omegas who needed the help.

But we'll be there for them, for as long as we're needed.

Max leans in to wrap his arm around my shoulders, and I turn to breathe in the scent of apple pie. He drops a kiss to my shoulder.

"Happy?" he asks gently.

I lean my head against his arm with a sigh, watching Luc and Bastien argue over ice cream flavors as Nikolai talks to Nash intently.

"I am," I say softly. "I wouldn't change our life for anything."

I wouldn't. Because at the end of the day, everything that happened, brought me to them. To Leo and Emery. To Max, Luc, Bastien, Nik and Nash.

To my family.
And I wouldn't swap them for the world.

THE END

Omega Lost playlist (in order)

Find it on Spotify

Broken Girl – Matthew West
Wires - Athlete
Save Myself – Ed Sheeran
Til It Happens To You – Lady Gaga
Take Me Home – Jess Glynne
September - Daughtry
Broken Ones - Jacquie
Stay – Rihanna & Mikky Ekko
Set Me On Fire – Bella Ferraro
Iris – Goo Goo Dolls
Fight Song – Rachel Platten
Like I'm Gonna Lose You – Jasmine Thompson
This Woman's Work – Kate Bush
How Long Will I Love You – Ellie Goulding
Rise Up – Andra Day
Titanium – Jasmine Thompson
Feels Like Home – Chantal Kreviazuk

A note from Evelyn

….and *breathe*.

Since Omega Found came out in March 2022, I've been overwhelmed at the amount of support I've received for Harper and Ava's stories.

Omega Lost is particularly special to me. Emery's story is based on my own experiences, except I was lucky enough to survive. This book is secretly dedicated to my own Nash, who is just as sassy and sweet as his on-paper counterpart.

Whilst Ava and Harper's story is complete, there is one more story still to come.

What happens after the Omega Creed falls? How do omegas integrate back into society? The impact of war doesn't end on the day the battle is over, and I'll be exploring this in *Omega Fallen*, Gabrielle's story. You've met her before, in Omega Found.

You can pre-order this here: https://books2read.com/omegafallen

These stories aren't always easy to write, and I sometimes question the level of detail I choose to include, knowing it's not easy to read either.

But I think when writing about sensitive topics, sometimes you can't shy away from the details – much as you can't in real life.

And whilst the Omega War trilogy is set in an alternative, dystopian world, there are some parallels I've drawn on from our world to create theirs. And isn't that a petrifying thought?

The world is a scary place right now. Take care of you.

If you'd like to keep track of my books and see what else I'm working on, I can always be found in my Facebook readers group, The Evelyn Flood Collective.

Evie x

Stalk me!

Facebook: https://www.facebook.com/groups/evelynflood/
Goodreads: https://www.goodreads.com/evelynflood
Bookbub: https://www.bookbub.com/profile/evelyn-flood
TikTok: https://www.tiktok.com/@evelynfloodauthor
Instagram: https://www.instagram.com/evelynfloodauthor/

Printed in Great Britain
by Amazon